ORR: Fatal DNA

By Lynn Marron

A Grace Farrington Mystery

Book and Cover Design By Lynn Marron
and Leonard J. Bloom, Jr.

Published by Kear Press
Stratford, CT

LIBRARY OF CONGRESS: 2016939778

ISBN: 978-1-942888-11-6

e-book ISBN 978-1-942888-12-3

To contact the author go to:

lynn@lynnmarron.com

This book is dedicated To

Doctor Anna Karidas

And those who work with her

Making people's lives so much happier!

Ann Alvarez

Rodanna Kokenas

Joanna Murzinska

Michele Sienkiewicz

Hui Ran

Nia Thomas

Nikki Lieto

Patty Bakes-Servos

Prologue

Captain Elijah Dell squinted at the thunderclouds closing in over the slate-gray sound. Hours till sunset but rolling fog already obscured distant Long Island, an evil omen for this day's work. Whitecaps foaming the crests of growing waves that now pounded the beach sand. Standing closer to the sea, his daughter-in-law Rebecca stared out, paying no heed as the advancing yellow foam lapped over her boot tips.

With such a Devil's storm brewing, would Christopher dare it in only a two-man sloop? Instead, should they take Elijah's fishing boat tied back in the harbor? It would handle the waves but stand out in Wallabout bay causing the British to question. Nay. Elijah shifted his left arm again, must've hurt it when the sail shifted, now it was numb and that added misery to the cold that sat on his chest, making breathing painful. Getting old, when all a man wanted was to be home soaking up warmth before his hearth fire.

But there was Eli– his youngest boy and Mae's last living child. Now Eli suffered with the rest in that hell hole of prison ship under the decks, in stinking July heat: Eli, Samuel, Willy, and Jacob. If Christopher would sail to Wallabout this day, and he would for enough coin, then Elijah must crew no matter how badly he felt.

Did they have enough to ransom Eli and the others? Elijah turned his eyes from the surf. Now in these times, he had to watch for dangers from the land too as his own former friends and neighbors might turn him over to the British as a traitor. Movement. He squinted, now he could see two figures coming out of the trees, down to the beach, two women in blowing capes. One unnaturally tall, Long Liz, his sister, her blonde hair streaming with gray, and beside her trudging in the sand, that brown faced servant, Posey. Liz was his sister, but her husband Seth was a wealthy Loyalist, siding with King George, who would have them all hanged.

Elijah sneaked a look to the whitening sea and cursed softly. Over the dark, rolling water he could see the top of a sloop's gray canvas sail. Better get Loyalist Liz out of here, before Christopher makes land. Elijah turned suddenly and felt dizzy, he had to stop and catch a painful breath, before he trod forward in the deep sand. Rebecca was hanging back as cold Liz's imperial manner always cowed her.

His sister waited above the black-green sodden mounds of seaweed at the high water line not wanting her fine linen cloak to get stained. As he approached, she looked directly into his eyes. Most women he always had to look down to, but Liz was his equal in ungainly height.

She spoke first. "Storm coming in."

"Hear the redcoats will be getting here first," he said a bit coldly.

"Our King's soldiers protect us." Her voice lost some of its hauteur and held sisterly concern when she said, "You look terrible, Elijah, your face is gray."

"Tis the poor light."

"You're an old man, who should be home before your firestead."

"Even the flames are cold without my Mae."

Liz looked away in shame. "I was not there when you laid your wife to rest."

"Half the town of Oyster River was not there," he said bitterly. "None of your good King's friends showed up to respect a woman they'd known their whole lives."

"They know your son for a rebel." There was a silence, then Liz said painfully. "I should have been there...but Seth forbid it."

Elijah nodded. "The Lord God has ordained that a wife must obey her husband. Mae would have understood that."

Looking pained she said, "What would the Lord think of our town splitting so?"

"I seek no war with King or Rebel. I only wish to fish and be left alone."

"But your son..."

"Eli listened to his fine friends. They joined a militia to battle the injustices of freeborn Englishmen not allowed to speak on their destiny, but a Connecticut Colony man should not have been fighting in New Jersey! Now Eli pays for his folly, rotting in a prison ship."

"Then you know where he is?"

"Perhaps imprisoned in Wallabout bay with Jacob Hoyt, Samuel Chapel, and Willy Jamison. That's where we think they took them after the battle."

"Seth says the military will subdue Connecticut, as they have Boston and New York. When that happens, the rebels–or anyone who treated with them--will be expelled. Where will you go? The Indies? Not west into the dark forests with the painted savages..." She actually sounded pained.

Battling the waves, the sloop was drawing closer. "Woman, why have you come?"

She hesitated, then started slowly. "My Posey heard from the indentured servant of the Jamisons that you are raising money for a ransom to free the soldiers?"

Would his own sister turn them in? "Is that of your business?"

She sounded agonized. "The British will hang you for a traitor! My very husband would turn you in."

"Aye, Seth would damned fool that he is," said Elijah sourly. "King George cares naught for him as little as he does for any of us. The rulers King George sends us will not be native born."

Liz smiled tightly. "Seth's a fool, always was, but the rebels are losing. I hear your General Washington had retreated from Manhattan and that the King's General Howe is gaining ground..."

"All I care is that my son starves in a prison ship."

"This ransom, is it official? Do the British know, or

are you just bribing some jailer?"

He just looked at her.

She turned to pleading. "My brother, they will take your gold and then laugh at you."

Elijah just raised his shoulders, but that brought a stabbing pain deep in his chest.

Liz looked back to the land. "I walked to Mae's grave today, the earth's still freshly mounded. There were newly picked flowers on it?" She looked back at him.

"Aye. I visit her–sometimes--before I walk home." He should hide his pain, but... "It's strange bedding by myself, after so many years beside her."

She looked away from him, her face a mirror of his pain. "Brother, you must let the dead lie in peace."

Did she see the sloop? "It's been nary a moon since she sickened."

Liz looked back at his face. "I have pleaded with Seth to write an appeal to General Howe's adjutant to see if he can get Eli and others released."

That surprised Elijah. Liz and Seth were a vainglory, peacock pair, fancying themselves the new world 'aristocracy.' His proud, King loving sister pleading for traitors?

She continued. "Seth told me to only mind woman's business, but maybe if you asked him?"

Begging was what she meant–which Elijah would have done gladly if he thought there was a shred of mercy in Seth. Elijah just shook his head.

She turned to the small maid beside her. "Posey, the casket."

A higher wave crashed into the sand with foaming spume, making the young woman's eyes widen, whites made all the whiter by her chocolate skin. The maid opened her cape to show she was holding a decorated box that was slightly larger than a loaf of bread, made of dark cherry wood, inlaid with ivory flowers and silver stems. Elijah had seen it before, the prize of his sister's bedchamber. Posey looked up questioningly to her mistress, and still tight-lipped, Liz nodded.

The young maid placed the polished casket down on the pale sand. From her apron pocket, she produced a small key, then struggled with the metal lock. Finally, it gave, opening to a white silk lined interior. Even in the low light, Captain Elijah could see gleaming coins and darkly colored jewels. Liz's wedding necklace, his mother's rings... some of the pain in his chest dissolved as he looked up in surprise.

Liz just nodded. "Eli is my only nephew. I have no children of my own." She looked to Rebecca, who still stood a safe distance away. "Eli's wife, she is with child?"

Elijah nodded.

"Then the babe should have his father to raise him. Take it all."

Elijah just there dumbly, more amazed than anything.

"You proud, stupid fool." Liz nodded to Posey. "Put the key inside, then shut the casket, and leave in the sand," As she turned, Long Liz looked back over her shoulder to her brother, saying, "in case some simpleton might wish to pick it up."

Resolutely Liz walked away with her boots sinking deep into the white sand as her dark cape billowed about her.

Posey looked from her to Elijah, and still touching the casket, the maid seemed reluctant to abandon it, as if the jewels were hers. Insolently, she seemed about to object.

"Obey her!" Commanded Elijah. Under his stern eye, she quickly released the casket and hurried after her mistress.

Rebecca walked to Elijah, looking at the chest in the sand. "Your sister gave us something for the ransom?" There was wonder in her voice. While he just stood there looking at the tall woman walking away, Rebecca fell to her knees and opened the casket. He could hear her sharp intake of breath. "Coins, gold. British crowns, French guineas, a necklace of gold and sapphires." As she held it up, Rebecca exclaimed. "A stoned bracelet." She looked up to Elijah. "So much? What if Master Seth finds out?"

"It is hers to give."

When the heavily pregnant Rebecca started to rise awkwardly, he reached out a hand to lift her, but it was his bad arm, and a stabbing pain cut his chest again. Watching the two cloaked figures retreat into the trees, his daughter-in-law murmured, "I should have thanked her."

Elijah looked back towards the rising sea, and now he could see the man at the sloop's stern. The wind was worrying him hard, but Christopher was a skillful sailor. "Add Liz's bounty to the bag. What else have we?"

Wrapping Liz's bounty in a silk scarf from the casket, Rebecca added it to the kid leather sack resting on her swelled belly. "The Jamisons gave us eight brass shoe buckles, and Willy's mother gave us six silver buttons. I did not ask Jacob's grandmother since Dame Alice is but a poor widow woman. We have Mother Mae's wedding ring, and the Hoyts gave us pieces of eight, the Scofields Irish farthings, and one Continental dollar. With my mother's ivory monkey-head beads and your sister's fine gift we have much, but will it be enough to free all of them?"

"It should be." Elijah pulled off his father's worn onyx stoned ring. "Add this to it." It dropped into Rebecca's bag with a soft clink. Pulling off his boots, Elijah waded hip-deep into the waves as Christopher fought the sloop in. Elijah grabbed hold of the prow, with difficulty turning it straight to the beach, as Christopher jumped out on the other side. They both strained to pull the bow above the high water line, even Rebecca got behind Elijah to help push.

Christopher shook his head, shouting over the surf. "Storms getting worse–wind from the northeast–we can't go this day!"

Rebecca looked helplessly from Christopher to Elijah. "They say small pox has broken out in the prison ships, and that they take the bodies of the dead from each hull every morning. You must go!"

Elijah squinted northeast. "Nay, lass. Tis only the devil's sea tonight. This light sloop will bounce like a drunken cork–no way to control it. Christopher, tie her to the downed tree..."

Christopher hesitated.

Elijah reached deep into his own leather pouch and handed the fisherman heavy coins tied tightly in a handkerchief. Christopher took them with a smile and without counting, stuffed them into his shirt, saying, "I had to trade two jars of whiskey for information, the lot captured at the Battle of Monmouth Courthouse was taken to the ship, *HMS Jersey*. From what the guards told me, that should be Eli, Samuel, Willy, and Jacob."

"Were you able to speak with them?" asked Rebecca her voice begging for hope.

"Nay. The prisoners are held below decks and never see the sun, but on land, when the officers look away, I've sold whiskey to a seaman on duty. They will talk to me. Have you raised a ransom?"

As they stood on the beach, salty rain droplets and sand were stinging their faces. "Aye. Rebecca, show him."

She opened the leather sack to him.

Christopher ran his rough hands through it. "Should do well, these seamen get little coin, but I'll need something to carry it in."

Elijah moved to pick up Liz's wooden jewel casket.

The sailor shook his head. "Nay, it must be something I could pass ashore easily." Christopher trod back to his sloop, and, from its deep belly, hauled out a large, milk-colored ceramic crock. He took the lid off, it was empty. "No one would question a soldier buying a crock of whiskey from some fisherman. Put your treasure in this, but seal it not with beeswax-- seal it with tar."

As Rebecca lowered the leather sack into the crock one coin slipped out into the sand. She bent to scoop it up, but her growing stomach made that an awkward move, and she started to fall back to her knees in the sand. Christopher bent quickly to help her up. He gave her back the empty casket and now took up the treasure-filled crock.

Elijah had been watching the shoreline, and he squinted to see a short, bent figure walking to them. "Someone's out." Townsman for sea catch washed up? Or one of the Loyalists, seeking to curry favor with their masters by turning Rebels in? Elijah spoke just loudly enough to be heard by Christopher over the crashing surf. "A rider came through this morning. They be moving the red coat line along the King's road so the lobsterbacks will be in the village soon. You will be questioned."

Christopher lost some of his cocky smile. "I have reason to be here. Helping my cousin build his new chimney."

Elijah reached out for the treasure. "It will be easier for me to hide this. Your cousin does not know why I summoned you?"

"Aye," Christopher said relinquishing the crock. "In these perilous times, I do not even know what way he leans this day or the next. Colony or King?" Christopher said to a worried Rebecca. "The storm clouds will blow over, leaving us a good headwind. Then Elijah and I will cast off tomorrow morn or the next."

Always a strong man, Elijah found this crock's weight more than he expected. God, it seemed so heavy, but lately even lifting his feet sometimes seemed too hard to do. "We walk back to the village, just friends meeting on the beach."

He started up the beach as Christopher finishing tying up the sloop to a trunk of driftwood.

The bent figure stiffly walked from the trees, and now Elijah recognized her, Jacob's grandmother, Dame Alice. As she walked, her cane sank deeply in the sand. Now she looked to the wind-blown waves. "Sea's too angry to put out this night."

"It will blow down by dawn," said Elijah confidently.

"Then ye sail to Long Island, to save my Jacob?" No emotion showed on her strong face.

"We'll try." Elijah just wanted to get home, this sea wind was making it hard to breathe.

The old woman still looked to the water. "My people were always of the sea. This storm is God's anger at the red coats! He will hunt them down for us!"

Elijah only grunted speaking took more air from his straining lungs.

Alice stamped her cane. "Back in the old world, God's wrath gave such a storm to destroy Philip's ships. Cursed be the Spanish King's proud Armada! Those galleons wrecked on the rocks before our cottages. For many years, my people walked the beaches, finding gifts from the sea. They found this." Pushing aside her plain gray cape, she used a skinny, veined hand to pull off something hidden beneath the neck of her coarse dress. A long, heavy gold linked chain that must have hung nearly to her knees. From it dangled a large, ornate priest's cross, studded with huge, dark stones that gleamed even on the overcast beach. "Tis rubies." She cackled. "Fine, clear burgundy ones, in the sun, they flash bright as flames. A popish foolishness most truly, a Bloody Mary's cross. Tis fitting it buys the return of my precious Jacob."

She dropped the heavy chain into his hand and turned away.

Lord, the widow, had bare enough to feed herself, yet she gave something of great value to his trust. With half the town Royalists and the red-coated army coming, Elijah must not let them find Eli's ransom. He must hide this fine treasure well. But where?

Chapter 1

Laboratory 5, Oyster River Research Facility
Present Day Connecticut

"No seance! Remember what happened last time?" Grace said to the phone tucked against her shoulder, as she typed in an e-mail to Brazil.

"You caught the murderer of Dr. Marshall." Freya came back on the other end. "This time we are going to try and contact Captain Elijah Dell, an ancestor of mine. Maybe we can find out where the treasure of Oyster River is."

"Treasure?"

"It's a lost ransom from the Revolutionary War."

While she talked, Grace started on another e-mail to Dr. Duwan at Woods Hole and asked absently, "We've got lost treasures in Connecticut?"

"Lots of them—did you know Captain Kidd may have buried loot on Charles Island in Milford? He was..."

If Freya got off on one of her history lectures, they could be doing this all day. "I'm sorry, a seance is just not something I want to do. You'll have to go by yourself."

"That's a problem, my van tire is flat, and Mac isn't home to fix it."

"How about if you take your boat over here, and I just lend you my car for a day or so?"

Freya voice turned coaxing, "At eight o'clock tonight, you have the reception for the New Head of Oyster River Research. You hate going to social events, which means you need me to back you up."

Grace had to admit with Sara overwhelmed by the toddlers, Bobby would probably not be coming, and it would be nice to have a friendly body beside her.

Freya coaxed more. "Grace, you know how you feel in fawning crowds. My energy beside you can have a great soothing influence."

At 6' 1", Freya Dell, the great, blonde braided, Viking maiden would be good to hide behind, and the slender, 5' 8" Grace Farrington could easily get lost. But another seance, oh no. "I drive you to Alma's, but I'm not joining the circle."

"You must!" Argued Freya.

"I don't want to."

"That's part of my deal!" Freya firmly insisted. "You have great energy–I know you don't believe in the spirit world, but Grace, I sense you're very psychic. That's how you've made so many DNA discoveries. Your classic theory that revolutionized everything..."

That annoyed Grace a bit. "I came up with the '*Popcorn Gene Switch theory*' by research. Whispers from the spirits and crystal balls had nothing to do with it."

"What about intuition?" Freya did not give up. "You've said that has helped."

"If you mean intuition as your conscious mind inputting data and your unconscious mind sorting it out into a new, understandable pattern, yes. Intuition."

"Some of it. Sometimes," Freya responded carefully. "But a lot of scientists endlessly research and are nowhere as successful as you. Grace, your genius is more than just twisting what you know into another angle."

Oh god, Freya was really laying it on, and as usual, Grace surrendered. "When do I pick you up?"

"Don't pick me up, I'll meet you at the Oyster River Research dock. First I'm gonna take my boat over to a dock by the Shoreline Motel and pick up someone else that I want you to meet."

That would cut more into her research time. "Another blind date for me? No way!"

"No. A woman who is a long, lost cousin of mine, Penny. Actually, her name is Penelope Barstall, descended from Elijah Dell's niece, Penelope Booth."

"You found her with your genealogical research?"

Freya was excited. "No, she found me! She was tracing her family and the lost ransom of Oyster River."

"What ransom?"

Freya's voice from the phone was distant, and she seemed to be talking to someone in her new age store, *Haunts of Wōden*. "That's forty percent off on the crystal-power wands," Freya spoke back to her. "I've got a customer now. I'll give you all of the story later."

Leaving her lab early, Grace decided to dress for both the ORR reception and Freya's seance. She didn't feel like a gown, opting instead to pair a traditional style, yellow silk blouse she purchased while at a Beijing genome symposium with black linen pants. Her car was still parked in front of her lab, so Grace walked over from her condo, and then drove it the little over a block to the entrance of the Research facility, which was just above Oyster River's dock. That's where she first saw Freya and Penny climbing up the metal ramp from the floats.

As a pair, Freya Dell and Penny Barstall where total conundrums for inherited DNA. Over six foot, Freya showed her Scandinavian fisherman's heritage, with a wind-reddened, white complexion, blue eyes, and a long, thick blonde braid. On the other hand, her newly found cousin was hazel-eyed, deeply tanned, with short, frizzy black and gray curls. Penny looked like she only stood 5' 5" inches tall, but Grace noted immediately that from her mastering manner Penny had the same dominating personality as Freya. With Grace's own slender height, blue eyes, and longer, black frosted curls, they would make a varied trio indeed.

"How did you find Freya?" Grace asked Penny as they started back to her car.

"She put her family tree online, and it matched up with mine."

Freya noted happily. "Yes, Penny's added a lot to

mine. On my tree, I had Long Liz dying without ever having children."

Penny quickly supplied. "After her brother, Elijah's death, Elizabeth and her husband, Seth Booth, moved to St. John's. That's in New Brunswick, Canada. Liz had a late-in-life baby, Penelope. Penelope later married an Armond Durlac.

"I haven't been able to get much on him, he may have been Paris nobility escaping to Canada from the French Revolution in 1794." Penny continued fast. "They had five daughters, which unfortunately meant that when they married, the Durlac name was lost, so I haven't been able to trace any of them, except my line from the original Penelope. Every generation, the eldest daughter is always named Penelope, as my many greats--grandmother, Long Liz wished." She finished triumphantly.

Grace turned her old Subaru Forester wagon out on to the main road in front of ORR across the road from the state fish hatchery. Freya twisted around to talk to Penny in the back. "I've got to get this all in my family tree program! You haven't told me much on Armond Durlrock."

"D-u-r-l-a-c," Penny corrected.

"I've got to get your dates, places of marriage, burials, then maybe I can trace Durlac's history for you!" inserted Freya.

"If we know more about the family, we might even find the ransom," Penny finished eagerly.

Freya snorted. "Lots of people have looked for that treasure."

Grace asked, "Looked for what?"

"It's in my first book, *Hauntings of Oyster River*." Freya was looking at her. "You still haven't read it, have you?"

Grace found herself flushing with embarrassment. "I don't read..." she nearly said '*fiction,*' then quickly finished with, "much outside genetics journals. Refresh my memory."

"During the Revolution, Oyster River was close to New York, and British occupied Long Island. The town was split almost evenly between Loyalists to King George and Rebels, such as Captain Elijah Dell's son, Eli."

"Elijah Dell was your great-great-whatever Grandfather?" asked Grace.

Freya nodded. "After a disastrous battle in New Jersey, four of the local boys were captured by the British and thrown into a hellhole prison ship in Wallabout Bay. After months of imprisonment, several of the townspeople raised a small fortune to bribe the guards to free them. Even Long Liz had her slave Posey carry her jewel casket to the beach. That ransom was entrusted to Captain Elijah."

But impatiently Penny broke in. "But the next day, British troops arrived to search Oyster River for Rebel guns and powder."

Freya finished. "Everyone in town knew who was a true subject of the King and who was supporting the Continental Congress, but the whole town stayed loyal to the code of neighborliness and said nothing to the soldiers."

Penny added passionately. "Because he wouldn't talk the soldiers killed the old man! With Captain Elijah's death, the whereabouts of the ransom was lost. I know about the treasure because Long Liz secretly gave all her jewels to save her nephew. When Elijah died she searched for the ransom too–but then the war ended, and she moved to Canada."

It had been awhile since Grace had attended one of Freya's Power Circles. Actually, it had been since last fall. Now, as they pulled up to Alma's, the mid-summer clumps of slender white birches were in full, green foliage. White birch turned to a bank of dark phthalo green pine trees that surrounded the low, contemporary Japanese style house, which was set among moss covered 'mountains' and several waterfalls connected Koi ponds. Parking the car near several others, they stepped under a red Tori gate, walking on round granite stepping stones set in the white gravel.

A petite, platinum-haired Alma opened up the black lacquered door with a warm smile. She led them past the glassed-in ateria, with its smaller garden of bonsai trees, rock lanterns, and another, moss-lined pond with its glinting gold residents. Waiting for them in the main room, the other guests were sipping jasmine tea in the blue, nubbed silk wallpapered room, with its juxtaposing of Sumi-e scrolls and stiff oil portraits of Alma's colonial ancestors.

Greetings extended, everyone headed for Alma's spacious, Orientally sparse dining room. It smelled delightfully of chrysanthemums from the fresh flower arrangements, and sandalwood incense. Grace hoped there would be somebody she recognized, and there was. Wearing one of her artistic, blue silk scarves, Linda Hertz was there, the trim, retired art critic from the New York Times, and also that young girl, Willow, that Grace had seen before.   And two more middle-aged women, that Grace recognized but couldn't name. They all sat around a rectangular, polished walnut table in Alma's dining room, Penny pushed past Grace to take the seat right next to Freya.

Freya started with, "Please take the hands of the persons next to you to form our energy circle." Grace found herself holding the dry, thin hand of Linda to her right and the moist, small-hand of Penny. Grace, as she would with any experiment, followed the protocols and tried to hold on to Penny's hand, but throughout the seance, Penny seemed to be restless and pulling away.

Freya did a blessing, that gave thankfulness and asked for protection for those in the circle. Then she closed her eyes, and all were silent. Eyes still closed and in a deeper than normal voice, Freya pronounced. "Mommy's here for Willow."

The girl gasped. "Mom?" Then stayed quiet, her eyes

growing wide.

"Don't cry, kitten. Mommy's looking over you, and it will get better, I promise."

Tearing up, Willow just nodded.

A silence, then Freya asked, "Are there questions?"

Lynda asked, "I can't find my keys?"

Freya shifted, squeezed her eyes tight. "Don't look anymore. Dropped on the tarmac-- shopping. They have your address on them, and some man you know will return them shortly."

Penny pulled her hand out from Grace's to wipe her forehead, then she placed it down on the table, and Grace had to reach out to take it up again. In the past and even a little now, Grace could feel a low surging of something like electricity when everyone was holding hands. Lord, she would love to get an electroencephalogram tester on all the participants during one of Freya's circles.

Seemingly annoyed, Penny looked at her, then turned to Freya. "Elijah Dell, we're here to contact him!"

Freya took several deep breaths that seemed to relax the tension in her shoulders, as she intoned. "Captain Elijah Dell. Elijah. We are your descendants, Freya and Penny. We call on you to join us tonight. Elijah Dell. Captain Dell."

In the following silence, Grace could hear the ticking of a clock in the distance as the others waited patiently. Freya's head fell forward, and Penny squirmed, looked about, then commanded, "Freya! Are you asleep? Contact Elijah Dell!"

An agitated Alma looked to Penny, saying urgently, "Please don't! She's in a deep trance. You might hurt her. Freya might not be able to come out of it!"

"She's just sleeping!" scoffed Penny.

A cool voiced Lynda gently admonished, "If the spirit chooses to come through, he will. If he doesn't choose to, there is nothing the trance medium can do to force him."

Ignoring her, Penny turned toward the head-bent Freya. "Elijah! That's what we're here for. The treasure!"

"Please!" Linda spoke with finality, a touch of anger in her voice at the danger to Freya.

With the rest of the circle glaring at her, Penny shut her mouth in a tight, resentful line. Then all of them looked to a closed-eyed Freya, who was still breathing heavily.

This seemed almost to be over, so Grace shifted impatiently as she wanted to be out of here, but Freya's chin sunk deeper to her chest. Her eyes remained closed, and when she spoke again, it was in a deeper, harsher voice. "Grace, beware! So many around you are betrayers. Osiris and Isis. They are not to be trusted, one more dangerous than the other, but the more wicked one is Bastet, the jealous feline. She will kill, but even she does not understand the duplicity of Osiris and Isis. Grace, Bastet will be afraid of you. Seeks to destroy you!" Freya's eyes snapped open and sweat now beaded her forehead as she looked around at the shocked faces staring at her. "What did I say, something about Isis?"

Willow piped up, "You were warning Dr. Farrington that..."

Grace cut her off. "That I could trip on or be bitten by a cat. I will try to be more careful, but I think we are finished tonight."

A frowning Alma immediately stood. "We'll have refreshments in the living room."

Penny hurried to a shaken Freya who still sat. "Nothing on Elijah! You didn't contact him!"

A pale Freya was still looking to Grace, and she was near tears. "I saw you frightened, in darkness. Coldness covering you, oh, Grace, it was terrible!"

Grace took her old friend's arm, wanting to get her away from that seance table as she said soothingly, "You know that might have been a flashback to the boat barn when

I was attacked?"

Shakily Freya stood up, looking doubtful. "I don't think so..."

"I'm sure it was. Night was coming on, I was frightened and cold, and I'm sure that's it." Grace looked at Alma. "Maybe you have something stronger than tea for Freya?"

"Of course." The relieved Alma hurried off, as in the living room Willow sat down beside Freya, hesitantly touching her arm and talking softly to comfort her.

Alma came back with a tray carrying a bottle of plum brandy and small, white porcelain, handleless cups. Despite Linda's angry glare, Penny was loudly murmuring to Freya, "I have a terrible headache, and this meeting is done. Can we skip your friend's reception, or maybe you could drop me off at the motel first?"

Freya fingers shook slightly as she took a sip of the brandy, but Grace was relieved to see a little color come back into her friend's face. Dropping Penny off at the Shoreline Motel was out of Grace's way and would make them late for the reception, but that is what Grace had to do. After Penny climbed out of the car, Freya asked Grace, "What do you know of this new Director of Research?"

"Dr. Huang Wong? He began his work in China, and he also hasn't gotten his Nobel yet, but he will be among the youngest ever awarded if they honor him soon. Adam's betting they will."

"How do you feel about that?"

If it had been anyone but Freya asking, Grace would have dismissed it, but she said carefully, "It kind of bothers me. I mean, him being just out of his twenties, doing a lot less research than I have, being honored. It makes me feel old and over the hill."

"You're forty-two, that's not over the hill!" Freya cried angrily. "You should have been head of Oyster River

Research!"

"I'm a scientist, not an administrator, and it's more of an honorary position. I hate the public relations side. Of course, from Wong's curriculum vitae, he has never run an institute before either. He made much of the fact that he's an *'accomplished level five' black-belt in Karate,'* and that his *'hands have to be registered as lethal weapons.'* A top scientist can be proficient in martial arts, but it not usually considered an academic bragging point."

"Oh, Lord, he'll get along well with that KKK friend of yours."

"Kurt's only likes to shock people–he's really a very good, dedicated scientist."

"Why didn't they make him Director?" asked Freya sourly.

"Adam Greenfield doesn't like him much. Kurt MacKay has worked his way up the hard way, his academic credentials are from the Internet and shaky, but his studies of sea creatures are definitely exceptional. That's what I'm worried about with Huang. I've read all of his papers, and early on, he made some really tremendous advancements in epigenetics, but he hasn't seemed to progress beyond those. So far as I see it, he's just been a Johnny-one-note."

"Do you think he's the one that is going to hurt you? Willow repeated what I said in the trance, and most of it came back to me. Perhaps Huang is Osiris, and you're Isis?"

Grace didn't want to get into this. "You said the evil one was Bastet, not Isis or Osiris."

Freya took a deep breath, stayed silent for a moment, then said. "Yes, the sister and brother are not to be trusted, but Grace, you should really fear Bastet–the jealous feline goddess. She is threatened by anyone who gets near what she feels is hers."

Talking like this with Freya was so frustrating. "What does that mean in the real world?"   Freya seemed to deflate.

"I don't know. ..but I know it's a warning!" She too sounded frustrated. "I know, like last time, we'll look back and understand the warning, but I can't be clearer than that. Perhaps Dr. Wong has a wife, who will be jealous of you?"

"Huang's a bachelor."

"Maybe he has a sister? I said..." then Freya corrected herself, "No, the spirits from the trance said..."

Grace shrugged her shoulders and said gently, "You said, the spirits said, isn't that really the same?"

Freya became annoyed. "No! It is not the same! The voices that come through are not me. Not my subconscious. They said Bastet, Isis, Osiris, those are all Egyptian Gods. Bastet is the cat or lion goddess." She thought about it. "Don't let yourself get scratched by some kitten with Bartonella henselae."

"What?"

"Cat scratch disease." Freya continued. "Set killed Osiris, then carved his brother up and spread out the pieces. Their sister, Isis, gathered all the pieces together and sewed him back to life, except she couldn't find his penis, which must have been a problem, because besides being his sister, she was also his lover."

"Freya! Too much information." Grace stopped for a traffic light.

"Horus, their son, took vengeance on their evil brother Set. How the cat goddess comes into that, I have no idea."

"It's not important," soothed Grace.

"**Grace, it is important!** The spirits know it's important! You were given a warning, regarding murder and death. Remember the last time, that seance at the Roost?"

Grace wanted to forget that. "Okay, if any Egyptians come into my laboratory carrying a cat carrier, I will immediately call security."

Freya sighed. "It's not like that. The spirits communicate in their language, their context, and we have to decode it. You said this new Head of Research at Oyster River is a young, ambitious man. A Set? He may be a threat to your career, like Set jealously murdered his brother for the throne?"

"Or since he is young, he may be a Horus, Osiris's son. Maybe Huang-Horus will avenge my dishonor?"

Freya sighed. "Like your DNA research, the spirits can be maddeningly complicated and almost impossible to understand at times."

"Prophecies that can only be understood after the event happens aren't too helpful."

Over the years, both of them had learned the futility of arguing against the other's strongly held beliefs. Reaching the State fish hatchery to the right, Freya brightly changed the conversational direction as Grace turned off the road onto the peninsula that Oyster River Research owned.

In the 1890's, ORR started with some wealthy summer visitors wanting to finance a cure for cancer. Over the years it expanded to bleeding edge research on cellular development and teaching. Several plaques testified to the Nobel Prize winners that had developed their theories here. The whole complex was a mix of architectural styles that started with the whaling Captain's mansard-roofed mansion, now called "The Roost," that in the early days housed Administration, but now the entire lower floor formed a large meeting hall, with the old library and conference rooms upstairs. Already the parking lot was filled up for the gala reception honoring the new Head of Research.

After Grace parked, Freya asked significantly, "Have you been seeing David Gardiner lately?"

Telling Freya anything would be cruel, like raising the hopes of a mother anxious to marry off her aging spinster daughter. "We've dated a few times, but I'm busy, and he runs corporations. And I don't think he's really that interested."

"He likes you. You went to the horse show to watch him jump his stallion. I saw the picture of you both that appeared in society pages."

Oh just what Grace needed, coverage in the society pages. "There is an opening on ORR's Board of Directors, and Adam's been trying to sign up David. So far he hasn't, but maybe tonight, we'll see how interested Mr. Gardiner is in seeing me."

Groups always made Grace nervous, and a hall full of noisy people–some wanting something from her--was pure hell. They probably weren't going to ask her to autograph one of her books, but the people here tonight wanted the celebrity to smile and acknowledge them as a special person and as an equal. And non-social Grace just wanted to run back to her laboratory and work.

Fortunately, or unfortunately, she was not the center of attention. Hearing shouting, Grace turned. A taller, thick-armed, stout guy was blocking Kurt MacKay's way. The guy's face was scarlet, almost as red as his unruly hair and chin whiskers. His thick arms started to swing at Kurt, but trying to get between them, the taller Adam Greenfield got hit in the chest.

"You damned interferers! Always getting into other people's business!" Thick arms shouted as Kurt tried to push Adam out of harm's way. Kurt stood about Grace's height, a lean man, tanned from an active, outdoors life. He was much stronger than he looked, but this chunky, red-faced guy towered over him, and if Grace guessed who he was, the gentleman had a nasty reputation for sucker punching.

She couldn't understand all that the angry voices were saying, but uniformed security guards were headed in.

"Is that?" Grace asked.

"Josh Jeffers," Freya whispered back. "He's the local nut case. Mac's been breaking up fights with him for years. His twin brother's supposed to be a good guy."

"I don't know about the brother, but Josh is supposed to be in jail. Last week he took his fishing boat and tried to ram Kurt's boat."

"Rammed Kurt's lobster yawl?" asked a shocked Freya.

"Yes."

"Josh could have overturned it and drowned the red-necked fool," grumbled a not too sympathetic Freya. " Why is Josh going after him?"

"Jeffery's angry about catch limitations. He blames *'stinking scientists'* in general and Kurt in particular."

Kurt raised his fists to defend his face while Adam still half blocked him, and Josh swung a punch just as security guards grabbed him from behind. It took three of them to haul a cursing, fighting Josh out.

To get out of the way, Grace stepped to the side and bumped into Freya. The tall, blonde braided mountain of comfort said, "Hope the real cops are coming, might be my son. Let's get a drink."

Grace eagerly nodded. Not that she really wanted a drink, but it was something positive to do, and something to keep her from having to socialize. Inside the Roost, they walked over to a bar built into the edge of the meeting hall.

Starting to take money out her handbag Grace stopped when Freya pointed to a discrete sign *'Complimentary bar courtesy of Affiliated Technologies Corporation.'* She would have to look around and see if *Affiliated's* representative, Brian Kancir, was there. *Affiliated* was sponsoring that lobsters' blue-fungus anomaly study she and Kurt Mackay were co-authoring, that showed possibilities for producing an ingredient in a new, powerful skin cell regenerating cream. Was their CEO here? Grant hunting etiquette required she should go and say hello. What was his name, something with a G...Gaydlan, Gaydon? He was young looking and what else did he look like? She hopelessly scanned the crowd, with

Grace's supposed genius, she never could remember people's faces or names even when it was important!

As she looked around the well-dressed crowd, Grace realized she should have worn a formal gown. She saw a few cameras and reporters, including Samantha Carson, the red-headed woman from *The Sound Times*. The reporter smiled at her, but respecting Grace's antsiness in crowds, Sam kept her distance. Grace would have to go over and make an on record comment, after the ceremony praising Dr. Wong.

She looked about more and saw the Wilshusens. This must be hard because Margey really wanted the honor of the Directorship for Fritz. Grace looked away, where were the Brewsters? In the late 1950's, Stewart Brewster had taken Oyster River from a wealthy men's charity to a top-level scientific institution, until times changed, and he fell into disgrace. Was Stewart or Joyce ill? Or had political correctness reared its head, so they weren't invited?

Grace took another sip and scanned the crowd again and froze. In the background was a man about 5' 8" but always standing with an air of authority. Now he was talking to his lawyer friend, with that boyish grin of his, she noted his sandy hair, pale blue eyes, and the way he was always impeccably dressed, that was David Gardiner. He hadn't called her lately, so she kinda of figured they were finished, but there was that opening on the Board of Directors, had David taken it? Did he want to see her more? With David's old and new money, Adam certainly would be pushing him to sign onboard.

Freya had spotted him too. "That's your David."

"Not my David."

"Why don't you go over and talk to him," Freya added with a little physical push from her elbow.

"Later." If David Gardiner were at all interested in her, he would take on the Board position. Grace just pretended to be looking for someone else in the crowd, to let him come to her if he was interested. Hearing a child's squeal, Grace looked around. Five-year-old Ginjer was running across the room with Bobby Jamison in hot pursuit, he only managed to scoop up his daughter just as she reached them. Ginjer had the red hair of their mother, but the boys were going to be like their father, stocky and strong with black hair. Grace could see Sara with a carriage and twin boys, Robbie and Willy. Ruefully, Bobby joined her saying, "Sara just had to get out and be among adults for a night."

Grace smiled gently as from the looks the Jamisons were getting, this was not a child-friendly crowd, but Sara deserved a night out. One of the Board of Directors was walking over, blonde, green-eyed Deborah Forbes. The wealthy Director was fitted into a very revealing dark bronze gown, which still looked good on the athletic, fifty-plus-year-old woman. She had a tall, dark-haired man on her arm, seemingly guiding him over, and he was a hunk, with wide shoulders, strong chest, and an athletic way of walking. Grace noted his very fair skin, unusual for a man who had such dark black hair, and she also noticed deep soulful brown eyes and a quiet, listening way of standing.

"And this is Dr. Farrington," Deborah babbled. "You know, '*Farrington's fusions*' and her *Popcorn Gene* theory? Grace, I'd like you to meet the man who will be funding your research from now on, Jack Stuart."

He looked slightly embarrassed at the gushing introduction. "Actually, it is the *Our Sisters Foundation* that will do any funding, but I've been very impressed with your work, Dr. Farrington."

"Grace, please." She offered her hand to shake as she turned to the woman by her side. "And this is my friend, Freya Dell."

"Freya," he repeated, as he reached out to shake her hand. "You're a researcher here?"

Deborah gave a thrilling, little laugh. "Freya's

definitely not a scientist! She's a trance medium, who runs the local 'New Age' shop– *Haunts of Wōden's* selling tarots and quartz and such. I don't know why Grace and she are friends." Deborah finished with a blazing smile.

Grace smiled sweetly back. "We're friends because Freya has such low standards."

Jack studied them quietly, before saying. "You know, when we first went into Afghanistan, I hired a Bakhsi--a local Shamen-- to bless our working sites. Did it as a show for the local workers.

"When Aret heard we were digging for treasures from the earth, he had me give him a sample of what we were looking for. This he held in his hand for quite a while, then he pocketed it, and he lit his pipe. He was smoking something that didn't smell like tobacco as he directing me to drive him all over our land. When he told me, I parked, then we started climbing mountainsides. Once in a while, he'd halt and take out that sample again, rubbing between his fingers. Aret seemed to commune with it, then he would point to a spot where when we dug, we'd find a seam of lithium or barite or anything else I gave him a sample of. Did better than all my staff of geologists. Tried to hire him permanently for my mining company and wanted him in Africa, but he won't leave Afghanistan."

Freya nodded. "I've done some successful water witching. I think it's a sensitivity to the fluctuations of the earth's electrical fields that can be fine-tuned."

"Interesting. What does it feel like?" He was taking Freya seriously, so Jack obviously didn't feel the need to speak only to someone with the 'label' of a scientist.

Impatiently Deborah intervened. "Tell Grace about your funding proposal."

Grace had the feeling that Jack hated these people mashes almost as much as she did and didn't wish to talk here, but after a slight hesitation, he patiently explained,

"Actually, Dr. Farrington, the Foundation I am with is interested in assisting your research on behavioral genetics. We've been looking at the equipment proposal for your lab that Adam presented. I think we might be able to do something, Eve and I wanted to talk to you about it, but not tonight."

Grace instantly liked this quiet man. "Eve is your wife?"

"No." He smiled briefly at the thought. "Eve Dupree is my partner, *Alcom's* chief financial officer with a chemical engineering background. We run *Alcom* and the *Our Sisters* Foundation together. "

Deborah again slipped her arm proprietarily around his elbow. "He's so modest, but Jack's a billionaire from his mining ventures worldwide." Obviously embarrassed, Jack was flushing slightly as Deborah firmly pulled him away.

After they left, Freya leaned down to Grace. "Well, Deborah's already got her claws into that one. Probably heard he's been renting *Windswept*."

"A windswept what?"

"That is the name of a real Tiffany-glass windowed, teak trimmed mansion closer to Cos Cob and Greenwich than us. Apparently, Jack's company rents it from the Van Rye estate."

"How do you find out things like that?" asked amazed Grace.

"That red-headed reporter you hate, Sam Carson."

"I don't hate Samantha."

"She wrote an article in the paper. *Windswept* now serves as world headquarters of *Alcom* and the home of the *Our Sisters* Foundation. Jack and Eve Dupree, also live there.

"Together?" Grace asked, not that she really cared if that handsome man was taken.

"Not as a couple. There are twenty-three rooms, so he

has the west wing, she has the east. The main building serves for entertainment and business office, not a bad tax dodge when you can live like royalty in exile. Eve lavishes funds to save the world, while Jack's the brains that runs the money train.   If you have anything put away, they've been letting friends invest in their foundation."

"Only friends?"

"Well, usually you need a million, minimum, but he seemed interested in you, and if Deborah hadn't physically dragged him away,   I would have diplomatically disappeared."   Freya looked around and made a sour face. "Great, look who's coming over."

Since this was a semi-formal reception, Dr. Kurt MacKay, obviously decided it was too warm for his fisherman's knit sweater, so he 'dressed up' with a clean white t-shirt, worn-brown leather motorcycle jacket, and his formal black jeans.

Chapter 2

"Ah, the prettiest two ladies here. Would've been over sooner, but Deborah was showing off that new fat cat." Kurt took a drink of his whiskey.

"Excuse me," said Freya pointedly as she walked off.

"They arrested Jeffers?" asked Grace.

"Just took him home to sober up, Adam didn't want ORR filing charges," Kurt said, ending that line of the conversation. He had trimmed his van dyke beard and seemed to be taking this party seriously. "Gaydosh, CEO of *Affiliated* had to leave before you got here, but he sent his regards to you. Seemed very happy with my-our- lobster study. Brian Kancir is over there talking to Fritz Wilshuen. Guy in the navy blue suit. Better say something to him before you go."

Grace looked at Kurt and softly commented. "I thought you and Deborah Forbes were dating?"

Kurt shook his head. "Not for long when you go out with that lady, you always expect a phone call whispering *'play Misty for me.'*"

She gave him a quizzical look.

"Ladies like Deborah are very possessive," Kurt explained.

Grace wanted to change the subject. "Have you been introduced to our new Head of Research?"

"In the men's room. His dick is in proportion to the rest of him–small."

Grace started to choke on her red wine. Getting control, she wanted to go back to the possible danger he was ignoring. "I thought Josh Jeffers was supposed to be in jail after he tried to ram your boat?"

"I convinced the judge the damage to my boat was just an 'accident.' Told the judge nothing was behind those threats, Josh just has a big mouth." Kurt took another sip of his whiskey.

Grace didn't entirely believe that. "Kurt, he looks dangerous."

"Naw." He just smiled.

She set her still mostly full glass down on a table, as Adam had climbed up to the podium set on the small, wooden stage and began his introduction of Dr. Huang Wong. As Grace had expected, just one achievement was highlighted, then Adam filled in with platitudes on the lines of *'such a young man for such great achievements'* and *'vast expectations of future scientific discoveries to come.'* Then Huang's mountain climbing and karate expertise were mentioned. Seeing him in person, Grace evaluated Huang at even less than she expected. He was about 5'5", with a thin body, but exaggerated movements as if he was always prepared and looking for an attack. When Huang spoke, he waxed elaborately on how he personally was going to wrestle ORR from its stultified, nonproductive ruts to the cutting edge of a new, young scientific universe.

Grace turned to shoot an arching glance at Kurt and found him in an eye-lock with a striking, tall blonde in a green business suit across the room. The natural blonde smiled at him, briefly parting her lips, and Grace could see Kurt giving her a wink and his shark's smile back. Okay, no after-meeting-coffee with Kurt MacKay tonight.

When Huang finally stopped to polite and thankful applause, Adam stepped to the microphone and looked at his speech cards. "And I have a further announcement. Since the death of Willard Lunquist, Oyster River Research's Board has been short a director."

Not even realizing it, Grace found herself looking expectantly to David Gardiner. He was standing in the back, peering at the podium with puzzlement, as Adam continued, "We have been honored that the vacancy will now be filled by Ms. Evangeline Dupree, CFO of *Alcom* conglomerate.

Besides running an International mining business, she also co-manages a worldwide charity foundation, *Our Sisters*."

Grace saw a brief flash of surprise and perhaps resentment cross Huang's face. Apparently, their new Head of Research didn't like being upstaged by the announcement of a new Board member, but a very tall, attractive thirty-year-old, gracefully climbed up the three steps to the small stage. Eve was dressed in a green business suit that still managed to radiate femininity and even a hint of sexuality. She smiled warmly as Eve took the microphone from Adam. Grace realized this was the woman who had been locked in eye contact with Kurt.

In a strong, but totally feminine voice she stated, "And as my first directorial act, I'm going to tell you a little bit about my personal passion, *Our Sisters*." She indicated the tall man near the podium. "I and my partner, Jack Stuart, do not run not a business, nor do we run a charity. What we've founded is a new kind of paradigm. We still mine raw materials in a number of countries, that's where the income comes from, but it doesn't go to our investors, at least not directly.

"A few years ago, a personal disappointment caused me to reevaluate my life. I had all the money I'm ever going to need, but somehow I felt unfulfilled. Something was missing–the reason I was here. Then one day I was with Jack, and we saw a woman in labor on a dusty street of Kabul. Her husband had decided the child couldn't be his, so he beat her horribly and threw her out. The village officials considered her the offender!

"Jack used one of our ore trucks to get her to what they call a *'hospital.'* The maternal death rate in Kabul is sixteen hundred per hundred thousand, and her child's chance of mortality was even worse. They don't even count the babies that die in the hills, or the women never seen by a doctor. No one counts the young girls denied schooling or the ones sold into a bondage marriage before the age of twelve.

"Afghanistan is not alone. And yes, nobody can save all of underdeveloped Europe or Africa, but Jack and I figured that we could do something, so we created a foundation." That was no surprise to the crowd, until she added, "It took some hard reasoning for a long time, but finally Jack agreed, and together we gifted *Our Sisters* with the entire assets of *Alcom Corporation*." Several sharp intakes of breath and Grace noted that even David Gardiner raised a quizzical eyebrow. Eve smiled. "We're not totally crazy. Like Bill and Melinda Gates, we know that by donating *Alcom's* assets to a foundation we get a great tax write off, and we still have complete control over our stock."

Standing on the stage with her, Huang was fidgeting as he glared at Adam, but Eve just continued. "*Alcom* has always been a privately held company, but now we are allowing—encouraging-- investors. Only our investors will have to prove a high level of creditworthiness, before being allowed to buy shares, because *Our Sisters* is definitely not your usual speculation." She looked across the crowd. "It does pay dividends back to its investors. What do you think of a return of thirty percent?"

There was a definite appreciative murmuring among the more financially educated members of the reception. Jack was also scanning the crowd, slightly shaking his head at the gullibility of humanity, as Eve started to laugh lightly. "No, an investment in *Our Sisters* does not pay thirty percent! I only wish. Our payouts have varied in the last three years, sometimes higher than market rate, usually a little lower, but not by much, check our website for the exact figures. For investors looking only for monetary returns buy *IBM*, but an investor in *Our Sisters* will be receiving far richer dividends.

"Because *Our Sisters* pays its '*preferred stockholders*' first: the beaten women, starving children, the frail, elderly men on this planet and others that need just a little bit of our help. Our Foundation just sent over two maternal scanners to Lashkar Gah in Afghanistan," she said proudly. "It pays school tuition in Malawi for two hundred children, donates vaccines to Guinea, and in Mozambique we delivered microloans to women wanting two goats for a cheese-making business. *Our Sisters* does not impose our answers. Instead, it respects and empowers the aspirations that people in need express to us."

Grace shot a look at the clock and wondered how long this was going to go on.

There was an approving murmuring in the crowd as Eve continued. "We don't want and won't take someone's 401K, but for those who are able to invest in million dollar increments, your money will be making a tremendous difference in people's lives! Both Jack Stuart and I feel that making this world a better place to live in is the greatest personal fulfillment that any person could ever wish. " Eve flashed a winning smile, as she singled out David. "Mr. Gardiner, you've been satisfied with your returns?"

David smiled tightly, not liking being put in the spotlight, and Grace felt he was saying just a little too politely. "Yes, I have."

She gave him a very intimate smile. "When you're buying again, keep us in mind. There is a lot of work to be done." Then Eve looked over the entire crowd, her face taking a serious expression. "*Our Sisters* is changing this world for the better, just as Oyster River has been changing the World of Science since the 1890's. So, I am personally very proud to be working for both!" Saying that Eve placed the microphone back on the podium and started stepping down from the small stage. Kurt had moved over gallantly reached up a hand to steady her, and taking that hand Eve gave him a warm smile as she stepped down.

Grace was sick of this. She needed another drink–no, she needed to leave. Turning to escape, she ran right into

Adam Greenfield and his wife, Rachel, and Grace had to force a smile.

Starting off sounding concerned Adam said, "I hope you weren't offended by Huang's *'totally new direction remarks,'* Grace. He talks a lot, but he has some good ideas."

"And you'll be getting your Nobel long before he gets his," Rachel finished confidently.

Adam took champagne flutes from a passing waiter's tray and passed them to Grace and Rachel, as they looked to the crowd clustering around their new director. "Because I recruited Eve Dupree as a member of our Board, *Our Sisters* waived minimum reserves and has allowed us to invest a portion of ORR's pension funds with them. So far the returns are excellent."

Grace took an obligatory sip and then pointed to the side. "Freya's waiting for me."

Losing her champagne glass on a passing tray, she hurried over to where Freya was joking with one of the hired waiters.   Grace joined them saying in a low voice, "Announcements over, we can leave now."

It would have been a good get away, but they were intercepted by Jack Stuart, who seemed to be leading his business partner over to them. "Dr. Farrington, I'd like you to meet Eve Dupree."   He turned to Eve.   "This Dr. Farrington, you know of her work."

"Please, call me Grace. It's easier to remember."

"Then it's Eve and Jack..." Eve returned as she watched Freya, who was staring in fascination at the large, pale-turquoise colored stone in Eve's pendant necklace.

"That is an incredible stone."   Grace's best friend reached out with her fingers and lightly touched it.

Surprised but acquiescent, Eve slipped the long, cleverly fashioned snake-scale gold chain off her neck and handed the pendant to Freya. "Although most of our mining is for commercial loads, we do some fine gems too. This was mined in Afghanistan. Legend claims that this stone brings peace and tranquility, and it will be a calming influence in difficult negotiations."

Turning the bright, powder-blue stone pendant in one hand, Freya pulled out one of the many necklace chains she wore. That one had a leather case at the end which she pushed aside to reveal a magnifying lens, which she lifted to her eye.

Surprised, Eve looked to Grace. "Your friend wears a jeweler's loop?"

Grace nodded. "Freya runs the New Age shop in Oyster River, *Haunts of Wōden*. She carries crystals, gemstones, and handcrafted jewelry."

"I also sell Tarot cards, Saint candles, and Voodoo dolls too," Freya added. "Beautiful stone. Hard to verify color under these artificial lights, but the hue looks even, probably not dyed or enhanced. Slight mineral inclusions. But this came from Afghanistan? It looks like Peruvian blue opal to me, and I thought they only came out of South America?" said Freya, as she handed the necklace back to Eve.

Seemingly embarrassed, Eve Dupree looked to Jack Stuart. It was Jack who smoothly explained, "Actually, you're probably quite correct. I gave the necklace to Eve as a birthday present. She must have just assumed it was mined in Afghanistan because I bought it from a jeweler there. The stone could have originated from South America."

Eve seemed to be considering something. "The *Our Sisters* Foundation represents women in business. Micro businesses, as well as macro. We have some jewelers--I would be showing you only the high-end goods–would you be interested in selling some of their work in your store?"

"Do you have pictures and wholesale prices?" asked Freya looking interested.

Eve nodded. "We'll have to factor in shipping and customs."

Freya dug out a worn business card, with a black raven and *Haunts of Wōden* on it. "E-mail me."

Jack seemed to intently be studying Grace. "You know, we should make an appointment to get together with Dr. Farrington and see if she is satisfied with the schedule for delivery of her equipment requests."

"No." Obviously embarrassed, Eve cut in. "Actually the equipment being delivered is going to Dr. Huang Wong ."

Jack looked at Eve. "I thought we agreed Dr. Farrington's work needed *Our Sisters* support?"

"While you've been overseas, I've been talking with Adam, Deborah, and the other directors. Dr. Farrington's laboratory is completely set up and functioning," explained Eve apologetically. "But Dr. Huang's isn't, so I thought we should start with his needs."

Grace hoped the disappointment didn't show on her face.

"But the importance of Grace's work..." Not looking happy, Jack's voice maintained a quiet level. "Let's discuss this, you and I, tomorrow before our conference call to Vietnam?"

Eve nodded.

Jack turned back to Grace. "We'll get this all straightened out and talk later."

Eve smiled graciously, and she and Jack moved off. Leaving Grace to wonder how much in the way of grants this new Director of Oyster River Research was going to allow her? Maybe she had better have a talk with Adam.

Chapter 3

Again Grace tried to get away, but in the back kitchen wing she and Freya ran into Adam Greenfield, who facing away from her and was looking down at Huang. Adam appeared to want this evening to be over even more than she did, but Huang was blocking him, speaking loudly to Adam with hands gesturing. "Foundation funding my work! Advanced work. You agree Oyster River doing old stuff. Now it finances true progress!"

"We will have to maintain a balance," tried Adam. "Dr. Farrington research is moving in very promising directions. She's got a lobster study that may have important commercial applications!"

"No commercial! Want Nobel–not advertisements on cosmetic bottles!" Huang glared at her.

With the wine warming her, Grace didn't give a damn. "Most of my research is funded through grants I obtain personally."

Huang narrowed his eyes. "For old stuff!"

Another voice behind her, male, not loud, but authoritative. "Dr. Farrington's reputation is worldwide, and ORR has pledged to support her." David Gardiner and his lawyer had joined them in this ad hoc kitchen conference.

Huang spoke with contempt. "You that other one? Study crabs, then eat them for supper? Squatting on your broken boat!"

"What?" asked a confused David staring at Huang.

Adam quickly intervened. "He's confusing you with Dr. MacKay." To Huang, he pointed out. "This is David Gardiner, one of ORR's patrons. Dr. MacKay is the man with dark hair and the van dyke beard, he's wearing black jeans and the leather jacket."

David ignored Huang and looked straight at Adam. "I thought I was being offered the directorship vacancy?

There was no mention of anyone else... "

Adam looked embarrassed. "You hadn't accepted. Then I heard you were leaving the country to live in Greece."

That admission came as a total surprise to Grace, who turned to look at David for an explanation. "You're moving?"

David looked pained. "Yes, but that shouldn't be a surprise to you." He looked back up at Adam. "I had intended to sponsor my colleague and lawyer, Alan Silverstein, in the directorship position. Which, if you had returned my phone calls, you would have known."

Adam and David were talking on, but Grace only focused on one thing. David was moving out of the country, and he had said nothing about that the last time they spend an evening together. Dinner and bed and goodbye? He had left early that night for a plane to London, the evening meant something to her, but not to him apparently?

David, Adam, and Huang were arguing about something, but she didn't care. Followed by Freya, Grace just slipped past them and walked away. She'd had enough of socializing for tonight.

Chapter 4

Tuesday was blue-sky bright and clear. At dawn, Grace drove to the Oyster River Library park to take her morning run and hopefully use the clear air time to work out a cellular division anomaly. Afterward she stopped, picked up a newspaper and danish at the Firehouse Deli, then headed to her lab, thinking she might have Dr. Branson's problem worked out. She tried a call to Woods Hole but couldn't get him. Should she e-mail him? No, she wanted the feedback as they discussed the matter live. As she listened to the phone answering machine start, Grace noted there was a scribbled note on her desk: *Board of Directors meeting at the mansion at 9 a.m. Need you to be there. Adam.*

Grace just wanted to ignore the note, maybe take her laptop back to her condo and work? But with Huang coming in, there was bound to be some changes so it would be better to attend the meeting and maybe deflect any harmful ones. Surely Kurt would be there fighting for both of them, but it was better she attended to back up his positions. Taking a folder that she could work on while they blathered on, Grace started walking up to the big, mustard-yellow painted mansion at the front of Oyster River Research.

Going in the back kitchen wing entrance of the Captain's Roost, she met Deborah Forbes. Deborah was wearing long strands of large pearls and a blue linen pants suit with the omnipresent cigarette in her peach stained lips as she stood right next to a '*please no smoking*' sign. Deborah gave Grace a bright smile as she poured coffee grounds into the top of the urn. "I filled it up to the thirty-two cups line because Adam said to expect a long meeting." She stubbed out her cigarette in a saucer. Grace always admired people like Deborah, Adam, and David, wealthy and very busy with their own lives, they still volunteered to take on unpaid directorships and run charities. Maybe since they had long family ties to the community, they actually felt they had a duty to work for the betterment of science and Oyster River.

In the center of the nearly two-story main hall, two long, plastic tables had been joined with folding chairs set around them. As President, Adam was there, and Huang Wong. Besides Deborah and Adam, Grace recognized a few more of the board members, and now, the latest member, Eve Dupree. Today Eve wore a lustrous bronze silk suit, that again managed to be both business-like and sexy, and Grace was happy to note her handsome partner, Jack Stuart, was also sitting in on this meeting.

"Grace, glad you could make it." Jack smiled warmly at her and got up to get her a chair by him. Grace realized what beautiful chestnut brown eyes he had. Standing that close, she could smell his lime aftershave, and even see the rim on his contact lenses. He must wear them–they looked a bit dark colored–was that his natural iris color or cosmetic lenses? But he was staring down at her intently and being female, Grace actually forgot about the genes involved and just found herself enjoying this handsome man's presence beside her.

She had to say something. "It's very nice of you–your foundation–to consider us." That sounded so stupid and awkward.

Jack got another chair when Dr. Fritz Wilshuen limped in and sat down, looking dapperly professorish. He would smile and nod his head and say nothing else that might make someone give him an argument. For the last thirty years, his scientific advances may be non-existent, but his students generally loved him. They were all sitting down on the long tables, as the recording secretary, Gail, passed out multi-page agendas. She flashed Grace a warm smile, but someone was missing, and the meeting was about to begin. Grace looked around for Adam, his chair was empty, so she headed for the kitchen, and as Grace expected, Adam had slipped into the kitchen for his cup of coffee. Grace found him waiting impatiently for the urn's ready light to go on.

"We can't start," she said. "Kurt isn't here."

Adam still watched the light. "He's not going to be attending."

"If this is charting Oyster River's coming year, he should be. I'll go get him."

"Grace, I do **not** want him here!" Adam sounded angry.

"Why?"

"We have a new member on the Board in Eve, and Jack Stuart is here to represent his company and the funding *Our Sisters* might be able to give us."

That was completely unfair. "Funding that should partly be going to Kurt's marine studies."

"But it isn't." Still staring at the coffee urn, Adam spoke with a touch of distaste. "MacKay is a redneck clown, hardly a leading scientist, or anyone I would want representing ORR to *Our Sisters*. Actually, MacKay agreed to this and he is voluntarily skipping the meeting."

"But his work..."

"You can represent his interests." The coffee urn's red light popped on, and Adam poured his coffee, stirred in the powdered creamer, and hastily rejoined the meeting. Reluctantly Grace followed. Now it was her and her alone that would be fighting for funding for herself, Kurt and Bobby, and maybe Fritz Wilshuen. She was preparing to fight, but Grace found herself sitting there while the full Board discussed building repair and increased landscaping allotments.

After an hour, they got on something about the ORR's endowment. Jack looked to Adam, saying in his usual slow, careful way of talking. "We've allowed Oyster River Research an investment of twenty percent of your institutional funds." Not looking too happy, he looked to his partner, ORR's new director. "These figures show a plan to increase that investment to thirty-five percent of their pension funding? I'm not too comfortable with that."

Adam looked worried himself as he stared down at the figures on the sheets before him.

Eve looked at Jack across the table. "You're right, this was another thing that was realigned while you were out of the country. Thirty-five percent is a lot, but their previous investments have had very low returns. This is just to let them catch up a bit."

Jack looked directly at her and took his time before speaking. "Funded by *Alcom's* profits, *Our Sisters* is certainly a sound investment, but in principle, I'm against anyone with limited, non-discretionary funds putting the majority of their eggs in one basket."

"Just this time," Eve pushed.

Deborah prodded. "Jack, that would be so generous of you. ORR is very aware of the good works being done by *Our Sisters,* and we want to be part of the solution. I've put my personal money in and, Adam, if Jack will let us, we should up the total allotment. ORR could liquidate and swing sixty-five percent. Jack, would you accept that from us?"

Before Jack could answer, Eve calmly said, "Yes, we will."

Looking overwhelmed, Adam shook his head. "With the market now, I-I just don't feel confident in making more of a change at this time."

"But, Adam, you have invested most of your construction company's pension funds with *Our Sisters,*" started Eve.

Jack weighed in thoughtfully. "His construction company is his personal business while ORR is a trust that Adam is responsible for, and I agree, he should not liquidate in a bear market. When handling the funds of others, prudence should be the utmost consideration. That's always been a main guiding principle for *Our Sisters*. Eve's made some very lucky picks, but basically, we've invested the Foundation funds very conservatively, with little of the money coming from outside of *Alcom*."

Eve glanced to Deborah, obviously her collaborator as she said, "Transferring from one safe investment to another safe investment, especially one that brings in a bit more of a return, I'd still consider that good business."

They all looked to Adam. Grace could see he was torn, but he said, "We have already agreed to dedicate thirty-five percent of ORR's endowment to *Our Sisters*. Any further investment, we'll table that for now."

Jack nodded approvingly. "That's a cautious position that I approve of."

Eve didn't look as happy. "The offer will remain open."

Grace felt that Jack did not look too happy at that.

Deborah changed the subject. "What are we doing about postgraduate student recruitment?"

Oh, no, Grace was so sick of this. Endless nonsense about websites, scholarships and grade point cut-offs, she wanted to scream. Finally, they got to *'budgetary allowance for support of scientific projects.'*

Huang started immediately, in a loud voice, "Focus must be to modernize! You must use entire funds to research in electrolytic cellular."

As usua,1 Adam insisted on maintaining order. "Dr. Huang, we try to keep a balance of projects, your research, Grace's genetics, Dr. Wilshuen's cancer studies, student education..."

It was Eve who added, "Dr. MacKay's marine biology..."

"No! No! Shotgun efforts miss target!" Huang insisted. "I come here to push you forward!"

Jack quietly interrupted. *"Our Sisters* is especially interested in Dr. Farrington's current studies of the genetic control of behavioral actions..."

Like a tag team member, Eve continued smoothly. "Yes, Grace, perhaps you could outline what you would like to see as support for your laboratory's mission?"

Before Grace could suddenly produce an unprepared presentation, Adam's cell phone rang. The ORR President looked at the call number, then looked sharply up at the clock, saying, "We've run way over today's meeting time. My construction company needs me now."

Jack looked down at his wristwatch and also spoke slowly, with regret. "Unfortunately, Eve and I have to attend an afternoon meeting in the city today." He glanced to all of them. "But something has to be decided before the full committee meeting Friday."

Deborah looked up. "You know–it's terribly stuffy in this old room. No wonder we can't work anything out! I propose an ad hoc meeting, tomorrow morning on my sailboat with just Jack, Adam, Huang, Eve, Fritzie, and Grace. No recorded minutes, just a few of us working things out before the formal meeting."

Jack didn't look happy. "Deborah, we need to get business finished, not socialize..."

"And we will," Deborah reassured him. "But nobody says we can't do it in a nice cool harbor. I'll provide lunch. Eve, you guys don't have a boat--really, living on Long Island Sound and not getting out on the water? That shouldn't happen."

Eve looked up from the note she was writing. "Well, buying a boat is a major investment of time, finances, and responsibility."

"No," Deborah protested. "I rent *The Merry Widow* from Girordano's shipyard. You raise the anchor and lower the sails all by pushing buttons. It's the shipyard's worry about maintenance, and if I need a crew, they provide it, and the docking slip, anchorage, and winter storage, all is included for a quite reasonable rate."

A resigned Jack was slipping his agenda into his briefcase. "Please, don't give my CFO any more ideas to spend money. As for your boat meeting, our time is taken up as it is, tomorrow I will be on a plane to Kenya."

"What about the scheduled Board meeting Friday?" Adam asked nervously.

"I'll be back for that, but I can't make this sailboat meet," said Jack.

"And you don't need to," Eve supplied. "I'm the board member, so I will attend. Deborah, I think it's a great idea."

Fritz shook his head. "With my hip, I'm not limping on a dock."

Huang just sourly demanded. "I must get funding!"

It was obvious that Deborah looked a little deflated when Jack said he couldn't come, but she still turned to Grace with a bright smile. "Can you make it?"

Grace didn't see she had any viable choice. "Yes, but could we keep the sailing and socializing to a minimum and get the budget done first?" And maybe she could get herself dropped off on land and get back to work.

Deborah laughed to the others.   "Grace is such a workhorse."

Disgusted that she'd just wasted a whole morning and had signed up for a bigger waste tomorrow, Grace just left, balled up her paper cup, threw it into the kitchen garbage can, and headed out the back wing door.   She was halfway to her laboratory when Deborah caught up with her. The woman was fumbling in her bag, as she pulled out a cigarette pack. "Wait, please." Grace stopped, allowing the older woman to light up and take a puff, before she said,   "I know this non-science business is so frustrating for you, but tomorrow..."

"Why go sailing?" Grace asked bitterly. "That just going to waste more time!"

"No." Deborah held up a staying hand. "No, Adam's tired and worn out. He just wants to get this ORR budgeting over with, but the way things are going now, he will be giving Huang everything and cutting you out! He's already dropped Kurt and Fritzie's from *Our Sisters* funding. But if I can get Adam on the water–you know Adam loves sailing–he will be in a much better, malleable mood! Then you and I can work on Eve, and I'm sure we'll get your full appropriations and something for Kurt and Fritzi too. Politics, Grace dear, you just have to go about what you want in the right way."

Right way? So far this day had gone into the toilet, and Grace didn't harbor any illusions that tomorrow's boat summit was going to settle matters more favorably. And there was something else she considered as Deborah walked away. Why had Deborah suddenly become her and Kurt's champion? Grace was usually a bit uncomfortable with people, some wanted something from her, some just wanted to be recognized by the 'genius,' but there were others that found her record of intellectual achievements rather off-putting, like almost a personal insult in a challenging sort of way. From comments Deborah had made over the years, Grace sometimes wondered if their relationship was less 'we girls' then as Deborah perceiving Grace as some sort of obstacle to be conquered?

Chapter 5

It was warm for an August morning, and it would be hot later in the day, but Grace grabbed a light jacket, because out on Long Island Sound with a stiff breeze it could be really cold. Actually, getting out of the laboratory, being about to breathe fresh air, did seem to perk her up a bit. At the docks, high tide leveled up the floats straightening out the ramping. Although the 36' Cabo Rico Cutter Kurt lived in was permanently moored to the dock, Grace was a little disappointed to see Kurt's lobster yawl was out. In front of her, Huang walked unsteadily, like he'd never stepped on a pontoon dock before. A zodiac motor dingy was tied at the end of ORR's dock, bobbed in the gold-flecked green water. Deborah herself was there to pick them up and motor them to *The Merry Widow*.

Plowing through smooth water in Oyster River Harbor, they had a clear day and maybe ten knots of wind. Deborah's white hulled, luxury sailboat was anchored offshore and true to Deborah's words, when they hooked both ends of the zodiac dingy up to the stern cradle, a button was pushed, and the ship hauled them neatly aboard.

Huang's skin had a natural yellowish undertone which rapidly seemed to be turning pea green, and as Deborah's boat's sails started billowing over the low waves, so he went below immediately. Deborah turned the wheel at the helm over to Adam, who in his navy blue captain's cap, was obviously relishing every bouncy chop as *The Merry Widow's* bow cut foam out of the Harbor rounding the point in style. On the open Sound, sails filled, and the boat leaned toward the water as they sluicing in virtual silence through lapis lazuli colored waves. Grace stretched out against the sage green cushioned benches and relaxed, as she caught an unobstructed view of the Connecticut shoreline receding with Long Island ahead.

Eve Dupree was already on board, in a light-blue denim blouse and matching shorts. The denim seemed to increase the intensity of her clear sapphire blue eyes. Soon she took a strawberry margarita from Deborah and then stretched out on the green cushioned seat next to Grace. "Have you ever been married?" she asked conversationally.

"No." Grace took a sip of her own strawberry drink.

"Didn't you want children?" Eve sounded surprised.

"My studies are my children. What about you? Any kids?"

Eve looked down at her drink. "I tried—years ago... with a man I loved. But we couldn't. A clinic in Switzerland said we were too genetically close to produce children. Can that be so, Dr. Farrington?"

"Please, just Grace. Well, normally a father and daughter crossing can produce a viable offspring, or a sister-brother relationship. That's done all the time to reinforce breeding traits with horses, dogs, cattle, still, if there is an underlying genetic problem, particularly a recessive gene, even two unrelated people can have genes so closely matched that they're unable to reproduce. Did they tell you what configuration seemed to be the problem?"

"No, we just lost babies," she said sadly.

"Have you considered having further testing done?"

Eve just smiled, saying brightly, "That was years ago. I've moved on, and, like you, my work has become my children."

Out on the Sound, as the sails caught even more wind, *The Merry Widow's* deck tilted at what to Grace looked like forty degrees as they raced faster. Deborah had moved off from them to smoke another cigarette, and the thin, white trail streamed out behind her in the wind. Feeling contented, Grace sipped her strong, sweet drink and settled back. Hopefully, they would get something done today, but she had to admit it felt good to get outside on a cerulean day like this.

After an hour, Adam swung back tacking upwind, headed for Oyster River harbor at a much slower pace. In too short a time they were back, and anchoring off of ORR's peninsula, but Grace had to admit Adam was in a much better mood, and Huang had stayed down below decks the whole time.

Lunch was lobster salad sandwiches and bar-be-que potato chips on the windy deck, then they decided to adjourn to the large main cabin below to begin the meeting proper. Taking the two long brass handles, and opening the two swing out hatch doors, Grace climbed down short stairs, past a neat galley kitchen into a plushly mint-green upholstered main cabin. It was a wide space, with its lily-of-the-valley pattern curtains beside closed, brass trimmed portholes. Deborah's boat was certainly luxurious, but Grace found it not as nicely compact as Kurt's smaller but better laid out Cabo Rico Cutter.

The meeting started off well–or would have--if everything hadn't been punctuated with Huang vomiting in the head further forward. Never-the-less Adam quickly sketched out appropriations for the next three quarters. Only after Deborah pushed--and Eve seconded it--was Kurt's jellyfish migration study funding added. Reluctantly, but for the benefit of ORR, Grace agreed to continue her undergraduate teaching for the summer and fall, with Bobby as her assistant, guaranteeing him at least half his salary, and the condo, with the rest to be made up by the joint Farrington-MacKay lobster study for *Affiliated Technologies*.

When Eve started suggesting further diversification of ORR institutional funds, Grace got up and walked to the open Galley with its convertible table. As she skipped another strong margarita in favor of ginger ale, Deborah came up behind her. "Such a shame David Gardiner is leaving for Greece."

"Yes," replied Grace, with as neutral a tone as she could manage. "He's been very supportive of research at

Oyster River."

"No, I meant personally for you.   There have been rumors, that you and he..." she left the sentence hanging.

"Are good friends,"   Grace noted that Deborah seemed to have an unusually keen interest in her answer. "Nothing more."

That seemed to relax Deborah.   "Oh, well the Gardiners have always been so insistent on the correct family connections.   David and I dated a number times in high school, but my family was in financial eclipse at the time. The Forbes go up and down."

"I thought Forbes was your married name?"

"No, the two times I was widowed, I've preferred to go back to being Deborah Forbes. Like the Gardiners, it's a very old family name in this area." She took out a cigarett but held off lighting it. "Of course the Gardiners marry money on money and still manage to keep at least one good merchant per generation. Much better than we Forbes. We have money, lose it all, and get it again." Deborah laughed brightly, then said, "It would be nice to be Mrs. Gardiner, with no money worries." She gave Grace a sly, side-long look. "Actually, it's a secret, but that might be in the future."

David and Deborah? That was a shocker.   Grace wanted to change the topic. "I understand your last husband owned a whole chain of garden centers?"

"Yes, actually I shouldn't have sold them. Both of my husbands did rather well, but they were tradesmen. Being a Forbes means something special around here as we go back to Colonial times."

"Like the Dells? Freya's family were colonists before the Revolution."

Deborah wrinkled her nose saying, "The Dells were always just smelly fishermen and farmers."

Grace found herself smiling politely back, and hoping her own distaste of Deborah's smug contempt didn't show.

With Huang laying on a bed in the bow with a wet cloth on his head, they managed to finalize a working proposal for the coming Friday Board meeting that included funding for her, Kurt, and Fritz's symposiums. It was after 6 p.m. before Grace was finally able to get into her laboratory, but she was satisfied with the division of funds.

Wind and sunburnt and tired, Grace should've just skipped the lab and walked back to her condo, but instead, she started on the stack of mail Inger mounded on her desk. Requests for her to give paid talks and even more requests for her to give free speeches. Offers of minor awards that--if she accepted--would require her to attend fundraising dinners out of town and give a speech, at her own expense. Once and awhile, she opened a letter with someone offering to fund her research. Not today. Just speaking requests, bills, and more bills

But under that mound of mail was a folder Grace dreaded. Her assistant gathered all letters, e-mails and phone messages together, and then once a month, the folder appeared on Grace's desk. These appeals were always the worst. Letters, some handwrote and some typed, some printed out from e-mails. Questions on genetics that had a personal urgency, a desperation. *Dr. Farrington, I've been diagnosed with the abnormal BRCA1 gene, and an MTDH, my mother, grandmother and two maternal aunts died of breast or ovarian cancer. If you were me, with two healthy breasts, would you agree to a preemptive double mastectomy?* Grace knew the gene expression statistics by heart, but she put that one aside before she answered it, she'd leave a note for Inger to gather up the latest detection, breast cancer treatment, and survival statistics. Maybe the survival prognosis had gotten better.

Reading the next, she signed and then started to type. "Yes, female hemophilia is very rare, but with both your family's medical histories it is a definite possibility that you must consider when thinking of children." Three more letters along those lines, with Grace finally writing, "Since Beta-thalassemia should be a concern for you both, did you ever consider utilizing donated eggs and sperm or pursuing prenatal genetic testing?"

Then there were the other appeals that were far worse—mothers writing their children were desperately sick, dying. Did the eminent Dr. Farrington have an answer? For the first one, Grace replied, "From your son's symptoms, your doctor might look into Canavan disease." Did that help? Did knowing what was killing your child make it any easier?

These letter writers didn't want a diagnosis or a treatment course, by the time they wrote her they unfortunately already knew what was available. From Grace, they wanted a miracle. Could--in her genius--Dr. Farrington recommend a study for a new pharmaceutical that would give their baby a chance at a normal life?

How many times had she written, "Gene replacement therapy is not at the stage yet that can be of help to your daughter. But progress is ongoing..." Yes, with just a little more time we might find a cure, but how much time did their sick baby have?

No matter how many of these letters Grace got, she answered them all, sometimes with her eyes welling with tears. Too rarely she could point some parent in the direction of a scientist, who was testing a new treatment for their particular brand of hell, but always, as she worked her way through that forlorn folder, Dr. Grace Farrington was so very truly aware of how empty and fallible her supposed genius could be.

Chapter 6

Friday early, Grace tried calling Freya at home again, still no answer. Maybe she was out hunting that treasure with her new cousin? The Board of Directors meeting at the Roost went well, Deborah's sailing strategy had worked. Returning from it earlier than she expected, Grace scanned her e-mail. Something coming in from Brian Kancir at *Affiliated Technologies*, politely enquiring about the final report on the '*Blue project,*' the blue fungus-mottled lobster study she had undertaken last Fall mainly to keep Bobby Jamison employed.   Preliminary results must be finalized and presented. For that, she would have to speak to her co-author, Kurt. She could e-mail him—Kurt did pick up his e-mails at least once a month. Instead she decided to walk down to the docks.

Leaving the lab open, she headed out in the hot summer sun. Most of the cars from the Board meeting were gone with just a few left behind the mansion. Deborah's tiny silver Mercedes looked like a cowering kitten next to Adam's cherry red 1500 Crew Cab truck. A black sedan was parked there, and for a second, Grace thought it might be David Gardiner's Cadillac?   She felt slightly let down when she realized it wasn't.   Two more cars parked near the Roost's back entrance, two snappy, matching Jaguar convertibles. One in silver, and one in powder blue.

Even a non-car person like Grace could lust a little after that fancy pair. Earlier she had seen Eve driving the blue, so the other must be Jack Stuart's. Truly dedicated, they must have stayed on after the meeting to talk about future goals. Grace stopped, almost wanting to go back inside. Jack Stuart, that tall, quiet man was so comfortable to be around, but more than that, he had an unconscious animal magnetism that made her wish she had worn something just a touch more revealing. What if she went in, just to see him, inhale his aftershave, and maybe talk a bit—what reason would she give? No, she had that lobster study to complete.

Low tide, the metal screened dock ramp with its wooden cross ties, was almost at forty-five degrees. Grace climbed down, then stood on the float, listening to the herring gulls nagging overhead, as she smelled rain cleaned wind just off the marshes at their end of the harbor.

Walking on the bouncing dock, she could see lights on inside Kurt's live-in sailboat, *The Lovely Lady,* with its smashed bow that Kurt was going to repair someday wrapped in a blue tarp. But his lobster yawl wasn't in its slip, which didn't seem right. With the exception of Bobby, Kurt didn't allow anyone else to take out his workboat. Hearing a diesel chugging, she looked further. The *Big 'Un* was chugging back to the dock, with Kurt at the helm. So who was inside *The Lovely Lady* lighting up his portholes?

As she watched the lobster yawl, puffing blue smoke was sliding into its slip in front of *The Lovely Lady*, and a cheerful Kurt tossed her a line to tie up. In pressed tan shorts and a blue polo shirt, he looked more spruced up than usual. His black van dyke beard was neatly trimmed, and Kurt looked like he had on brand new deck shoes. He hopped off his diesel, carrying a large, brown shopping bag.

"Hey, Gracie, you out of your lab before midnight?"

"Brian Kancir of *Affiliated* e-mailed. They need those data sheets on the lobster study. I want to get that finished."

"Yeah, the lobster project." He shook his head. "Been meaning to bring those over to ya. Will do that early tomorrow."

"You have them done?"

"I do, they're in my boat."

She looked to the white-hulled, Cabo Rico Cutter. "So I'll pick them up now and send them out for you."

He didn't seem to want that. "No, I-I gotta find them. I'll bring them over tomorrow and buy ya breakfast."

Obviously, Mr. MacKay didn't want her going on his boat, so he must have a lady on board, but Kurt was not usually this secretive about his other lady friends? Now Grace and he shared a bunk now and then, but with a clear understanding that neither owned the other, so who he was sleeping with was none of her business. Still feeling like teasing a little, Grace started to his sailboat. "Or, I could just climb down your hatch and find them myself," she said sprightly.

"Hey–y, Gracie, no..."

Yes, he didn't want her going over, so she hurried up a bit to the gangplank on the side of his boat. She was headed toward the main hatchway, but he was faster and got ahead of her. From below decks, she could hear the deep, pulsing, rising music of '*Ravel's Bolero*' playing. Grace gave Kurt an arch look. "She's started without you?"

Kurt ignored her teasing and walked to the open hatchway, calling out, "Are ya decent? We have company, Grace is with me." But as Kurt looked down that steep ladderway, the leer faded from his face. Not seeming to think, he put the paper-bag down on the sailboat's deck, then looked back to Grace, his face tight and haggard as he harshly ordered, "Stay there!"

Hearing that authoritative tone, she just stood there listening as he climbed down. The music stopped, but no feminine voice giggled from below. Kurt was taking his time–she half thought of following him down just to tease him with some new, naked lady, but Grace found herself staying put. She didn't hear his rubber-soled deck sneakers on the ladder, but when Kurt came up grim-faced, he was pulling out his cell phone from his front pocket.

"Could you give me your data on a flash drive?" Grace started.

Kurt looked at her, as if he had never seen her before, then he spoke in a low, urgent voice, "Grace–go back to your lab! You were never here!"

"What?"

But Kurt's eyes were already scanning the shoreline. "Shit! Students coming down to the dock. They've seen us and probably recognized you. Better not lie then, Grace, just stand there. Don't look down the hatch. I've got to call the police." He turned away to look out at the water, as he listened to his phone ringing.

Not into obeying, she moved to the companionway. Looking down, Grace could just make out a women's legs in blue pedal pushers, sprayed out at an awkward angle on the deck below. "Kurt–she fell?"

"She fell forward, but the back of her skull's caved in. Looks like someone bashed her good." Then the phone must have been answered because he spoke in a louder voice. "My name is Kurt MacKay, I have to report a death."

Chapter 7

As he ended the call, Grace started to go down into the hold, but Kurt grabbed her arm painfully, stopping her.

Grace argued, "Shouldn't we try CPR?"

"Her skull's caved in at the back. Been awhile, blood's drying."

"Who is she?"

"Eve Dupree," answered a pained Kurt.

"Who was planning to spend the night with you?" The competition for Kurt just upped to the max; that was an unpleasant surprise for Grace.

Kurt looked down at the brown paper sack he'd left on the deck. "Aaup."

Not saying anything, they just waited until the police came in two cars, but not Mac or Ben or any other town patrolman Grace recognized. The first cop moved to them, while the second when down below. "This is your boat, sir?"

"Yes."

"Did you know the lady?"

"Didn't move her body to see her face, but I figure it's Eve Dupree. We were getting together tonight," he gave a sidelong look at Grace, "to have some chili and wine. She was standing on the upper deck when I left her."

"Anybody see that?"

Kurt looked along the bank and shrugged. "Maybe."

The cop looked at the tarp wrapped bow. "You were going out sailing in this boat, sir?"

"No, I live aboard her. *The Lovely Lady's* permanently docked, see the hookups to sewage and electricity."

The other cop coming up asked, "And when you left her, Ms. Dupree was alive?"

"Aaup."

"Why did you leave her?" The first cop started again.

"The lady wanted white wine and such, so I took," he

indicated his diesel lobster yawl, "Over to the town dock so I could do some shopping." He pointed to the bag on the deck.

Grace added. "He has an alibi with me. Kurt just went down the hatchway, there wasn't time to kill her."

"Unless I killed her before I left to go buy the wine," Kurt helpfully commented, giving Grace a look that indicated he knew exactly what he was doing to himself.

Oh, shit. He was always such a stubborn blockhead!

The cop slipped his notepad in his pocket and reached down into the bag, exposing a wine bottle neck. "Have you been drinking, sir?"

"Not yet."

"The lady, was she drinking?"

"Not that I know of. In fact, I doubt it, she just came from a Board of Directors meeting up at the Roost." Seeing what was coming Kurt looked grim.

"The Roost?" The second cop asked.

"Captain's Roost is that big, yellow Italianate mansion up on that hill there, that's used for Oyster River Research's meetings."

The other cop bent down and was rummaged in the brown paper sack. Reaching deeper, he pulls out a red and white can of whipped cream and a small cardboard box of '*super ribbed*' condoms. He looked up, saw Grace, and dropped the box back in the bag. Grace looked at Kurt and noted he seemed to be coloring under his suntan.

"Sir, you were planning a long night?" The first cop asked.

"Was," admitted Kurt. "Course the lady would've had the final say to that," Grace noted that Kurt was not saying anything about the back of the head wound or the fact that he thought someone had hit Eve from behind.

The cop was looking to Grace. "You are?"

"Dr. Grace Farrington."

"You were joining the party?" The cop asked knowingly.

Grace did not like his smart assed assumption. "No, Dr. MacKay and I are co-authoring a scientific study. My lab is up the hill, and I walked down here to discuss our report and pick up some data. When I reached the dock, I saw his diesel coming back."

"Did you see anyone else on the dock?"

She had to think about that. "No, but there were people about. Students...and up by the mansion, the Board of Directors meeting was breaking up. I didn't see anybody else on the dock, but I wasn't really looking." She was rambling, and so Grace tried to focus. "I waited there at the slip to help Kurt tie up and then walked over, and we found the body."

Kurt immediately corrected. "Grace didn't find the body. She stayed on the upper deck of my sailboat when I went down below. In fact, I think you can let her go because she's told you all she knows."

The cop looked a bit annoyed at being told his job, but his partner who was now radioing in nodded. "Let her go. I know where to reach Grace if we need her."

Great, the cop obviously knew who she was, and Grace had no idea of his name. The first cop nodded that she could leave and that now seemed more like an order. Grace looked at Kurt. He just moved his eyes towards the mansion. "You better talk with Adam."

Three ORR postgraduate students were down on the dock untying one of the small, yellow, wooden motor boats as they curiously stared at the cops and Grace. Trying to look normal she just marched past them and headed up the hill. Almost all the cars were gone now, with just Adam's truck and the two Jaguar convertibles parked behind the Roost. Before the meeting, Grace had seen Eve getting out of the blue one, and she'd left the top down. Someone was going to have to put the top up for her before it rained tonight.

Sighing, Grace climbed the back stairs to the rear addition.   In the kitchen, she smelled the coffee still percolating in the urn as she walked through to that two-story meeting hall. Most of the chairs had already been folded by the other board members as they took their leave. Now at the two tables, only three people were left, Adam, Huang, and Jack Stuart. Across from her, Adam could see Grace walking in, but Huang and Jack's backs were facing her.

Huang was talking excitedly.   "Finances must be focused on my work! Mine is new! Grace's work is past!"

Jack's voice came flat and firm. "As I have already stated several times, *Our Sisters* will be funding Dr. Farrington's research and yours. We will also see what can be divided among Dr. MacKay and Dr. Wilshuen."

"Wilshuen–old fool! MacKay's doing nothing-- he brings that Jeffer's thug to my reception!"

Jack must have seen a reaction in Adam's face because he turned and smiled to see Grace. "Dr. Farrington, maybe you should be included in these discussions." He looked at Adam. "Or perhaps it should be just between the President of ORR and myself?" With old-fashioned politeness, Jack stood up to unfold a chair for her while in a quiet voice he continued, "But Grace, I promise you your interests will be being protected."

Grace spoke, her voice sounding upset to her. "Those convertibles out front–-yours and Eve Dupree's?"

"Yes." Jack flushed a little bit. "Actually they're both rentals belonging to *Alcom*. Eve picked them out, a bit too showy for my taste, but I've got to admit they're fun to drive. If you like, I'll take you out for a spin sometime. Maybe we could have dinner?"

"You go out with her? What? Talk about grants?!" Huang demanded.

Jack turned and looked down at Huang from his dominating height, his face impassive, yet Grace could feel anger. Still he spoke softly. "I will talk to Grace or anyone else, about anything I wish to talk about, and that, sir, is none of your business."

Not knowing what to say, Grace automatically sat down and waited until Jack also sat down beside her. She started to talk. "Uh, there's been..." She started, but no one was paying any attention.

Adam was back pointing to sheets alongside his laptop. "We've been going over the Foundation's research grant to ORR. Huang really wants..."

Jack quietly spoke up. "All of it. But... " He looked directly at Adam. "As I explained, both Eve and I feel that Grace's research is vitally important and needs to take precedence. Eve has agreed to vote that understanding." Jack looked at Grace. "We've been following your research for some time..."

"Eve is dead." Grace hadn't meant to blurt it all out like that.

Adam looked shocked, the blood seemed to drain from Jack's face, but he only looked at Adam and asked, "Is she joking?"

Adam shook his head. "Grace wouldn't joke."

Jack looked back to her trying to understand something he couldn't accept. "Eve's hurt?"

"On the dock. She fell..."

He was rising, and Grace tried to put a staying hand on his arm, but he gently pulled it off as he was striding across the room. Grace hurried after him. "Down on Kurt's boat. There's an ambulance coming, but Kurt said she's gone. She was by herself–she must've fallen and hit her head."

Three cops cars were now parked blocking the dockway. Behind them, Grace could hear Huang's shrill complaining, "ORR involved in death! Not in my name!"

Although Jack was striding not running, with his long

legs, he was way ahead of her when he slipped between the police cruisers. A 6'5' inch uniformed officer was stringing yellow crime scene tape over the dock entrance, and Grace was glad to recognize Mac Dell, Freya's sandy-haired son. Mac stepped in Jack's path to stop him, but Grace called out. "He works with her. He can identify Eve."

Mac nodded and stepped back, allowing Jack to proceed to the police standing on the boat. Not fully realizing what was happening Grace looked at the yellow tape. "They're closing off our dock?"

"Fraid so." Answered Mac.

"Why?"

Mac looked down at the ramp. "Being treated as a crime scene."

So the police now think Eve was hit in the head by someone. "Do the detectives know Joshua Jeffers was arrested for attacking Kurt at the reception?"

"He wasn't arrested," Mac corrected. "Adam Greenfield didn't want charges pressed because of the publicity, but I'm sure the detectives will be talking to Josh."

Grace looked to the end of the dock and Kurt's boat. Jack was now on it with a policeman blocking his way and was talking, arguing with his hands. He seemed to have convinced the first cop to let him go down, and with the other cop preceding him, they all went below.

Kurt stood on the deck, quietly between another two officers. Was he going to be arrested? Finally, they said something to him, and he started walking up the dock by himself.

Adam had joined Grace and several of the students standing watching. Anxiously he asked, "Did Eve fall on our dock?"

"No, down the ladder of Kurt's boat," Grace explained.

"Why would she be there?" He spoke with disbelief.

Grace didn't want to answer that, so Adam continued, "Is MacKay under arrest?"

"Doesn't look like it, and he didn't do anything! I was with him when he found the body."

Kurt boat sneakers rang on the wood cross pieces of the low tided ramp as he climbed up.

Grace asked, "Are you under arrest?"

"Nope. But they won't let me on my boats, even to pick up a second pair of jeans."

Which meant he had no place to sleep. Grace should offer the spare room in her condo, but she could still see the brown paper bag sitting on the dock with its wine bottle and box of condoms.   Adam was still speaking. "Huang is living in the guest lecturer's apartment until he finds a place to buy, and the student dorms are filled, I think. I could ask the Wilshuens as the house ORR gives them is big enough for you to stay awhile."

"Aaup. Don't want to go to the expense of a motel, and this kettle of sea slugs looks like it's gonna take some time to straighten out." He didn't look worried, just inconvenienced.

Grace was watching the hatchway of Kurt's sailboat. Finally, Jack climbed back up and away from the cop, almost as if in a daze. As he walked out on the float and climbed to the upper docking, Mac quietly lifted the yellow tape on the dock railings to help Jack get through, and then stood beside him.

Adam, Grace, and Kurt walked over, and Adam started to say something, but still looking at the boat, Jack said, "Please, I rather be alone."

Kurt nodded, so the others left, and Grace herself pulled back across the road, watching Jack. Wishing she could think of something she could do, Grace just watched helplessly as that huge man stood with his shoulders bent in grief. Jack stood there for hours while the police photographer arrived, followed by the coroner and his bulky case, who Mac had to help down the ramp. Obviously, in agony, Jack's eyes followed the white ambulance, turning off the Main Road to ORR. The State police cars that came with it and State Police Detectives, Grace presumed they would soon to be interviewing her. She watched them as they parked down the road, in front of her lab.

She should go and talk to them, but instead-- compulsively--she still kept staring at Jack Stuart. As Grace watched him, Jack's eyes followed the folded, metal frame carrier rolled down the hill, then lifted over the dock ramp. Watched as he saw the green sheeted body removed from Kurt's boat and loaded on to the ambulance. Only when the ambulance slowly pulled away, when Eve was truly gone, when whatever he could do for her was finally over, did a bent shoulder Jack start to walk on to the road.

Chapter 8

Grace moved to Jack. He had moved away from the dock but was just standing there in the middle of the roadway, staring at where that ambulance had gone. She took his arm, guiding him out of the road toward the cars. "It's going to rain. You've got to close up her car."

He still stood there, then finally seemed to shake himself awake. "I don't have her keys."

That's a problem, and the police won't give them up this soon. "I'll call maintenance and have Sam put a tarp over it," Grace said slipping her arm into his. "Come with me, we've got a cafeteria here. Let's get something hot, maybe some tea? Coffee?" They headed in the direction of a brick and glass 1950's building, that held the new administration offices, cafeteria, and science library.

In the café, Grace brought over a cup of black coffee to Jack, who sat there, not drinking it. She hated to but felt she should push. "Does Eve have a family to notify?'

Those deep brown eyes turned to stare at her. "No,...no family. Eve was an only child, and she lost her parents early. I'll make all the arrangements for her. I have her power of attorney, and I'm her executor. Funny, I'm older, we always thought I'd go first, and that she'd be running *Our Sisters* alone..."

"Don't even think about that now." Grace wanted to get his mind off of it. "How did you start *Alcom?*"

His face lightened a bit, glad to overlay other memories. "My father was a mining engineer and geologist. Great with finding whatever you needed, but he was always finding it for other people. Since the age of ten, I traveled with him. Mom stayed home, especially after my little sister was born. Dad died in a mining accident when I was nineteen, that left me, mom and my younger sister to support. I started working for the company he had, and I seemed to have the business sense my Dad lacked. It wasn't long before I had my own company going, then Mom died of lung cancer. Smoking."

"Where's your sister now?"

He stopped and looked away from her. "Kristen died young." He said nothing, she waited, and then he spoke with pain, "Drug overdose. Obviously, the wealth I could give my sister probably helped kill her."

Jack finally drank some coffee, then said, "Alone, I just concentrated on the business. Growing and growing it more became an obsession with me. Sometimes good, sometimes bad. Eve was working for me as a chemical engineer during one of the bad times, and she started helping maneuver the finances. She was good at it and managed to help me save the company." He stopped, more pain crossing his face. "I didn't manage to save her either."

"You can't blame yourself for an accident?" Grace protested.

He stopped and drank some of his coffee, which must be getting cold. Finally, Jack started again. "It was Eve who realized that both of us were pouring our entire efforts into just pure business ventures and that our lives had no real meaning other than trying to add another zero to the bank balance. So that day in Kabul, when we helped that beaten woman, we saved ourselves too."

Grace so wanted to help this man. "*Our Sisters* will be a fine memorial to Eve."

He sat up a bit straighter. "I'll have to organize a funeral here and memorial services at the other company locations. Grace, I would take it as a personal favor, if you would come to Eve's funeral?"

She definitely did not want to utilize her time that way, but Grace just nodded. "Of course."

Grace offered to drive him home, and Jack said no, he would rather be alone. When She walked him back to his car, it was starting a cold rain, but because of Grace's call, Sam had already covered Eve's Jaguar convertible with a blue tarp, roping it all around against the wind. Jack looked at the car. "I'll tell the rental company to come pick it up."

She watched him drive off, then feeling tremendously empty herself, Grace walked back to her lab, entering it to find the phone ringing. It was David's clear voice. "Grace, I've been trying to get you."

"Yes." She let her voice stay cool. "You should call now, it'll be a long distance call when you have to telephone from Greece. That was real news that you're moving." *A real kick in the head type news.*

He sounded surprised. "I had discussed Greece with you. We just haven't arranged when you're coming over..."

"You want me to visit you?" David wanted her to just drop her work for a vacation lying on some Mediterranean beach?

"Visit?" He sounded mystified. "Grace, you seem confused about all this...I don't think we should be discussing it on the phone. What are you doing for dinner tomorrow?"

"I'm having my weekly dinner at Freya's."

"You could change that."

She was in a contrary mood. "No, I'm afraid I can't."

"Then how about New York on Wednesday?"

So he can brush her off nicely? Grace didn't want to waste the time. "The City will take too long."

"Then we'll stay local, what restaurant would you like?"

David wasn't a man who gave up easily, and she had to eat dinner anyhow. "There's a new hibachi restaurant on the Post Road towards Greenwich, *Mountain of Fire.*"

"I'll pick you up at your lab at 5:30, and we can get this all straightened out then."

She was just putting down the phone, as two huge, suited men walked into her laboratory.

"Dr. Farrington?"

"Yes."

"Detective Loomis and Detective Kimball, State Police." They flashed I.D.s, faster than she could see and Grace wondered if they choose detectives that looked big to intimidate suspects. Loomis was continuing. "We were told that you were there when Mr. MacKay found the body of Ms. Dupree?"

She stood up to greet them and walked around her desk. It was ridiculous, but the police always made her start to perspire. "I was there–yes."

"You knew Ms. Dupree?"

"Yes, she's a–was a--Director of this research facility."

"Any problems with her?"

"Problems?"

"Did you feel that she might have insulted you or wronged you in some way?"

"No."

"Then no arguments?"

"No arguments or bad feelings. I just met the woman a few times."

"Have you ever dated Mr. McKay?"

The last time she lied, Grace got into big trouble. "Yes."

"Sleep with him?"

This was entirely too personal, so Grace evaded the question. "We are friends and scientific colleagues on a marine study. I was aware Eve was on his boat socially, and I didn't have any problems with it."

"What about Mr. MacKay?"

"Dr. MacKay. Had a cordial relationship with Miss Dupree, and I think they planned to spend the evening together. He went out to get wine, and when he came back, I saw him find her. He was terribly shocked."

"Did you see anyone else in the area?"

"On the dock? Before he came back?" She tried to picture it, but she had so many other things on her mind this day. "No, I'm sorry. But I had just arrived, and this is an open campus, people are always walking about, going down to use the motor boats for research..."

As Detective Loomis finished writing that down, his partner looked down at her. "I understand that you had something to do with finding the murderer of Dr. Marshall?"

"Yes, I did." *If they knew that, it might be points in her favor.*

He frowned. "For future notice please leave this investigation to the professionals."

Grace deflated. "Of course."

They left with Grace having the distinct feeling they were not treating Eve's death as an accidental fall, but as murder, and that she and Kurt were chief suspects.

Chapter 9

The next day, she was finally making progress on sequencing alleles from Woods Hole, until another unwanted guest strolled into her laboratory. A woman dressed in a pants suit, with a red coat jacket trimmed with a black velvet collar. Her '*hunting pink*' outfit was accented with matching jewelry displaying expensive looking gold and diamond foxes. That was Deborah Forbes.

"Grace," she said. "Always working! I came down today to have Gail run off the agendas for our next Board meeting."

"That's good." Grace tried to be polite as she wondered how long this will this take?

Unfortunately, Deborah seemed in the mood to gossip. "Adam is very angry about the body being found on Kurt's boat."

"Isn't he more unhappy that Eve is dead?"

"Of, course! But a murder here, it's just terrible publicity for Oyster River," Deborah fretted.

And not too great for Eve, Jack, and Kurt, Grace thought. "It could have been just an accident, she fell, hit her head..."

"Not with the police questioning everybody. Sending out divers by Kurt's boat, probably looking for a weapon. Of course, I know Kurt couldn't have done it." Her face changed, looking doubtful. "But he is wild. If she fought him..."

"Kurt did not kill Eve Dupree!" Grace said a bit too firmly.

Deborah looked sharply at Grace. "I didn't even know he knew her. Was Eve going after Kurt? Were they lovers? They'd just met."

"As a new director of ORR, I think Eve wanted to get to know all of the researchers here, so she was having a bowl of chili with Kurt." *Forget about the condoms in Kurt's shopping bag.* Yeah, Eve must have moved fast, and Kurt MacKay wouldn't have been objecting.

Deborah didn't look like she bought that '*just a friendly*' meal bit. "But you're a detective, at least you were with Dr. Marshall and that girl. Who do you think killed Eve?"

"I have no idea." Grace looked at her computer screen again, but Deborah didn't seem to take the hint. "And I've really got to get back to my work."

"Oh, yes. I've got to go, too." Deborah started to turn, then looking conflicted, she stopped and came back at Grace, lowering her voice. "I shouldn't say this. I haven't told the police, but after the board meeting, I stayed and went to Gail's office for some of the papers. When I walked back to my car, I looked down at the dock, and I saw David Gardiner near Kurt's sailboat. I don't know what David could have been doing there, since Kurt and he are hardly friends? I'm sure it was innocent, but I didn't say anything as the police might not understand." Then brightly smiling Deborah left.

That little nugget of information about David seemed to hit Grace almost as a blow. For today, all work was finished. She stood up, took her lab coat off, and headed back to her condo. She could do a fast run to release some tension before she showered and changed for Freya's.

Once a week Grace and Freya tried to get together for dinner, either cooked at Freya's house or at a restaurant if it was Grace's turn to treat. With narrow old roads along the harbor in front of Freya's house, Grace parked in the Town lot. She brought French bread at the cheese shop and walked over on a cross street coming out on to an old lane that ran along the shore, where 1800's one or two-story stores gave way to older 1700's wooden houses. Freya's was a two-story wood clapboard, with peeling white paint. A house on the water that grew with the generations passed down through the

Dell family. Tucked away on the side, a recent addition of wooden stairs led to the tenant's apartment on the second floor. Freya had the full first floor and the back kitchen stairs to the attic storage, while Mac rented his apartment downstairs in the basement, with its own Bilco door entrance at the back.   Climbing the porch, Grace knocked then just pulled open the front door. Freya had already stopped using those new locks Mac had installed last fall. Inside, as she inhaled the rich smell of tomatoes, sausage, and meatballs, Grace realized how hungry she was. That fresh garlic sauce must have been simmering in the crockpot since Freya left for work in the morning.

In the foyer, the now no longer used main staircase and hallway divided two large, high ceiling front parlors. The one to the left was curtained off and filled with Freya's many craft and Viking wood projects. In the parlor to the right Freya did her private tarot and psychic runes readings for clients, so Grace was walking through rich dark reds and blues, heavy brocade curtains, Empire furniture, and Tiffany-like glass dragonfly lamps.

But going through the jewel beaded glass curtain across the room, Grace was in Freya's Swedish modern dining room. Ahead was the door to a county kitchen, remnant of the original Colonial farmhouse with its old gray slab wood cabinets. In there Grace put down her bread and looked around. A bottle of white wine was already opened, but it was down to its last quarter. Unusual because even with Mac, the three of them rarely finished a full bottle. Grace poured herself the rest in a glass goblet decorated with a climbing dragon, and carried it toward the back of the kitchen, pushing open the screen door to a porch that overlooked the harbor. Freya might not have much money, but she had a view most millionaires would envy.

There were usually three chairs on the cramped little fire stair porch. Today there were four. One empty for Mac, one for Freya, and Penny was there, holding out her glass. "While you're up—can you get me a refill?"

"The bottle's empty," Grace said.

Penny giggled. "Just open up another one. Freya, where do you have more wine?"

Before Freya could answer, Grace, put her goblet on the table before Penny. "Not necessary. I haven't touched this one yet, and I really don't feel like wine tonight." Grace sat down and scooped a taco chip into the onion dip in a bright green, cabbage-leaf shaped dish. Thinking about the seance, she asked, "Tell me more about this treasure you guys were trying to contact Captain Dell for?"

Freya happily slipped into her tour guide, dramatic recital, "During the Revolutionary War, Oyster River Harbor was evenly split between the Loyalists to the King and the Patriots or Rebels, depending on your politics."

"My ancestress, Long Liz was loyal to the King," Penny provided proudly.

Freya continued. "Several of the young townsmen had signed on with the Connecticut Militia, which came under General George Washington's command. Four of these soldiers were captured at the Battle of Monmouth Courthouse and thrown into a prison ship in Wallabout Bay."

"Wallabout Bay?" Grace asked absently as she dipped another chip.

"Across the Sound, off of Long Island. Now it's called Brooklyn Bay where the shipyard was."

"They were shipping our soldiers out?" asked Grace.

"No," Freya shook her head sounding pained. "Those prison ships were vermin infested, rotting hulks, permanently anchored to hold captives for years."

"The only way out was death," Penny added, sipping from the second wine glass.

Grace wondered about that. "No prisoner exchange?"

"No, General Washington especially didn't want to

exchange imprisoned Colonial green militia for trained British soldiers who would have just gone back to the line against the Patriots."

"Sad," said Grace thinking of the young lives lost.

Freya was getting worked up. "Those poor young men. The British were hoping bad conditions would force the imprisoned colonists to become turncoats and join the British navy."

Grace looked up, not really too interested. "They became galvanized Yankees?"

Freya shook her head. "No, that was a Civil War term for Confederate prisoners who were freed to join the Union army and fight Indians in the Western territories."

Penny tried to get them back on track. "So Elijah Dell raised a ransom for a bribe to free the soldiers. He contacted a fisherman friend, Christopher Coe, who lived on Long Island. Christopher and Elijah were to sail to the prison ships and try to make a deal."

"But it didn't happen," said Freya sadly. "Captain Dell died before the soldiers could be rescued and no one knew where he had hidden the ransom from the British."

"The important thing is the treasure!" Penny interrupted. "We have to find it! It's ours!"

Freya took another sip of her wine. "Actually, you could make a case that it was the property of most of the villagers of Oyster River Harbor."

"That treasure was hidden by my great–many times–granduncle, Elijah. It's mine by inheritance!" Penny pronounced her face flushing from the wine.

Grace thought about that. Actually, it was Freya who was the direct descendant of Elijah Dell while Penny's line only descended from Elijah's sister, but she noted Freya was content to say nothing. And since they didn't have the treasure to parcel out, and might never find one, it seemed a waste of time to figure who was entitled to ownership. Grace wondered out loud. "Perhaps the Red Coats discovered the ransom, said nothing and took it with them?"

"No," Penny quickly responded. "The family story passed down said that Long Liz never believed that. She and most of Oyster River, especially Elijah's daughter-in-law, Rebecca, was reputed to have spent years looking for the treasure."

"Oh, yes!" Freya brightened. "That was in my second book, *More Hauntings of Oyster River Harbor*. Rebecca's ghost is still heard in the Captain's Mansion restaurant that overlooks the harbor, it used to be Elijah Dell's home. She can be heard rapping against the wood paneling, looking for hollow spots where the ransom could be hidden."

Grace felt out of the loop. "While she was alive, why didn't she just take out all the paneling in her father-in-law's house?"

Penny seemed to be focusing on prodding Freya. "It could be elsewhere. This house you live in, Freya, it once belonged to the Paul Coe, Christopher's cousin."

Freya shook her head. "Only this kitchen wing is left from the Revolutionary War. The rest in the front was built in the whaling boom of the 1820's."

Looking at her now empty goblet, Penny said plaintively, "You must have another bottle of wine?" Ever the gracious hostess, Freya left to get another bottle.

Hungry, Grace took another chip and scooped up some more dip. They should be setting out the spaghetti now, but instead, she asked Penny, "How did Freya miss your branch on her family tree? She's always researching the censuses and whatever."

It was Freya bringing back another bottle who explained. "Elizabeth Dell had married into the colonial aristocracy, and there was some talk of Seth Booth becoming the Royal Governor of the Connecticut Colony. He owned a large ship's chandlery in Oyster River, but most of his money came from his trading schooners. Unfortunately, Elizabeth or Long Liz as she was known never managed to get pregnant and produce an heir for Seth. When the Revolution came, both Elizabeth and her husband remained loyal to King George, unfortunate because when the British lost, the life of the loyalists in the colonies was pretty intolerable."

Penny joined in. "He and Long Liz fled to Canada on one of Seth's ships, *The Osprey,* with their two slaves, Henry and Posey, while the Colony of Connecticut declared his property abandoned and confiscated it. In Canada, Seth petitioned the Royal government for just compensation for his losses. He never got much–some land in the wilderness of Saint Andrews–, but he still had the remains of his schooner trading business. Then," Penny looked to Freya, "Long Liz was blessed with a late-in-life baby, a daughter she named Penelope."

"You've still got to give me the dates," insisted Freya. "Your line and what you know of Penelope's other daughters? And do you know where Seth and Elizabeth are buried?"

Penny shrugged. "Somewhere in New Brunswick, but Long Liz raised Penelope with stories of the casket that she had given to Elijah."

Freya nodded. "That empty jewel chest was found in Elijah's house. My grandmother donated it to the whaling museum, it's on display, and it's beautiful."

Looking annoyed at Freya's interruption, Penny continued. "Long Liz told her daughter that those jewels were her birthright! Her sapphire wedding necklace, and those coins. Can you imagine–gold coins from 1778? That's what we should be researching!"

Grace was curious. "When the ransom was lost, what happened to the imprisoned soldiers?"

Taking another sip of wine, Penny shrugged her

shoulders, obviously uninterested. "I don't know, maybe they raised another bribe?"

"That would have been hard. Everything of value had been donated," said Freya sadly.

They ate dinner in the kitchen, and Grace was looking forward to having some time with Freya, but Penny cut it short. "Grace, I know you're so busy, you don't have to help Freya with the dishes. She promised me we could search her attic tonight, and it's going to be just old family stuff."

"Grace could help us," Freya proposed.

"She'd be bored," insisted Penny.

Grace looked into those green eyes of Penny. Did she see jealousy? Suspicion? Could she possibly think that Grace would be after '*her*' treasure?"

Whatever, shortly after that, Grace found herself out on Freya's front porch, wondering what to do with the rest of her evening.

Next Wednesday's dinner with David Gardiner seemed even shorter. Impeccably dressed as always David picked her up on time in his luxurious black Cadillac. He wore a tan suit, with a pale pink shirt, and even knowing that he was moving away, Grace still felt a little thrill that the two of them were going out.

"Where is this restaurant?" he asked.

"*Mountain Fire*. Take a left on the Post Road, and it's on the way to Greenwich. It's the new Japanese hibachi place."

"Never had hibachi myself. They have steak?"

"Yes," answered Grace, then they drove in unaccustomed silence. Grace wondered why, if he was just going to brush her off, was he even bothering with this dinner? Still, she always enjoyed sitting next to him, feeling the strength and power of his personality, being comfortable in the fact that to him, Dr. Farrington wasn't just an important scientist to be shown off publicly. Too bad he was moving out of the country without bothering to tell her.

Mountain Fire was both rural brown wood and understated elegance. A purple kimono dressed hostess seated them before a rectangle of steel set in a wood border, with eight seats in a 'u' shape around it. David seemed to be in unfamiliar territory, but when another Kimono dressed waitress handed them large food menus, he started looking.

Grace ordered plum wine, California rolls, and a shrimp and scallop combo meal. After ordering a whiskey and soda, David seemed to be spending an inordinate time studying the menu. When he looked up, six more people were being seated at their table, frowning David politely pointed out to the hostess. "They aren't in my party."

She looked at him surprised and bowed smilingly. "Hibachi."

Grace put a restraining hand on his. "They seat others with you."

"On my bill?" A perturbed David asked sharply.

"No, they'll have a separate check of their own." Grace looked at him in surprise. "You go to Japan regularly, you've never eaten hibachi before?"

He raised a quizzical eyebrow over those poached blue eyes and sounded rather defensive as he stated. "I have eaten all over the world in restaurants that serve steak and baked potatoes. They have them in Japan and Bora Bora too."

"Have you ever eaten sushi?" Grace persisted.

"Raw fish, no thank you."

The young laughing couple settled in opposite to Grace and David, and an older woman obviously the grandmother sat next to her daughter. Then twin boys, about six, were ordering Japanese sodas, and next to David was a squirming little girl, who gave him a big smile as she placed her stuffed teddy on the counter. To his obvious displeasure, the teddy's yellow ribbons slopping into David's drink, so distastefully, David took them out and held up his drink for the waitress to see he wanted a replacement.

A waiter delivered Grace's sushi. Six black seaweed and sticky rice wrapped crabmeat in two inch high rolls served with a shallow dish containing soy sauce, torn shreds of pink, pickled ginger, and a ball of green wasabi paste. Grace dropped a torn piece of ginger into the brown, salty soy sauce, then with her fork, she stirred in a tiny portion of the green ball.

"What's that?" David asked, his nose crinkling.

"Wasabi. A very hot, spicy paste, you'll find a little goes a long way. It will flavor the soy sauce, and the crab meat in the center of this roll is cooked–not raw."

With a quizzical eyebrow raised, David watched her take one of the rolls in her fingers, soak the end in the soy mixture, and then put the whole thing in her mouth. After she finished chewing, she challenged him. "Try one."

He followed the procedure and ate one, admitting, "Not bad."

"You enjoy raw lox on your bagel, so you might like to try some salmon sushi?"

"Let's do this slowly," he replied.

As the hostess brought David another whiskey, the tall, red-hatted Japanese chef arrived, pushing a cart of raw chicken, beef, shrimp, scallops, and vegetables. Standing behind the grill, he turned on the gas flame, then began the cooking show ritual that Grace always enjoyed. David followed Grace, in opening his mouth for a long squirt of saki, from a red plastic squeeze bottle. The waitress delivered Japanese, 'glass marble' sodas for the boisterous boys, and a Shirley Temple with tiny paper parasol for the little girl beside David.

As part of the ritual, for show and probably to cleanse the grill, the chef squirted bottles of oil and rice wine on the hot steel, then the chef set a flame that exploded into a three-foot high fireball. All at the table expected it, except David and the little girl next to him. Terrified, she pushed to the side and would have fallen off her chair, if David hadn't dropped his drink on the counter and grabbed her with his right hand. His left arm also darted out in front of Grace, fingers ridiculously spread as if to shield her as in an outraged voice he yelled at the chef, "**Careful!**"

Grace looked at him. "They always do that. It prepares the grill."

With whiskey and ice was dripping on to his lap and the little girl next to him was crying for the Shirley Temple she overturned, David icily ordered the chef, "**Don't** do that again!"

The waitress was hurrying over with towels as David ordered, "Please bring my third whiskey and soda." He looked at the tearful girl. "And another fancy drink for the child on my bill." Then as he brushed ice off his lap. "And another plate of those California rolls." He nodded to Grace. "Not bad."

The chef hammered steel blades to the grill, then balanced a raw egg on his knife, dancing it a bit, then started chopping cucumber, broccoli, and chicken with his flashing blades. While they sizzled, a small, flat rimmed bowl of pink ginger dipping sauce and another of brown was set before each diner. Noodles and mounds of white rice, which soon became brown fried rice were prepared, and swiftly the cutting blades clanged against the searing grill, as the chef rapidly chopped up cubes of shrimp, steak, and scallops.

When he finally did get to drink some of his whiskey, David mellowed a bit and actually seemed to be fascinated by the rapidly prepared food. But he still seemed to have difficulty trying to pretend not to see the energetic family beside him, even if the laughing parents seemed to have no trouble ignoring their offspring.

But finally, David turned towards Grace. "You seemed surprised at Greece. We had discussed it, several times."

"We did?" Grace was clueless.

"Yes. The last we went out to the Pier."

Oh, Lord. She remembered him talking of the beauties of Greece and his island and going on and on. She had just nodded and tuned out, while her mind had been on an article about the possible gene switches of trilobite fossils several millions of years in the past.

"Don't you remember?" David asked, a bit perturbed.

Better be honest here. "Actually no..."

"Several of my companies are involved with developing a large shopping center in Greece. Years ago, my late wife and I bought an island, planning to build and spend winters there perhaps." For a second he stopped to remember, then came back and focused totally on her. "Have you ever gone to the Mediterranean, Grace?"

"Only to look out at it from hotel windows during some genetic conference."

"The water is warm, clear, beautiful, and I've finally begun executing the plans I stopped when Sylvia died." He seemed to realize something. "Actually I started that just about the time we met. The work is progressing on the main house, and it'll be liveable by December. Just when it's starting to freeze around here."

"We'll miss you." Grace tried to say that brightly, but it fell flat. She really would miss him.

He looked at her surprised. "But you'll be coming with me."

"What?" *What in hell had she nodded agreement to while she wasn't listening?*

"I thought that was settled," David said.

This conversation was frightening her. The way he took it for granted that she'd agreed, she must have said something she shouldn't have. "David, is this a marriage proposal?"

He looked embarrassed. "That's not exactly what I intended. We're both adults, and I have grown children. However, if you wanted children, and women are having them later, then, of course, there would have to be a marriage first. Maybe we could work out a trial period before we married?"

She cut him off. "David, I have my work, my laboratory, and my commitment to Oyster River Research. I just can't get up and leave! I have a contract with Adam."

"I donate enough money for the new student dorm Adam wants, and ORR will be more than happy to release you," he said wryly.

"I don't want to be released, I want to work!" he just seemed to be ignoring what this life change would be for her.

"I've settled all that. Scientists can work all over the world and still be in communication. In your Greek lab, they've already scheduled the installation of a world-class communications headquarters with video cameras and screens.   *Oh, my God.* "You've already started building a lab?"

"Yes," he said proudly. "A bigger laboratory laid out by the Beaton Architectural firm. They specialize in the design of advanced scientific facilities. Doing a lot for the Chinese. The plans for yours are a bigger clean room, better offices, and a fully wired video communications studio, but you can be on camera in any room. I haven't ordered any equipment or hired staff, because I felt you should do that."

What had this already cost him? "No!"

"You want the Beaton firm to equip your facility?" He sounded surprised. "They've already planned for the equipment they said you would need..."

Oh, this was getting way out of hand! Yes, she'd heard of the Beatons–they do great work, at even greater prices. "No!"

"No what?" he asked a trifle annoyed.

"No, I am not going to overturn my life, and move to Greece just for your convenience." The others at the table were looking avidly at them, and Grace found herself flushing with embarrassment. "David, I don't want to hurt you, but no thank you!"

"Grace, you said yes to all my plans..."

She probably did by just nodding her head and saying nothing to the contrary. "I'm so sorry. Sometimes people talk to me, but I'm deep in my own thoughts, and I just keep agreeing to be polite."

He stopped, thought, and then said, "Obviously this is all new to you, and you need time to think about it. I'll have the Beaton Firm send over complete plans for your laboratory. It's under construction, but it can be modified. I'll also send pictures of the island, and perhaps I should have my lawyers start drawing up a prenuptial outline that we can discuss. I will have to protect my children's inheritances, but I'm sure my lawyers will suggest a graduated arrangement so that the longer we are married, the more you will receive. But Grace, I can assure you will have quite a bit even if you chose to leave me in the first year. "

What had she gotten herself into? The chef was using his board knife to pile noodles and steak cubes on to his plate, and David had turned his attention to his alien meal. They finished eating in silence, Grace said she had a slight headache, and he drove her home, leaving without comment. Which was good, because she really didn't know what to say.

She'd spent some happy times with David, he was a very skilled and considerate lover, and he fully supported her in her genetics work, but of a woman he married he'd expect attention from her, and with her self-imposed workload Grace didn't have time enough to spare as it was.

And as Grace drifted off to sleep, she found herself

having another of those fantasies where a bare-chested Jack Stuart was climbing into her bed.

Chapter 10

The next day, Grace was coming out of the clean room when she was startled to see a man there. Big man, in a dark blue business suit. Dark hair, fair skin, Jack Stuart.

"I hope I didn't frighten you," he said, always speaking in slow, measured tones.

"Not frightened, just surprised actually. Pleasantly surprised." God, seeing that hunk of a man gave her a little warming feeling all over. Made her want to stand up taller, and wish she was wearing perfume.

"I wanted to talk to you about your equipment allocation," he said.

Grace spoke a touch bitterly. "I understand Adam is working that out with Huang."

Jack smiled tightly. "I really don't care what Adam and Huang are working out. With Eve gone, I'm the one who going to be writing out the checks. Now, have you had lunch?"

She looked up. Surely it was too early? Nope, it was 1:30. "Not yet."

"Would you like to come out with me. Steakhouse or Italian?"

Grace shook her head. "Actually, I'm pretty busy. I was just going to run to the Admin building and get something from the Cafeteria."

"Sounds good, may I join you?"

Grace took off her lab coat and paper booties and then wished she had chosen her green blouse and orange pants to match a little bit better today. At his suggestion, they bought take-out and carried their lunches over to the picnic tables under the oak trees, where they had a nice, cool breeze from the harbor and a fabulous view of sun sparkling water. Grace usually ate alone, but she really enjoyed being with such a handsome, quiet man, who radiated an almost magnetic sexual attraction. Nothing serious would come of it, but if David was leaving, it was rather reassuring that another attractive man wanted to eat with her.

Jack carefully unwrapped his roast beef on rye, bit into the long dill pickle, and said, "What are you doing for your retirement?"

Grace nearly spit out the coke she was drinking. "I look like I need to retire?"

He colored deeply. "No, far from it.

She took two bites of her ham sandwich, then finished chewing. "I don't plan to ever '*retire.*' I just plan to keep working until I die. My great-grandmother Harriet canned twenty jars of tomatoes before she sat down in the kitchen, closed her eyes, and died. She was ninety-two."

Jack nodded at that. "Wanting to retire and being able to retire are two different things. Now, I've been told that you should be getting a Nobel, and there is the money that comes with it. That would be a substantial start to your estate planning."

She took that and her sandwich with a grain of salt. "I haven't won it yet, and it looks like I might not."

He smiled confidently. "Before starting to commit *Our Sisters* funds, Eve and I studied quite a number of deserving scientists and institutions. We were the most impressed with your continuing body of work that has advanced the study of genetics immeasurably. You deserve the Nobel, and I'm certain you will get it."

"Do you think Dr. Huang will?"

Jack took a long time to think that one over. "His one discovery in epigenetics was pretty good, at very young age, but I think they are going to want to see something more before he gets it–if ever. Let's get back to you. For your retirement, what have you planned?"

She chewed some potato chips. "Most of my money goes for new lab equipment so don't have anything saved."

He looked down at her in surprise. "You accept grants in your name. You must be a financial entity that pays taxes?"

"Oh, yes."

"Self-employment taxes?" he pursued.

"I don't..." She tried to picture what her tax guy said. "Yes, I think I do. That makes me eligible for a Social Security pension, right?"

"Great." He continued drily, "With that income around here in Oyster River you can live in a tent in the woods and eat potatoes from a hundred pound sack."

"As I said, I'm not going to retire."

"You also have a small pension coming from Oyster River Research."

"I do?" She asked in surprise.

"Yes, at the meeting didn't you hear us discussing ORR's institutional obligations, that would include pensions?" He always seemed to stop and think before he slowly spoke. "You are vested."

"So ..." she pushed.

"You will be able to afford some government cheese with your potatoes," Jack finished tartly. He was being a bit intrusive, but Grace had the feeling that Jack really cared for her, as he continued, "Look, *Our Sisters* does take investments for retirement accounts."

She picked up a dill pickle. "Starting at a million dollars?"

"What could you write a check for?"

Grace thought about her obligations. With Bobby part time, she now had three assistants and needed an upgraded computer station, so how much disposable income did she really have? "Five hundred dollars. That's it!"

He thought about it, looking at the sunlight dancing on the harbor. "Maybe you could buy shares with some of your friends? Freya owns a business, how is she preparing for her golden years?"

"Freya couldn't even write a check for five hundred. I don't hang with a solvent crowd."

"I've been told you're very good friends with a number of the Board of Directors, and all of them are business people of substantial means. David Gardiner is already one of our investors. You know the Brewsters and the Hoyts?"

She smiled wanting to get off this. "Hopefully, they already have their retirement arrangements."

Jack nodded. "Okay. We're not waiting for the Nobel. Write me that check for the five hundred and put your social security number on it–we're going to open a retirement account for you with *Our Sisters*. The Foundation is going to match your funds, dollar for dollar so your account will start with one thousand dollars. I will see your contributions are matched up to a maximum of twenty-five thousand dollars."

"Are you kidding?" she asked.

"Nope, and when shortly *Our Sisters* issues you a experimental grant, a percentage of that will go directly into your IRA. *Our Sisters* is set up to improve the world, and I cannot think of a person who is doing more of that than you. Your *Popcorn Genes* theory ignited fires under a lot of scientists, exponentially spreading your influence. So, young lady, I want to see you taking as much of a positive interest in your personal affairs as you do in the slime on a blue-mottled lobster."

After eating, they just talked for awhile, and for a change, she was doing most of the talking. Jack had a quiet way of listening, seeming to digest all of what she said, before-- occasionally--commenting on it. Jack obviously knew very little about genetics, but he seemed to quickly grasp processes, being able to clarify with carefully chosen words what should be obvious, but what to others usually wasn't. They didn't speak of Eve and finally--reluctantly--

Grace said she had to get back to work. Jack's silver Jaguar was parked behind the Roost, above the entrance to the dock, and unwilling to part from him, Grace walked to it and stood watching as Jack pulled away.

Yet it was such a nice mellow day, cool for August, that she didn't want to go inside to a stuffy lab when her assistants could finish the schedule. She didn't do her run this morning when she should have, and Grace figured she could work out her lobster study definitions mentally in the sunlight. After changing to a pair of running shoes she kept in her lab, Grace started to walk towards the dock that was still closed off with its yellow crime scene tape. Now, a patrolman's car and a small van marked 'State Police Crime Scene Unit' was there. She also saw two inflated yellow zodiacs's anchored in the water off of Kurt's sailboat, as divers with tanks and blue wetsuits were emerging. Just seeing them in that water gave her a rush of coldness and a feeling of fear, but of what?

As she was standing there, Grace heard the roar of a motorcycle and looking up she saw Kurt's big, black Harley-Davidson. He had someone behind him, holding on tightly to his waist. For Grace, Kurt had a backrest installed so this new lady obviously didn't need to hold him so tightly, she just wanted to.

Hell, that was classic Kurt MacKay, his boat home was taped off as a crime scene for the death of Eve, and he already had another woman warming his back. Kurt parked just above the dock, in front of the police van, he got off and walked to where he could survey the anchored zodiacs, with their neon orange floating markers, as the suited divers sank down again.

Seeing Grace, the trim, big boobed passenger stayed with the bike, but when she took off the helmet and shook her red hair free, Grace recognized Gina Miakos, one of the waitresses at the Alpine biker bar and the widow of the supposed '*great*' modern artist, Miakos.

Reaching Grace, Kurt spoke quietly. "You see them bringing up anything small?"

"A gun?" she asked.

"Nope."

"Something missing from your boat?"

"Aaup."

She was getting mad. "I don't want to play games—what?"

"I did some diving on a WW II wreck. German U-boat off Montauk Point."

"So?"

"I found a spanner and took it home as a souvenir. Used to keep it in my main cabin to weight down the charts when I unrolled them."

"And it's gone?" Grace didn't really see much of a problem.

"Aaup." Kurt's face looked hard, but she couldn't read the expression.

"So, a spanner--it's a European wrench, in a harbor, full of boats, with engines that constantly need repairs, how would that tie to you?"

He looked grim. "It's been sitting there on my table, jes as you came downstairs."

"So?"

"Think that's what cracked open the lady's skull."

Oh, God. "When Eve fell, you think it accidentally dropped on her?"

"Nope, it fit in someone's hand. Caving her in her skull that deep wasn't an accident."

Trying to remain calm, Grace pointed out. "If they find a wrench in the bay, the saltwater could have washed off all her DNA, blood, even your fingerprints. It could be anybody's wrench, from any boat."

Kurt smiled ironically. "It was from a World War II

U Boat. It was proudly stamped..."

"With what?" Grace asked, already forming a hypothesis.

"A Nazi swastika."

She closed her eyes at the stupidity of it. "Yhep, you're the only boat around here that would be expected to display a tribute to Hitler's Third Reich!"

"Whal, I know a few guys that hang out at the Alpine, that might ride with an Iron Cross or Prussian spiked helmet..."

She glared at him. "Maybe after those divers leave, you and Bobby should put on your wetsuits and...."

"Me and Bobby go in that water, and we'll be jailed for interfering in a murder investigation." He squinted out over the harbor. "That killer, if he had a good baseball arm, could've thrown a wench in a radius of fifty or sixty feet, maybe more. The water drops off steeply into the harbor, so if those guys are trying to run any archeological grid pattern, they are gonna have problems. If they don't have a metal detector, there's a chance those police divers aren't gonna find it in that muck."

Grace frowned. "On the other hand, maybe you should help them find it. Tell them you just realized it's missing, help them look for it, and DNA or fingerprints might lead to the guy who killed Eve."

"Blood, fingerprints, and DNA are probably washed off, but that swastika stamped wrench is gonna lead them right to my companionway."

A thought excited Grace. "Kurt, what about that guy who rammed your boat?"

"Josh Jeffers?"

"Don't you think he did it?"

"Why would he hurt Eve?"

"He's got a grudge against you, against Oyster River Research, against the world from what I hear. Maybe Josh went to your boat to hurt you and found Eve instead? Or saw you leave and deliberately attacked her to implicate you? Maybe the next time they question you, you could push the police to grill him?"

"They've already questioned him. Hear Josh has got an alibi."

"A good one?"

"Better than mine," he said sounding tired.

She had to work this out. "You think Eve fell forward, accidentally or was pushed?"

"Don't much matter, the real damage was when she was on the floor and was hit in the back of the head."

"Okay, if she was off balance and fell or was pushed down the ladder, anyone could have overpowered her?"

"Aaup, if she wasn't expecting it."

"The Board of Directors meeting was still breaking up, people were about. Eve is killed, and the murder strolls back to his car or boat?"

"Or his dorm room. I hear they questioned all our postgraduate students."

"Wouldn't the murderer be covered with Eve's blood?"

Kurt thought about it a bit. "Some spurted out from the back of her head. Nothing from that swollen bit on her forehead in the front. Mostly gray brains from the skull hit my bulkhead. Don't think a man's shirt or pant's legs would have gotten stained."

What had David Gardiner had been wearing when Deborah saw him by Kurt's boat? Should she ask? "I don't understand, how could the killer have been sure that you were going to leave her alone, to go out and check your research?"

He kind of colored. "I actually wasn't logging any data."

"You had a hot date waiting, what exactly were you doing in your boat?"

"Whal, things were going kinda good."

"How good?"

"She wanted white wine and some of those ribbed condoms, and so I motored over to the town dock. Walked over to the liquor store and pharmacy."

Grace just stared at him.

"And she wanted some whipped cream. Had to go to the cheese shop for that...you know, what a man and woman in bed can do with a can of whipped cream..." Those dark eyes stared into hers.

She cut him off. "How could the murderer plan to kill someone on your boat...pretty much out in the open with everybody walking to their cars and dorms. How could he or she be sure that you weren't motoring out to the first buoy, pulling up a lobster pot, and then hurrying back?"

"Grace," he sounded exasperated. "Only someone like you would first plan out a murder in a lab blue-book! Some guy sees his girl heading towards another man's bedroom, he loses it, and kills her in a blind fury! Happens all the time."

"Or," she mused, "It could have been a random killer, seeing a woman alone..."

"On ORR's dock? At the end? C'mon, Grace, a stranger in amongst the directors and students strolling about? And Josh or his boat would've been remembered."

Two more cars entered from the main road. Blue and white, state troopers, and another dark, unmarked car with a light on the dashboard. They parked on the road, above the dock and then the three men started walked toward the narrow gate booth, carefully spreading themselves out.

Kurt watched them, and then said firmly, "Aaup. Gonna need a lawyer. What was the name of that jewboy who defended you in the Marshall case?"

"I thought you were worried about them taking over the world?"

"Grace, if I'm hiring a butcher, I'm hiring Pole. If I need electronics built, I'm hiring a Nip. But if I'm gonna need a sneaky lawyer, I'm looking for a Jew."

The first big man in a suit said, "Mr. Kurt MacKay?"

"Yes, sir," Kurt said politely.

Still standing by his bike, Gina looked apprehensively at Kurt.

.   "We would like you to come with us, just to clarify some issues?" The plainclothes man said.

"Actually, that's not too convenient at the moment. I..." Kurt started.

With his hand on his holstered gun, one of the uniformed officers cut Kurt off. "You have to come with us, sir, we have a warrant for your arrest."

Kurt nodded. "Jes a second. I am going to take out my keys out and throw 'em to that lady over there. Okay?"

The detective looked at his friend, then nodded, saying, "Just do it slowly."

"Gina!" With exaggerated deliberateness, Kurt pulled out and tossed her his motorcycle keys. "Honey, you can use the bike, until yours gets fixed." Then he turned to her. "Grace, can you call that lawyer for me?"

Wanting to cry she only nodded.

Chapter 11

Back in her lab, she finally located the lawyer's number. "Hi, Mark, this is Grace—Grace Farrington."

"Getting around to making that will we discussed?" Came the friendly reply.

"No, actually, I'm calling for a friend. A friend of mine has been arrested in connection with a possible murder, Kurt MacKay."

The lawyer was silent for a moment and then said, "Oh, I remember Mr. MacKay. Is he going to wear a white sheet and hood to the arraignment?"

"They're just questioning him today."

"If there is any justice in the universe, he'll get Judge Rubin. The judge's grandparents died in the Holocaust, and Rubin loves getting those white supremacists in his court."

"Will you defend Kurt?"

"The name is Silverstein. I don't think Mr. MacKay would want a Jewish lawyer defending him."

"Actually, he asked if you could meet him at the police station."

Mark stopped and seemed to think about that. "I'm surprised he even remembered my name."

He hadn't. Grace felt she should explain. "There are 'people people' who remember names and faces easily because that's important to them. Those people often place extraordinary value on what others think of them and are guided by that. Others, with minds like my own and Kurt's, take different paths, focusing on other things as important. We have a terrible time with names and faces, but we solve a lot of the world's problems."

Mark didn't sound impressed. "That's unfortunate in this world, people often need people."

She had to make him understand. "When I started formulating my *Popcorn Gene* theory, the prevailing opinion held that I was wrong. If I cared to conform, cared what other people said about me, I would have stopped my research. If I listened to my critics and stopped pushing, no one would have funded me."

His voice sounded neutral. "But you knew you were right."

She smiled wryly. "I wish it was that easy."

"You kept going to find out," Mark amended.

"Fortunately for me, I had Eric Larsen."

"Didn't he get a Nobel?"

"Eric. Yes, he had his Nobel and the prestige and influence that went with it. He got me hired at Oyster River Research when I was radioactive poison to the rest of the scientific community. It was Eric as Head of ORR who told me, *I'll support you, but don't know if you're right or not. You'll have to determine that.*

"Kurt's the same," Grace continued. "That's what makes him such a valuable scientist. If the politically correct opinion is that the cold water lobster die-offs result from man-made global warming, Kurt will dare question it if he discovers the warm water crabs are also dying off. If he finds the town sprayed insecticide in the marshes to kill off West Nile mosquitoes, and he thinks that is contributing to the die-off, he will work his ass off to prove it.

"And when he does, the powers-that-be aren't always terribly happy having Kurt rub their noses in it. In the scientific world, he and I swim upstream, and that can be hard to do at times. I cope by withdrawing from society as much as I can, and he responds to disapproval by making a show of flipping the world off."

"So being a shithead is what makes him a good scientist?" asked Mark skeptically.

"Partly."

There was a pause. "Well, it's been slow lately." Mark gave a little laugh. "My Uncle Alan will be just thrilled when he finds out our firm is defending someone connected to biker gangs and the KKK."

"Kurt's also a member of the Masons and Mensa."

"Interesting mix."

"He's not a bad guy, he has friends in all sorts of groups. I once asked, if you're drinking with your black friend, and your KKK guys come in the bar, and a brawl breaks out, who do you fight with?"

"What did he say?" Mark asked with real curiosity.

"You fight with the guy you came in with."

Mark was silent for a time, and then said, "Well, hopefully, I can keep this out of Judge Rubin's court."

"Then you will defend him?"

"For today's questioning at least. Then I'll see if he seems willing to tell his Jewish lawyer the truth, the whole truth. Otherwise, he can find someone else."

Back in her lab, she started on letters and e-mails that had been winnowed down by Inger, with only a few hundred left. Some letters, a lot of kids told by their teacher to write someone '*important.*' Grace wrote a 4-B for Inger on this pile, one of several boilerplate responses she sent back encouraging the kids to think of science as a career. Grace then signed each of the printed out letters from her last batch. The e-mails that might possibly lead to decently paid speaking jobs she dragged to her Conference folder. When she got through the e-mails, she started on the phone messages.

Most could be discarded, but not the one from David Gardiner. Wanting to take her out for dinner Friday. That's today. Grace would have to get back to him to say no, he was going to have to accept her decision. Which she would be firm about if she could just convince herself the answer to a loving, luxurious life with him on the Mediterranean was a '*no.*' Already depressed, she started typing the first response to the Conference folder as she picked up the ringing phone.

"Laboratory 5."

"Grace? This is David Gardiner." A silence, what was she going to say? Finally, he continued, "I've left several messages for you?"

Grace didn't answer, her mouth dry. She didn't know what to say.

He continued. "After we spoke, I thought you would be getting back to me? I mentioned another dinner..."

"I'm sorry. I was getting back to you–later. David, I'm very busy..." That sounded so lame!

"I didn't realize that Greece was going to come as such a surprise for you."

Oh, it was, buddy!

When she didn't speak, he continued. "But actually dinner tonight is out because I have to be near a phone."

Perversely she said, "You have a cell. You can take that to the restaurant."

"It's not a secure phone that I want to transfer considerable amounts of money over. Could you please join me for dinner at my house tonight?"

He sounded a bit harried, but his voice held that touch of the warm friendship that she so hated to lose. Taking the line of least resistance was the weakling's way out, but to get him off the phone so she could go back to work, Grace agreed and hung up.

A cowardly act that she regretted that evening. David had his house and stables in an area know for its pastures and forests of oak and elm. For an estate of its size and wealth, there was no imposing security gate, just a small, bronze plaque stating the street address of 936, set like a diamond in the mounded banks of manicured red and purple azaleas. She turned on to an asphalt driveway, more like a road, and was soon driving through a screening thicket of trees.

Trees gave way to white boarded horse fences, and then his rambling gray-shingled, two-story house. It was once a simple, colonial farmstead that was added on to by generations of the Gardiners. She parked in the rear on the cobblestone courtyard formed by the house, the five-car garage, and the stables. A sandy-haired girl was brushing down a beautiful sorrel hunter. Grace noted how young and pretty she looked and regretfully realized how David's money could attract any female company he wanted.

Before Grace could knock on the back door the butler, Caine was opening it for her. Grace headed inside to the coolness of the slate floor and ancient timbering. As he escorted her to the front, the ceilings got higher and decor became male and leather, and when she entered the living room, she noted that this time an open laptop had been placed on one of the brass-studded drum tables.

Standing by the huge, square stone fireplace, David was totally engaged in a phone conversation. Seeing him always gave her a little thrill. His sandy-hair, boyish looks, those strong shoulders, and legs slightly bowed from a lifetime of riding. She wanted him to put his hand on her arm, reach over and carelessly kiss her, but his conversation on the phone seemed not to be going very well.

Grace tried to get her mind off the problem of the move to Greece. Above the mantle, she studied that huge, yellowed map of the world. The legend read 1931, and it was marked with red lines going from England to New York and different continents with another label in the Pacific Ocean that read 'Travels of the Prince of Wales.' She wondered if this was the original, once owned by the Duke of Windsor? It might be, the Duke's household furnishings were auctioned in Paris after the Duchess' death.

That phone call did not get better. When David hung up he looked flushed and annoyed, but then his iron control quickly returned. "Grace, forgive me. This European shopping mall deal is proving to be very complicated, with the landscape constantly shifting."

"Well, when you're in Greece it might be easier," she said non-committally.

He looked directly at her. "Yes, I wanted to talk to you about that."

She started to speak, "David, I can't..."

He held up a hand. "First, let Caine get you something to drink, you'd like ginger ale wouldn't you? Let's have some of the appetizers he's bringing in, and then let me at least show you the architectural drawings for the laboratory I'm building on my island."

She owed him that. It was a state-of-the-art laboratory, and the architects David had chosen knew what a scientist required, what a scientist dreamed of. As they looked at the plans, he commented. "Your current clean room isn't negative air, is it?"

Actually with a building that old, Grace was lucky she had any air at all. "David, how much did you spend on these plans?"

"I certainly don't care, and you shouldn't either," he said. "Even if my drawings don't get used, I'll have had the dream of us being together. Of me being able to sit in your lab on my island and watch your amazing work. "

She laughed. "That would be so boring."

"Not to me." He stared at her intently. "Especially knowing that you would be coming home to my bed–our bed."

"At what? Midnight? Two a.m.? I wake up in the middle of the night, turn on the lights, and start writing protocols."

He laughed now. "I've noticed."

She blushed. "I can't see you sitting around an island, waiting for me to finish work."

"Grace, I won't be. My business affairs are fairly engaging but as important as our work is, I think we both should take some time out to savor life. Living as husband

and wife on the island. Traveling..."

He did make it sound so inviting, but she couldn't do this. "You need a wife totally dedicated to you, someone, like Deborah Forbes."

"How does she come into this?" He asked sharply.

She hesitated. "Um...just thinking of someone in your social circle."

"Has Deborah said anything to you?" David was narrowing his eyes.

"No," Grace lied.

His face got grim. "There was a problem, years ago. After several board meeting that we were both on, I took her out for coffee. Then it got back to me Deborah was telling people we were engaged to be married! I spoke to her, but the rumors kept coming back. Finally, I had to have my lawyers formally tell her to stop spreading baseless nonsense."

Grace wished she'd never brought the subject up. "Sounds like she's a little too infatuated with you?"

He snorted contemptuously. "Deborah's infatuated with marrying money, and she always has been."   David picked up his drink, then chose to change the conversation. "This death of Eve at Oyster River, the police aren't bothering you are they? I mean, perhaps you should speak with my attorney's nephew again, Mark Silverstein?"

"That might be a conflict of interest. Kurt Mackay just hired him to defend himself against a possible murder charge."

That surprised David. "The Silversteins are the best, but they can't work miracles."

"By that you mean?"

"Eve Dupree was a woman of substantial means with powerful friends. If MacKay murdered her, even an outstanding lawyer can't sweep it under the rug."

Grace couldn't believe this. "Why would you think

Kurt would kill a woman?"

"A romantic encounter. Perhaps Eve was teasing him a bit, but then she sobered up. Tells him she's leaving, and maybe says something dismissive of his romantic prowess?"

"Kurt is not going to kill a woman for brushing him off." If he had, Grace would have been dead many times over.

David was continuing. "I can't understand why a cultured, intelligent woman like Eve would have even talked with a buffoon like MacKay, much less planned to spend an evening with him?" Left unsaid was why would Grace also '*talk*' to him.

"He has his ways," Grace returned coolly. "Kurt feeds us his famous chili, that he puts heroin in. Keeps the ladies coming back again and again."

David looked at her, then flushing slightly he smiled ironically. "Yes, you are correct. It is none of my business."

Before he could speak further, his butler entered. David was obviously unhappy about the interruption, sounding annoyed as he asked, "Yes, Caine?"

"A Mr. Jack Stuart is at the door."

"Tell him I can't see him today."

The butler hesitated. "He says its very important, regarding your investment..."

Grace started to get up. "I can go."

"No!" David looked strained. "We still have to eat dinner...please. Could I just get Jack over with, and then you and I could talk?"

He was trying to please everyone, and she could understand that. "Fine, do you want me to leave the room?"

"No." He looked to Caine. "Lead Mr. Stuart in, please."

Grace was just nibbling salmon spread on a cracker as Jack entered. He looked terrible, even worse than he had looked when Eve died. David stood up to greet the much taller but sagging man. Not even seeming to see her, Jack just sank into one of the leather chairs and looked at David. "You have called in your investment with *Our Sisters* Foundation?"

"Yes, I'm developing a shopping mall project in Greece, so I'll need to raise quite a bit of capital."

"We–I can't meet that," Jack said in a broken voice.

"You can't...?" Asked a disbelieving David.

"Eve Dupree ran the financial side of our businesses. Since her...accident, I've been trying to sort everything out. She had her office staff in Paris that issued dividends, but they're not answering. All the accounts I've found so far are empty. There's nothing!"

David looked at him in horror. "What?"

"You knew our business affairs—well, we went through a rough patch–about two years ago. Sabotage to our equipment, the economy slowing down, and warfare breaking out near the mines. I was constantly dealing with the day-to-day logistics of rebuilding the business and had to keep asking Eve for more and more money. She said not to worry, Eve claimed she had some insider investments that were doing well for the Foundation. Eve said she was making fabulous returns! That's what she told me."

"And?" David said.

"There weren't any insider investments, at least nothing I can find, everything is mortgaged, and the accounts are empty. She must have been paying off the shareholder dividends in *Our Sisters* with newly invested funds."

When David's responded, his voice sounded dead. "The classic Ponzi scheme."

"No!" Jack protested. "Not a deliberate cheat! Not Eve! I think she got in over her head, and Eve figured if she could just keep the business afloat, we could work our way out of the red ink. We'd gone through hard times before, but what I can't understand is why she didn't tell me? Get my help?"

Grace spoke softly, "Maybe it was a matter of pride. She didn't want to be seen as a failure in your eyes?"

Both men were silent at that, and then Jack stood up to his full height. "I'm going through everything now. We still own some mining equipment in Afghanistan, Canada, Guinea, and Indonesia. Eve talked about opening offshore accounts, but she never did, at least I can't find anything. David, I can not honor your withdrawal at this time, but I will be getting back to you when I've seen what I can salvage." As he was leaving, Jack looked at Grace. "And you—your promised project funding...I-I don't know what..."

"Forget it! Just try to take care of your investors," she said, gently touching his arm briefly.

He nodded and left.

David stood there staring after him, his face unreadable, not showing surprise, shock, or even pity. He walked to the laptop open on his drum table and started tapping into something as he intently read screens. He tapped more and Grace realized she was now totally forgotten as he delved further. David absent mindedly dismissed the butler when Caine came to say dinner was on the table.

Grace was hungry and getting a bit of a headache, when finally after nearly half an hour she had to ask, "What is it?"

He sat back, still glaring at the glowing screen before him. "*Alcom* has been an established mining company since 1986, and its website lists Jack Stuart as one of the founders. That website also gives the impression that their Chief Financial Officer, Ms. Eve Dupree, was a long-term employee."

"You knew that?" Her headache was getting worse.

"Oh, yes. Yes, I did check that before I invested, but what I hadn't checked from independent sources was just when Mr. Stuart and Ms. Dupree started to be listed as responsible officers for the firm.   Jack Stuart first appears three years ago, and Ms. Dupree only a short time after that. *Our Sisters* was founded exactly three years ago."

She thought about it. "Jack said he owned a number of mining companies. If one of his firms had bought *Alcom,* and *Alcom* was the larger company or, the more marketable name, Jack might have dropped his company's name in the merger. That could be why he would still be a founder, even though he doesn't appear on the lists of officers from *Alcom's* earlier years. If you did more research..."

His face grim, David pushed his laptop away. "Actually, I will be paying people to do just that." His voice had a deadly coldness she had never heard before.

"Do you think Jack was in on a deliberate Ponzi scheme?" David didn't answer, but Grace couldn't believe it. "I can't see it, he seems so honest, so open."

"Yes, a very charming man, and a man to be easily trusted. That can be a very bankable trait," David said, in a neutral tone.   "But I'd prefer not to discuss this anymore, after all, we should be having dinner."

A horrible weed of an idea had taken root in her mind. "David, you invested with *Our Sisters*?"

"Unfortunately, yes."

"A lot of money?" She asked.

"Over five million."

"Then with that money lost, to the police, you will have a motive to kill Eve?"

"Do you think I did?" Those pale blue eyes of his had turned on her and gone icy.

She had to think about it before she said, "No, no, I don't."

"Thank you for that," his tone a bit flippant, underscored with bitterness. "Grace, look at that painting over there? That's a Monet. My great-grandmother purchased it and several others when she was in Paris during the Impressionist period. There's at least sixty million dollars worth of paintings on the walls of this room."

"That you don't care about the five million you've lost..."

At that, he exploded.   "I'm **damn well** not happy about it!" He stopped to get control. "But that is the way of the world, if one lets one's guard down, one loses..."

Caine entered, knowing it was a bad time, but the dinner must be deteriorating. Still, Grace had enough. "David, I don't think either of us feels like eating or talking right now. I've got a bad headache, and I'm sorry, but I've got to go."

"Of course," he said in a steel clipped tone. "I have finances to rework, and I am packing for Greece. Will you be coming with me? Or will you be staying here to hold Kurt Mackay's hand?"

Chapter 12

She left David without giving him an answer, and he was too much of a gentleman to press. It was unkind of her not to settle matters one way or the other, but she honestly didn't know what she wanted to do! Her mind was so muddled, she just couldn't think. She kept seeing Jack sitting there in that chair, broken by his losses. She could not see that man as part of Eve's financial sleight of hand, but he was going to be paying the price.

As she drove back into Oyster River Research, a tall police officer in a light blue uniform was pulling off the yellow crime-scene tape from the upper dock's railings, and Grace relaxed, recognizing the sandy hair of Mac as she walked over. "Adam got the docks back?"

"Actually it was more Kurt's lawyer. He couldn't get Kurt's live-in sailboat freed, it's still the crime scene, but his lawyer convinced Judge Rubin that Kurt needs his lobster yawl to carry out his livelihood."

"Mac, remember I asked if the detectives were going to question Josh Jeffers?"

"They did. Had an alibi, he was with his twin brother fishing out on the Sound up by Stamford."

"Josh's alibi is his brother? That's not exactly a disinterested party."

Mac sighed. "I know you want to help Kurt, but..."

"Did anyone else see the brothers out on the Sound?"

"I don't know, and I couldn't tell you if I did, but if I were the detective in charge, I'd be thinking that if Josh had planned that murder, especially if his identical twin brother was willing to help him, he probably would've worked out a better alibi."

"Yes." She had to agree.

"And Grace, I've been handling calls about Josh for years. If he had killed Eve to get back at Kurt, he would have done it publicly, or at least stayed hanging around there to take the credit."

"That would be crazy," she said.

"That's Josh Jeffers."

"Yeah." She stood there looking out over the water, then said, "Your police divers are gone." Grace wanted to ask if they found anything but didn't.

"Might be back." Mac squinted up to the dark clouds rolling in from the East. "Thunderstorms expected today."

Grace decided to try another sore subject. "I haven't heard from Freya lately?"

At that, Mac's face hardened. "Ma's stuck with that *'newly declared'* cousin of ours. Miz Penny Barstall." He pronounced it with a tinge of contempt.

"You're unhappy with that?"

"Ma's an adult woman, she runs a business, and raised me as single mother, but she never seems to learn! Do you know how many people she's had living upstairs that have left owing her for months of rent? The last clown ripped out the brass lighting fixtures and sold them for drug money. You can't get a reconstituted turquoise, a dyed diamond, or a radiated tourmaline past Freya, but my mother gets ripped off time and time again by her so-called *'friends.'"*

"Freya's a good person," said Grace sadly.

He was really angry about this. "But she never seems to learn! One bum hardly finishes ripping her off when Ma is just opening up her arms to the next one!"

Grace felt she had to defend Freya. "Finding a whole branch of her family tree must be something."

He wasn't listening. "Then there's that ridiculous treasure."

"The Revolutionary war ransom?"

"Aaup," he said it dismissively.

"You don't think it was collected?"

"The family histories say that it existed and that Captain Elijah Dell had it in his hands. The next day, the Red Coats marched into Oyster River. Some soldiers questioned Captain Elijah rather vigorously until he died, then the troopers marched out of town, and the ransom was never seen again."

"So?"

"I think it is pretty obvious what happened, the British soldiers tortured the old man until he handed over whatever he had of value. Then the soldiers split it between themselves and marched off. That treasure's been gone from here for two hundred years! The fact that so many of the townspeople searched for the ransom and couldn't find anything confirms that." To Mac, it was a done deal.

"It doesn't hurt to look a bit more."

He gave a disgusted look at her naivete. "I just found out that Cousin Penny talked mom into buying a metal detector."

"Oh, no, I think Kurt has one I can borrow for Freya. Can she cancel the detector order?"

"It's here already. Penny insisted that they needed this overnight express, with Freya paying for the extra shipping. And it isn't just any old metal detector, it is an X 4000, three D display with a color screen. Penny pushed Freya into going for the added night package, with video eyeglasses and extra probes. Aaup, Freya's van transmission is slipping, but she now has a 4000 that can discern between gold, silver, and iron. The 4000 can display earth cavities in color, and even tell you how deep your treasure is."

"That must have cost at least a thousand," said an unhappy Grace.

"The basic package alone was $6,889. That's without taxes, overnight express and all the extras, like the video glasses."

"Oh, God, that was the money Freya was saving for

a used truck?"

"All spent and the rest put on her credit card at twenty-one percent interest! With Penny cheering Ma on, telling her she can repay it all when they find the treasure."

"I've got to talk with Freya."

"Maybe that'll help," said a weary Mac.

But Grace didn't think so. "Is Penny staying at your place?"

Mac gave a firm. "No! You know how my mother always wants to take in strays? I finally got a rule that neither of us can have *'friends'* staying overnight, so Ms. Penny is at the Shoreline Motel, complaining bitterly to Freya about what that is costing her. I'm hoping Penny gets fed up and moves on to leach off of somebody else."

"With all the genealogical research Freya has done, it's strange she missed a whole branch of the family."

"Aaup. And if I stopped Ms. Barstall for speeding, with that antsy feeling she always gives me, I'd have central run a complete background check on her."

"Can't you still do that?" Grace asked hopefully.

"That can get you into a lot of trouble," he sighed. "I don't have the password to the databases, so I'd have to put it through the Sergeant. I'm sure she'd do it for me, but you can't be using the police databases for your own personal curiosity." He stopped. "Yet, every time I see Ms. Penny, all my cop alarms go off. I've warned Ma, but she's still feeding her at our house and treating Penny to meals out. They just went to the Captain's Mansion house for lunch, and Penny doesn't have a car, so anywhere they go it's on Freya's gas."

"Penny could chip in."

Mac gave a tight smile. "Doesn't. Has to pay for the motel, remember? And this looks like it is going to last until that non-existent treasure is found."

He drove off, and Grace headed back to her lab. She tried to start working, but thinking about David's ultimatum was still giving her a headache. Well, if she couldn't work out her life, maybe she could solve a two-hundred-year-old puzzle.

When she worked on a DNA problem, Grace often set up a spreadsheet to focus her mind on the various factors. For each possible outcome, she assigned very arbitrary percentages, and those with highest total 'points' became her working theories. Later as she studied the matter more, she could refine those percentages, testing different theories until--usually--the correct answer stood out.

Grace set up a spreadsheet titled *'Location Oyster River Ransom'* with headings for *'Disposition,'* *'Motive,'* *'Means,'* with two columns for *'Pro'* and *'Con.'* Each item would have a guessed at a percentage, added or subtracted in the final *'Total'* column. From spreadsheets such as this, she often developed a *'To Do'* list or visualized her final hypothesis.

For the ransom she started with a row for Elijah, *Motive* greed 2 %, as for *Means* he had possession and was going to hide the ransom, so 10%. The *Pro* was he had possession 20 %, the *Con* he died before the ransom for could be paid, but since it was for his son, he probably would have given it up, so Grace figured that was a - 40 % giving Elijah a total of zero, since Grace didn't place minus percentages in her *Total* columns.

His daughter in law Rebecca could have been greedy 5 %, might have seen where Elijah hid the treasure 5 %, but seemed to have been honest 5 %, and searched for the ransom the rest of her life, giving her a - 10 % for *Con*, adding up to a *Total* of 5 %. While Christopher Coe was known to be money hungry 30 %, he might have seen Elijah hide the ransom 5 %, and he was a rumrunner, spy, giving him a whopping 20 % *Pro*, but on the *Con* side the neighbors would have been watching, giving him, - 10 %, leaving Christopher's Total as 45 %.

The Red Coats marched into Oyster River when the ransom disappeared. For *Motive* she would give poorly paid soldiers 50 % for greed, the *Means* were torturing Elijah 30 %, *Pro* they left the area immediately so 10 %, but for the *Con* column the neighbors didn't see or report anything - 10 %. Ransom being taking by the British Soldiers finished first with a whopping 80 %.

But there was still Long Liz. Greed? She was a wealthy woman so only 2 %. Elijah's sister certainly knew of the treasure 10 %, could she have donated and then had second thoughts 5 %? But she didn't have to give money to ransom her nephew - 10 %, giving Liz an overall score of 7 %. What about her maid, Posey? Standard human greed 10 %, she was on the beach when Liz gave up her jewels, but thinking of *Means* a slave didn't have too much freedom - 5 %. For the *Pro* column, Posey could have dreamed of escaping with the ransom to finance her freedom, 20 %. No knowledge of her escaping and not much ability of a slave to spend treasure - 20 %, added up to a weak *Total* of 5 %.

That left two choices, *Unknown Person*, with the motive of greed, could be anyone in the area from the 1770's till the current year, 30 %. For *Pros,* they might have just stumbled on to the treasure 10 %, and they could have passed the ransom off as a family inheritance, 20 %. But for a Con, the ransom never officially showed up - 10 %. So Unknown Person came in at a substantial 50 %.

That left the final row on the spreadsheet that intrigued Grace, '*Still Hidden.*' No motive, but Elijah told his daughter-in-law he was going to hide it from the Redcoats, 30 %. For Pro, no one has ever seen any of it over the years, 40 %. But a big - 20 Con stood out: with all the building in two hundred plus years why had the ransom not been found? *Still Hidden* came in at a total of 50 %.   Laying her suppositions out in a spreadsheet, giving purely subjective percentages to the various alternatives, zeroing out minus numbers, firmed the alternates in her mind usually gave Grace ideas for her '*To Do*' lists. Who might have benefitted? Christopher should be a higher possibility. He knew Elijah had the treasure, and unlike Rebecca, he lived on Long Island so locals wouldn't have seen him spending it.

Rebecca kept searching for the treasure, so she probably didn't believe it had been stolen, so if she believed Christopher had taken it, Grace doubted she would have kept searching. Looking at the numbers, Grace knew Freya would be unhappy, but it looked to her like the British soldiers forced an old man to talk, found his hoard, and then marched away with it.

Her was phone ranging so she answered, "Laboratory 5."

"Grace, this is Mark Silverstein. Do you know where Kurt is? He's not answering." The lawyer sounded stressed.

Instantly Grace was worrying, she didn't want Mark to quit defending Kurt. "He might be out on the harbor. There's not much cell phone coverage..."

"There is a bench warrant issued for him," Mark stated with annoyance.

"Why?" Grace found herself going cold.

"They found out he's fleeing the country."

That was ridiculous! "Kurt isn't fleeing anywhere!"

"His passport has a visa for São Tomé and Principe. He also has airline reservations."

"Which he has had for months! He's being paid to go on a two week, international ocean study off the coast of Africa for the *Science Channel*. He'll dip some nets in the ocean on camera, do something scientific looking, and make some comments to be taped for a special on ocean currents."

"When was this arranged?"

"I don't know...January, he was talking about it." She had to think before saying, "There must be a record of when the airline reservations were made. Ocean currents have been an ongoing focus of his research for years. Everyone knows about this, and I think the whole thing is partially funded by the government of São Tomé. They're a tiny, island country, trying to increase their profile for tourism. His upcoming trip's been listed on the ORR website for months."

"But nobody told me, his lawyer!" Mark didn't sound happy. "Or the District Attorney's office. Or the Judge. São Tomé and Principe have no extradition treaty with the United States."

"Will this interfere with his travel?" And his work thought Grace.

"I should say so. He's being arrested and placed in jail, as a murder suspect and a flight risk."

"Eve's death is definitely being treated as a murder?"

"Unfortunately yes. Can you look for him for me? Call me if you find him, I want to highlight our innocence by making arrangements for Kurt to turn himself into the police before they take him into custody!"

She locked up her laboratory and walked across the road and down to Oyster River's docks. Yellow tape still on his sailboat and Kurt's diesel was tied up and waiting, but so was a State trooper there to arrest him.

Chapter 13

After checking Kurt's shared lab, she walked past another cop while trying to look innocent, as she headed for the big mustard-yellow mansion. Behind it, there was a livery stable, now a maintenance barn. Kurt kept his Harley stabled there. It was gone.

There were a number of places to look for him, but she figured the *Alpine* for the best bet. Soon she drove to a stretch of the road that had few houses and just some pastures and deep piney woods.   It was the middle of the day, but already twenty to thirty motorcycles surrounded the Swiss 'A' frame-shaped building, a frightening biker bar, with family picnic tables under the tall trees around it. Grace parked and started in.

A male voice yelled from the side. "Hey, mama, what you doing here?   Slumming?"

Grace stopped noting the two leather-jacketed punks that were snickering at her, as they moved to block her path to the door. She just lowered her head and started to walk around them, as if she hadn't heard. One of the guys stepped directly between her and the door. "You listening, mama?"

Grace lifted her head and would have replied, but a voice from the side thundered out. "Shut your mouths, that's Grace! She's one of Kurt's ladies!" A mountain of rusty red hair and beard looking like a troll on steroids stood there. Even Grace recognized Wayne, a biker friend of Kurt's she met at her first visit here.

Grace smiled with relief. "How's the bike?"

"Got a new front tire--Continental TKC 80s Twinduro Dual Sport! You gotta see it," he said proudly.

"Later, now it's important I find Kurt."

"Inside, eating lunch with Gina."

Inside a permanent blue fog of tobacco and whatever

smoke blanketed the *Alpine,* making it hard to see. Kurt preferred a table in the back, away from the dart board and its sharpened steel points. Grace was terribly grateful that big Wayne was following her in through the rough looking crowd. She found Kurt sitting in a tall, wooden booth, eating a bowl of chili, with Gina sitting close to him. The shapely barmaid must be on her lunch break.

"Grace?" He sounded concerned. "Hey, didn't I tell you not to come here by yourself?"

"Wayne gave me safe passage," Grace said, sliding into the red leatherette covered booth on his other side.

He nodded to her protective mountain angel, as Grace told Kurt, "Your lawyer called. There's a warrant out for your arrest."

"Why?" Kurt sounded genuinely surprised.

"They consider that São Tomé trip *'fleeing the country.'*"

"Shit. I didn't even think of it, but I'll be back in sixteen days."

"There is no U.S. extradition from São Tomé." Grace looked at him hard. "Mark wants you to call him, and he'll arrange for you to turn yourself in."

A worried looking Gina put a comforting hand on Kurt's arm as he looked around the room and then spoke flatly, "Not turning myself in, that makes it too easy for the cops. Besides, I promised to take Gina for a ride up Route Seven today." He put an arm around her waist and pulled her closer, and Gina responded by snuggling against him.

Grace felt herself getting angry. Kurt was playing his tough guy image to the room when he should have been worrying about his life! "They've got a cop waiting at the dock, so try not to ride there!" Saying that Grace turned and strode out. She didn't need Wayne's escort, anybody who dared get in her way would have gotten a punch in the mouth!

Yhep, that was Kurt MacKay, stupid, stubborn, and

probably scared. A man who loved being outdoors as much as he did, who built his whole life around it, might prefer death to imprisonment. Suicide by cop? Oh, hell, she was getting overly dramatic, but the thought of not having Kurt around to bounce her ideas off of really bothered her more than Grace would have expected.

Chapter 14

Back at her lab, she decided to start another spreadsheet. This one to find '*The Murder Of Eve Dupree.*'

First Suspect up was Kurt Mackay. His *Motive* was weak, Eve refused sex 10 %. He found her long dead, but he could have killed Eve before he went for the wine so *Means* 25 %. For Pro she went to his boat willingly, 20 % and the Con, he wanted her alive for sex, -20 %. So a total of 35 %, and much as she didn't believe it that was a significant showing.

Now Josh Jeffer's, his *Motive* was to frame Kurt, 30 %, and he certainly knew where Kurt's boat giving him 20 % as *Means*, and 30 % for a general craziness in *Pro*, but in the *Con* column, Josh has an alibi - 20 %, and he would have been recognized at ORR -20 %, so Josh finished with an overall *Total* of 40 %.

Who else was connected with Eve Dupree? She hadn't been in Oyster River long enough to have created close friends much less enemies. Well, there was Jack Stuart. What *Motive*? Jealousy? Grace gave him a weak 2 %, and *Means* for Jack consisted of the fact he was in the area and physically strong enough to kill, 20 %. She had to dig some for a *Pro*, he worked closely with Eve, perhaps anger she hid the state of his company from him? 10 %. But then there was the *Cons*, Jack appeared to have no sexual relationship or jealousy in relation to Eve, and he seemed genuinely grieved by her death, so - 40 %, giving him a Grand Total of 2 %.

Huang Wong. For *Motive* it would always be monetary gain, 10 %, he was in the area 20 %. For *Pro* column, Huang resented that he wasn't getting 'his full share' from Our Sisters, 2 %. But it would have been a foolish attack, that even he must realize would gain him nothing. *Con* - 30 %. She just about zeroed him out a 2 %.

Adam Greenfield. *Motive* lost pensions 20 %, *Means*

he was there and strong 12 %, and a strong *PRO*, he lost his company's and ORR's investment with Eve 40 %. For *Con* Adam's married to a lawyer, he would have sued Eve, so - 50 %, he came in at a Grand *Total* of 22 %.

She had to widen the scope of her investigation. Unknown Lover? Jealousy 10 %, People in the area, 20 %, but *Con* if this lover came from Eve's past they might have been recognized by Jack - 20 %, and ultimate *Con* there was no evidence this person exists - 20 %. Weak *Total* of 5 %.

Okay, the *Motive* was wrong. How about Unknown Thief with *a Motive* robbery gone wrong 30 %. *Means* people are always around ORR 20 %, and for the *Pros* the Thief thought Kurt was out and was surprised by Eve 35%, but why wasn't this person seen? That left a *Con* of nothing was stolen and no robberies in the area lately - 10 % giving Unknown Thief 75 %.

Yes, this was obviously a very limited sampling of the people around Eve, and as Grace found more suspects, she would enlarge the spreadsheet by adding more rows. But Eve's murder didn't make sense from the beginning. Right now, if she ignored Kurt as a possible suspect, the two strongest choices were Josh Jeffers and Unknown Thief. The police focused on Kurt early on and apparently stopped questioned Jeffers because he had an alibi. Grace wondered just exactly how steel hulled that alibi was? Maybe that was something for her '*To Do*' column. But was it a murder? Could there still be a chance that Eve accidentlly fell and the police overreacted?

The next day her assistants were off so any work in the clean room would have to be done by Grace. She planned to attempt some DNA extractions from the volcanic vent seaworm samples sent by the French research ship. She was in lab coat and pants, had pulled on a paper hair cap and she was about to pull on shoe covers when there was a polite knock on Grace's laboratory entrance door. People didn't knock, they usually just opened the door and walked in.

Reluctantly Grace headed over, opening the door to a shamefaced Samantha Carson. Her face was almost as red as her hair, as she started talking fast, "I'm so sorry about this! You know I didn't interview you at all about the new research head of Oyster River, and I didn't try to talk to you concerning the murder of Eve Dupree..."

Grace icily cut in, "It could have been an accidental fall."

That stopped Sam. She stared at Grace in a surprised fashion, then carefully explained. "The police are investigating it as a felonious attack. Eve either fell down the steps or was pushed and then Dr. MacKay or someone else smashed her skull in."

Even thinking that herself, it still came as a blow to Grace. "Then they're sure?"

Sam did a fast check of her notes. "The police found the weapon when they were diving off of ORR's dock. It's a wench tied to Kurt MacKay, I don't know how. They may have gotten fingerprints from underwater, but with corrosive salt water that's really hard. They're not saying..."

"Thank you." Grace tried not to show her horrified reaction, but she knew what tied the wrench to Kurt.

"I'm sorry. You didn't know any of this?" Sam asked sounding surprised.

"I know that Kurt–**Dr**.--MacKay did not kill Eve Dupree."

Sam spoke hesitantly, "My editor has insisted that I try to get a comment from you. Your name..."

"Sells newspapers?" Grace bitterly finished.

"No, not a scientist. Scientists aren't really bankable, like a big-time movie actor, but locally and internationally, your name is at least recognizable."

"Thanks," said Grace, drily.

"Could I have a something?" Sam asked that as if she

expected a no.

"Quote me as saying that Dr. Kurt MacKay is a scientist, not a murderer." Sam was scribbling that down. "If he wanted to kill someone, he could have done a much better job of getting rid of the body." Then Grace raised her hand in a stop gesture. "Please don't write that part! Could you just give a little of his background, his discoveries..."

Sam nodded. "I've researched him: saving the oyster crop, working on ocean currents, trying to increase the lobster catches...I'm going to point that out in the story, and that the São Tomé trip that caused his arrest warrant was planned originally last December."

"Yes," said Grace relieved. "Yes, I'm sure it was!"

"Do you know if Oyster River Research is going to raise his bail?"

"Kurt's in jail?" That sounded too emotional to be professional.

Sam's quick eyes took that in, as she scribbled more. "He was arrested this morning when he went to his lobster boat."

Oh, God, he knew they would be waiting. "Has bail been set?"

"I don't know yet. He was going into court early today."

"Excuse me." Grace had to get Kurt out, that meant raising bail money. David Gardiner? Never. But first, she had to get rid of this reporter. "Umm...can you just say that Dr. Farrington is steady in her belief in colleagues' total innocence and that she wishes people would wait until all the facts were in before they make their judgments?"

Sam nodded and scribbled some more.

Grace was pulling off the disposable, sterile cap. "I've got to speak with someone."

Sam helpfully added. "You know if he gets bail you don't have to raise the full amount. You can look up a bail bonds man on the Internet. They've got a calculator that tells you how much you have to raise, then you arrange with the bail bond company to pay a percentage up front or put up something you own as collateral."

"Thank you." Not even looking back at her, Grace hurried outside. No cop by the dock, well, they'd picked up Kurt and found the wrench so no need for a guard anymore. No cars parked by the Roost, but when she looked down the road, she saw Adam's shining red truck parked in front of the new Administration building.

The building was new in the 1950's, with large expanses of glass wall windows and brown firebrick. As with most of ORR, it faced the road and then the harbor. Inside a large reception area, Gail's desk sat in the center, she called it her 'fishbowl'. To her left was the cafeteria, which as she'd shown Jack which was actually not quite bad, more of a café. To the right was the glass-fronted scientific library with its rows of bookshelves largely being preempted by its Internet terminals, but still used quite a bit by the students. And right behind Gail's desk was a short hallway with storage rooms on either side that led to the President's office. As Grace walked up, Gail stopped typing on her computer, and the self-proclaimed '*Polish doll*' looked up with a welcoming smile.

But Grace started abruptly, "Kurt's been jailed."

Gail looked guilty. "I know, that's why Adam's here. I was ordered not to tell you, I'm sorry..."

Grace understood. "He's your boss."

"Oyster River Research must make some kind of official announcement, I'm typing it now. Do you want to read it?"

Getting Kurt out was the most important thing. "I need to talk with Adam."

Gail shook her head. "He's in with Dr. Wong now. If I buzz him, he'll just say no." Gail looked back toward the office. "But if you just walk in...?"

Taking the hint, Grace headed into the President's office without knocking. Adam was at his desk, leaning as far away as he could, from the man sitting in front of him. Huang was furiously sputtering. "Shame Me! Shame Oyster River! Caught killing woman! Running to Mexico! Fire his ass out!"

Grace walked up and defiantly sat in the other chair fronting Adam's desk. "Kurt is in trouble because of the São Tomé trip to Africa, they claim he was fleeing this jurisdiction! Adam, that trip was arranged months ago by Oyster River because you wanted the favorable publicity of having Dr. Kurt MacKay interviewed on television."

"Woman killed on his boat! Him stupid!" shouted Huang.

Ignoring Huang, Grace concentrating on Adam. "Kurt needs bail money," Grace said firmly. "Oyster River was responsible for that trip, and so they are responsible for raising his bail!"

"No! No! He killer!" Huang kept yelling, even as they ignored him.

"Adam?" Grace asked, holding her breath.

The big man swallowed. "You know I'm not paid to be President of Oyster River. This is a voluntary job that has given me nothing but headaches!"

Huang cut in. "Bail MacKay? No! Stay away from him. Bad press!"

Adam looked from Grace to Huang really wanting to be out of there. "Oyster River Research will not be raising his bail." Huang smiled triumphantly at Grace, but that smile hardened as Adam continued. "I have been contacted by Kurt's attorney, Mr. Silverstein. Oyster River will be providing an affidavit as to why Mr. Mackay was going to São Tomé and the dates he originally arranged his travel."

"It is **Dr.** MacKay," Grace finished coldly. "And if

I remember correctly, Adam, you approached Kurt with the cable television proposal, saying if he appeared on that *Science* channel it would increase ORR's footprint in the scientific community." She stared at him hard, daring him to deny it.

A basically fair man, Adam finally acknowledged her point. "Yes, now that you mention it, I did bring up the opportunity to..." He hesitated, and then finished, "Dr. MacKay's attention."

She started again. "Kurt never has much money about, so he'll need cash for bail, it's only fair..."

Looking sick Adam said, "Grace, are you aware of the *Our Sisters* situation?"

"Now that Eve's dead, Jack can't find any assets? Yes," answered Grace.

Like it was his worse nightmare, Adam just repeated in a dead voice, "With this *Our Sisters* mess, my whole construction company just lost most of its pension fund! We've also just lost twenty percent of Oyster River Research's entire endowment! I am not authorizing expenditures for anything now!"

Defeated, Grace returned to her lab and picked up the phone to dial Kurt's lawyer. "Mark, how much is Kurt's bail?"

"Actually, he's being bailed out as we speak, but the paperwork should be completed soon."

"That's good news," she said feeling a bit better.

"Not exactly." Mark sounded pessimistic. "Quite a number of his biker friends showed up in court with a bails bondsman, when Judge Rubin set bail, they passed the hat in the courtroom. The judge didn't look too pleased."

"Why was Kurt even indicted?"

"I've been told the police found a wench they think is the murder weapon, and they've tied it to Kurt, I don't know just how yet. If this goes farther, I'll be filing a discovery on that, but..."

She cut him off. To help, he needed the full truth. "There was a wench missing from Kurt's boat, one that he used it to weigh down charts in the main cabin." She reluctantly continued, "One he found scuba diving on a wrecked U Boat. It has a swastika on it."

Mark quickly replied, "That's why the judge sustained a bail request, even after I proved São Tomé was a work-related, previously planned trip. A Nazi souvenir which my client never mentioned," he ended angrily.

It sounded like Kurt just lost a lawyer. "Mark, he won't admit it, but Kurt's afraid. To an outdoorsmen like him, prison would be worse than death. And when someone panics, they often do stupid things."

There was a pause on the line. Grace expected to hear Mark say he was quitting, but instead, he asked. "Do you think Kurt knows who killed her?"

"No. I saw his face when he came up after finding her body. He was in total shock because he had gone down there thinking she was alive." There was silence on the line. "Do you think he has a chance?"

"It's not going well for him," Mark admitted.

"But he's innocent. Will you still defend him?"

He didn't answer for a moment and then said, "Kurt and I will have to talk. He's got to be a lot more open, or I can't help him."

"There was a man, a known nut case with a public grudge against Kurt, Josh Jeffers. He rammed the *Big 'Un* in the harbor, and the night of the reception Josh started punching Kurt."

"Kurt didn't mention him," said Mark thoughtfully.

"He has his code, and Kurt tries to protect people. I hear the police have questioned Josh, but supposedly he has an alibi that he was out fishing with his twin brother. If you pressed and police looked harder, and they couldn't find any other witnesses to confirm that, it would be good, right?"

Mark thought about it some. "No. It's not to our advantage. If the police find another, impartial witness it strengthens Josh's alibi, so we want them not looking. If they don't have corroboration, and if Kurt goes into court on a murder charge with only the brother's word for Josh's alibi, I might be able to cast some doubt in the jury's mind."

"Is it going to court?" Cold fear flooded Grace. "Kurt will be on trial for his life?"

"Connecticut doesn't have the death penalty anymore, but let's wait for a trial date, before we panic, okay, Grace?"

After she hung up, Grace pulled up her murder sheet again, but she saw no help there.   She was missing something. She knew it. Like a protein that was there right in front her, but her tests hadn't detected it. Grace studied the suspect rows again.   What had she overlooked? Remembering Freya seance warnings, she was so desperate that Grace almost inserted rows for Osiris, Isis, and Bastet.

Tonight was her regular dinner with Freya, Grace's treat at Neptune's Grotto. She rather felt relieved at the thought she could forget everything, have a glass of red wine and eat something she wouldn't have dared trying to cook at home. She parked in the Oyster River town lot, seeing a number of shoppers walking in front of upscale stores. In the 1800's, Oyster River didn't get as much whaling traffic as Sag Harbor, but it had enough of a romantic seafaring history to draw tourists today. Grace headed along one and two-story wooden stores to the steps that lead down to the basement shop with its hand carved *The Haunt's of Wōden* sign. As she entered the new age shop, the brass bell that hung at its coil high on the door jangled out.

Freya's black-lace bloused, part-timer Lilith, was sitting at the central desk. Grace walked over and saw the goth girl was studying an algebra text. Lilith didn't even look up to see if a customer had walking in, so Grace just waited a bit before finally asked, "Is Freya in the backroom?"

The black and purple haired, fair skinned girl looked up, blinking her eyes as if surfacing from underwater. Lilith looked around briefly, then said, "She's not here," and looked back at her book.

"Not here?"

Looking a little annoyed at being disturbed again, the part-timer looked back up. "Yeah, she left. Oh, you're Grace, right? Penny came by and wanted to borrow the metal detector and said she had a definite feeling that the treasure might have been buried in the park behind the library, just above the high water line..."

"They're going to dig up the town park?" That didn't seem like a good idea to Grace.

The girl just shrugged her shoulders. "Freya said to tell you dinner is off tonight."

"Did she say why?"

"The cousin needs Freya to drive her somewhere else."

"Great," Grace said disgustedly, but before leaving, she noted something. Lilith had black hair but the very, pale-white skin usually associated with a red-haired woman. "Excuse me, is that your natural color hair?"

The salesgirl looked up like Grace was crazy. "No, I dye it purple."

Grace shook her head. "No. No, I mean the black hair. Brunet hair can go with skin that fair, but genetically it's an unusual combination..."

"The black's dyed too. I'm in a rock band. You know Elvis Presley' hair wasn't black? He dyed it to make himself more dramatic on stage."

"Thank you." Outside, it was hot and muggy. Maybe a storm tonight? Well, she could go to *Neptune's Grotto* by herself but didn't want to do that, or she could go home alone and heat up a frozen fried chicken dinner, that didn't appeal either. Grace looked up and down the street. Across the road was the three-story, grey house, constructed in the 1800's it was built into the rising hillside with wood planking on top, stone masonry on the bottom receding into the hillside. Abe Hoyt lived upstairs in the old family house and, in what started out as a basement, he now had his bookstore. It'd been too long since she browsed his new and used books.

The stone walls inside were white-paint shiny. Abe was lean, shortish, with thick-lensed glasses, and a thin graying-brown goatee. His eyes tended to be merry, although usually focused on a book page. You normally found him sitting at his central desk in a nest of book piles. He was reading when she came in, but today he actually stopped and looked up.

There was a couple browsing through the tourist section, but Abe must have figured they wouldn't know who she was, because he didn't loudly proclaim, '*Hello, Dr. Farrington*', instead he just put down his book and leaned toward her. "Grace, you having dinner with Freya tonight? I found a local history she might be interested in." He held up the worn blue book he'd been reading. "A WPA project that has some mention of Revolutionary War sites."

"No, Freya's off with that new-found cousin of hers." Grace tried to say it with a neutral tone.

"Penny?" Abe also spoke in a definitely crafted neutral tone.

"What do you think of her?"

Abe put his glasses back on as he seemed to be carefully phrasing what he was going to say. "Funny, Freya not finding any record of her. Freya's done research for me in the past, and she's very thorough."

"Well, with Long Liz having a late-life baby in New Brunswick..."

Abe shook his head. "If'n Freya suspected there was some family history to be dug up, she'd have been on the road to Canada long ago." But trying to be fair he finished with, "But I can see where at Liz's fortyish age, nobody would have suspected there'd still be a baby. And a girl gets off the records pretty fast, as soon as she marries and changes her name."

"Why did Liz and Seth move all the way to Canada?"

"Had to. Seth and Elizabeth Booth were staunch Royalists during the Revolutionary War, so they didn't leave as much as they were kicked out with the rest of the British sympathizers. Seth, Liz, and their two slaves were shipped off. The British government gave them some remuneration–just lands–nothing like what they lost."

"They held slaves in New England?"

"Aaup and in Canada then too. The poetess, Phillis Wheatley was bought as a child by a Boston family. During that time period--under British rule--Boston Harbor was one of the great ports in the African slave trade."

That actually surprised Grace. "Slaves worked the fields in Connecticut?"

"Not as great a percentage as the South. New England had lot more indentured servants, where the passage to the new world was paid for by seven years of work. For slaves, Seth Booth had a manservant for the horses and chickens, and his wife had a maid to help with the housework. In New England, hardscrabble farms couldn't afford to feed a large population of slaves, so you just had more kids to tend the cattle. Most slaves in New England had to have a trade, like an ironsmith, and there were a lot of free blacks and escapees. Down south, they needed field hands for the plantation and were responsible for them until they died. Up north, if you had a mill worker, you could work'em to near death, and then just release 'em on the mercy of the town, who farmed their care out to the lowest bidder."

"Seth and Long Liz were farmers?"

"Not really. Seth owned the major dock in Oyster

River and some shipping. Toward the end, he had a ship's Chandlery, sort of marine hardware. Then they had a fancy mansion, biggest in town, and he owned some farmland he rented out. That mansion was full of clothes and fine furniture when it got burned."

"Accident?"

"Nope. Feelings running sore in town. After that Seth and Liz were forced out, and what was left their property was claimed as '*abandoned*' and sold at auction for the town's benefit. Local town boys had died in the Patriot militia, and folks weren't too happy about that."

"Then Long Liz probably never returned to her home?"   "With the town ready to tar and feather her and her husband?"

Grace kept probing. "Maybe her body could have been shipped back and buried in the family plot?"

"Doubt it. Lotta trouble and expense as bodies deteriorated pretty fast in those days and why bring her back? Her parents and her only brother were dead. She'd have been buried in New Brunswick, probably alongside her husband. Why is that so important to you?" He asked.

"Wish I could do a DNA on Long Liz or maybe her mother. She's buried in Oyster River isn't she?"

"Probably. You gonna go to a judge and ask permission to dig up somebody?" Abe sounded like he thought that was a ridiculous notion.

And it was. Exhuming a body for its DNA, just to satisfy a point of her own personal curiosity. Grace flushed slightly. "I get carried away sometimes. Forget that my extracting some DNA isn't the most important thing in this world."

"Aaup," Abe thought about it. "but you'd want some if you could get it?"

"Yes." Grace was positive on that. "Long Liz's mother would be an ancestor of both Freya and Penny. Now when you see Freya so tall, blonde, and big-boned, while Penny is so petite, olive-skinned, and green-eyed, the DNA might provide a very interesting look."

"Might have some," Abe said carelessly.

"Have somewhat?"

"Colonial DNA," he said quite matter of factly.

Chapter 15

"You do?" She scoffed. "Pressed in some book, like flower petals?"

He laughed, getting off his stool. Abe looked around his bookstore seeing the two tourists were still looking through a book on sea otters. "You folks, if someone comes in and wants to buy anything, I'd be obliged if you could tell them I'd be right back. C'mon, Grace." Abe moved back behind his sale counter. He was leaving his bookstore wide open with strangers in it, so Grace thought he might at least be locking up the cash register, but instead, he was only picking up a heavy duty flashlight from under the counter.

He saw her look. "You can always trust people who love books." Then he headed through the back bookshelves to where a wood door opened up to a Bilco door with cement steps dug into the back hillside. Mystified Grace followed out into a small gravel parking lot, in front of an old, gray, two-story livery barn. There was chain and a padlock on the wide doors, but Abe just pulled at the hasp, and Grace saw it only appeared to be locked. Well, normally in a small New England town like Oyster River nobody much worried about petty thievery or murder. She followed him into a dark, wide-planked barn, that smelled of old book mold, leather, and dusty wood. God, the place was an antique pickers heaven!

"My Dad used to sell second-hand furniture in the store below, but I was just interested in the books. Though I still pick up a good piece now and again, you'd be surprised what fools will be draggin' out to the curb." He looked around. "Now somewhere in here..." He flashed the light over a red velvet upholstered, two horse sleigh, an old soda shop sign, a Model A Ford, and cartons labeled 'books.' "Naw. Might be upstairs."

As she followed him up a steep, narrow wooden staircase, Abe commented, "Most of those early settlers had genes a lot smaller than us."

Grace corrected. "Actually, it wasn't the genes. More poor diet and early childhood illnesses stunted their growth."

"Well, be careful on these stairs, treads are mighty short for modern feet."

She wouldn't have thought it possible, but the loft was even more tightly packed than down below. The walls were hung with horse collars, hand saws, and moose antlers. Above her, she could see someone had put flooring on the beams, so more stuff could be piled up in the double hayloft. If anything happened to Abe, he should will this place to the Smithsonian.

Now seeing these cardboard boxes stacked upon barrels, stacked on top of crates, and steamer trunks, Grace could readily believe that Abe would have the skulls and thigh bones of generations of the towns' people entombed up here. What she couldn't see as possible was him ever being able to find them, buried under the assorted anvils, spinning wheels, and milk cans.

Yet, Abe just kept casting his flashlight over the piles, until finally he zeroed in on a distant, tall, maple specimen cabinet, with rows and rows of narrow drawers almost buried behind barrier reefs of junk.   "Dr. Floyds', several generations of doctors, starting as Lemuel Floyd, barber and herbalist man, did the town's only surgery, bleeding, and bandaging. Later Floyds were doctors, and the last of the Floyds was a veterinarian up on Long Ridge Road in Stamford in the nineteen forties." Abe looked around vaguely. "We've got to clear a way to get to it."

"What about the store? Your tourists?"

"Didn't seem interested in buying. Jes breaking in my books a little." He shook his head in despair. "Course, I don't see how we're ever going to get back to that cabinet..."

Clearing a path through this hoarder's nest looked like a major job for ten strong men, four dumpsters, and a television crew. Grace shook her head. "These Doctor Floyds, what did they do? Snip diseased tissue and save it in formaldehyde? If so, I'm probably not going to be able to extract any decodable DNA. I've tried that before, but the formaldehyde or alcohol degrades it too much."

"The Floyds came to be mostly dentists. Member, the first was a barber? Barbers did a lot of surgical cutting and sewing in those days and teeth pulling. The first Floyd started a collection of all the teeth he pulled. Rest followed suit."

"Why?"

He shrugged. "Ask the Floyds. Generations of very anal men kept years of teeth, all labeled with the townsmen's name and dates in tiny manilla envelopes, and wrapped with red tie strings. You can get DNA out teeth can't you?"

With the electric jolt that a chance of making a discovery always gave Grace, she quickly agreed. "Yes! Sometimes, if they were preserved without moisture and temperatures were correct, they've gotten DNA out of three-thousand-year-old Egyptian mummies." With eager eyes, she looked around. To clear the path, they were going to have to move a lot, but there was nowhere open to move anything into...clearing this pathway would be like reorganizing a life-sized Rubric cube. Some of it would have to be hauled downstairs, and some piled perilously higher. She mentally worked out a narrow route of least resistance to the cabinet.

"I don't think we can reach it..." he started, sounded crestfallen.

There might be centuries of DNA in there! Allowing for no disagreement Grace stated firmly, "We **will** get it!"

Chapter 16

She reached down, picked up a cardboard box, and handed it to Abe. "Take this downstairs--temporarily--to make room. Shoo those tourists out and lock up your shop! Come back with more flashlights. No–get a lamp! See if you can find or borrow a long extension cord, a couple of them to bring power up here from the store. We'll need more light to do this." She wiped her nose with the back of her hand, disturbing ages of grimy dust was clogging her sinuses

He looked doubtful but obediently said, "Yes, mam."

Soon they had a seashell lamp from his store--with the price tag still hanging on it--lighting the wooden planking, while Grace was sweating and covered with dirt. She and Abe had been clearing for what seemed like hours, and they were not quite there yet. Still blocking her was a solid dark wood chest on top of a bar stool. The chest was nearly two-foot square and had a built-in lock in the front with an ornate key still inserted. When Grace wiped dirt off with her sleeve she could see the top lid had an elegantly engraved plate, '*India Princess.*' "Abe, what's this?"

Carrying away two life-sized, wooden Canadian Geese decoys tucked under each arm, he turned back to peer at the polished wooden box. "Captain's medicine chest."

Grace's genius and her fatal flaw was her insatiable curiosity. The case's top was hinged. She found the locked lid opened upwards, and there seemed to be, at the bottom half of the box, two drawers that pulled out frontways. Grace tried to turn the key but found it stuck. She jiggled it free, and the lid opened. Inside was a thick, yellowed paper pamphlet on top of a wooden honey-comb with each segment containing a glass bottle, either square or round.

Abe was explaining, "Whaling ships couldn't return to home port until their barrels were fully loaded with oil, so men were sometimes gone three to five years on the open sea. Only had room for workin' crew, no fine, educated doctors. A man got feeling poorly, the captain looked up his symptoms in this book." He took the paper treatise from on top of the bottles and handed it to her.

Grace very carefully turned the aged paper page dated 1826 and noted it wasn't crumbling. She read: *'Head pain, blood cough, two drops nightshade, teaspoon, mixed with whiskey.'* She turned a few more pages, *'Burns, scorched skin–red, weeping, place picric acid on muslin. Have patient held firmly...'*

In the box, Grace counted fifteen square or pillar-shaped, glass-stopped bottles. She pulled out the first bottle, empty except for a dark red stain, it was labeled *'Malaga wine,'* and she carefully slipped back.   Some still had protective, brown paper wrapping them, like a Worcestershire sauce bottle. Grace picked up another half filled with a fine, white powder labeled *'Opium'* in a spidery hand. "Abe, is it legal to possess this stuff?"

He shrugged.

The first lower drawer held an assortment of grim looking metal knives and tools, the second held smaller bottles and round ointment tins, and a stack of woolen squares–for bandages? "This should be in a museum or at least sold."

"Couple of months ago, I promised to donate it to Maryanne at the Whaling Museum.   Never got round to digging it out.

"If it was promised then we have to get it downstairs."

"That's heavy. Two of us can't carry it down those narrow stairs."

"I'm sliding it forward, and then we both will take an end. Looks like there's built-in brass handles on the sides so we'll just pull them out and carry it down. If we are going to get to the Floyd cabinet, we need to clear this!" Getting that medicine chest down was a major horror, but they deposited it outside on the gravel, alongside the clock yard winder, goose decoys, and boxes of tax records. Grace nearly ran back, now only the stool, some bonnets, and a water-stained, whaleboned underskirt stood between her and the tooth cabinet.

Finally, the moment Grace had been waiting for! They reached the five foot, maple cabinet, and Grace ran her hand along the grimy but still smooth wood. The cabinet looked like it came apart in two sections. The uppermost had thirty, small square drawers in the top section set up library card catalog style, and the bottom had four six inches high, three foot wide drawers.

Abe held the flashlight for her as she slid one of the small, topmost drawers open and saw gold!

Chapter 17

The drawer was filled to the brim with little, mustard-colored envelopes, carefully sealed with red tie strings that wound around cardboard disks. Most were white labeled or had faded ink scribbled directly on the envelopes, but a lot of that brown ink had faded, of course, the barn's light was terrible. Grace started pulling samples from the drawers and found the older dates seemed to be in the top row drawers, and some seemed to be boxed in by the family's last name. Her fingers trembled a bit with the excitement of holding possibly centuries of DNA in her hands.

Grace fished and found a packet labeled '*Alice Hoyt, 1777*', and there was an another, George Seawell, with three dates: '*1772, 1776, and 1781*'. She untied it, pulled out the envelope's paper lip, and peeked inside. Three yellowed teeth with deep, black cavities. It was a long shot, but if these samples had been maintained dry and at the proper temperature, it might be possible to extract DNA. "I need something to carry these..."

Abe looked around, unable to move out of their narrow, cleared pathway, and then he reached high and pulled out a stained Nantucket basket which he passed to her.

But just a basket of these riches wasn't enough. "Abe, this collection. " She indicated the Doctor Floyd cabinet. "How much?"

"What?"

"I want to buy this."

"The cabinet or the teeth?"

"Everything. How much? "

He shook his head. "Cain't sell it. Cain't get it out of there." He pointed to the buried front of the barn. "Used to bring stuff up by opening that hayloft door and hauling it up here with a rope and pulley. Cain't get to that door now, sorry."

"It could be carried down the stairs."

"You and I couldn't lift that cabinet, much less carry it down those narrow stairs." Abe sounded like he knew it was impossible.

There was DNA here! Grace started grabbing a few of the 1700's envelopes for her basket saying, "I'll send Bobby and Nick over. They will get it out of there. How much?"

"You get it out of here, you can have it, free."

"No! That's a valuable piece of furniture. How much is just that wood cabinet worth?"

He squinted his eyes as he studied it. "Wholesale I'd say $500 to $700."

"Will you take $600?"

"No! For you, maybe $100."

"No," Grace said firmly. "$500."

He sounded angry. "I'm not gonna do that! $150 tops! Grace, that's my last offer!"

"$400," She said stubbornly.

"Grace, that's not fair at all! Maybe $200, that's all I'll go!"

"$350." She said finally.

Abe looked beaten. "You're not being fair! My final price, $225, and that, mam, is as firm as concrete! Take it or leave the cabinet!"

She looked to the cabinet. "I don't have my checkbook." Grace thought about her bank balance. "Look, Abe, could you wait until my next grant comes in?" He nodded, so she felt obliged to add, "That may be awhile."

"Worry about the eminent Dr. Grace Farrington paying me? I'll trust ya, and now let's get out of this dust mine."

Reluctant to leave the trove of DNA, Grace headed down with him, carrying the basket with samples. "Could you at least padlock the barn?"

He made a face but said he would. Outside she could breathe again and noted that the Captain's medicine chest was just sitting there with a bunch of odds and ends on the parking lot gravel. "Do you know the valuation of this?"

"If I ever get it down to the museum, it's free. Gonna donate it."

"Well, how much are you going to ask for in a letter of donation? For your taxes."

He looked blank.

"It's a beautifully crafted chest, and it must be valuable. Abe, you are going to guard it, while I bring my station wagon up here. After we load it safely in the back, we're going down to your shop and look up the value of an antique captain's medicine chest on the Internet. Then I'll take it to the museum, donate in your name, and see that you get a receipt for the full value!"

From others sold on e-bay, a captain's medical chest, in merely good condition and not complete with all the bottles looked like it might be worth $ 900 to $1,500. Grace didn't like the idea of leaving something that old and irreplaceable sitting in her van overnight, so she drove down Main Street past the town stores, to where old houses lined the tree-shaded street near Oyster River's Museum. Two small, one story buildings housed a museum dedicated to Oyster River's years as a whaling ship harbor.

Inside the main room was dominated by a thirty-foot whaling skiff. On board that fragile wood boat, five brave men, and a sixth rudderman rowed from the mother ship to get the harpooner close enough for his throw at a forty-ton Sperm Whale. The harpoon was attached to a long coil of rope, seventy-five fathoms worth, but when that rope reached its end, a strong whale swimming forward could pull that boat at incredible speeds, which was the origin of the famous '*Nantucket Sleigh Ride*.' And if the whale suddenly dived deep, he might take the boat with him under the icy water, probably drowning all aboard. Truly the whalers were '*iron men in wooden ships.'*

Coming over the curator smiled at her in recognition. Maryanne Morgan was a short woman, with light cocoa colored skin, gray curls, and hazel eyes. "Dr. Farrington." Like a number of people, Maryanne had told Grace to call her by her first name, but when Grace asked her to do the same, Maryanne still preferred to refer to her as '*Doctor Farrington.'* She always looked so honored to have Grace there. "We love having our members come in."

"It has been awhile," Grace admitted.

"Dr. Farrington, I understand that with DNA you can trace where a person's roots are?"

"The *Genographic Project* sponsored by the *National Geographic Society* is doing that now."

"How can they do that?" Maryanne sounding intrigued.

"It's believed we all roughly shared a common ancestor, an 'Eve,' and an 'Adam.'
That as the original humans spread across the world, there were genetic mutations. By discovering the locations where a particular change took place, you can take modern DNA and trace it back to a geographical area and time where that mutation first appeared. From this, you can work out a progression of your early ancestors."

"My family is mostly Louisiana on my father' s side. I've got two white great-grandparents on the paternal side, but Freya once held a ring I got from my maternal Grandmother Pat. From that Freya said my mother's ancestors had once lived in Oyster River," said Maryanne in a questioning tone.

Grace hesitated, then said carefully, "I know of no recognized physical basis for one of Freya's '*strong feelings.'" She thought about it and had to honestly add, "but I also know Freya has been right about things that she should have had no conventional way of knowing."

Maryanne continued. "The strange thing was that Grandma Pat said she was descended from free Negroes living up north. Grandma Pat spoke French and was a Home Economics teacher in the City schools. When we lived in Harlem, she said that way back some of her people came from the Oyster River area, of course, I had never heard of Oyster River Harbor then. When you're a teenager, you don't care much about history, and Grandma Pat died while I was in college. I so wish now that I would have asked her more questions about our family, and about why she thought we came from here. Funny how I wound up in Oyster River, this job opened up, and when I moved here, it felt like home. I was wondering your genetics tests...? "

"DNA won't point out the difference between Harlem and Oyster River, or even between Louisiana and New York. Maybe someday, but still we might be able to find out something interesting. I've done DNA profiles on a lot of people from Oyster River, and I might be able to pick up your family's migration with a simple test."

"How much will this cost?"

"For you, free." Grace opened her leather fanny pack and started looking. "I try to keep a few sterile tubes in my bag. Yes." She pulled out a small, screwed topped plastic vial and started to open it.

Maryanne looked apprehensive. "Does it hurt?"

"No," Grace laughed. "You can do it for me. Just take the little wooden stick out, then swab the inside of your mouth three or four times with its cotton tipped end." When Maryanne was finished doing that, Grace told her to replace it back in the vial to be recapped, then with the black sharpie, she always carried Grace labeled the tube with Maryanne's name and date.

The curator was still talking. "You just missed Freya and that woman, Penny."

Grace caught a slight undertone, and she decided to probe. "What do you think of this new found cousin of Freya's?"

Maryanne seemed to need to straighten a yellow silk parasol with whalebone struts hanging on the wall. "Oh, she came in here pushing Freya to ask about that *'treasure.'* And while Freya was reading one of Rebecca Dell's diaries, Penny was walking around, looking at what we have here." Frowning, Maryanne looked back at Grace. "Some people...the way they stare as if some of our objects were theirs, you get a feeling you don't want to leave them alone near anything that could walk."

The curator's frank assessment surprised Grace, but she realized she had that very same feeling about Penny.

Maryanne was still talking. "Penny didn't have any interest in the harpoons or the baby quilts, she just focused on the gold and ivory. The broaches, stick pins, and coins. And Maryanne said rather dismissively, "That mythic lost ransom."

"The treasure? You don't think it existed?"

"Oh, it did! I've read about the ransom from several independent sources, and later generations did search for it."

"But?" Grace prompted.

"Well, what could it have been? There is a diary reference to the Jamisons giving shoe buckles, Willy's family gave six metal buttons, maybe pewter and Rebecca Dell gave up her monkey faced necklace, probably handpainted wooden beads. There might have been a few farthings, but no real coinage, these were poor fisherfolk. They bartered crabs for corn, piglets for firewood, and they wouldn't have had silver coins or gems."

"I thought Penny's ancestress, Long Liz, was well-off?"

"Oh, yes. Squire Seth Booth and Elizabeth Dell Booth were quite well-to-do by Colonial village standards, but the well-off citizens tended to support an orderly society and the King. The Booths would not have contributed to a bribe for a royal prison guard."

"Penny and Freya seem to think..."

"Oh, you know the way Freya always exaggerates. Just look at those lurid pamphlets of hers. I told her that light switch over there is kinda of wonky, and she held a seance and '*intuited*' a Chinese maiden whose tortured spirit is attached to that porcelain teapot we have on display over there. The ghosts of our museum are chapter three of her booklet on the *Hauntings of Oyster River Harbor*. We sell her books here in the gift shop, and Freya's yearly seances are a good, reliable fundraiser." Maryanne frowned. "Her ghost tales do bring the tourists in, but the Board would not allow her to bring her midnight Haunt tours into the museum."

Grace wanted the curator back on track. "Do you think the ransom treasure is still lost? Or that the soldiers got it when they killed Elijah Dell?"

Maryanne looked at her in surprise. "Captain Dell? The British didn't kill him."

"No?"

"Oh no. Come with me." Grace followed her out of the main building, under a covered walkway, and into another small building that housed the gift shop, kitchen, children's birthday parties tables, storage, and small curator offices. Maryanne lead Grace back to her tight office with its filled bookshelves, two chairs, a book-cluttered desk, also holding an old style CPU and computer screen.

"We're working on a special show on the Revolutionary War, which will be referencing our permanent collection, and I've been studying all the diaries and histories of the local families." Opening a red-bound book to a yellow index card marked page Maryanne recited, "Mrs. Seawell wrote '*Captain Elijah was well liked by both the loyalist and rebel elements. As British troopers were searching all the houses looking for guns and powder, his daughter-in-law had run out on to the street crying for help for Elijah, who had fallen down and could not rise.*

"*Several soldiers responded, and they carried him upstairs to his bed. Uncle Joseph said his face was purplish, his breathing painful and laborious.*" Maryanne searched through papers on her desk for another book. "It's documented from several sources that he had been feeling poorly for some time. His daughter-in-law, Rebecca, kept a diary until her child was born. Then with her husband and her father-in-law gone, it must have been an extravagance she couldn't keep up."

"Or do you think she died in childbirth?" wondered Grace.

"No, Rebecca lived and had a boy who became one of Freya's ancestors. Both Rebecca and her son appear later in the town tax records." Maryanne selected a long, thin black ledger. "Tax listings for the Town of Oyster River. Yes. A Rebecca Dell was alive in the early 1830's and paid taxes on the property on Main Street that her husband inherited from Elijah."

"Did her husband, Eli Dell, come back from the prison ship?"

She glanced at her piles of reference materials. "I don't really know, Dr. Farrington. Some of the prisoners did. Let me look into that for you." Maryanne located a crude, board covered book. "This was one of the dairies of Rebecca." After a few minutes of reading, Maryanne continued. "Yes, here's more on Elijah's death: '*The soldiers were very kind and respectful. They didn't even search the house. They stayed with the Captain, while I got Doctor Floyd, but Father was dead before dawn. The doctor said the cause of death was 'Pleurisy.'*'"

Maryanne stopped. "From the symptoms that she writes about, her father-in-law was probably in the late stages of cardiac failure. His son being imprisoned, gathering the ransom, and then the British coming would have only aggravated his existing condition. The British Major in charge was very upset about the incident. Elijah's brother-in-law was Squire Booth, and the king's men did not want to offend the population unnecessarily. He had his soldiers dig the grave for Elijah in the Dell family plot, that's the old burying ground on the hillside.

"Seth Booth wrote and demanded a settlement from General Howe for the family because of the loss of his brother-in-law, but I have no record as to whether he got it or not. I'll look into that and see if I can find if the son Eli Dell returned."

That sounded like days of wasted research, "I couldn't have you doing that," Grace protested.

Maryanne just smiled gently. "It will be a pleasure, like you I immensely enjoy my work. Now, was there anything else?"

"Yes, I have a donation from Abe Hoyt. I wonder if the Museum could issue a receipt letter for the object, showing a valuation of a thousand dollars?"

Maryanne's face grew stern. "That's quite a lot of money with the museum's name on a receipt that could be given to Federal Income Tax Auditors. I don't think the Board would allow that amount..."

Grace cut her off. "On the Internet, a similar item sold for $1,325. It's for a captain's medicine Chest, I have it in my van. Do you want to look at it?"

The curator's face lit up. "Oh! Abe talked about donating that..." she thought back, "It must have been over two years ago! I'd given up hope he would ever find it for me."

When Grace opened up the back of her Subaru Forester, Maryanne looked as she was twelve getting a palomino pony for Christmas. "I never saw it before!

Beautiful joined chest. Is that the original key still in the lock?" She opened the top lid, and her voice rose with amazement. "All the bottles are intact! The manual is complete–that alone is worth $ 400!" She raised several bottles in turn. "There are residues of the original medicines in these, we could test their purity–oh..." she held up a bottle in the sunlight to squint at the faded label. "Some of this is stuff is quite poisonous! It will have to be displayed under glass."

Grace looked down. "There's two lower drawers with smaller bottles and tins."

Reverently, Maryanne slid out the bottom drawer. "Oh, my Lord. Surgical tools! I'll have to get the Board of Directors' permission, but I am sure we can accept this. We will have a brass plate made up for the display to give Abraham Hoyt full credit for the donation!"

"And give Abe a letter of credit for a $ 1000 valuation?" persisted Grace.

"Oh, no." Maryanne looked up at her in horror. "No! Not a thousand. I know the one you saw on the Internet for $ 1,325. I've seen the picture of that one. That chest was nowhere in as good–as excellent condition--as this is," She held up a scalpel, "it's still stained! Think of an untrained captain operated on a man, on a rolling ship with no land in sight for weeks. This chest will be the centerpiece of our whaling case! I'm sure we can get a valuation for at least $ 2000, maybe more. Could we keep it in the museum until we get the letter?" Maryanne almost begged.

Grace looked back the museum. "Is there anyone else here to help us carry it?"

Small, frail-looking Maryanne reached down and grabbed for the chest. "We can carry it!"

Struggling, they lugged that heavy chest into her office, which she now locked up.

With the warm feeling of having done something

worthwhile, Grace headed home to her condo, but that happy feeling evaporated when she checked the phone messages. One was from David. "I'll be on the plane before you get this. If you do change your mind, you can reach me through my New York office." The New York office, was he selling his house? He hadn't mentioned it. It was all so final. Grace knew they would end someday, but she just didn't expect it to be so abrupt, and so soon. And although that's what Grace said she wanted, she really felt horribly sad.

Chapter 18

The next day, back in her lab, Grace pulled up her Ransom spreadsheet. She had to change 80 % guilt for the Red Coats'. Lowering *Motive* to zero and *Means* --without torture--to zero. The remaining "left area, 10%" she balanced out with neighbors didn't see anything, "- 20 %". Simplifying the negative to a "zero %." The more Grace learned about Rebecca, the less the loyal daughter-in-law seemed a viable candidate for ripping off her husband's ransom, Rebecca's motive was removed and zeroed out.

She also zeroed out Long Liz. If Elizabeth had stolen back the hidden ransom, why would she bother to tell a daughter--born after the event--about its loss? Did Long Liz send her slave Posey by herself to deliver the jewel casket? Could she have stolen it? Grace would have to ask Freya about that, she typed in a *'To Do.'* What about the other more likely choices? Christopher, with Grace's guess percentage of 65 %. Must research what he did after the Revolution. "*To Do*': Check Internet. Talk to Freya and Maryanne re casket and Coe.

Unknown party secretly finding the ransom still came in at 80 %. Without knowing descriptions of the specific items in the ransom to trace or having a confession, there really was no way to trace this. *'To do'*: ask Maryanne if in her readings she'd seen any note of a sketch or of a specific description of the pieces in the ransom, or perhaps later of sudden, unexplained wealth in a local family in the following decades–a real long shot.

But looking at the figures, Grace felt still felt the strongest candidate, was *'Treasure Hidden'* and still waiting to be found, which she upgraded to a 90 %. Elijah had only that one day to hide the ransom from the coming British soldiers, and even if he didn't know it, he was dying. How far could an ill man walk or ride? Well with him being a seaman, he probably would have traveled by boat. That might open up sites on the shoreline as possibilities, but a storm had prevented him and Christopher from going to Long Island, so a boat was probably out. And even if the ransom was hidden, where could Elijah have found a place around here that would have been undistributed for over two hundred years?

There were a number of pre-Revolutionary houses, barns, and spring houses that still existed in Oyster River Harbor. A lot had been preserved, but most of it had been remodeled, repaired, or added to. And supposedly most of the population of Oyster River knew of the lost ransom and spent time trying to find it.

Elijah must have hid it where it wouldn't be found unless he passed it on to someone else. Another caretaker? She went back to Christopher again. What were the logistics? He had an open boat beached that the soldiers could've searched, and he was staying with his cousin, building a chimney in what now was Freya Dell's house. That would have been searched. And wouldn't have Rebecca have suspected Christopher? She probably would have known if he followed Elijah home or if Christopher visited when the old man was dying. By spending the rest of her life looking for the ransom, Rebecca seemed to believe it was still in Oyster River.

Loyal Rebecca waiting for her husband to return, was that for the rest of her life? Such a sad, foolish waste of a woman's life. But what about Grace herself? She let David go. Pushed him away and now, perversely, Grace desperately wanted him back. But she wanted David comfortably living in a house nearby so she could visit when she wished, and that wasn't fair to David. Probably not even fair to herself, but was her life just to be all research and that's it? And what about the attractive Jack Stuart, who kept inserting himself more and more into her thoughts? She couldn't marry David while she was having fantasies of Jack undressing. Her mind shifted again. What about Kurt? A convenient boyfriend, but also a KKK biker who was halfway to being convicted of murder when he just walked into court?

Grace pulled up another spreadsheet, *The Murderer of Eve Dupree* and studied the rows once again. Knowing Kurt, she zeroed out his total column, and nearly deleted his row, then had second thoughts. However she emotionally felt about him, she had to be objective. Kurt could have killed Eve, then knowing she had been seen on his boat, he left, bought wine, and came back, pretending to find Eve's body with her as a witness, but Grace still couldn't see a motive. Kurt wasn't going to kill a woman for refusing him, and if she taunted his sexual prowess, that would have probably have turned him on more. Grace raised Kurt's '*Total*' to 24 % and didn't believe it one bit.

She skipped to the less likely candidates. Adam Greenfield: what if he had secretly discovered the Ponzi scheme? She was pretty sure he hadn't, but if he had, Adam would've been trying to get the money back out of *Our Sisters* not kill Eve. At that last meeting, he seemed to be considering investing more. Would he have killed Eve if he realized he'd lost his construction company's pensions and the ORR investments? Murdering in a sudden rage? Grace couldn't picture Adam doing that. '*To Do*': Ask Gail if she knew whether Adam's Construction Co. pension losses might have been covered by insurance? If so, that would lower Adam's percentage.

Huang Wong: He bragged about his martial arts prowess, and he yelled that Eve and Jack were financially favoring Grace, but that was a very weak motive. Grace had consistently seen his raging outbursts, would they always remain just empty posturing? Or if thwarted over the loss of possible grant money, could Huang lose total control enough to kill a woman?   Yes, the attack would be foolish and wouldn't gain him anything, but crimes of passion usually have that exact problem. She upped Huang to 30 % but didn't know how to test that short of provoking him to murder her.

Unknown Thief sounded good: would be convenient, but she down downgraded '*him/her*' to 0 % on the grounds that nothing was stolen and the police hadn't come up with any indication that a murderous thief was operating at ORR. '*To Do*': Speak with Mark Silverstein about unknown thief as a possible defense for Kurt?

She considered zeroing out Unknown Lover but stopped. Again she had no evidence this person existed. Eve was new to the area and wouldn't have had too much time to create a madly passionate attachment with a local. If it were a former lover who had followed her to Oyster River, that person probably would have been recognized by Jack or seen by someone in the area. Still, Grace didn't zero out Unknown Lover, the brutality of Eve's bludgeoning indicated some hatred on her killer's part. With no confirming evidence, Mad Lover Man existed Grace should just zero him out, but Grace had learned over the years to trust her instincts and leave an investigation active, however unpromising, so she left Unknown Lover at 2 %.

That left two wild-card players, Jack Stuart and Josh Jeffers. Did Jack find out about the Ponzi scheme and in his anger kill Eve? That seemed to run contrary to his evident shock and grief at her death. Grace had the distinct feeling that if Eve confessed her money manipulation to Jack, he would not only have kept her secret but would have worked to financially extricate the both of them. Grace left Jack Stuart at 30 %, but Grace wondered how much his masculine magnetism influenced her?

That only left Josh Jeffers: Prone to violence, grudge against Kurt and Oyster River Research. The police weren't going after him because he had an alibi, but was it really that tight? Despite what Mark said, somebody should be looking into it more.

Where was the hard copy phone book in her lab? Grace found one, but there was no listening for Joshua Jeffers and no yellow page listing for 'fisherman.' What did that twin brother work at? She didn't know. There was a residential phone listing on for a G. L.Jeffers. The brother? A relative? There was also a Paul Jeffer's Gas station on Shore Road. Should she call it?

Grace tried the Internet and got newspaper articles on Joshua Jeffers' battle with his neighbor; his fight with the Town; his struggle against the Department of Maintenance; his run-ins with the Coast Guard. Still no address. She dialed her best source of knowledge, and after eight rings, she finally got an answer.

"Abe's bookstore."

"Abe, this Grace Farrington."

His loud response jarred her ear. "**Dr. Farrington**, calling to see if I've got your *Molecular Biology Theories* in? Sorry, not yet. A day or so." Abe was trying to impress someone standing at his counter.

"Do you know the address of Josh Jeffers?"

"Aaup." His voice muffled, he must be speaking to a customer with the phone tucked under his chin. "You need a bag for that?" Something indistinguishable, and then Abe was back. "Know where Josh lives."

"I'd like to talk to him."

A silence, then he said, "Not a good idea, Grace. He's mighty touchy, even that brother of his can't always hold Josh back."

"Abe, the address, please."

"Can Kurt go with ya?"

"Kurt's in jail."

Another silence on the line. "Hadn't heard that." A

pause, then. "Even if they found the woman's body in his boat, didn't think the police had enough on him?"

"It's just a simple misunderstanding, he had a long planned business trip to *São Tomé*, but the court thought he was fleeing the jurisdiction, but he's getting bailed out," Abe said nothing, so she pushed it. "Abe, in the directory there's a Paul Jeffers' Gas Station listed?"

"Aaup. On the Coastal Road towards Old Greenwich. You've seen it, been there before I was born, and looks it."

"Is Paul any relation to Josh?"

"Paul was Josh's father, but he's been dead for years. Josh started seriously going off the rails when Paul died."

"Josh runs the gas station?"

"Nope. Father had more sense than that, left the station and the boat in brother Greg's name. I think Josh was in jail when Paul died, had beat some guy up. Greg repairs cars and boats real good. A bit of a temper, but nothing like his brother. Josh fishes–or used to--from their old boat, *The Ellen B.* Lately, Greg reopened the bait shop for Josh, that the twins used to run as kids selling worms, herring, and such. Josh digs them up or nets them. Course it's a short season."

"Can Greg support his brother?"

"Has to. Fisherman, who can't fish is out of it."

"Thanks, Abe." She started to hang up.

"Grace! You don't get a notion to go there, do ya?" Abe sounded really worried.

"Why is that problem?"

"Josh Jeffers is tipping more and more over the side. I mean, Kurt went down there, and Josh clipped him one in the jaw."

That she didn't know about. "Why did Kurt go there?"

"Feeling sorry that those fish catch limitations is puttin' boatmen out work, Kurt tried to offer Josh a job collecting seaweed samples for his research, more to help Josh out, I think."

"And he hit Kurt?"

"Aaup. Josh and Greg have had terrible tempers since they were kids."

"Thanks."

She hung up. Well, she has been warned off, but Kurt was in jail, and the police didn't seem to be doing anything. Grace turned to her assistant. "Inger, how is the monitoring coming on lobster blue mold project?"

Inger gave her the usual confident smile. "So far good, they are tolerating the tanks well. I've copied the data to your laptop, and I've started a rough draft of your report to *Affiliated*."

"Thank you. I'll be back later, and make sure Nick prepares karyotypes for the specimens I've listed." Grace picked up her fanny pack and started out. Being warm in the lab, she didn't feel any air conditioning, but as Grace walked outside to her car the late August heat hit her, and she felt her blouse sticking to her back. She wasn't dressed to go visiting but didn't matter, not for this call, one Kurt's lawyer did not want her to make.

The car seats were burning, her old car's air conditioning was dead, and it would have been a great day for a swim off the point. Not too much time left in the summer, but instead, she headed out on along the meandering coastal roads. Not a way she usually took, bypassing small towns she drove on an old road hugging the curved inlets. Not here the mixture of new million dollar houses, not yet anyway, she figured it must still be protected lands. Just long, lush strips of thick green marsh grass cut with salt water rivulets regally presided over by tall, elegantly-stepping white herons.

To her right, a small farmhouse house with an old tractor alongside a good sized field with corn reaching six foot or so. More marsh, then a lip of land with several beat up old buildings. Two shiny new gas pumps that didn't look like they belonged in front of a paint-peeling dump like this old wood framed, three-bay garage, with some parking room to the left side. On the right was a one-room *'Live Bait'* shack set by a pier, with a narrow plank gangway that extended eighty or so feet over the marshland out to the open Sound and deep water.

Even with the heat haze, she could see Long Island across the way. Was that where they'd held those poor Revolutionary soldiers? A man, stocky and taller than herself was working on a car in one of the bays. Oh, hell what did Josh look like? At the confrontation at ORR for Huang's reception, she just noted he was frighteningly taller and more muscular looking than Kurt. He had a bright red face–probably because he was cursing madly–as he was being bodily dragged out by three ORR Security guys. Really all she knew was the man terrified her, but she couldn't call up a face or a hair color.

Why could she never recall people's faces unless she'd known them for years? That was a behavioral genetic question she must look into some day. She could picture hundreds of DNA profiles in mind, but couldn't remember the color of her waitress's hair. Freya said it was shyness, and David said she just had an internal world too busy to register most of the people around her. Whatever, it was a definite pain when her blind spot inhibited her functioning like right now.

Grace parked in front of the *'Live Bait'* shack. Way down the dock, two boats were tied up, one a fancy, new Chris craft launch, and the other an old Steiner fishing boat at least sixty foot long. That was probably Josh's boat, which might mean he was here. At the garage, a reddish-haired, stocky man in blue overalls was now filling somebody's tank as he was looking at her. One of the Jeffers brothers? They were supposed to be twins. Identical or fraternal? Maybe

Grace could say she was doing another twin study, except the last time she had seen Josh he was damning all scientists to hell!

Locking her car, she walked into the bait shop with its freezer case and strong, fishy smell. An older man and twentyish guy were looking at bright, neon yellow and orange twisting plastic lures. Fish went for those? They looked fake to her. There was nobody behind the counter, but having normal looking people around made her a little more comfortable. Not knowing just what to do, she browsed among open water pots of bloodworms and leeches. Grace glanced out the dusty front window, as his customer drove off, the gas station guy hurried over to the bait shop. When he came in, his men customers looked up, but the square faced, red-bearded mechanic was looking nervously at Grace.

"How much for a flat of bait fish?" Asked the older man.

Without looking at him, overalls recited. "Flat of sardines $35. Flat of mackerel $30."

"We'll take the mackerel." The older man put two twenties on the counter while his son gathered up the box. Nervously, the mechanic glanced away from them towards the open door as he made change by reaching deep into his overall pocket.

Grace looked from the red rubber worm baits to huge, sailfish hooks, and to the vicious looking tuna gaffs.

"Good fishing, sir. Hear the bluefish are running off the point." The mechanic politely stated as he handed over the man's change. Nodding the man and his son left, walking out along the dock which meant Grace was going to be by herself now.

The mechanic looked at her. "May I help you, mam?"

"You're Greg Jeffers?"

"And you're Grace Farrington, aren't you? One of those scientists over at Oyster River? Saw your picture in the paper a few times." He sounded nervous.

God. Bet he remembers his waitress' tattoo too, at least he didn't sound like he hated her. In fact, he looked afraid of her. "You're Josh's brother?"

"Yeah."

"I wanted to ask you about...you know a woman was killed?"

"Josh didn't do it!" he said fast.

"You're his alibi," Grace acknowledged. "I just wanted to know how sure you were?"

"My brother was with me the whole day," Greg said defensively.

Okay, this was going good, she thought sarcastically. Grace might as well just leave now, but she couldn't. "You're sure of that?"

"Hear they arrested Kurt?" asked the nervous mechanic.

"He didn't do it," Grace said.

"Naw, Kurt's ain't gonna kill a woman by hitting her in the back of the head," Greg agreed.

"How did you know that? That Eve was hit in the back of the head. It wasn't in the newspapers?"

He reddened. "Heard things."

"From where?"

Greg shut his mouth, having said too much.

She wanted to get him to admit more, but still, Grace realized how isolated and vulnerable her position was, and that she should leave. "Your brother has a grudge against Kurt?"

"Scientists' putting catch limits killed his livelihood!"

She wanted him to understand. "The limits may be temporary to allow the stocks to build up again."

"Temporary?!" Greg had some of his brother's excitability "H-H-He's got to stop eating and living 'temporarily' for a year, maybe more? While everybody and his Canadian brother are fishing off our shores? And how do you scientists figure stocks down? You got barcodes on the tail fins of all those fishes?"

Getting closer and louder he was frightening her, but Grace would hold her ground. "You fisherman have said the stocks are down."

"They go up, and they go down–if you don't understand nature's rhythms, you shouldn't be tinkering with her!"

Darkness shadowed the shop as another figure entered, a duplicate to Greg. They appeared to be identical twins, except Josh looked a bit more unshaven, a little bit rougher, and wilder eyed as he said, "What's she doing here?"

Greg turned. "Buying bait, what else? But I ain't got any that she wants, so she's leaving now."

His brother turned on Grace. "You're one of those power grabbers! Shutting off the sea to honest men!" Josh was blocking the door, but Greg had moved to him, trying to pull at his brother's arm.

"She's leaving now," said Greg.

"No–she ain't!" Josh spoke with a dead voice. "We'll fillet her and just drop her off the dock to feed the crabs, that'll show MacKay and his friends!"

Grace found herself looking for a possible defense weapon. Which, looking at the height and muscles of these guys, would probably be a seriously stupid move. Why didn't she bring Kurt's gun?

Greg sounded like he was pleading. "Don't pay my brother no mind! He jes talks big." Greg stood tall against his brother, looking directly in Josh's eyes. "I said she's leaving!" There was a scuffle of arms.

Apparently, Greg was dominant, and reluctantly Josh stepped aside from the door, going behind the counter. Grace found herself making a humiliating retreat, scurrying past him, and basically running from the two red-haired, bridge trolls.

Outside she took a deep breath and headed for her car.

Damn it! She locked it! Grace was fumbling for her keys from her bag when one of them–was it Josh?--came up behind her. She turned in terror, but the man's voice was reasonable, so it must be Greg. His eyes were pleading. "My brother gets carried away, especially making a dramatic show, but he don't really mean any harm. Please, we don't need no trouble."

"Eve Dupree was killed..." Grace started, trying to sound reasonable to him.

"Look, if that woman was punched in the mouth, yeah, I'd say my brother probably did it. Especially if there were witnesses about, but hitting a woman he didn't know in private from behind that's not Josh!"

"If he wanted to get back at Dr. MacKay? By killing her on his boat to implicate Kurt?"

Greg guffawed. "You really think my brother plans anything that well?"

"Kurt didn't kill her," repeated Grace equally as sure.

"Naw, he's one of the white knights. Kurt wouldn't beat on a woman."

"They're putting him on trial," Grace said, knowing she sounded anguished.

That seemed to set Greg back. "Mam, I don't know who did it, but I know my brother didn't, Josh was with me."

Grace hated to say this, but, "It's only your word."

"No! No, it ain't! The police asked around, and I know they spoke with Nick at the Neptune. He saw us pulling out, and both of us talked to Ray down in Stamford Harbor, he had his boat tender out. Unless you think me and Josh snuck back, with a fifty-eight-foot boat and what? Used a cloaking device to come up invisible as we docked at your research place in full view of everyone? No, Mam, yeah, he's my brother, and I'll do anything I can to protect him, but other people say he was with me on our boat. Josh couldn't have killed that woman."

Not nearly as sure, Grace tried to hide the fact that her hands were shaking as she attempted to open her car door. Both Greg and Josh were outside watching her, as she turned the car around. Josh's boat and the two of them were seen out on the water, but what if one swam ashore? If Josh had a car parked at the beach? Drove back, killed Eve, and then returned to the boat? Even if a number of people had seen the brothers on their boat, they probably weren't staring at them for hours. They were identical looking twins, one goes into the cabin and comes out wearing his brother's shirt, and a watcher would think he saw the two Jeffers onboard.

Of course, Joshua would have been easily recognized if he showed his red-haired head at ORR. Unless he shaved, temporarily spray dyed his hair? She was getting ridiculous. Could Josh have made it? Possibly, but probably not. But one other thing was totally clear, the Jeffers brothers had enough outside witnesses to shore up their alibi in court, and that left Kurt MacKay hanging from the yardarm.

Chapter 19

It was the next day, as the two of them stood in Grace's lab, and Penny excitedly said, "Freya had a dream."

"Vision," Freya intoned.

"She saw the ransom deposited in an excavated shaft," finished Penny.

Grace looked at Freya. "Shaft?"

"It's awfully vague," Freya admitted lamely. "Must be sunspots, bad spirits or I'm coming down with a cold, but lately most of my perceptions seemed blocked."

Grace wondered to herself if Freya was blocked by being around Penny and her constant greedy focus on the treasure. "Shaft...could be a foundation excavation? Like the foundation of a chimney?" Christopher's cousin's chimney?

Freya closed her eyes in an attempt to concentrate. "Narrower... I was thinking a well, maybe. Dry well even?"

Thinking about that Grace said, "Or the shaft of an old outdoors toilet? That's an excavation. They would dig them, then when the hole filled up, they'd move the upper outhouse over a new hole."

"That's disgusting," Penny said.

"But, Grace is right," Freya agreed. "They find a lot of stuff when they excavate sites where old outhouses once stood, and the soldiers wouldn't have looked there. Anyhow, " Freya looked to Grace. "Today, we wanted to look through some of the local journals in the old library at the Roost, and we're trying to get permission to take the metal detector to some possible old well sites on ORR's peninsula?"

Grace shrugged. "Just the detector? I guess I can give you permission to look.   You have to ask Margery Wilshuen if you are going to be tramping around her flower gardens."

"You need to give us written permission," Penny insisted.

That didn't seem necessary to Grace. "To dig, yes, but now you're just walking with the metal detector, right?"

Freya flushed in embarrassment. "There was an incident. We were looking in the park behind the Library, down from the grass on that narrow rock and sand area where the stream joins the harbor?"

"Near the small bridge?" Grace asked.

"Yes, the detector sounded gold, so we got a shovel from the car and dug just a few inches."

"And?"

"Somebody saw us. A policeman arrived while we were digging."

Oh, God. "Your son showed up?"

"No." Freya looked humiliated. "And it wasn't Ben, but we had found somebody's wedding ring, and I got a lecture from the cop about unauthorized digging on Town property. And of course the big mouthed cop had to tell my son, so I got another lecture from Mac about the necessity of a policeman's mother being above suspicion."

Penny sounded outraged. "But Freya told the cop about finding the ring. She could have just pocketed it! When she told him, we had to turn it in!"

Freya looked at her. "Of course we turned it in. It was someone's wedding band, with the initials LM + LB. Maybe the police can find out who lost it."

"It was solid gold!" Penny looked from Freya to Grace for confirmation. "It would have helped Freya pay for the metal detector. Right? Finders keepers."

Grace thought about it. "For written permission at ORR you'll need a letter from the head office, and I think Gail might be able to do that. In the meantime, you guys want to check the old library, right? I can get security to open it for you, just make sure the door locks after you leave."

"Thanks," said Freya. "I've heard there's a lot of old town records collected up there."

She called security, and then as the two cousins walked off to the Roost, Grace knew should go back to her workload, but she decided to take a look at that DNA she was sampled recently. Before Grace suited up for the Cleanroom, she called the Oyster River Research Administration line. "Gail? This is Grace. Freya Dell and her cousin, Penny Barstall, are doing some research in the old library in the Roost. Freya has my permission,"

"I'll call security now to open it up."

Grace thought about it. "She may be coming back when I'm not here..."

"I'll see that it's opened for Freya if she comes again," promised the ever helpful Gail.

"And this has to be a little bit more formal. They would also like to be allowed to walk the peninsula with a metal detector. They're trying to find some Revolutionary War artifacts, maybe even dig a little. How can they get written permission?"

Gail thought about it and said, "I'll put in a request with an e-mail to Adam. He should allow it, but either way, I'll have an answer for you by tomorrow. If he okays it, I'll type permission up, and then I'm authorized to sign it."

She was authorized to sign it, but Gail's status was still 'temporary secretary,' and she still was an employee of the Temp agency, Grace was going to have to do something about that! As she continued to suit up for the Cleanroom, she couldn't get her mind off the waste of it all. Rebecca, spending the rest of her long life searching for the treasure, and her waiting year-after-year for the return of a husband everyone else told her was dead? Maryanne said some of the imprisoned soldiers had made it back years later but had Eli? Did Rebecca ever reach out for some happiness and maybe marry some other man? People make decisions and have to live with them, but sometimes in retrospect, the choices seem so wrong. Grace found herself wondering, would her own life be the same wasted chances?

Chapter 20

Grace was sweating under that sterile cap, this old building's air conditioning never worked too well even in the Cleanroom. With warming and cooling temperatures factors in DNA degrading, she had used her grant money to buy top of the line, no defrosting cooling equipment, but maybe the next grant she should seriously prioritize upgrading the air conditioning in here. She came out into the main lab pulling off latex gloves and reaching down to strip off the disposable booties. What she saw made her want to go back and hide in the Cleanroom.

His back to her, Huang was gesturing wildly as he yelled at Inger. "Where is Grace! She work here! What you do here?!"

Inger saw Grace, and her eyes seemed to suggest Grace should head back inside, but Huang had turned on her. "Grace! What you do?"

"I was..." She started to explain, then stopped. It was none of his business! "Dr. Huang, did you want something?"

"Trashy boats still tied up on dock!"

"Dr. MacKay has two slips as part of his contract with ORR."

Inger explained, "I think he means the *Vengeful Valkyrie*."

Mac had renamed that old boat when he was fourteen years old when Freya christened her purchase with her home-brewed mead. Now Mac was an ex-Navy seal, a town cop, and that old lobster diesel kept chugging on. "Oh, you mean the boat of my friend, Freya?"

"It no stay here!" Raising his hand, Huang emphasized his command.

Grace tamped down her distaste at the foolish display and tried to quietly explain, "It has been Oyster River

Research's general policy to allow any visitor to tie up temporarily. You can confirm that with Dr. MacKay, who is in charge of the dock."

Huang glared up at her. "It looks like garbage scow! People come from road, they see floating junkheap!"

"It's an old boat, but it's kept up." Grace was wondering if he could make trouble with Adam.

"What Freya do here?" Huang demanded. "Tell fortunes? Bad for scientific establishment!"

"She's doing some historical research in the Roost library."

"I no give permission for that!"

Grace hated confrontations and hated dealing with this mean, little man, who didn't seem to understand that '*Head of Research*' at ORR was pretty much an empty honorary title. "Freya doesn't need your permission, she has mine! I told her she could research."

"She's alone?"

"No, I believe she has a friend with her."

"You believe? You don't know?" Huang was yelling again now that he had an excuse. "We do government research here! This facility does lots of government research!"

"I know that. I do most of it!" Grace slipping from annoyed to angry.

"But street people walk about. Freya dress like beggar, police may arrest her–I call them!"

"Freya is the mother of the local policeman, Mac Dell, and she is a well known, local business owner. She and her associate have my permission to dock here, and research in the Captain's Roost!"

"This not permissible! They must have someone watching them! I call Adam!" Saying that he turned and stalked out before Grace could answer.

Inger watched him go. "Do you want me to go up

and stay with them until this gets straightened out?"

"This is a public campus with students and guests constantly coming and going. What's he going to do, fence the place in with razor wire?" Grace complained.

"I've been talking with Gail," Inger pointed out. "She says Adam is trying to appease Dr. Huang, at least until he settles in more."

"Great." Grace stripped off her paper gown. "Just what we need, another control freak. It's time I stopped for lunch, and I'll take care of Freya. If Adam calls, tell him to get me on my cell!" Grabbing her fanny pack from her desk drawer, Grace headed up to the Roost.

The old library was upstairs in the mansion, and some of its books came down from the Roost's builder, the whaling captain Benjamin Smith. The mansion stayed in his family until it and its contents were sold after his spinster granddaughter's death in the 1890's. In the fifties it was Stewart Brewster who kept the collection from being dumped, feeling that keeping the journals, ship's logs and diaries were sort of a tribute to the town and the people who had lived here.

Today the cleaners were working on the first floor, so Grace got in the back entrance, heading through the kitchen and reception area into what would have been the mansion's original main entrance hall, located inside the tall, square, central tower. The tower ultimately lead up to the iron-railed widow's walk atop the mansard roof were some claimed the ghost of Jersillda Smith still watched.

Grace never walked on that parquet floor without admiring the skill and artistry of the carpenters that had created that intricate inlay of exotic woods. A ten-foot diameter compass rose of ebony, maple, oak, and rosewood spiraled out from the center, and alongside the tower, walls were the edged borders with alternating rosewood blocks and ebony stars ambled around the edges of the room. Crafted by ships' carpenters in the 1800's, a narrow, curving staircase rose in the back of the two-story foyer, in a tight curving of the polished wooden banisters up that steeply turning spiral. The carpentry skills involved always fascinated her.

On the second floor, she headed through a curved arch of eighteen foot tall, yellowed bull elephant tusks and walked into a room flooded by sunlight. To her left was a carved limestone fireplace that she could almost walk in, to the right a wall of wide windows overlooking the sound, and except for the three doors, the rest of the room was covered with custom built dark wood bookcases.

She found Freya and Penny sitting in the center at a heavy rectangular mahogany table with piles of logbooks, diaries, and local histories before them. Freya looked upset. "Grace, I'm so sorry–that Dr. Huang came in and started yelling at us. He ordered us to get out, but I just stayed here. When he figured he couldn't lift me, he left, and I felt we could just keep researching until security showed up. I didn't get you in trouble did I? You wouldn't interrupt your work if it weren't a problem."

"No, it's not." Grace came over and sat down across from Freya. "I've told Dr. Huang, you have my permission to be here. I may have to speak to Adam about it, but Huang is out of line."

Freya still looked worried as she gathered up her things. "He also complained about me tying up to your dock."

"I'll speak with Adam. Don't worry about it."

"I don't want to get you in trouble." Freya kept repeating.

Grace ignored that. "Did you find anything?"

Carelessly, Penny tossed a leather-bound volume down in disgust. "Only two more listings of old wells..."

But Freya looked saddened. "Actually, we found quite a bit. There is no doubt that Elijah knew the British soldiers were coming, so he hid the ransom. Then he died."

Penny was always pushing. "He had time to tell his daughter-in-law. Freya, isn't there any family tradition passed down? Or something written in a book or the family bible that might give us a clue? Rebecca must have known where to find the ransom, but she was hiding it from the rest of the town's people?"

Freya looked down at the books before her, looking discouraged. "I don't think so. Elijah probably didn't tell Rebecca where he hid the treasure, because he didn't know he was dying."

Grace looked around the library as sunlight reflecting off the harbor danced on the bookcases on the opposite wall. "Did you go through everything?"

"No, far from it." Freya held up a worn, board cover book with lined pages. "This is the log of a local farmer, Nathaniel Thomas. Every day of his adult life, Nathaniel would write the date and the weather for the previous day. Sometimes he would enter an event with the frustrating briefest of notations. Opening the book she read, "*June 20, 1778, Clear sky. Warm wind from South. Rebecca's mother-in-law, Mae Dell Died.*' That was Captain Elijah's wife."

"But that tells us nothing!" Penny testily pointed out.

"Still it's fascinating," said Freya her eyes on the book with its view of a vanished world. "These manuscripts are giving us other viewpoints of the same story." Freya was wrapped up in the saga. "We know from other sources at the Whaling Museum, that Nathaniel loved Rebecca from childhood, wanting to marry her, and followed her throughout her life."

"Did she ever marry him?" asked Grace.

"No. Thinking her husband might still be a prisoner on some British ship, she raised her son, eking out a living as the town laundress and seamstress. For extra money, Rebecca cleaned out rubbish and carted it to be thrown into the sea, that was all hard labor. I don't think she would have done it if she had ever found the treasure and was secretly spending it. And if she had found the ransom, and was unable to use it to free the prisoners, I think Rebecca would have returned it all to its original owners."

"You think so?" exclaimed Penny in a disbelieving voice. "Why would she do anything so stupid?"

Freya frowned at her. "Because she was that kind of person Rebecca. Honest, generous, that's why Nathaniel said he loved her."

Grace asked, "Anything about Christopher Coe?"

Freya nodded. "A month or so after Elijah died, Rebecca's diary said the fisherman, Christopher, drowned in a storm off of Long Island. His cousin, Paul, inherited Christopher's land holdings over in Cold Spring Harbor: a second boat, a dock, and farm, that couldn't be accounted for from a mere fisherman's earnings."

"That proves he stole the ransom!" Penny cried in a fury.

Freya shook head. "Actually, Maryanne at the whaling museum says it was known that Christopher was smuggling whiskey to soldiers on both sides, and it is suspected that he was part of Sally Townsend's spy ring for General Washington."

"What about the imprisoned Continental soldiers?" Grace asked.

As a mother herself, Freya seemed to find this exceptionally painfully. "In 1783, with the war over, Willy Jamison managed to survive the prison ship. Released, he started limping home, and a fisherman took him the rest of the way. Even Jacob Hoyt came back years later. He had been impressed into the British navy, and he jumped ship in the Bermudas. Later he caught a winter whaling ship back from Key West, and his grandmother, Dame Alice, just lived to see him return."

Freya continued sadly. "The Jamisons never knew

what happened to Samuel Chapel. He was alive in the prison hold the last time Willy saw him, but he probably wound up as one of the 11,000 plus unnamed bodies buried in the marshes, that are memorialized at Fort Greene Park in Brooklyn."

"Elijah's son Eli Dell?" Grace asked.

Freya spoke with pain. "Probably dead before the ransom was even raised. The four of them were taken to the prison ship *HMS Jersey*. Within a short time, Jacob said Eli had broken out in what they called '*blood protuberances,*' probably smallpox blisters. One morning he was taken out of the hold, alive, feverish, and swelling. He didn't return, Willy and Jacob thought he died.

"But Rebecca never accepted that. She always waited for Eli to return for the rest of a very long, hard life." Freya stopped unable to continue, her eyes tearing at the sadness of it all.

Grace put a hand on her shoulder and spoke softly. "Freya, it is sad, but it was over two hundred years ago. All of them are dead and out of pain now."

"And?" Penny spoke dismissively, "What were they? Slavers? Whiskey smugglers? Spies? Thieves?"

Freya leaned back and looked at the shelves of books regretfully, saying, "There's still more I can study, but that boss of yours says we can't come again."

Grace felt herself flushing with anger. "Huang is titular 'Head of Research' for Oyster River, but he is in no way, my boss! You will be allowed to return! I will be speaking with Adam about this, you will come again whenever you want, and if anyone asks, you are researching for me, don't tell them anything else."

"Then let's get lunch, Lilith is minding the store, and I'm starving," Freya said, back in her usual optimistic state. "At *Neptune's Grotto*. My treat."

Penny looked up to Grace hopefully. "Maybe you

could drive us?"

"No." Freya rejected mostly firmly, "She's not wasting her gas. The *Vengeful Valkyri* is moored at the dock, and I'll bring back Grace later." Freya had tied up just below the tide ramp, because on the deeper end of the dock and Kurt's sailboat depressingly still had rings of yellow crime scene tape sealing it off, but at least his lobster diesel was free. Freya's boat was older than her car by about fifty years, but *Vengeful Valkyri* ran a lot smoother. Like Kurt's diesel, it chugged loudly with blue smoke pouring out, but it cut through the green water smartly. Here at the harbor end, the river from the Congregational church lake entered the marshes on its way to the sea. Contented to just ride, Grace watched as in the tall green grasses a gray heron stabbed a sharp beak into brackish water and came up with a silvery fish. Blackbirds with red striped wings swept low over the cattails, as Freya swung around and headed to the town harbor. Quietly Grace just enjoyed the physical and mental acceleration being out on the water always gave her. Penny didn't look so happy, she had her arms wrapped tightly around herself, and was trying to keep her feet from getting wet from the rainwater sloshing under the slatted decking.

The *Neptune Grotto's* dock was just before town proper, and with a spin of the wheel, Freya expertly eased her boat into the slip. Grace jumped off to tie up, and fortunately, with high tide, there was less of a climb up the ladder to the pebbled tar parking lot off the main road. Grace eyed the snack bar, with picnic tables outside. "Freya, wouldn't it be really nice to eat out here? I'd love their fried clams." *And it would be a lot cheaper.*

Penny tossed her head. "With the wind dust and the gasoline smells? I want to eat inside!"

"Yes," Freya said. "Forget the price we should celebrate our ancestors today." So she lead them inside to a room that had been decorated to resemble a grotto undersea.

Mock stalactites hung from the ceiling, and the tables were topped with a clear resin poured over sand and drift-wood designs, with starfish, shells, and pirate *'coins'* scattered about in the *'water.'* The place was pretty empty, but as the hostess guided them in, a familiar hand raised up. "Georgia, bring the ladies over here. I'm celebrating my freedom."

Freya looked as if she was about to object but then tightened her mouth, walked over, and sat down. Kurt was already eating his shrimp linguini as the hostess passed out menus to them.

Grace looked directly at Kurt. "Your lawyer wants to talk with you."

He nodded. "Got an appointment to be in his office at 2:00 p.m."

"You have a way to get there?" She pursued.

"Gina brought my bike to the courthouse."

At least he seemed to be taking this seriously, so thinking of the Nazi wench Grace said, "You didn't mention that item lost if you aren't honest with your lawyer, Mark says he'll dump you!"

"Aaup." He acknowledged and obviously wanting to change the subject Kurt looked at the other two women. "I know voluptuous, vivacious Freya, and this pretty lady is?" He leered.

"Penny Barstall, a long lost cousin of Freya's," Grace supplied.

The waitress had her pad out, looking at Freya, who ordered. "The chicken salad with apple and pecans. And a glass of cranberry juice."

The waitress turned to Grace. "I'll take the crab cake sandwich and iced tea."

Then it was Penny's turn. "I'd like a glass of Sangria–make that a pitcher and a two-pound lobster."

Kurt pointed out. "That's market rates here. Lobsters kinda high in Connecticut, but if you like lobster meat, I can bring all ya want over for Freya to boil up free."

Penny just gave him a little dismissive smile as she continued. "And for an appetizer, I don't know if I'll have she crab chowder or the shrimp cocktail. " She studied the menu again. "I'll have both."

Grace looked at Freya. "I split the check with you."

"No," Freya said firmly. "I have a credit card."

Kurt held up his empty glass for a refill. "Grace, you and I got to get together on our lobster project."

Not wanting *Affiliated's* top secret project discussed openly, she gave him a watch-what-you're-saying stare.

He continued more carefully. "Looks like our friends think our results are promising and will want to continue. With an extended contract, we gotta renegotiate our shares." Then to change the subject, he turned to Freya. "You brought Grace over by your boat?" As the waitress brought over their drinks, he wound up another fork full of linguini.

Freya looked embarrassed. "Yes, but that Dr. Huang says I can't tie up at ORR anymore."

Kurt looked up sharply from his plate. "He says what?"

Looking downcast Freya said, "Dr. Huang told me not to use his dock anymore because my boat looks like a '*garbage scow.*'"

Kurt's face shifted from puzzlement to cold anger. "My contract with Adam gives me two free boat slips and makes me Dock Master, in charge of Oyster River's Research boats and pier. Until that's legally changed, Freya, you have my permission to tie up whenever you choose." His tone finished the matter.

Freya responded with a surprised, "Thank you."

Even being nice, Kurt managed a shark's gleam in his glance. "You tall women always intrigue me so. Makes me hot to jes have ya around."

Oh, God, why did he always have to start? Grace wanted a change of the conversation. "Freya and Penny are hunting for a lost treasure. A ransom."

Freya explained to Kurt, "During the Revolutionary war, coins and jewelry were entrusted to Elijah Dell to ransom several patriot soldiers held captive on a prison ship in Wallabout Bay."

Penny pointed out. "Most of it came from Elijah's sister, Elizabeth Dell Booth."

Freya finished. "The ransom was lost. Later as loyalists, Elizabeth, her husband and their household were expelled to Canada after the Revolution."

"Household? Their slaves you mean," said Penny bitterly.

Kurt thought about it. "Aaup, they did have slaves in the early New England colonies. Not too many though, and they'd have to have been converted from slaves to servants when Canada outlawed slavery in 1830."

Penny glared at him. "Most of the founding fathers were slaveholders."

Kurt fired back. "Paul Revere? Roger Sherman? Samuel Huntington, arguably the first President of the United States, never heard of them owning slaves."

Penny seemed furious. "Benjamin Franklin did!"

"Two. To work in his shop when he was young, but later he became a leader in the Abolitionist movement."

Penny's face darkened with outrage. "White Europeans went to Africa and dragged Black people from their families! That wasn't right!"

With a bit of smile, Kurt looked long. "Ms. Penny, are you a believer in Black Liberation Theology?"

Penny sat still, just staring back at him.

"What's that?" Freya asked.

Kurt gave a small smile. "A belief system grounded in Marxist Socialism. A lot of progressive-oriented whites and the more radical black groups hold that Whitey owes Black's compensation for the slavery of their ancestors, so because of that, Black people are entitled to steal from Whitey whenever they can, to get back what is theirs by birth. With that logic, some Black liberationists refused to pay their income taxes. Didn't go over well with the IRS."

Penny glared at him. "Our founding fathers had men, women, and children kidnapped."

Kurt moved his head to the side. "With the hostile coastal tribes, Europeans could never have penetrated the African continent. It was the coastal tribes that enslaved their fellow Africans, that dragged their brothers and sisters to the Arab traders, and then to the slavers' ships."

"Those dead white guys owe every black person in America!" Penny spat out.

"Mam, the majority of the Black people in this country today are not descended from slaves. They emigrated to better themselves, just like my folks did, but regarding compensation, I agree. Those White, male plantation owners that raped Black women produced mixed babies, so their descendants do have some money coming! But not from Uncle Sam. Since they are both part White plantation owner and part raped, Black woman, they should write a check and pay themselves."

"This is getting ludicrous," Grace said, giving Kurt a '*shut up*' look.

As ever Freya seemed to be trying to keep the peace. "Well, there should be fairness...an equal playing field today."

Before Kurt could start, Grace gave him a murderous look. "You have that meeting with at 2:00."

He nodded and signaled the waitress, "Georgia, I need my bill. I have got to go see my lawyer." Kurt looked at them. "Normally as a gentleman, I would pick up your checks, but unfortunately I'm facing some heavy-duty legal fees."   Having created his predictable chaos, Kurt got up. "Whal, ladies, since nobody wants to be serviced, I've got to be on my way." At Freya's glare, he left with a smirk on his face.

Freya didn't wait until he was entirely out of earshot before she turned to Grace and loudly commented, "Why do you have anything to do with that shithead?"

At times Grace wondered herself, but she wanted to turn the conversation. "If you find this ransom, what are you going to do with it? I bet they would love it at the Whaling Museum."

Penny looked up. "Donate it? No–No--it's mine! It belonged to my ancestress, Long Liz!"

Her vehement outburst caused both Freya and Grace to stare at her. Licking her lips, Penny corrected herself. "It's mine and Freya's since she is a descendant of Elijah Dell."

Grace said carefully, "Others in the harbor had donated, and some descendants of the original families are probably still living in Oyster River."

Penny seemed to think about this, "But when they donated to Elijah for the ransom, they gave their property away. And finders keepers!"

Freya looked a little concerned. "If we find it on somebody's property, we would have to share..."

 "Not necessarily." Penny was picked the last meat out of her lobster claw, as with an ingratiating smile, she turned to Freya. "What are you going to do with your half? I mean just one revolutionary period gold coin could bring two thousand dollars or more? Especially if it was a rare coin in fine condition." Penny encouraged Freya. "You were talking about those Caribbean pirate tours?"

Freya's face lit up with joyful thoughts. "Those are great! I tried to get a free trip as one of the expert tour guides, but the guy running it said only if he adds a Viking segment to the tour. I send for each year's brochure." She continued dreamily, "Your yacht sails from island to island, with a history expert dressed as a pirate for your guide. They have barefoot, seafood bakes on private islands, re-enactments of a pirate crew burying its treasure by moonlight. It's eight days of pure bliss. They do pub crawls, and they go to one Blackbeard actually patronized. In Jamaica, you can sit a scarred-wood table where he drank ale." Freya turned to Grace. "You'll come too, Grace, as my guest, because you haven't had a real vacation in years."

"What do you mean?" Grace protested. "Last year, I traveled to Hong Kong, Berlin, Hawaii, and Rio de Janeiro."

"All as a paid speaker at some DNA conference." Freya made a face. "The pirate trip will be no work, no phones, no e-mail, no test tubes, and positively none of your genetic swabbings! Just us on a private cruise where we'll wear flower print sarongs and drink cold rum, pineapple concoctions."

The thought of six foot Valkyrie maiden Freya and skinny her in a sarong, with deep pink passion flowers in their hair made Grace laugh. "We haven't found the treasure yet. Let's just see if we can pay the lunch bill." She started reaching into her fanny pack.

"My treat," said Freya grandly, pulling out a credit card as she signaling the waitress.

Grace insisted on paying Freya cash for her portion of the bill, and she noted that Penny just sat there, toying with the last of her key lime pie. Freya motored them back across the harbor, taking her time tying up, looking like she wanted a confrontation with Huang.

Not what Grace wanted, but there was something else. "Penny hasn't seen my lab yet, has she?"

Freya smiled widely. "Oh, you have to see that! When Grace gets her Nobel, I'm going to be leading the *Grace Farrington Popcorn Gene* tours around here." Penny looked mildly interested as she followed them up the hill and across the road.

Inside Grace's lab, Penny looked about. "I thought you'd have hi-tech equipment?"

Penny was standing next to a seven hundred and fifty thousand dollar microscope, but Grace ignored that. "There's some real hi-tech stuff in the Cleanroom. Take a look at these microscopic pictures here." While Grace was showing the photographs, she tried to make her voice sound very disinterested. "Penny, your hazel eye color is so lovely. Is that natural? Not a colored contact lens?"

"Yeah, why are you interested?" Penny always seemed suspicious.

"I'm interested in everything related to genes," Grace said speaking casually, reaching for one of her tubes. "You know, I'd like to do a fast swab on the inside of your mouth."

Defensively, Penny backed a step away. "Why?"

Freya laughed. "Grace's always testing everybody's DNA for something."

"No, I don't want to." Dropping her pout, Penny laughed nervously, "You just want to compare me to Freya?"

Grace shook her head, saying as casually as she could sound. "Oh, no, I'm not taking Freya's sample, her eyes are just plain blue. I'm just studying the genetic composition of hazel irises. Your eyes have a greenish cast, with amber, gold, and blue, and I've always been interested in the genes switches that turn eye color on or off. You know, they now sell a pharmaceutical that you can apply to your eyelashes that actually causes them to grow thicker."

Freya looked up. "Nice."

"But..." Grace continued. "One of its side effects that they warn about, could-- in rare cases--darken of the iris color to brown permanently."

"A permanent change?" a concerned Freya asked. "Eye color is genetic, isn't it? A permanent change, that's strange. What's going on to cause that?"

"That's what I would like to know." Grace reached out with small, q-tip sized swab on a stick.

Penny drew back slightly, but Freya was there, pushing her towards Grace. "It doesn't hurt at all. Just a swab inside your cheek, Grace needs it for her research." Penny just stood there, mouth closed.

Frowning, Freya asked. "Why wouldn't you give it to her?"

Penny couldn't seem to come up with an answer to that, and so, after a long moment, she reluctantly opened her mouth a little. Grace swabbed and slipped the stick it to a test tube, which she labeled *'Penny Barstall, Oyster River'* and the date.

Penny still seemed to be uneasy. "How long will that take?"

Again, Grace tried to sound disinterested. "A week or two, after I get time to work on it, but it might be several months in the freezer until I get around to the iris project."

"Don't the police do it overnight? I mean a DNA profile?" Penny asked.

"Police DNA profiles are rather limited, the FBI has standardized 13 specific points or loci on a person's DNA, that have been designated to produce a unique *'DNA fingerprint.'* Even that limited processing takes a minimum of five days."

"That long?" Freya asked.

"We're working to shorten it, but now it's five or four days, counting from when the evidence is bagged, and delivered, and assuming the police laboratory doesn't have a fourteen-month backlog. The shortest period of processing is five days, maybe in an emergency situation--say a kidnapping case--they could pressure it to four."

"That's long," said a concerned-sounding Penny.

"If it's degraded material, like say a body underwater

or bones out in the elements for months, extraction and culturing can take way, way longer. The 3,000-year-old King Tut extractions took months and months of work to get even a partial profile. That police profile is specifically designed to not contain any identifying markers for disease tendency or physical characteristics like eye color and height. If you are going for a more detailed analysis, say possible ancestry routes, it takes longer."

"When will you have my results?" Penny asked.

Grace hoped her words sounded careless enough. "I probably won't be able to get to process your DNA until next month at the very earliest. Sometime in September maybe, unfortunately, I've got a lot of work that takes precedence to my just-curiosity-stuff."

That answer seemed to relieve her a little, but when they left the lab, from Penny's backward glance, Grace had a feeling that Freya's cousin wanted to snatch her swab back. When they were gone, Grace wanted to suit up for the Cleanroom and start processing, but first, she needed to work on her e-mails. Several genetic questions to respond to, more in-house questions from *Affiliated* on the Lobster study, even a message from Jack Stuart. Just looking at his name on the e-mail gave her a little pickup and made her want to check her lipstick.

Before Jack had written that the funeral service for Eve was postponed, due to the authorities being difficult about releasing her body, but now Jack said his lawyers had forced the coroner to finish all his tests. Jack was holding her service at the Fergerson Funeral Home at 6:00 p.m. tomorrow. There was a map attached, but Grace knew where the home was in Old Greenwich. God, she hated funerals. But she hit the reply button: Yes, she would be there. Maybe she could talk Freya into going with her?

Grace needed to run her test work on several profiles for the *Science* journal paper she was writing, but as she suited up for the Cleanroom, she decided to give into her curiosity and begin the process of extracting Penny Barstall's DNA, or now as it would be known: OR50357.

There was another purely personal curiosity that she wanted to satisfy. Eve Dupree had said she was unable to have children because of a genetic problem, but Grace had never found out what that was exactly. Either it was a misdiagnosis, or a fatal gene hereditary problem, or something that recently mutated. DNA that left an individual sterile would be a problem that Grace should look in to. Eve had readily agreed to give her a sample, but she had never gotten around to doing it, always rushing off before Grace could pull out a swab kit. Grace needed a sample of Eve Dupree's DNA, but she couldn't face disturbing Jack at this time to get his permission. So the funeral tomorrow would be her last chance to acquire some of Eve's DNA.

Chapter 21

The day of Eve's funeral was sunny, as Grace picked up Freya, glad to have a friend with her. The Ferguson funeral home was a Greek Revival building, two stories high with four tall, white columns up front. The attendant didn't have them park in any special order, so apparently, there wasn't a graveside reading, which Grace was silently thankful for.

As she signed in the guest book, Grace was surprised to see how many people were there. The large double room was filled, with a lot of them local people, attending for a woman most of them barely knew. Apparently being a victim of murder gives you fans. There was a line before the pink metal casket, where each person stopped and talked to Jack Stuart. Grace held up in the back, wanting to stop a moment and reevaluate her problem.

"You okay?" Freya whispered down to her.

"Yes." She looked ahead. "It's a closed casket."

"So you never like open caskets."

"I know." But she liked this one even less. Grace had slipped a small pair of nail scissors into her jacket's pocket, and she planned to go up to the casket, bend over as if praying and snip or scrape her sample. But you can't even snip a small lock of hair with that lid shut. The line moved forward, and they just had to follow. Grace saw the Adam Greenfields already sitting in the front and the Wilshuens. There were a number of other corporate-type people in business suits, employees of *Alcom*? Investors in *Our Sisters*? Curiosity seekers?

Grace found herself sighing as she got closer. God, she hated funerals, but then Jack looked over and smiled to see her. Again she noted the paleness of his skin, contrasted with those warm brown eyes, dark hair, and bright red nose. She reached out her hand to shake, but he shook his head, speaking with a nasal voice, "No handshaking. I'm

contagious, on top of everything else, I've got a bad cold. "
Yes, she could see his swollen nose and redden eyes. The
funeral director brought up a box of Kleenex, and he placed
a clean waste paper basket right next to Jack, who remained
standing by the casket when the others sat as the minister
entered.

Passing the closed casket, Grace and Freya started to
walk to the back of the room, but Jack saw that and said,
"Please, Grace, sit in the front row. Both of you—you at
least knew Eve." So they got a front-row view and couldn't
sneak out the back. Grace didn't recognize the minister. He
seemed to be from some local protestant church, and, as he
droned on, it became evident that like a lot of other men of
God, weddings, and funerals to him were now heavy duty
venues for proselytizing his particular brand of religion.
Grace seemed to remember that the funerals of her childhood
were focused on the deceased and their grieving loved ones,
that really seemed better, especially if you were paying for the
minister's time.

Finally, it was over. Freya started up the aisle to the
exit, but Grace pulled at her elbow. "I've got to go to the
ladies room."

"Fine, I'll meet you out by your car," Freya answered
carelessly.

"No!" Grace said quietly. "You come too."

Freya gave her a funny look, but they went into the
ladies room, where Grace got online for a stall, and then redid
her lipstick. Twice. When the last older woman in the
bathroom left, Freya asked in a whisper, "Why are we in
here?"

"We're waiting for the others to leave."

"Why?"

"I just want to get something."

"What?"

"A sample."

"What kind of sample?"

"Some skin cells or hair follicles."

Freya looked horrified. "We're—no, **you're** going to open up Eve's casket and cut the corpse's hair off?"

"Just a few strands."

"Grace, that's desecration of a body!" said Freya sounding very much like her son the cop.

"I need you to watch the door."

"Oh, Goddess," Freya moaned. "And I didn't think funerals could get any worse!"

After a few more minutes, Grace peeked out. She could hear someone down the hall, probably the funeral director. In a dignified manner, they quietly walked past the white lettered sign saying '*Evangeline Dupree*' and into the pink and yellow flower display banked viewing room.

"Should I pull the doors shut?" Hissed Freya.

"No, they might see it."

Freya stood hiding at the doorway, as Grace hurried to the casket. It was a polished pinkish pewter colored metal. She tried to lift up the lid, but it was too heavy. "Freya. Help me," Grace whispered.

Always a loyal accomplice, Freya hurried over and they both tried to lift the lid.

Sounds of someone walking down the hallway. They both froze, but the footsteps went past. Freya whispered, "It's screwed down."

Grace looked helplessly at Freya, and giving in Freya pulled up her massive handbag. "Boy scout knife has screwdrivers."

It was only screwed on two sides, with Freya at the feet and Grace at the head, they lifted the white satin lined lid and looked inside.

Eve's casket was empty.

They were standing there, staring in to it, when Grace heard a firm voice behind them. "May I help you?" Grace turned to see the funeral director facing them both, looking very unhappy. She lowered the lid carefully.

"Yes," Grace started. "Yes, you might be able to. Eve Dupree's remains are supposed to be in here?"

The director just stared at her.

Grace continued, "Actually. You see, I wanted a lock of her hair..." She ran out of words.

Freya came to the rescue saying soothingly, "For the Ceremony of the Winds. It's an American Indian tradition. We are Ministers of the Native American Church of the...Dancing Eagle Feather."

"Dancing Feather," Grace repeated, wanting to just run now.

Freya continued, "We must release Eve's spirit to the winds..."

"Of course," said the man, trained to please. "But unfortunately that casket was just placed there as background for the service."

"Could we see her body?" asked Freya.

"You want me to go get it?" He asked incredulously.

"That would be so helpful," Freya said brightly.

He turned and left the room, and when he did, Grace looked down at the wastebasket on the floor, with its mound of used tissues. There was another question bothering her. Jack's interesting skin versus hair color, she kept wondered what was the ethnic background mix he had? People sometimes got embarrassed when she asked for a sample, and with Jack in mourning, she couldn't do it now. Grace moved over to wastebasket. Digging into her purse, she pulled out a small, sterile collection bag, and she then took several clean tissues from the Kleenex box to shield her hand as she reached down and grabbed up a handful of dirty snot rags.

Freya stood there, straightened to her whole six one height and said quietly, "I do not know you."

Grace had just finished stuffing that disgusting mass

into her handbag when the funeral director returned, carrying a twelve-inch high bronze urn, sculptured with gracefully entwining vines.

"Jack had her cremated," Grace said to Freya. The chances of even a bone fragment with DNA surviving that kind of heat was nil.

"Yes, ma'am," The director replied. "I believe Mr. Stuart plans to do a private release, over the ocean she loved."

"Lovely idea." She turned to Freya. "I'll speak to Jack, and we can do the Dancing Eagle Feather ceremony then." Grace smiled back at the director and started walking out. "Thank you so much." Outside in the parking lot, Grace said in a sotto voice to her partner in crime. "Church of the Dancing Eagle Feather?"

"Didn't hear you coming up with something better!"

On the computer screen in her lab, Grace reviewed her finished write up of her share of *Affiliated*'s preliminary study on the blue lobster fungus and its application as a long-lasting skin regenerator. Actually, she thought it looked very promising. What *Affiliated Technologies* thought of it, they'd find out. She clicked to send the e-mail on its way. Grace turned around from the computer platform and found a figure was standing there. It was David Gardiner, dressed in a pale blue shirt, dark blue suit, and red striped tie. From suit to a swimsuit that man always looked so distinguished. "I thought you had moved to Greece?" She started.

"I have. It's not Mars, Grace, it's just a plane trip away." He looked about the old white room of her lab. " I've been standing here watching you for awhile because I didn't want to disturb your work, but you know, with you always so deeply engaged, we really should install a security door, so you'll have to buzz something before someone can just walk in behind your back." He bent down and kissed her forehead.

She didn't want to face this. "David, I haven't gotten back to you..."

"Which, as a businessman, I took *'no word'* as a *'no'* to us living together in Greece. Dearest Grace, you are very hard on a man's ego." He pulled up a rolling chair to sit beside her.

"I'm sorry..." She started. "It's not you, I really like you.*" Maybe even love you.* "But I like my life here."

He raised his hand. "You're quite right. I asked you to give up your whole world to come live with me, and then I hedged my position by suggesting we remain, lovers, instead of an honorable offer of marriage. That is really unfair to a woman, so I intend to sweeten my offer." He reached into his pocket and took out a small, brown velvet ring box. This he opened, showing a large diamond in an antique setting. "It was mother's, but we can have it reset, or you can select something else." Those pale blue eyes stared into hers. "Grace January Farrington, will you do me the honor of becoming my wife?"

Oh, my God. "I can't think..."

He gently put up two fingers up to cover her lips. "You can't envision it now, and I will not try to force you. All I'm asking is that you think about what our life could be together. I have work that engages me, but it's not totally fulfilling." He looked at her quietly. "Since Sylvia's been gone, I've never found a woman that I could be so comfortable with until you. Someone who knew so much, felt so much, someone I wanted to share my day with." David stood up. "I will be regularly meeting in New York for months, and I'll be calling you...maybe we could do dinner and show?"

"David..." Helplessly she started.

"All I'm asking is that you give it a little thought, Grace." He closed the ring box and placed it down beside her.

"No!" She said firmly. Grace picked up the ring box and handed it back to him. "I'm not turning down your ring, but it's your mother's---that's just too important to you, and too valuable for me to have it lying around here. You hold it...for now...and I promise to give serious thought to your proposal."

"I was here earlier, hoping we could go out to lunch, but you were out. Unfortunately, I've got a flight to catch, but I'll be back next month. And even if you are still just thinking my offer over, we can have some enjoyable evenings together? I think I'm getting to like Hibachi. " Those blue eyes smiled, and then he kissed the top of her forehead again, he turned and started to walk away.

She so wanted him not to leave, but there was something she had to know. "David, I've got to ask you..." Grace stopped, not wanting to do it.

"What's the matter?"

He looked back, as she stood up and walked to him. "The day Eve died, you didn't attend the Board meeting, but someone saw you down on the dock near Kurt's sail boat?"

David looked shocked. "Who saw me?"

"It doesn't matter. Were you there?"

He had reddened, obviously angered. "Do you think I went on to his boat and killed Eve Dupree?"

"No." Grace could say that with total certainty. "But if you were there, you might have seen something you didn't realize."

He wouldn't meet her eyes, staring off into the distance, his face tightly drawn.

"Please tell me," she coaxed.

"I was there for a meeting with Adam, which he couldn't make. I was at the top of the dock and saw I Kurt's smoke pot chugging across the harbor towards the village, yet I saw lights on in that broken-down sailboat of his."

"Do you think Eve was still alive?"

"I don't know." He shook his head. "There was no one else about. I walked down to the floats and heard music–romantic music—but I didn't see anyone. Feeling like an idiot, I left."

"Why did you go at all?"

"I was curious..." Embarrassed, he looked down at his shoes. "Jealous, perhaps."

"Of Eve and Kurt?"

"No! I didn't know it was Eve, I thought you might be with him."

"You didn't tell the police?"

"No. I won't lie if they ask me, but my lawyer suggested that I don't have to bring it up."

"Kurt may be on trial for murder."

"But there is nothing I could tell the police that would help Kurt, other than to turn them on to me as a possible suspect."

He was silent. She said nothing in the awkward moment, so David started again, "Now, Grace, I won't contact you for a month. You're an intelligent woman, think about it, and compare what I have to offer you to MacKay's broken down boat..."

That was unfair. "David, that isn't the choice..."

"Isn't it?"   He seemed to be calculating odds. "Whatever." He smiled confidently again looking directly into her eyes. "My family didn't get to where it is today by giving up easily," saying that, he moved in and gave her a solid kiss, which she found herself returning, then he left.

She watched him leave, knowing that in David's mind, she preferred Kurt to him, but did she? The only thing she knew now was that David was going away, and she'd miss him terribly, but she just stood there, while he and that his pocketed engagement ring walked away.

That night, she went out for dinner alone, eating fried oysters from Neptune Grotto's outdoor grill. It was the end of

August, getting cool at nights, and the open grill would be closing for winter soon. Now as the sky darkened, she sat at the picnic table, shivering a bit, and feeling terribly alone.

Afterward, she did the week's food shopping, and it was dark when she returned to ORR. Grace was driving towards her condo, but strangely the lights were on in her lab. She pulled her car into one of the parking slots in front. It wasn't a day for the cleaning crew, so who in hell was in there?

In the lobby, her double doors had been wedged open with chairs, and she could hear male cursing.

"**Your other left!**" Bobby's voice hollered out.

Inside, a sweat and dirt streaked Bobby and Nick were raising the top section of Dr. Floyd's cabinet on to the bottom half, and setting it where Grace had indicated, along the front west wall. All the cabinet drawers were out, and in the middle of the room, there were half a dozen brown packing boxes with publishing company logos. Looking around she could see the four long, bottom drawers stacked up on the floor. The envelops and small top drawers must be in the book boxes from Abe's. Nick had a big, fresh purpling bruise on his cheek, and Bobby's hand was wrapped around with a cloth, his makeshift bandage showing blood.

Grace was delighted. "You got it!"

A not too happy Bobby muttered, "Your cabinet nearly got us! Nick fell down the damned barn stairs. My hand got cut up by a rusty iron rendering pot, I'll need a tetanus shot. Talk of the curse of Oyster River, that barn of Abe's is a death trap!"

She headed for the boxes in the center. "Thank you guys, so much! Are the envelops in here?"

"Yhep, and the little drawers," Nick said, heading for the door.

"No, wait!" Grace said, then bit her lip. "I know it's late." She looked at Bobby. "And Sara's expecting your home for dinner."

"I missed dinner two hours ago," he sarcastically commented. "But?"

She was taking a precious envelope from the first box. Reminding herself, she couldn't open them until she got them in the Cleanroom. "I need a place to sort everything out before it goes back into the cabinet. Can you guys get two of those long, plastic folding tables from the Roost? Set them up here?"

"There's no room," said Nick.

She surveyed the large room. "We'll have to move these desks and tables with the equipment on them over to the side walls and get everything out of the center of the room. If I had two of those long, folding tables, we could set them upright in the center."

"It's past nine,"   complained Nick. "The Captain Roost's locked up, and maintenance has gone home."

Grace said, "But there's still a guy doing a security patrol, he can open it. I'll call him."

Nick was shaking his head. "Maybe tomorrow."

But as a married man, Bobby knew the drill. "The lady is hot on a project. Needs it now! Then he added sternly, "Grace, don't you try to move any of those wood tables or that heavy equipment while we're gone! Nick and I will do that when we get back."

She did some move some chairs, screens, and CPUs, then started fitting the small drawers back into the top section of the Floyds' cabinet, finding they were good, tight fits. Before she was done, Bobby and Nick had carried back two tables. As they moved furniture and then set up the tables in the lab area, Grace said. "Nick, tomorrow tell Inger we are going to start a spreadsheet and inventory numbers for all of these envelops. And have her print me a new number sheet for any DNA specimens, these will all be the DF00000 series for 'Doctor Floyd.'"

Then they were gone, leaving Grace to sort little paper envelopes into century and decades' order. Excited she found a *Rebecca Dell*, dated 1802, and one just labeled *Elijah*? The date, October 5, 1762, looked right. To do a maternal line with Penny, she needed Elizabeth Dell Booth, but so far she couldn't find a period dated envelope for Long Liz.

What else could she do? If that Elijah was Liz's brother, he should have some markers in common with Liz, even mitochondrial DNA, which Freya wouldn't have because it's passed through the maternal line. To confirm, what she really needed was a maternal ancestress of Penny. What were Elijah Dell and Elizabeth Dell Booth's mother's name?

Grace dialed a number, and a just awakening voice drowsily answered. "Grace?"

"Hope this isn't too late?" she said feeling guilty for not thinking of the time.

"It's...after midnight," slurred a sleepy Freya.

Grace ignored that. "What were the names of the parents of Elijah Dell and Elizabeth Dell Booth?"

Nothing on the line as Freya had to think about that one. "I think he was Ebenezer."

"Ebenezer?"

"It's Biblical. Actually, a very common name, before Dickens wrote Scrooge into his Christmas Carol."

"And Ebenezer's wife, Elijah's mother?"

"Oh, lord, I don't remember. I did research that through the First Congregational Church records, and I've got some of those notes...I think they're in a box under the eaves. Could this wait until I get home from work tomorrow?" Freya kind of pleaded.

When Grace didn't answer, Freya sighed. "No, if it has something to do with your precious research, it can never, ever wait. I'll have to call you back if I find something."

And she did. About an hour later, the phone rang with Freya saying, "Figured you'd still be in the lab."

"You got a name?" asked Grace excitedly.

Slurring a bit from lack of sleep Freya said, "Ebenezer's wife was Freelove Dell. She was a Scofield before her marriage."

"Freelove?"

"Another common Colonial period name, that sounds funny today. I don't think it meant the same as what we think of free love currently. Now, can we both go to bed, please?"

"Sure." And Grace was tired. She did so want to go back to her comfortable bed in the condo, but there was so much to do here! All those possible hidden gene treasures in these little yellow envelopes were tempting her. She set out a collection tray and turned up the lab lights to the max, trying to puzzle out the faded handwriting of generations of Dr. Floyds.

Grace started on the stacks of envelopes that seemed to come from the 1750-1800s period. Picking up more envelopes, she began searching the spidery writing with a magnifying glass.

It appeared Eli Dell never ate sugar or got tooth decay, but Grace had better luck with Ebenezer Dell–two teeth in an envelope. And another one. Very faded. Freelove D.? It could be Freelove Dell or Freelove Dominick?

The Freelove D. envelope was marked 1760, 1761, and 1773 and those dates were a possibility for a woman who could have been Long Liz's mother.   Not suiting up but masking and pulling on latex gloves, Grace unsealed that envelope and peered in. Three teeth. One so dead and rotted out that Grace didn't think she could get any DNA, but with three teeth, there would be two more chances.

She should just wait until she had Inger and Nick to help her, but Grace suited up for the Cleanroom. Carrying a tray of Dr. Floyd's envelopes, she headed inside, and there she first checked the progress of the vials holding Maryanne Morgan's swab from the Whaling Museum and several other specials she had in process. Then she hand numbered a preliminary inventory sheet and labels for the new "FD" series so she could start the extraction from the envelopes on her tray.

Had the teeth been maintained properly in a cool, dry atmosphere? Did the tightly sealed little envelopes protect the aged DNA? No water damage discoloration on the envelops or bleeding of the in--which was a good sign! Those cabinet drawers had been a very tight fit, another good sign that something might have been preserved. Feeling hopeful, Grace did her drilling and then started mixing extraction chemicals.

Then she held her breath as she began with FD00001, the "Elijah" tooth. When Grace next looked up, hours had passed.

She'd only be getting an hour or so of sleep before it was time to get up again, but before Grace went to bed, there was one other thing she might as well do. She kept thinking about that mismatching skin and eye color, what genetic varieties had mated to produce that? Grace decided now would be the time to start the yucky process of extracting trace DNA from the tissues she had stuffed in her handbag at the funeral home and later transferred to the lab freezer.

Even with the mask, disposable suit, and latex gloves, she found handling someone else's used Kleenexs really distasteful, but--as always--her curiosity over came her dislikes. She filled out the lab log, then picking up a pipette, she took out the collection zip-lock envelope with it's three disgusting, balled up tissues, with Jack Stuart's snot from Eve's funeral. She put one of Inger's pre-printed labels on a vial, and Jack's snot became OR50358.

Chapter 22

The next day, Inger printed out new sheets of inventory numbers with "FD" for the Floyd collection and logged in the numbers Grace already began. Inger was set to sorting the envelopes first to be logged in on a spreadsheet by name and date(s), then put back into the cabinet--in newly labeled drawers--after they were inventoried. Grace kept one pile of envelopes for herself to sort, any that by date or coloration or spidery handwriting seemed to come from the 1750' to 1830s. These she focused on, picking one up from 1774. Grace studied the longer than usual notation, written in rusting ink: "*October 1774. Posey, African serving girl of Elizabeth Booth. Pulled as punishment for theft.*"

A coldness flooded Grace. In that time period, teeth pulling was done without the benefit of any anesthesia other than maybe whiskey. And if it was done as punishment, Posey probably didn't even get the whiskey. The 'dentist' took a pair of wrought iron pliers and pulled a tooth deeply rooted in her jaw. Oh, God, the pain must have been horrible.

Grace emptied the contents of the envelope into the palm of her gloved hand: one molar, roots intact, and no evidence of decay or damage. Long Liz had a reputation for haughtiness, coldness...but to have a tooth ripped out to discipline the household staff?

Again curiosity spurred her, Posey was a Connecticut house slave, could her DNA determine what part of Africa Posey or her parents, had been kidnaped from? Grace had only one chance, but she decided to attempt a DNA extraction from this tooth. She picked off the next label of the new FD sheet Inger had run off: FD00004.

God, this obsession of hers with trivial DNA questions was leaching all her time away from her real work, but Grace still didn't have an Elizabeth Dell or Eve Dupree sample. Should she go to Jack and explain, *I just have this curiosity to sequence Eve's DNA*? Did Eve leave a brush with hair or used band-aid in the waste paper can that might have a little of her bloody pus or her skin cells?

No, the man was sick with shock from his company's CFO's murder and his financial troubles. Despite Jack's spoken admiration with her work, as a non-scientist, he'd probably look at Grace like she was some sort of ghoul with a twisted fetish for the remains of murder victims. She was not quite up to facing that. Eve's car? If she dropped by Jack's, would it still be there–no, he was having the rental company pick it up. People slough off skin cells all the time, so if in that mansion she lived in, her bed sheet or her lipstick might still have skin cells—where were Grace's brains? Or more specifically, where were the remains of Eve Dupree's bloody brains?

The sky wasn't yet graying before dawn as Grace hurried out of her lab in the moonlight and headed toward the ORR dock. Kurt's lobster yawl was still in. Good sign and the yellow taping was gone from around his sailboat house, and, yes, the portholes on his main cabin were lit. Walking aboard, Grace knocked on the teak trim to the hatchway, waited, and then knocked again.

Finally, a gruff voice drifted up from below decks. "C'mon down. Ain't talking to you until my lawyer's present."

Grace climbed down the ladder wondering how she would bring this up? Kurt sat at the dining room table, which was now his computer station. He was studying sea charts and looked up, smiling pleasantly to see her. "Lady." He looked at his screen, typed something in, and pushed it aside. "Heard you were also trying to raise my bail, thank ya."

"You're still on bail?"

"Actually, no. The state can't seem to get its case together. Course, my São Tomé interview is on hold until the judge releases me."

Regretfully she could only say, "Forgot that."

"No, I figured I had lost that gig, but since they've got footage on me in fall, winter, and spring, the camera crew is still kinda hoping to get a full year in. And they want me swimming off the ship too."

"They have any idea how cold the Atlantic is even in August?"

"Be shriveling my balls," he laughed.

Actually, that did sound like good news. *"Science* channel exposure is great for grants. Prestige."

"Unless they interview me on my views on Alien invasions? Might get on that program, if I can comb my hair high enough." There was devilry in his dark eyes, then Kurt softened as he voice took on a serious tone. "You know, they've already said they'll pay for my assistant to come with me. We could have two weeks lying around those São Tomé white sand beaches doing whatever in the cabanas?"

She stopped for a moment. Being on the beach and carefree with Kurt would be fun. "Sounds nice, but not at this time."

He expected that. "Why are ya here? Realized that a stud like me may soon behind bars, and you want your last chance for supreme joy?"

"No," Grace shook her head not really paying attention as she looked about.

"Then what?" he asked suspiciously now.

"I can't just come to visit?" Grace asked primly.

"Before dawn on a workday?" He laughed. "Lady, when you want something underhanded, you're about as subtle as the Queen Elizabeth docking."

She looked at his built-in table by the hatchway and sighed. It had once been upholstered in cotton brocade in a red anchor pattern, but since it was probably splattered with blood and Eve's brains, the police had cut the fabric out. "I wanted to see if I could extract Eve's DNA from any stains on your upholstery."

"Why?"

"Eve said she was infertile for genetic reasons, and I'd like to know more."

"Police got samples," he said.

"Won't give them to me."

"Ask Jack for access to her body?"

"She's allready been cremated."

"Grace, trying to squeeze out Eve's DNA is going to be a lot of trouble and work for what? To cure her infertility? The woman's dead."

Good question. Still, she appealed to him, "Kurt, don't you sometimes do things that you don't really have a reason for, but you just know you should?"

He looked at her, those dark eyes radiating a sort of innate understanding. "For the rest of us, our subconscious comes up with some socially acceptable excuses for our weird behavior, but not you, Grace,...well, lady, you find any stains left on that upholstery, you're welcome to them, but I think the police off cut out anything seeable."

Grace agreed. There was a rough three-foot square hole cut in the upholstery and yellow foam back padding that stopped only at the surrounding wooden trim. "Kurt–did you see her blood?"

"More brain splashes."

"Where was it?"

He stood up, walked over, and just pointed to a rough circle near the floor, where the fabric and carpet was ripped out by the police. "Didn't chart it. Had my mind on other things."

She pointed from the hatchway. "She was lying here when I looked down. The head must have been here. Splashes that police found and ripped out there, toward the floor."

"Deck," he corrected.

She studied it more closely.   "Kurt, that fabric continues under the frame.   It was built in when the boat was constructed."

He saw where she was going and immediately started protesting, "Grace! You are **not** ripping the wood trim off my boat! No way!"

"Just a little wood—over there. Just a little!" She tried inserting her fingernails in the trim. It wouldn't budge. "Do you have a crowbar I could use?"

"Oh, shit." He looked about and came back with a huge Bowie knife. "I'll do it! Not you! You don't touch my boat!"

"First put on latex gloves—don't contaminate what's there!" She commanded.

The frame came away with a splintering of teak wood and a cursing from Kurt, but Grace could see another six inches of stapled fabric that had been covered up. She used Kurt's penlight and was delighted to see there were several stains that had wicked under the frame.

"Lady, it will take you days—weeks to process all those stains! You're probably gonna find nothing but fish blood and beer!"

Ignoring that Grace said, "Let me have that knife to dig out the nails from this fabric! Let me put on gloves first."

Late that morning, after Grace gotten some sleep, she returned to her lab finding Inger greeted her with a wide, excited smile. "I've been taking a closer look at some of the Floyd collection. A number of the envelopes I had to set aside because their legends were so faded, and I couldn't put them on the spreadsheet, but from the student's lab, I managed to borrow a black light. See how it brings up some of the ink? This one came up." Inger handed Grace a faded envelope, now resealed in a clear plastic evidence bag. Inger's new white labeling neatly lettered 'Beth Booth 1764'. "Isn't Beth another nickname for Elizabeth?   And her last name was Booth after her marriage?"

Inger turned off all the lab lights, and Grace studied the envelope under the purplish-black light seeing Beth's name. Yes, Elizabeth was called Long Liz, but she might also have been called 'Beth' by Dr. Floyd. It's a softer name, maybe left over from childhood. The time period is right, according to Freya's family tree, Long Liz was thirty-eight in 1778 so Elizabeth would have been about twenty-six in 1764. Could have been married to Squire Seth Booth at that date?

This would be so great–if they had something! But Grace had to admit, "Booth was a common name in the area. Still, if we can link her Mitochondrial-DNA with Penny and Freelove D., we'll know we've got the right one!"   Grace lightly pressing her fingers on the polythene bag to feel the paper envelope within it, disappointingly it only held one small bulge. Only one tooth. One shot only at a viable extraction from a tooth over two hundred years old, who might be Elizabeth Dell Booth or might not. "Let's suit up!"

In the cleanroom, as they worked, a masked Nick was grinding up the fabric taken from Kurt's boat and then cutting it into small, numbered squares. As soon as he documented each, he would starting trying an extraction from dried blood or brain matter. One particular leached stain looked recent, so Grace took that one to work on herself. Dark, with grainy material– was it brain matter? When Nick passed her the chemical solution, she started soaking the fabric in a small pointed vial. At the counter across from her, Inger began the painstaking process of grinding down the teeth, while Nick mixed more of the chemicals Grace hoped would extract two hundred plus years of dry DNA. With her 'Beth Booth' and Inger's 'grid cloth number OR50362' soaking, Grace checked on her other extractions. The one labeled OR50038. Jack's sample. Perking nicely.

She wanted to do a geographic study on Jack with a DNA profile tracking the spread of his ancestors. Grace should have just asked him for a sample. It certainly would have been more ethical—she was sure he'd have given it to her–but with Eve's death and Jack's losses in business, she felt very awkward bringing it up at this time. His snot should be enough to harmlessly satisfy her curiosity.

Five days later she had several sequences to study. She started with the geographic profile she was working up for Maryanne Morgan, finding that the Whaling Museum curator's DNA had processed perfectly. Grace wished she could have gotten some of Maryanne's Grandmother's DNA, but with what she had, Grace made a call to a friend working on the *Genographic* project. With Kermit's help, Grace tied Maryanne's Mitochondrial DNA's to something she thought the museum curator would be fascinated by.

She next looked at Freelove D.'s extraction, automatically rechecking the number with her master list, FD00007 as she picked up one of the small, pointed vials. The woman might be the mother of Elizabeth Dell Booth and the many time's great-grandmother of Penny Barstall, which would mean they should all have identical Mitochondrial DNA. FD0007 could also tie to the line of her presumed son, Elijah, FD00001. If FD0001 and FD0007 shared DNA loci, Freya Dell could have retained paternal DNA from the both of them–or not, as the chromosomal dice mixed itself up.

Grace was really excited to get a peek at the samples that might tie a whole DNA genogram of the Dell family tree profile. She looked under the microscope. A major problem, FD00007 failed to replicate. Frustrated for a second, she just stood back half wanting to throw the vial across the room, then the discipline of years of failing and starting again from scratch kicking in.

She did the only thing she could do, go back to the

original sample envelope and try to do another extraction. The first tooth seemed a total loss, the second was gone, but she might get something from the third tooth now being labeled FD00010. It would put all her work back another six to ten days. With such an old, probably degraded sample, a lot more time would be needed, but it was her only chance.

A long, long nine days, but soon Grace was at her computer screen. She had a clear compilation on Penny Barstall and a good partial on the tooth labeled "Beth D." that might have come from Elizabeth Dell Booth. Grace started with the tooth of her presumed Elizabeth, FD0009 or 'Beth Booth.' Pulling up a computer screen with scribbled lines, with valleys and peaks, she noted the DNA had degraded a bit, and a lot was missing, but still more than enough to get a police profile. She began by familiarizing herself with the numbers of loci that she had. Locking the pattern into her mind, she blanked the screen, and Grace pulled up Penny's profile.

To her frustration, nothing worked. A quick glance told her nothing looked close to a match.

Grace split the computer screen so she could study both limed profiles at once. No matches. She got up and walked over to the second Freelove D. test. Still perking. She could try it, but that would be taking a chance she'd ruin it. No, it wasn't ready, and there would be no second chance. No, better she wait. Damn—waiting was so hard!

Grace went back to the computer, this time taking the trouble to overlay both the presumed Elizabeth and Penny's profiles on the screen. Not a match, not even a close miss, but maybe there would have been a match, in the missing segments of FD00009's sample...but...

Okay, there were a number of reasons for this. The most likely being that the 'Beth Booth' sample she had was not the Elizabeth Dell Booth who was Penny's ancestor, or Penny, in her assertion that she was a direct maternal descendant from Freelove and Long Liz, just got it wrong.

An honest mistake? The family story was right, but somewhere along the line a wife slept with a lover, well that wouldn't effect Midacondronial DNA. But suppose one of Penny's ancestors couldn't have children and had adopted a little girl? In those days, the children were never told of an adoption.

Grace would have to wait for confirmation from the third and last tooth from Dr. Floyd marked as *'Freelove D.'* envelop, perhaps that would be a match with Penny's. Unfortunately, Freya had said that Freelove was a common woman's name in Colonial times, and it was very possible the *'D'* didn't stand for *'Dell'* but *'Donavon or Darby'*? A wrong attribution with her Colonial samples would certainly show as the divergent mass of results as she had before her, but Grace had been so positive she would find a match! Perhaps with the other samples still processing she had a chance, but Grace found waiting for a sample to gel one of the hardest things in life!

There was one other member of the family that could be tested. It was highly unlikely, but still possible, that Freya retained some remnants of FD00009's DNA or the DNA Elijah shared with his sister, Elizabeth. And Grace had saved every DNA profile she ever had run, although some of them were on drives that weren't even in the current computers. She sat down and typed in an instruction to Nick's workload, *'Check the master lists until you find the DNA profile numbering for Freya Dell. Then pull it up for me—it should be with the first samples I took in Oyster River.'*

Chapter 23

Getting a solid week of work in, Grace deciding she deserved a long lunch, so she headed over to the Whaling Museum first, figuring she might remind Maryanne about that tax letter for Abe. Maryanne positively glowed when Grace came in. "The Board of Directors has commissioned a plexiglass case for the Captain's Medicine Chest, but I still don't know exactly where I'm going to put it. Either at the end wall or over here."

Grace walked with her back toward her office. "Abe's tax receipt?"

"Oh, I have it for you at my desk, Mr. Delmotto did the appraisal. He thinks it may be preRevolutionary War to possibly the 1860's, and he said the bottles alone were worth over a thousand dollars. And with the original book and surgical tools, Abe's receipt is for a full 3,600 dollars." She handed Grace an envelope with Abe's name on it.

"Thank you."

"Oh, thank you for nudging Abe along on this! It's going to fit in perfectly with the material I've been finding on Oyster River during the Revolutionary War period."

Funny that missing treasure was getting to even Grace. "Anything more on Elijah?"

"Yes, I'm going to put it in the computer, as a story display," Maryanne spoke reverently. "It's not about the ransom, just an excerpt from a period diary by a neighbor, a story about how Elijah loved his wife so. Mae had a favorite brown wool knit shawl that she kept on the bench by their hearth fire, and she would wrap up in it on cold nights. He kept it there after she died." Maryanne turned to Grace. "A knitted shawl was a very difficult thing to make in those days. In the spring, someone would have to shear the sheep, the wool would have to be washed, and combed, the wool fibers would have to be spun into yarn, sometimes dyed with vegetable stains that you had to collect, crush, and mix by hand, and finally the yarn had to be knitted. The whole process could take months, so when a piece of clothing wore out, they would unravel the yarn to reuse it.

"That shawl should have gone to her daughter-in-law, or at least a close friend of Mae's, but after Mae was buried, he stubbornly kept the shawl on her bench. Then one day seeing a storm coming in, he walked to Mae's grave and placed the shawl over her earth mound. One last act of love.

"When Elijah died, the British Major was so upset about his soldiers being in the Dell house when he died, the Major ordered his soldiers to help Rebecca by digging Elijah's grave. When they got to the Dell plot, they saw the sodden shawl, still covering Mae's grave. The diary says that the soldiers carefully moved it aside, then they dug Elijah's grave next to his wife's. With the townspeople standing there, the soldiers lowered his coffin, and then shoveled back the soil. Just before marching off, one of the red-coated soldiers carefully moved the shawl back, so that now it was covering both wife and husband."

Grace felt a lump in her throat, for the husband whose love and consideration for his wife went even beyond death.

Maryanne continued. "I'm made copies of the source for Freya since the Dells are ancestors of hers, she might want the story for one of her books." Maryanne handed Grace a large envelope. "You'll probably see her first." Then Maryanne stopped, hesitated, before finally saying, "Did you find out anything from that saliva I gave you?"

"Oh, yes," Grace had nearly forgotten. "Lots."

"Nothing bad medically?" Maryanne asked in a nervous voice.

"I hadn't planned to a disease possibility test, because there are so many unless I know what you are worried about? But I did do a preliminary geo-genetic study with your Mitochondrial DNA. That's the DNA passed directly from mother to daughter. I've printed it out for you." Grace dug the paper she'd brought out of her handbag. "I've placed all your markers on this world map, your female line originated in Akosombo ho. That's in Ghana, Africa today. And there are markers here in Louisiana in the 1800's."

Maryanne's face lit up. "That's so interesting!"

"There may be additional facts I can tell you, but I just need more time to study it."

Maryanne reverently examined the papers in her hands. "Thank you so much, but your time is so valuable! I should reimburse you..."

"No," Grace said firmly.

"It's so fascinating–to know about one's own family! The good and the bad." She stopped. "I mean it's personally interesting, not for a museum display." Maryanne stopped again and looked about, thinking more. "But maybe if we could trace some of the long-term Oyster River Families, and do some sort of family origin flow chart on a map along the wall over there?"

"That's possible," Grace said. "Actually, I'm currently running profiles on a treasure trove of ancestral Oyster River Harbor DNA that I got from Abe."

Maryanne looked very excited. "It would be so good for the children! Bridging dusty history with cutting-edge science!"

"We'll work on it, but not today." Grace nodded and was turning to leave when Maryanne hesitantly started to speak again, "That Penny person was here yesterday."

"With Freya?"

"No, she walked over from the motel. I think she wanted to talk to me while Freya was at work." Maryanne suddenly seemed like she didn't want to finish.

"And?" Grace gently prompted.

"I know she is a distant cousin of Freya's, but she was trying to sell the museum an artifact. She wanted a lot of money for it. Penny claimed it came from a whaling ship wrecked in Newfoundland, it was a green-glass deck prism."

"A what?"

"For whaling ships crews, managing resources over three to six year voyages was hard. Down below decks, you didn't want to waste precious candles or oil lamps, so the ship builders laid large diamond-shaped glass prisms flush with the upper decks. Those prisms drew and magnified the sun's rays down to give light below decks."

Grace had a feeling there was more to this than a simple transaction. "Was this prism worth what she was asking?"

Maryanne spoke hesitantly. "I'm not really an expert, but I think it was only a twenty dollar reproduction that anybody can buy up at Mystic Seaport. It was scraped and scratched, in fact, it looked like someone had sandpapered it with a rough grit, but the glass was very clear, and there were no bubbles. Very modern looking, but Penny still swore that it had been in the Barstall family for a hundred and fifty years."

"But you think she wasn't telling the truth?"

"There was more..." Maryanne appeared to be really having difficulty getting it all out. "When I wouldn't buy it, Penny started walking around the museum. Pointing to pieces, saying that harpoon was worth five hundred, and that captain's log would bring in maybe two hundred. She asked if the museum had any extra artifacts in storage that they didn't need."

Again Maryanne didn't want to go on, so Grace prodded. "And?"

"Penny told me she had connections in the antique business, and that if I would just '*lend*' her a few items, she could show them around and make us both money."

"By 'us' do you think she meant the Whaling Museum?"

"No."   Maryanne was firm.   "I think that those transactions would have just been between herself and me." She thought about for a moment. "Well, she never really came out and said we should steal the museum's property, but I got the definite impression that's exactly what she was planning. My grandmother used to say *'If you hang around friends who steal, it's not if they will steal from you, just when.'*" Maryanne stopped again, finally saying, "But she's Freya's cousin, I can't say anything. What should I do?"

Chapter 24

As for what Maryanne should do about Penny, Grace didn't know, and when in doubt, she always turned back to her work. That afternoon in the Cleanroom, Nick called her over as he studied a microscope screen. "This is a sample from Kurt's fabric. Looks bad–I'd say we got prokaryotes."

Grace looked through and saw simple cells with no nuclei. Definitely not human. "The last time I was eating in Kurt kitchenette some of the lobsters got out of their bucket. Probably slime from something like that. This one is?"

"OR50360." After first writing the cell decision on the lab log, he showed her several more samples. All cell-less stains or simple life forms, but Nick had saved the best for last, "Take a look at OR50362."

Grace did, and the excitement of the chase shot through her. "Human. Definitely, from Kurt's upholstery?"

"Yhep," Nick said proudly. "Shall I start replicating?"

"Yes, sir!" It's was a long shot, but maybe Grace had gotten her Eve Dupree sample.

The mass of worthless material from Kurt's upholstery made Dr. Floyds' teeth seem easy. Still, decoding Revolutionary period DNA took time, making it excruciatingly slow, and it was four more days, on Thursday, before she could check on FD00010, the third Freelove D. tooth extraction.

Eureka! The sample was a bit degraded, with much missing, but it was still readable. With enough mitochondrial and nuclear DNA, she should easily be able to tie it to a maternal line descendant. Grace looked at the squiggly lines across her screen, valleys and peaks, loci that should match with Freelove's maternal line descendants. Grace pulled up Penny Barstall's mitochondrial DNA, and again the valleys and peaks squiggled across the screen but nothing matched. Scanning fast, Grace wasn't seeing a recognizable pattern. Nothing looked like a single loci match.

She flipped back to the FD00010. Grace split the computer screen and studied Freelove and Penny's profiles at the same time. Then she took the trouble to do what she should have done in the first place, overlay a blue lined OR50357's profile on top of a green lined FD00010's.

Not one of the locis matched. Not even close.

Again, there could be several disappointing reasons for this: Freelove D. was not Freelove Dell, Grace's third tooth sample was contaminated, or there could have been a break in the maternal transmission. Penny swore the female line from Long Liz was not broken, but an ancestor could have been adopted and grew up without ever being told of her biological beginnings? And like Maryanne, Grace had the uneasy feeling that Penny was not always exactly truthful. Still, barring mutations, mitochondrial DNA was always passed intact from mother to daughter in the maternal line, and definitely, there was no way these profiles were of a mother/daughter relationship.

Grace removed FD00010 and just stared dispiritedly at OR50037. No match. No game. No win. But as Grace stared at the screen, her mind began visualizing one of her famous *"Farrington fusions"* as those lines across her screen were forming a familiar landscape. A landscape that she had recently studied, not once, but twice.

Grace rapidly scrolled through her recent profiles. And she found the other two that matched! One two hundred years dead, and the other one walking the earth now. Proof of a true story from a time of human suffering, turmoil, and pain, proof that the human spirit continues to soar and conqueror. Proof of something Grace should have suspected all along.

But there was something else she felt was familiar.

She started with overlaying FD0009 and FD00010, and hit the jackpot! FD0009's blue lined Mitochondrial DNA matched up perfectly with the red lined profile that appeared on the screen, proving the mother-daughter relationship. This could be verified and enlarged upon. Grace checked one more of the Floyd teeth profiles. Confirmation on five loci's on parental DNA, linking that FD00010 to FD00001 and FD00001 to FD00009. From the dates on the envelops probably mother-son, sister-brother.

And Nick had found Grace another sample in her past records, OR00056, to try to match against this growing family tree. Eagerly she called it up and overlaid the gene replication of OR0056 matching it to FD00010! Even with the degraded FD00010 sample that was missing so much and having over two hundred years between them, there were enough marking loci to strongly indicate kinship from FD000010 to OR00056– **yes**!

She tried for a match between OR00056 against OR50357 and as she expected, no matches, which if her hypothesis was correct made perfect sense. Grace wanted to pick up the phone right now, but there would be a confrontation. No, she should wait, solidify her data, and live with it a bit. Grace needed more ammunition before she went into battle, and she also had to ask for permission to release one test subject's name to another subject.

That call she made now. Getting no answer at the work number, Grace decided to put off dealing with it all until Monday. That might be cowardly, but Grace needed all the information she could muster for one fatal shot. Maybe the DNA couldn't give her the location of the lost ransom, but it could explain a lot of what happened two hundred years ago!

Chapter 25

Monday evening, it was raining heavily. Grace took extra care to place her laptop in a huge waterproofing, Ziploc bag, before placing it inside its carrying case. She had all the relevant profiles on it, and as she entered Freya's house for their usual dinner, she already had made a cell call, making sure that Penny Barstall would be there.

Freya had eggplant Parmesan in the oven with home-baked Italian bread, and a flushed faced Penny was already on a second bottle of Freya's burgundy. Freya seemed to have started buying it by the case. As Grace shook off her raincoat, Freya poured her dark ruby wine in a green mermaid stemmed goblet.

Grace asked Freya, "Can I set my laptop up on your dining room table?"

"Only if you eat before you work!" Freya warned as she pulled on red oven mitts to take the bread out of the oven.

"How's the ransom hunting coming?" Grace asked them both.

Her old friend looked discouraged as she carried the melted cheese and garlic-smelling bread to the table. "Not too good. We've got two more possible well locations to check after this storm lets up, but it doesn't look promising."

Penny looked furious. "And I've used up all most all my money staying at that stupid motel! Since we're family, Freya, I can't see why I can't stay with you!"

"Mac..."

"This is your house! Not your son's! I'm family to you too!"

"Well, let's talk about that, Penny," said Grace, cutting her off as she pulled her genetic profile directories up on the laptop's screen. "You know, I came across a sample of Freya's DNA that I had taken for verification of a geo-genetic project." Penny stared at her, the foolish, alcohol-fueled pugnacious look disappearing as Grace continued. "Freya's descended from the male Dell line of Elijah. From the Dr. Floyds' teeth hoards, I was able to do a profile on a male labeled Elijah with the correct dates." She turned to Freya. "Even in your DNA you still share markers you inherited from the Captain."

Freya looked at the screen, fascinated, as Grace pointed to the two overlaid genetic profiles. "Both you and Elijah show Scandinavian, Ukraine and Middle Eastern heritage. That heritage is also shared by a tooth labeled "*Beth Dell*" and her presumed mother, *'Freelove D.'*"

"So?" Penny asked.

Grace continued. "I profiled that swab you gave me, Penny."

Penny's eyes narrowed at Grace. "You said you weren't going to compare my DNA with Freya's."

"Well, I guess we all don't tell the truth sometimes, don't we? Penny, you claim to be descended in a direct female line from Elizabeth Dell Booth, sister of Elijah, whom Freya is descended from."

"Freya's from the male line," pointed out Penny warily.

"Yes, so she wouldn't have any mitochondrial DNA from either Elizabeth or her mother, Freelove. But as I've said, Freya does share genetic markers with our Elijah Dell and with his presumed mother, Freelove, and our presumed Beth Booth or Long Liz. You, on the other hand, Penny, do not share any DNA markers with Freya or Captain Elijah. More importantly, you do not share mother-daughter Mitochondrial DNA markers with the tooth labeled as '*Beth Dell,*' or the tooth labeled as '*Freelove D.*'" Grace voice stayed in a flat lecturer's cant, but she felt the exhilaration of trapping her prey.

Penny sat up straight and glared at Grace. "Your samples were obviously from the wrong people."

"I don't think so.   Elijah and Freya show a gene sharing with Beth Dell and Freelove D., making me suspect that I am correct that Beth is Elizabeth Dell Booth or Long Liz, and that Freelove D. was her mother, but again, Penny, you do not share a single marker with any of them?"

Freya started to protest. "We're going back over two hundred years! Couldn't things have shifted or mutated? Just because Penny hasn't shown a genetic relationship to someone in Oyster River Harbor, that doesn't mean..."

Penny's mouth had stiffened as she silently glared in fury a at Grace.

Grace cut Freya's excuses off. "Actually, Penny does have a mitochondrial profile in common with someone in Oyster River in the 1770's. Penny perfectly shares Mitochondrial DNA with two profiles in my possession. One currently living in Oyster River now, and one from a 1770's profile. With the teeth from the Floyd cache I was able to run a profile on a tooth labeled 'Posey, African slave of Elizabeth Booth.' Penny, both you, Posey and Maryanne Morgan from the whaling museum all share the same mitochondrial DNA.

When Penny said nothing, Grace continued. "I've already spoken to Maryanne Morgan today, not revealing your name to her but saying she might have a long lost cousin. She has given me permission to reveal her name to whoever that cousin is, and she's actually very excited to compare family notes with you since all three of you share a DNA heritage that matches up with territorial markers pin-pointing a genetic, geographical origin of your maternal lineage to the Akosombo ho area."

"Akosombo?" Freya asked.

"Akosombo ho. It's in Africa, and today it is called Ghana. My research tells me many of the New England slaves came from that area."

Penny's voice dripped poison. "Posey was dignified, educated in needlework, and she performed elegant, intricate music on the harpsichord. Elizabeth treated Posey as a daughter, and Long Liz should have adopted her! Posey should have inherited all that was Liz's!"

"What did happen to Posey?" Freya asked quietly.

Penny spoke bitterly. "Oh, she was 'freed' in Canada. Allowed to marry a quarter-blood man, a coarse tradesman. A widow then, Elizabeth generously," Penny barely spat out the words, "paid for Posey's wedding feast. Posey changed her name to Penelope, but she could never forget she was born a slave! She had to treat Long Liz like a beloved 'godmother' when Elizabeth condescended to visit so Penelope would get some piddling gifts of cloth for her five daughters."

Freya cut in. "When they were forced to go to Canada, Seth and Elizabeth Booth had lost most of their wealth. Seth never recovered his shipping line, and when he died, Elizabeth probably was barely hanging on with just one ship."

That didn't appear to impress Penny. "Henry was their slave too, but when Seth Booth died, Liz gave Henry half an interest in her ship's cargo! She allowed him to stay and run her property like a son, and she made him her heir. As a daughter, at the very least Penelope should have gotten the jewels, but Elizabeth had handed them over to save her rebelling nephew! That ransom jewelry is mine by right of descent! By right of sufferance!"

Freya sighed. "Well, before we argue about who is entitled to what, the fact is we don't have the ransom. Unless Penny, you know something more then you've told us?"

Penny's eyes focused on the distance, she really seemed to be recalling every passed down the story. "My many–greats grandmother was ordered to carry that jewel casket down to the beach, and Posey was forced to leave it there in the sand. Elijah was a sick, old man, and he died the next day. He couldn't have carried those jewels far!"

"Rebecca took them?" offered Grace.

"Long Liz never believed that," Penny answered. "She believed her brother had hidden them somewhere."

Grace started, "The boatman...he was on the beach."

"Christopher Coe." Freya nodded thoughtfully. "He's a distant cousin to myself too, so I've researched him. A young man, Christopher was very successful, and when he died, he had two boats and his own dock in Oyster Bay."

"You think he paid for that with the ransom?" Penny demanded.

Freya shook her head. "No, he didn't live much longer than Elijah, and he already had the boats before the ransom was collected. As I told you he was supplementing his fishing with whiskey smuggling, and he was suspected of being a member of George Washington's spy ring on Long Island, so he probably had income streams we aren't aware of."

Penney sat back, looking challengingly at Freya. "Your ancestor, Elijah, stole that ransom from mine! We've got to find it–then we can share it–but I can't afford to keep renting a motel room in Oyster River. Freya, you have to let me stay here with you or pay my rent at the motel! You owe me!"

Chapter 26

When Freya didn't answer, Grace did. "No, she doesn't! Whatever wrongs were done to the first Penelope, she and all those around her have been dead for over two hundred years! No one owes you anything when you're born. Someone may have gotten good parents, maybe they didn't, but by the time you're over thirty, you have to take responsibly for your own life!"

Freya looked worn and tired. "Fighting over a ransom that we just can't find doesn't accomplish anything." She looked at Penny. "If you can't pay for the motel, maybe it's time you went home, where ever that is."

Penny looked furious, but she only said, "You promised to search those last two filled in wells–you owe me that!"

Freya nodded, saying wearily, "Yes, I'll take you back to the motel today. And as soon as it stops raining tomorrow, we'll check those wells with the metal detector, then whether we find anything or not, I'm finished looking for the Treasure of Oyster River."

The next day Grace meant to call Freya but didn't. She was getting behind in her work schedule, with Kurt's near trial, and Freya's unhappiness, but Grace's mind keep flying back from her paid consultancies. Finally, she just gave up and pulled up her '*Eve Dupree's Murder* Spreadsheet. Kurt was in trouble, and from the police's standpoint it still looked like he did it, but it would have been a motiveless murder. He didn't kill women for rejecting him, because, with Kurt MacKay, hope was eternal, so if Eve wouldn't go to bed with him today, there was always tomorrow. And if he wanted to kill her, why couldn't he wait until dark, and then do a better job of getting rid of the body in the harbor? She zeroed Kurt out.

She added a row for David Gardiner now the most serious contender. David had no reason to be on that dock, but Deborah had seen him there, and he hadn't told the police that. He admitted being jealous of Grace and Kurt, and he was suddenly moving out of the country. Still, Grace couldn't actually believe someone as sophisticated and totally civilized as David could suddenly go mad with jealous passion. And even from behind, no one could realistically mistake the taller, curvaceous Eve for Grace's angular body. No, David was not a probable, no matter what the numbers.

Thinking Adam Greenfield did kill Eve was just desperation on her part, so she zeroed him out as well and with no new evidence, but the brutality of the killing dropped Unknown Lover to 2 %. Again she studied Josh Jeffers with his protective brother as his main alibi. He was the strongest candidate for *Motive*–craziness, but the *'Means'* were weak. He would have been recognized if he was walking around on ORR's dock, still was he just too crazy to care?

Finally, there was that other man, she couldn't believe did it, but he was growing stronger as a candidate. Jack Stewart, although the *Motive* wasn't clear unless it was a concealed jealousy? But that didn't seem to be right. Maybe Jack was in on the Ponzi with Eve, but she could no longer stand the guilt and wanted to confess? Did Jack want to stop her from going public, so he murdered her? Grace remembered his silent agony, watching the police take Eve's body away, she couldn't believe Jack could ever kill her. Damn! The answer was there in the spreadsheet. Grace was sure of that, but she just wasn't seeing it!

In frustration, she closed that one and pulled up her *'Location Oyster River Ransom.'* Again, as she stared at the spreadsheet, there was something nagging at her. Something not right that she was missing. Yes, 'Ransom Still Hidden' seemed to be the answer. She seemed sure of that, but there was something else there, some pattern that she should be seeing.

And then suddenly, with a '*Farrington Fusion*' she did!

"Inger, I've got a job for you. Up in the library at the Roost there's a diary of Nathaniel Thomas that is in the bookcase closest to the left of the fireplace, it's about this thick," she put her thumb and finger at four centimeters, "with black bookends and faded red cloth binding and no title. On each day, Nathaniel wrote at least a line, giving the date, and a notation about yesterday's weather. I want you to start on June 17, 1778, and go through until you reach July 22, 1778. Write down the weather for each day, and copy any notation that mentions Rebecca, Mae, or Elijah Dell, Long Liz Booth, Posey, Christopher Coe, or British soldiers."

Inger was busy rapidly writing that down. "Long Liz? That's also Elizabeth Dell Booth, or Beth Booth, right?"

She nodded, and Inger left. With one problem possibly solved, Grace could finally get back to her regular work. After an hour of working on banana skin coloration gene switch data, Grace started dialing her conference call to Brazil. It took a long hour and a half before she finished. Standing up to un-stiffen herself, Grace heard the main door open.

An embarrassed Inger was closely followed by Huang, who waved papers in his hands. "She just sitting. Looking at old books! Why isn't she working for you?"

"She is working for me," Grace replied coldly. "I sent her there."

"To read old books?"

"Why I sent her there isn't actually any of your business." And what in hell was he doing in the Roost Library?

"She on ORR payroll!" Huang yelled, throwing down the papers on Grace's desk.

"No, she is not! Inger is on my payroll, from my

personal grants!"

Inger spoke up. "My job is to assist Dr. Farrington, in any way that she feels will further her research."

"I speak to Adam about this!" Huang yelled turning to go.

After he left, Inger apologized profusely. "I'm so sorry. I was absorbed in the diary, and he came up behind me and just grabbed the loose leaf papers and started reading."

"It's not your fault! I'll this straighten this nonsense out with Adam. You work for me, not Huang or ORR." And she would make that clear to Adam! "Did you have time to finish?"

"Yes, I was just reading a little bit further, after the funeral of Elijah Dell. I thought I might find something you would want."

Grace picked up Inger's neatly printed sheets and moved to her Ransom Location spreadsheet as she studied the loose leaf sheets for dates and weather notations. Warm, normal summer days, some light rain, but major storms on June 23rd, July 6[th,] and one on the night of July 15, 1778. Bingo! That cinched her hypothesis for Grace. "Inger, I need the notes I typed of my Brazilian conference sent to Dowan at Wood's Hole. I've got a personal errand to run, can you lock up today?"

Inger nodded and moved to her desk.

Grace dialed Freya's phone number. "Where's Penny? We've got to get together."

"She gone," said Freya in dead, flat voice.

"Gone?" There was no answer on the other end of the line. "When will she be back?"

"She won't be coming back–ever. And I don't want to talk about it!"

There was a silence as Grace digested this, and then when Freya added nothing further, Grace said, "Well, get that metal detector and meet me..."

Freya's voice sounded muffled. "When Penny left, she took my van..."

Over the phone, Grace could hear her sniffling, either Freya had a cold or had been crying. "You lent it to her?" asked Grace.

There was silence, then Freya admitted. "No, she just took it."

"Oh, Freya..."

"And she stole my handbag, with cash from the Springfield mineral show, credit cards, and two locked, display jewelry cases that I had taken to the show, with a few hundred dollars worth of gems and jewelry, and that expensive metal detector that I still have to finish paying off." Freya stopped, "She had me put that in the van, too, so it must have been the plan all along."

"Have you called the police?" No answer. "Freya!" Grace demanded firmly.

"Yes–I called them. But I waited...awhile, for her to come back."

"How long?"

"Hours. Mac's furious with me."

"Your credit cards, you have to cancel..."

"Mac has already done that. She used them for gas and food and some expensive luggage, but since we reported it so soon, he doesn't think I'll have to pay for any of it. She didn't check out of the motel or pay her bill, but her room at the Shoreline was totally cleared and had been cleaned with bleach wipes, so no fingerprints. The police in Massachusetts found my van, abandoned with my empty pocketbook and the smashed, empty display cases. Mac's been running her name on the police data banks, and he thinks '*Penelope Barstall*' never existed. She had no driver's license, no address in Boston, and no entry permit into this country from Canada."

Freya stopped, trying to get control. Mac must have

been really reading his mother the riot act, but she seemed to be calming down as she got the story out, "Grace, Penny walked over to my house and wanted to borrow my van. I wouldn't give her the keys, I said I'd drive her instead. She had me put the metal detector in the van because we wanted to check out a filled in well by the church. But before I started to drive away, Penny said she felt sick–she asked me to go back to my house and get her some aspirin and ginger ale. When I started to get out of the car, Penny asked me to leave the key in so she could continue listening to the radio." Freya stopped, then started sounding pained. "When I got back, she was gone." Again silence before she spoke brokenly, "Grace, why am I always such a fool?"

Grace couldn't bear for her friend suffer so. "You aren't. You're an honest, open, good-hearted person, who can never really see bad in someone else. So you've got Mac and me to look out for you, and this time we did a lousy job of protecting you." This changed things, but Grace just had to work this out. "Now, Kurt has a marine metal detector he uses sometimes, let me see if I can borrow it from him. I'll pick you up at your house as soon as I get it. Do you have a shovel? A pick?"

"What are we going to be doing?" Freya asked.

"Robbing the dead."

Chapter 27

When Grace reached Freya's, she had a map of Oyster River that she spread on the kitchen counter. "Where did they bury people in the late 1700s?"

Freya looked blank. "There were at least four church cemeteries in Oyster River, in the late 1770 and some family plots on their own properties. Most of them have disappeared, plowed under and the stones recycled."

"We're looking for something that was within walking distance of Elijah's home."

"Which is now the Captain's Mansion restaurant," said Freya studying the map.

That surprised Grace. "His place was that big?"

"No, it was remodeled extensively during the whaling boom of the 1830's." Freya slowly shook her head. "Walking distance for a man in the Colonies, that leaves a lot of ground to cover."

"You have other family members buried up on Church Street at Burying Hill, right?"

"Yes."

"Then we start there."

"Start what?" asked Freya.

"According to Nathaniel's diary Elijah's wife, Mae Dell, died on June 19th and was buried the next day, on June 20th, 1778. Her grieving husband Elijah stopped by the cemetery almost every night. From the diary, we learn that between June 20th and July 16th, which was the day Elijah died, there were three major summer storms."

"So?"

"Only on the last storm, on the night before he died, did Elijah walk to the cemetery and lay Mae's precious shawl on her grave. Why? If he wanted to cover her from the cold rain, why hadn't he done that on the earlier storms?"

"He was feeling poorly. Dying...maybe he sensed that

this would be his last chance to visit his wife's grave?"

"Sick and dying are reasons not to climb up a steep hill, but that night he did. He didn't cover her mound before or during the other storms, but he covered her that night."

Freya just sat there as she got it.

"Yhep." Grace continued. "He wasn't protecting his wife, he was hiding something under the shawl. He didn't know when the British soldiers were coming, and he could have met them on the road. Elijah probably was using the shawl to cover up the ransom as he carried it up Church Street and then he used it to cover the new digging in a grave that already had loose dirt."

Freya looked at her. "He buried the ransom in his wife's grave?"

"I think so. He did such a good job that when the redcoats came to dig his grave alongside hers, they respectfully moved the shawl clear, buried him beside her, and then replaced the shawl over husband and wife."

"Wouldn't they see the ground newly disturbed?"

"Nope. Remember, the night before he died, a storm was coming in? Nathaniel wrote in his weather diary that it rained heavily throughout the night. That would've soaked through the shawl and have helped wet down the newly disturbed earth."

"But you don't think that the soldiers digging probably found it?"

"Possibly, but probably not. They were under the watchful eyes of the townsfolk in the funeral procession. Their Major was already unhappy that a prominent local had died during their searching. I think they would have dug Elijah's grave, buried the body, and gotten out of there as quickly as they could."

"Yes," Freya nodded in agreement. "Yes, they would have."

"And Elijah probably never realized he was dying.

When he collapsed, he had the soldiers who carried him upstairs in the room with him. Then he had the British regimental surgeon there, so he didn't have a chance to tell Rebecca where the treasure was buried."

"I think you've got it!" Freya exclaimed.

"Now just where exactly are Mae and Elijah Dell buried?"

Freya looked blank. "I have no idea. I've never been able to find their graves. They aren't in the two Dell family plots up in Burying Hill. When I was doing the family tree, I looked a few times, but I didn't find anything. There's no cemetery maps earlier than 1820. The Revolutionary tombstones were mostly carved on slate. The inscriptions have worn pretty badly from the acid rain and two hundred years of icy winters."

"It never comes easy, does it?" complained Grace bitterly.

Chapter 28

They parked on the grass off an asphalt road, in front of the cemented stones that formed the gates of '*Burying Hill*' cemetery, of course, like a lot of New England burial areas, the early town fathers choose land that was too thin and too steep for planting crops. The iron gates had long ago fallen off the cemetery entrance, but Freya said turning a station wagon around in there was hard, so they'd do better walking. Grace looked nervously around as Freya unloaded the bulky metal detector from the station wagon.

The horse cart narrow lanes between the rows of tombstones were packed dirt with remnants of once graveled paths. Up front, Grace could see some contemporary stones, one with a new, sad mound of wilting flowers, but Freya led her higher, toward the rear. Here the stones changed from polished gray granite to washed, white marble.

"Victorian period. 1840's to 1900's." Freya pronounced in sonorous tones as if she were guiding her '*Haunted Halloween Graveyard*' tour. Grace carefully stepped past a lot of '*as I am today, so shall ye be*' and some sad little marble lambs over babies' graves. Freya stood amid black iron pole fenced plots, pointing East and then Southwest. "Dell family plots. My mother used to have us go up on Grandma's birthday and put her favorite black-eyed Susans on the grave, but when it was just me and Mac, I planted perennials for both plots. I know all the stones in those two plots, three born in the 1700's, but no Elijah or Mae Dell there."

So they started walking to the higher areas, climbing over a low dry-fit stone wall. Here the grass wasn't even cut, and small, thin rectangular slate grave markers hugged the ground. Grace studied one, '*Patience, wife of Gunther.*' The 1700's dates seemed to be in the ground as if the stone had sunk over the ages or the ground got higher. Another one had a fat-faced cherub's head, with wings on each side, and Grace saw some winged skulls too.

"Grace, over here." Freya had spotted a line of broken stones that had been leaned against the rock wall, and Grace joined her.

"*Mary Scofield. Bart Hoyt*." Freya squinted, as she read off the names, then she stopped and froze. Two stones touching together. '*Mae, Wife of Elijah Dell 1778*' and '*Elijah Dell 1778.*'

Yhep. They found the stones, but where were the graves they came from? "Vandals broke them off?" asked Grace dispiritedly.

"I don't think so." Freya pointed to a huge, five-foot diameter tree stump. "When that came down, it must have broken up a lot of them."

Grace looked around, disappointed to have gotten so far and now come to a dead end. "You're sure the cemetery people don't have any records?"

Freya was fooling with Kurt's metal detector. "How do you turn this thing on?"

Grace looked at the handle and found a switch, and knowing Kurt's protective love of mechanical tools, there would be working batteries in it. The metal detector lit up and beeped softly.

But Grace looked about without much hope. There was a quarter acre of burying ground that these headstones probably came from, and with the sun slanting low, soon they wouldn't have any decent light. "Maybe we should come back tomorrow?"

Freya hefted the metal detector. "Got to work out some sort of grid coverage. I'll start in that corner of there."

But without stakes and markers to know what they covered, it all looked rather a mission impossible to Grace. Still, she found some straight branches to stick in the ground and mark off the rows they'd done.

When Freya reached the first row, the pings started immediately. "Grace, I've got something!"

Grace hurried over. "Indicator says metal. Iron?" She pushed the probe into Freya's hands around a bit, walking a four-foot pathway with resulting small pings. "Seems to be a rectangular pattern. Probably nails. Coffin nails."

Freya made a face. "Oh, great."

Moving to the next row, Freya got a different, higher sounding 'Ping.' "Indicator says gold!" she said excitedly."

Grace looked at the screen. "Small."

"Either very tiny and close to the surface. Or bigger and farther down? But it's definitely gold!" Freya looked at the headstone, *Helen, beloved wife of Johnny Blackstone.*

Grace nodded. "Bet he buried her with the gold wedding ring."

A car passed on the main road and Grace flinched. If someone in authority showed up, how would they explain this little expedition? "Maybe we should have gotten the cemetery association to authorize this little grave rob?"

"Forget it, they haven't held a meeting in years. The full committee still can't agree on allowing motorized hearses," said Freya disgustedly as she moved off down the row, with a series of small 'pings' and 'dingings.'

Grace looked back at the northeast section where the huge tree stump was, rows here weren't too evenly laid out. Of the slate stones that still remained, most had lost their carved inscription, or were so worn by weather and time, that they were barely readable. She turned on the pen-flashlight she had brought, trying to light the inscriptions from an angle so that the shadow effect would make the wording stand out just a little more.

Near the treed stump she saw a brownstone, like one of those leaning against the wall. The man's name–John D... The stone next to it was slate, Grace thought she made out an

'EB..N...,' she turned the light to the one next left of it. This stone was even more washed out, but she made out the letters *'F..elove...'* "Freya!" She called out loudly, "What were the names of Elijah's parents again?"

"Freelove Scofield Dell and Ebenezer Dell."

"Over here!" Grace was down on her knees, ripping weeds away from the broken base of the stone next to Freelove's as Freya hurried to her, and placed that unwieldy metal detector down on the ground before she started helping Grace clear the overgrown area.

Grace pointed, "I think that broken base would match up with Elijah's headstone over there. If those were his parents, and he was buried next to Mae, she would have been here between them?"

Freya rose and hurried to pick up the metal detector, then she swung it across the brown earth. Nothing. Sadly Freya put the detector down.

Grace stood up and walked to look at the detector–it was turned off! Grace reached over and switched it on again, and the metal detector went wild! Pinging its little brains out!

Chapter 29

"Gold! More! Metals! Silver! Iron!--Grace--this must be it!" Freya shouted.

"Keep your voice down!" Nervously Grace looked around at the houses about the cemetery. Even if this was another Dell family plot, they didn't have permission to dig, but Freya had gone down on her knees and was digging into the muddy dirt with her hands.

"Stop!" Grace nervously looked about. "I'm going back to the car, to get the shovel and pick."

"Hurry up!" said an excited Freya.

"What if somebody comes by and sees me carrying a shovel?" asked Grace nervously.

"We're digging a hole to put flowers on my great grandmother's grave," explained Freya reasonably.

"Too bad we didn't think to bring any flowers," Grace finished off.

It took them over half an hour to get a hole only two feet deep, especially with an elated Freya, who just had to keep lifting the metal detector up again to hear that wild pinging. It was Grace's turn to dig when the metal shovel thudded against something. Both she and Freya got back down on muddy knees and started clawing at the dirt with their fingers. "Not a treasure chest. It's a cylinder?" questioned a surprised Grace.

"A ceramic crock." Down on her knees, Freya was feeling around it. "They used to use these for cow's milk and whiskey. They sealed them with wax."

The two women pulled it up with difficulty, surprised at how heavy it was and Grace asked, "Can you open it?"

Freya tried to twist the lid off. "No"

Grace knew that Freya was strong. "The wax hardened?"

"No--this wasn't sealed with wax. It's black and thick

and hard. Tar? They used heated tar to use to caulk ships with. Damn! Stuck good!"

"Great." Grace stood up and looked around the cemetery nervously. "Maybe we should just take the crock with us."

"Good idea!" Freya said joyously. "Grace, fill the hole back up."

"Freya, with the crock gone it is going to leave a depression."

"Well if the groundskeeper gets curious, he can ask Mae Dell." Freya lurched up with the huge crock under her arm and the pick, as Grace shoveled back what dirt she could. Then she tried wiping her drying muddy hands on her pants, God, she hated having dirt under her finger nails. Picking up the metal detector and wishing for a shower, she headed down after Freya.

Freya had just stashed the crock, pick and metal detector in the back of Grace's old Subaru when the police car came up the hill. Any hopes of it just passing them were dashed when the cop car pulled over beside them and stopped. Well, at least the neighbors would be treated to a show of flashing blue lights and sirens as they were arrested. Like a dummy, Grace stood there with dirt covered hands holding the shovel.

"Hi, Ben," said Freya cheerfully waving to the cop, as she firmly slammed shut the rear door of Grace's station wagon.

He leaned out his lowered his car window. "Got a call, some teenagers were in the cemetery?"

Freya just smiled. "Probably just Grace and me. Doing genealogical research on my family and realized I had clean up the graves a bit." She indicated Grace's shovel, then embellished more. "Planning a new Revolutionary War Ghost tour to pair with the Whaling Museum's upcoming exhibit."

Ben had that cop's, *'I know you're up to something here'* look as he studied the both of them. "Grace, you're sure covered with dirt?"

Grace's throat closed, but Freya cheerily jumped in, slipping into her best tour guide cadence. "She uncovered Harold Grayson Scofield's memorial, it's a cenotaph you know. A cenotaph is placed for a memorial when there is no body to be buried. Harold was drowned, well to understand that we have to go back to 1812, during the war with England, General Winthrop Scofield..."

Ben cut in, talking fast. "Yeah, Freya, I'd love to hear all about that sometime, but right now I'm on duty and on the taxpayer's dollar. Gotta drive through this cemetery here, just to make sure everything's peaceful and quiet." Still talking, Ben put the car in gear and made his escape. "Dinner with you and Mac soon, okay?" Ben yelled as he drove away.

Giving him a big smile, Freya waved. When he had driven out of sight, Freya said to Grace in an undertone. "Wet your pants yet?"

"I'm just standing here picturing the newspaper headlines, *'Grace Farrington, esteemed Nobel nominee sinking to robbing graves,'*" she finished.

"That's us, Burke and Hare. C'mon, Hare, let's check out the remains at my house."

But at Freya's, before they could touch the crock, she insisted on a ceremony. Freya had Grace stick ten, tall, white candles into two candelabras and light them while Freya opened and poured dark-amber mead into silver wine-goblets. The wiped clean crock was set on a cream linen tablecloth on Freya's dining room table with the flaming candelabras standing sentry on each side. Then Freya handed Grace a cold goblet. "We must toast Elijah, Rebecca, Eli, and the soldiers that suffered and died for our freedom. May your spirits rest easily now, your ransom has been found!"

With Freya, Grace took a long, bracing sip of the

sweet, pungent alcohol.

Then Freya pronounced. "That crock is an important Revolutionary War archeological artifact. Maybe even a historic site itself! We have to document all stages of opening it up."

Impatient to just get this done Grace asked, "You have a camera?"

"Somewhere..." Freya looked about in the large hutch, but impatience overwhelmed her. "Does your cell phone take pictures?" Borrowing Grace's phone, Freya began by photographing the crock from all sides, or as Grace called it *'documenting our crime,'* then after kitchen knives failed to pry the lid off, Freya spread thick newspapers under the crock and then got some carpenters' wedges and a wooden mallet from her shed.

Two hundred years gave up slowly, but Freya and then Grace took turns chipping little pieces of the black sealing away while heating the tar with flames from Freya's bar-be-que fire lighting wand until they finally managed to slip a wedge tip under the crock lip and jack it open.

Inside it was filled to the brim with something soft gray that was once fabric, but now was cracked and crumbled like stale saltines. "Residue of a leather bag?" Freya guessed.

Again a photograph was taken, and then with trembling fingers, Freya reached in. The first item out was a heavy onyx stoned gold ring. "Grace, try it on."

She tried. "It's a man's ring–way, way too big on me."

"Maybe it'll fit Mac?" Freya started to lift a long, yellowed bead necklace, but the rotted stringing gave way, and the monkey-faced carved beads cascaded back into the crock. Freya lifted up a bead and studied it closely. "Rebecca's prized necklace. Ivory, probably carved in Africa."

Soon on the newspaper and tablecloth, Freya began lining up gold French guineas, Irish farthings, and three pewter Continental dollars. Grace tried her hand at dipping out treasure and added a Celtic cape pin in bronze and blackened silver buttons. A stiff, white silk scarf still wrapped around two fist fulls of women's jewelry: Sapphire necklace, emerald rings, bracelets, obviously from a wealthy woman.

"Long Liz's contribution to saving her nephew," Freya said reverently, lifting that out, they both saw something the bottom, gleaming in the light, coiled like a snake. Freya reached in. "Gold chain?"

"Real gold?" asked Grace.

"From the weight, I would say so." She and Grace both started to carefully lift out thirty inches of rectangular links, and then they saw the massive gold cross dangling from it, its carbuncle polished rubies still flamed in the dining room's lights.

Freya took the cross and placed it between her palms, closing her eyes.

"What are you doing?" Grace asked.

"Psychometry. Feeling vibrations to get mental images from an object that has been worn or used closely by a person. Metal works best. Some sensitives use hair." She breathed deeply for a minute, then said, "This cross is ancient." She paused again. "This is not an English made piece."

"Age and origin, you could guess that by the design," Grace pointed out. "That's not really a psychic attribution..."

Freya did not open her eyes. "Grace, please!"

Grace fell silent.

Freya continued. "An elderly woman cherished this piece her whole life after her Grandfer had given to her the last time she ever saw him. Gave it to her before she traveled by sail to the new world. Grace, she left her family knowing she'd never see them again. This cross was her only treasure and comfort, but she gave it up for her grandson, to buy him back from hell.

"The cross is far older." Freya continued. "A priest–high in the true Church—very devout. He is old and infirm, but he comes aboard a ship to bless its venture...a galleon to save the souls of the people of England from damnation. There's a storm. He prays desperately, but to no avail.

"Then I see people on shore, watching with open joy as the storm wrecks the ships. As foreign sailors and soldiers drown. Ships sent to invade them, the Spanish Armada." Freya squeezed her eyes harder and was silent for a long time. Then in a dreamy voice, Freya spoke again. "The stones–pigeon's blood rubies–they were returned to Spain. Plunder from a crusade." She opened her eyes, studied the stones and spoke normally. "Originating from the Balkans, I think."

Then Freya's eyes closed again as she still fingered the cross. "But the gold...the gold is far older. A relic from the new world! I see bare-limbed Indians bringing offerings to their Lord. Gold on a platter with bundles of long, green feathers for Lord Inca, a descendant of the Sun. Gold, the blood of the sun, the Inca's workmen cast and polished a chest piece, for the living God...

"Then the Spanish soldiers came...the gold was ripped away, shipped to Spain. Melted down by a Jewish smith in Castile. Heretic gold, purified by fire for the Holy Church." Freya opened her eyes and hands to stare at the cross in total awe.

Grace thought about it. "I don't know if metallurgy could trace melted gold to Peru, but it might be able to. I'm sure the workmanship and design could date the cross to pre-Revolutionary times, possibly Spanish, but I've never heard of a Spanish colonist family in Revolutionary Oyster River

Harbor? I don't know how that cross could have gotten here from Spain?"

Freya just smiled at her gently. "It'd be fun to test for the origin of the metal and the gems, and it would be interesting to have the design checked out. Still like your theories, sometimes proof is hard if not impossible, but Grace, I don't need your tests. I **know** where the cross was forged, who suffered and died for it. I've seen the old woman who treasured it through the long, cold New England winters, as she wept for her family left behind. I saw all of it in a vision."

Grace wanted to avoid arguments at times like this. "Well, even with just the coins and stones," she said surveying the magnificent ransom. "I think you will be able to repay what Penny stole and have enough left over for your Pirate Cruise to the Caribbean!"

Chapter 30

Back happily in her laboratory, Grace answered an e-mail from Brian Kancir with a question on their study of the lobster slime derived skin regenerator. *Affiliated Technologies* would either drop it here or go to contract for further investigations, either way, she and Kurt had done a remarkable study that had given *Affiliated* some positive results for their money. The study had only really been undertaken to give Kurt and Grace a way to keep Bobby working when the last ORR Head of Research had fired him. Grace noted that so far, the volatile Bobby had managed to feed Huang's ego. It seems being a father of three dampened his quick temper a bit. Hearing the door open behind her, Grace didn't even bother to look up, until she heard a woman's voice behind her.

"Grace, you are always so immersed in your work."

She turned to see Deborah Forbes standing there. As usual, Deborah was casually, but expensively dressed, today in lime green silk with a sparkly, bronze-stoned, arrow-shaped necklace that coiled around her neck. But where the coifed, dyed-blonde hair and fashionable green-shaded prints should have signaled youth, the heavy lines in Deborah's face showed her maturity. Had she suddenly aged, or had Grace just never seen her in such poor light before?

"Have you heard from Jack Stuart?" Deborah was asking. "He hasn't answered my calls."

"I got an e-mail from him..." Grace started.

Deborah cut her off as she took out a cigarette. "I did too! He thinks he can recover some of my money that Eve stole."

"Not stole as much as just lost," Grace said, just wanted to get back to her work, but she felt she had to defend Eve. "Maybe it was just poor investment judgment."

As Deborah's face hardened, she looked even older.

"Eve was a thief, and you know it! We all trusted her." Her bitterness trailed off, and she seemed to be making an effort for lightness today. "But I'm not here for that! As directors of Oyster River Research, we've got to get together and go forward.   All the plans we made, well, now there's no funding for them so we'll have to start from the beginning again. The Board needs a new director to replace Eve, and the loss of *Our Sister's* funding has to be made up. We have to reconcile Huang's needs with yours."

"And Kurt's," Grace reminded.

Deborah smiled with tight, thin lips at that, as she lit her cigarette. "And Fritzie Wilshsuen. What I am proposing is another conference on my yacht, *The Merry Widow*."

Grace shook her head. "That doesn't sound like a good idea..."

"Huang has agreed.   He has an anti-seasickness prescription, and since Oyster River is so marine connected, as Head of Research he wants to go with the flow..."

She didn't want this. "Would this be during working hours?"

"Adam had trouble with that too, but we have so much to work out, and Huang is pushing Adam a lot. You know, how Adam loves being on the water, and if I get him out on a boat like last time, he 'll really be in an amenable mood for all of our proposals."

Tired of this waste time, Grace said slowly, "Can't you hold this without me?"

"No, no I can't!" Deborah stopped to order her argument. "We need your clear, direct mind, and you'll be the one there lobbying for science and Kurt and Fritzie. It's only going to be the two of us fighting for them now. Kurt has refused to come, he says he must be out in the water doing salinity tests all day so, Grace, I need you! How about tomorrow at noon?" Deborah was pleading.

Grace shook her head. "That's going to lose me

another half a day. I just can't..."

Deborah held up two fingers to halt Grace. "Alright, I think I can get the others to agree to six p.m. I'll make sandwiches for dinner, and Adam can sail a bit. We'll anchor at sunset, and then we can plan out Oyster River's new agenda. See, it will be after your work day is done?"

Actually, it wouldn't be, but Grace wanted to get this over with. "Fine. If we can just talk as soon as possible and keep the socializing and sailing to the minimum?"

"That's what I had in mind." Even though Grace wished she would leave, Deborah continued to talk quietly. "We have to focus on your funding, so you can continue to keep probing with that magnificent mind of yours, just as you always do, Grace. Maybe we should start planning now." Deborah stared down at her with a narrowing eyes that actually made Grace feel like a sea slime specimen under a microscope.

To get her to go, Grace stood up. "Actually, I was just about to leave...I have an appointment." For a moment, she thought Deborah planned to just stay in her lab, but the woman was waiting to walk out with her, so Grace had to actually lock up. Now, she was outside with her fanny pack and Deborah, still in the parking lot, so Grace walked to her station wagon. She did have an errand that needed running. Jack Stuart's e-mail had talked vaguely about perhaps still being able to get some funding for her behavioral project from an industrialist friend. Could he?

Where was this *Windswept* place? From her car Grace called Abe and had him look up the address in his bookstore, so soon she was on a road that paralleled the water past Cos Cob headed for Greenwich. Some original fishermen's houses still there, but mainly all she saw were gated estates, most of them shielded from prying eyes by seven-foot-fences and old oak trees.

The *Windswept* estate had a whitewashed, seven-foot

high brick wall with a two-story gatekeepers cottage built in, but the six-foot-tall, wrought iron ornamental gates were just swinging open. Grace drove in, seeing a wide stretch of green lawn perfectly mowed. Ahead was house perched on the top of a small knoll, or did it only look small, because of the huge size of the mansion?

Apparently, this was the back side, because the driveway took her around to the 'front,' a two-story central portion with a long porch, that wrapped from one one-story wing to another. The pale-blue clapboard house looked like a giant bird just resting, before it took off to fly across the green waters of the Sound ahead of it. Grace got out of her car and walked to the entrance. Parked in front of the double doors, Jack's silver Jaguar convertible's seat and trunk were overflowing with suitcases and boxes. The man himself came out carrying a briefcase and large, black laptop bag. He looked surprised to see her.

"Are you leaving?" Grace asked.

"Leaving? No." He always seemed to spend time thinking before he spoke. "Well, am I leaving here. Yes, I've managed to sub-let this albatross of a house." He looked up at it and then the car. "I've already returned Eve's Jaguar to the rental agency, and this one will be next." He touched the smooth iridescent silver polish. "Actually, I'll miss it, it was fun driving." He placed the laptop on top of the stuff in the passenger seat. "But I'm getting a much more practical hybrid rental to replace it, with four-wheel drive for the mining sites. And I'm moving to a hotel suite to run *Alcom* from." He looked at the estate around them. "Eve felt founding *Our Sisters* in *Windswept* would give us an even footing with wealthy donors in this area, and easy access to finances that would have increased our efforts. Since I thought we had enough money from *Alcom*, I didn't see why not, but now *Our Sisters* is going to have to be moth-balled while I get back to the core business. Mining, that's where

I've always made my money."

She was kind of sad to see him leaving. "How will we know where to reach you? I mean David and Adam and the others?"

He looked down at her with those intense brown eyes. "Actually, I don't care much about the others. My lawyers will be keeping in touch with them, while I see what can be salvaged and repaid." He stopped again, still staring at her. "But personally I was going to give you my address as soon as I settled somewhere." He stopped awkwardly. "I'm not a billionaire anymore, but I really want to keep seeing you..."

"I'd like that," Grace said sincerely.

He smiled and again she was stunned by what a truly handsome man he was, as Jack continued. "Then let's make it a date when I get back. Grace Farrington, how about sandwiches at...Chez MacDonalds?"

He didn't even seem to be trying, but again Grace felt her body responding to the full force of his animal magnetism. "Hot dogs at my condo sounds better."

He smiled gently. "Yes, I'd like that too."

In the meantime, Grace realized he had a mansion to clear out. "Can I help you move today?"

He looked at her. "Move?"

"To your hotel suite."

"Actually,... it's all done. The courts have already subpoenaed all of Eve's *Alcom* and *Our Sister's* records to try to straighten out the missing money situation, so they're gone. As for the house itself, all the furniture here was rented, and the company has already picked it up. All of Eve's personal possessions I had donated to the hospital consignment shop, so," he looked at the boxes and luggage in his small sports car and said, "This is about it."

With him looking so forlorn with his few possessions, she didn't want to just leave him. "So let's go to your hotel, I'll help you settle in. Do they have a restaurant there for lunch?"

"Room service," he said, then stopped. "But, I hadn't booked that suite yet. I won't need it until I get back."

"Get back?"

He stopped again, and spoke slowly as usual. "From Ontario."

"Canada?" That seemed a world away to Grace.

"I'm flying out today to check some leased sites *Alcom* has. See if they're worth developing in the short term. I think one of them might just work out to something big,...don't tell David and the others what I'm doing, it might raise unwarranted hopes." He looked back at her. "But it won't be long until I'm back, and maybe, if you don't mind, we could develop something on a personal level." He laughed shaking his head at his own ineptness. "That sounds so awkward. So business like..."

"No, it doesn't. I'll miss you," she said sincerely.

He held with those intense eyes. "Not as much as I'll miss you, Grace. I–we've just met, but I feel like we just should be together." He took her into his arms, kissing her hard and long. "We will be after I get things straightened out." He pressed her hands one more time, and then he turned and got into his car.

As he drove away, she stood there feeling empty and disappointed, she needed him, needing more. Since Grace first saw Jack, she'd had a kind of schoolgirl fantasy about him, about what his kisses would be like, the touch of his hands, and his bear crushing hug. Before sleep, Grace actually had fantasies of what it would be like to be in bed with such a magnificent man, but now somehow, it all felt a little hollow.

David Gardiner's protective pressure against her arm as he guided her into a restaurant, and Kurt's swat at her behind while they were varnishing the deck of his sailboat...those felt real. Something about Jack was too perfect, to godly to be true, and as his power car pulled down the driveway, she was left with that '*where did all the good stuff go*' feeling she always got from eating pink-cotton candy.

She hadn't had lunch, so Grace stopped in Oyster River and walked to *Haunts of Wōden*. Freya was inside her new age shop, frantically scribbling with a red pen into a loose-leaf book. She looked up joyously. "Grace! I just started the first draft of my new book, '*Oyster River's Haunted Ransom*'!" With no customers in the shop, Freya had spread loose leaf papers all across her glass counter with printouts of her family tree, photos of the Prison Ship memorial statue in Brooklyn, and some prints of the treasure photos. Freya was frowning. "Penny never got around to telling me where Long Liz and Seth were buried or those dates she promised of her family tree, of course, we know the reason for that."

"Don't you think she was lying about it all?"

"No." Freya looked over her papers. "So she stretched the relationship with Long Liz a bit, but I think most of the facts she gave me about the 1700's Penelope was true. The insider stuff Penny knew about, the ransom, Long Liz's life after Oyster River, that could have only come from tales passed down through family. As far as I know, no one has ever seen anything in print about Long Liz's donating her jewels, so Penny had information that could have only come from a source very close to Elizabeth Dell Booth."

Grace nodded. "By the DNA, Penny was descended from Posey, Long Liz's slave."

"Yes, and in a way, I could see how Posey felt she was Long Liz's adopted daughter and entitled to the treasure. I'm going to put Posey, Henry, and any of their descendants I can find in my family tree as '*adopted.*' Don't tell Mac, he's still furious that Penny ripped me off."

"Freya, she stole your van."

"I got that back!"

"And your credit cards, and that fancy metal detector you still have to pay on..."

"I took two of those gold ransom coins, which turned out to be rare Elizabethan coinage, and I sold 'em for the money to pay for the metal detector and everything that Penny cost me. Had money left over to replace the van's transmission, and I even saved one gold coin for Penny's share, if she ever comes back."

Her friend was so hopeless! "Oh, Freya, you expect Penny back?"

"Not really," Freya admitted. "But she seemed most interested in the coins Liz had donated to the ransom. If she ever shows up, the numismatist I consulted said he thought that coin might be worth quite a lot, if she wanted to sell it."

"After car theft, false identity, unauthorized use of credit cards, and your stolen jewelry from the display cases, I don't think you'll be hearing from her soon." Then thinking about it, Grace continued, "The rest of Elijah's treasure, you're going to get your trip to the Caribbean right?"

Freya's face lit up with a bright sunshine smile. "Oh, that pirate cruise, you, me and Mac on that white sand beach with the turquoise water—that would have been wonderful." She stopped, and the golden smile faded from her face as she continued, "but I've already donated the rest of the Oyster River ransom to the Whalers Museum."

"No! Freya, you work so hard—you need the money!" Grace objected.

Freya held up a hand. "Don't lecture, I've got my cop son for that! And I've already donated it! Well, I kinda fudged where we found it, claimed it was buried on my property near where Christopher worked on the chimney. Otherwise we'd have had all sorts of problems with the Cemetery Trustees. And I also only put three of the ivory monkey head beads back for the display. The rest, I'm restringing for myself with onyx bead separators. There's over thirty of them, a gift from Rebecca, my great–whatever–grandmother.

"And the onyx stoned man's ring fits Mac perfectly." Freya's eyes unfocused at bit. "I think it had a connection to Elijah or his father." Then back in the real world again, she said calmly, "The rest really belongs to the townspeople of Oyster River Harbor, who originally raised the ransom." She reached under the counter and lifted out a silver chain with a dollar sized coin holder pendant, enclosing something blackened silver. "It's one of the Spanish coins from the crock. It's been circulated but is still in very good condition. Your reward for finding the hoard."

Accepting that her friend just threw away a fortune, Grace took the necklace from her. "It's beautiful."

Freya continued, "As a silver intact '*Pieces of Eight,*' with a documented story, it could be worth a new car for you?"

"I'd rather wear it," Grace said, slipping it around her neck. "Thank you."

Freya's face darkened, her voice dropped down a tone. "Grace, I selected a silver coin instead of gold for you because silver is the metal of protection. Remember that vision I had of you buried...dying? That feeling is still around you." Freya seemed to be trying to shake herself out of it, but couldn't. "Please wear the silver, and think a white light about yourself for protection, and be careful! I know you think it's silly, but please for me!"

Chapter 31

The next day, she got into her lab before dawn, because she planned a full ten hours of working before having to do that wasteful director's cruise bit. Hours later, satisfied she had gotten a lot done with her regular work, Grace decided to take a further look at the results from Kurt's sailboat. Nick had prepared and uploaded all the samples that she, Inger, and he had extracted from *The Lovely Lady's* upholstery. Two fish blood, one slime, a non-DNA stain, and three human samples. Nick listed them as all from one subject, with the best being OR50362, so Grace began screening with the OR00362 genetic profile. Human female. Was it Eve Dupree? It might or might not be as Kurt had a lot of female traffic on his boat.

Grace looked at the DNA readout, valleys climbing to peaks. Suddenly a shock that was almost electric ran through her body. Something matched in her mind that shouldn't. Grace scanned quickly through her profiles, finally pulling up OR50358. Holding her breath, she keyed instructions into the computer and the two profiles overlaid on the screen. Actually, it was hard to see an overlay since the ascending and descending blue and red lines were mostly on top of each other. Oh, the twenty-third chromosome was completely different, but, of course, that was to be expected.

It was the rest that blew Grace's mind away. Chromosome four, fifteen copies of gene three–a perfect match. Loci after loci in common, the blue and red graphing lines overlaid more than they separated. She removed OR50358 from the screen and started a more detailed analysis on OR50362. As she suspected this sample, like Freya and Elijah would have genetic inheritance including Scandianian ancestry, that would explain hair and eye color most likely.

She closed that profile and reopened OR50358. Grace decided to a geographic study first, then to look at the genes for hair and the three for eye color. As she suspected OR50358 came up with Scandinavian ancestry too, which explained fair skin, but not the mixture of dark hair. Well, the Vikings had invaded the British Isles, and there were dark-haired, tanned skinned 'Black Danes.' Still, Grace looked at the gene patterns more closely and noticed a configuration for hair that should have manifested differently.

Doing a full study could take months, but she could do a did a fast run for a major genetic mutation that caused a specific disease. But there was something she wanted to check on OR50362. Yes, as she suspected, nothing she could prove without further samples, say from the autopsy of a resulting Edwards Syndrome afflicted infant, but it looked to her like OR50362 would have a definite susceptibility to Trisomy 18, that would have increased with maternal age.

She cross-checked. On the 18th chromosome, OR50358 also had the same look about the gene linkage. A coldness flooded Grace. She knew what she was seeing on the screen, but emotionally, she couldn't accept it, but now she understood why Eve Dupree had to die.

She needed to call Mac or somebody. Did she have the business card of one of those State detectives? But explaining the significance of the synchronized sequencing to the police would take time. Hell, explaining chromosomes to the police would take time, and she didn't really want to make an accusation so bald, so damning until she had to run more tests, accumulated more confirming data.

But she was pretty sure what those tests would show!

The phone rang, breaking her revery. Before she could even answer, the voice was calling out, "Grace? It's Deborah."

"Yes?" Grace answered still absorbed in studying her screens.

"It's really late, dear." Deborah sounded highly aggravated. "We were supposed to sail at 6:00. Now we won't get on the water to until after 7:00."

That stupid sailboat meeting, she'd forgotten all about it. "This isn't...

Deborah cut her off. "You must come! You've agreed. I know you hate meetings, but you have to do your share! I'm waiting for you at the dock with Huang."

"Another day..."

Deborah's voice lowered as if she didn't want someone to overhear. "I'm not supposed to tell you this, but Huang is pressuring Adam to fire Kurt MacKay."

"He can't–Kurt's got a contract!"

"Kurt's mixed up in a murder, and there is a morals clause in all your contracts. You must come with me, and together we can get behind Kurt and save his job!"

Reluctantly Grace closed her screens and grabbed up a jacket as she headed to the dock. Deborah had anchored the zodiac dingy and was smoking a cigarette on land, while she waited impatiently for Grace. As Deborah herded her down to Huang, Grace automatically looked to the empty slip where Kurt's lobster yawl was normally docked. She was a little saddened to see his boat was out on the harbor. If his job was on the line, Grace wanted to talk to him, but an irritable Deborah was ushering her toward the zodiac. "We're running late."

"Kurt should be at this meeting." Grace could see him moored across the Harbor.

Firmly Deborah said, "Kurt has agreed with me, that with his antagonism to Adam and Huang, you and I should be speaking for him!"

Great. That left her one against two, or three probably. Grace could see Huang standing on the dock above the floating dingy, with a bright, new navy jacket with white yachting pants and sneakers. His anti-seasickness pills seemed to have mellowed him, and he gave Grace an ingratiating smile. "Fine day to be on the water. A fine day for cooperation!"

Wanting to punch him out, Grace just smiled back. With Grace holding him from the dock and Deborah's helping hands inside the dingy, Huang managed to climb aboard, then Grace threw the tie lines aboard and climbed in herself.

As Deborah guided the dingy's little--nearly silent--electric motor, she made a comment that seemed odd to Grace. "Dear Grace, always so smart, I can never seem to keep up with you." Saying that Deborah smiled brilliantly at her, but Grace had the feeling that she was being mocked.

Adam was already on board *The Merry Widow,* but Grace expected more of the directors, it was only the four of them. Well, Adam always looked more relaxed and happy when he was on the water, and he looked better than Grace had seen him looking for weeks. Could he actually be firing Kurt? She wanted to let him get in the best mood possible before that came up. They sailed for about an hour on the Sound, then returned to the sheltered harbor, just as the sun lowered behind the trees. Deborah pushed a button to drop the anchor in deep water, opposite the rocky point of Oyster River Research's peninsula.

The sailing had cheered Adam up, and Huang seemed to be doing well on his seasickness prescription, so when they went below to sit in the main cabin, they all started agreeing on projects to be funded. Deborah let them talk as she busied about the cabin's small kitchen, getting the men drinks, putting out chips, avocado dip, and citrus shrimp. Great, because Grace hadn't remembered to eat lunch or supper. Nibbling shrimp, she waited for the subject of Kurt's firing to come up, but they were starting on the coming student year teaching assignments.

Deborah announced they should work out a year's schedule, and then a new five-year plan without *Our Sisters* funding. Boring, but it had to be done sometime, might as well be done now. Still, Grace found her mind going back to the consequences of those two DNA profiles. It only meant one thing, but how could she explain it to the police?

Deborah asked, "Anyone need a drink before I come back below? I may have to move the boat. Otherwise, we'll be slipping into the channel current as the tide goes out."

Grace looked up. "Do we need to help you?"

Deborah just gave a trilling laugh. "This ship is made to be run by one person. Everything winches electrically, while I'm furling the sails and lowering anchor, I can even smoke my cigarette."

Huang only wanted Adam to tell him, "Where do my travel symposium money come from?"

"How many do you want?" Adam asked.

Grace found herself thirsty, she looked over, but Deborah had gone up on deck closing the double hatchway doors to keep them from being bothered by the sounds of the engine. Still, Grace felt confined. Well, at least she could get herself some ginger ale and move a bit.

She got up and walked to the galley, just under the hatchway doors, and found a green bottle in the cabinet. With the sun setting it was so dark in here, she pushed a button for the overhead light. Why had Deborah closed the hatch doors? With only closed portholes, it was getting dark and stuffy in here. Grace opened up another cabinet and pulled out a squat glass. Ginger ale? Or would orange juice give her more staying power? She had to pay attention because Huang always seemed to be trying to tip the planning in favor of his projects, and Grace didn't understand why Kurt's dismissal hadn't come up yet? In fact, Adam seemed to be writing him right into the budget.

Bored, her mind wandered to her DNA. When she got back on land, Grace was going to do a full work up on OR50362. As she poured the foaming soda, Grace idly looked out the round, glass port near her. Smooth harbor water had been turned to molten gold by the last rays of the setting sun. There was a small boat silhouetted on the waves, and with a start, Grace recognized it as *The Merry Widow's* dingy. It was free of the ship. Actually, Deborah with her back turned from them was motoring away in it.

Adam and Huang were still at the table, scribbling out schedules and publicity releases. Grace looked to the hatchway, its double doors were closed, so she moved to it and pushed at its polished teak boards. The split doors didn't smoothly swing out in unison as they should have. Grace looked for a counter to put down her glass and tried again, pushing with both hands. The two doors should have just swung up, but they didn't. "**Adam!**" God–her voice sounded frightened–but she felt trapped. "I can't open this door! Please help me!"

"It's stuck? Damn mugginess," Adam grumbled, as he came over to help her. "The wood keeps swelling." He was pushing with two hands against the wood. It wasn't moving. "This must be jammed. Maybe something on the other side... **Deborah!**" Adam yelled.

"Deborah's out in the dingy! Look out the..." Before she could finish, Grace smelled something, a smell terrifying on a boat. "Smoke and gasoline?"

"Help me!" Adam commanded, heaving his weight against the door. "Huang!"

Adam was using his shoulder, and Grace was pushing with all her might when the sound of the explosion shook them. The hatch seemed to bounce but stayed solidly closed. It was the boat itself that started to tip, rolling, as it slanted downwards from the stern. The carpeted deck they were standing on was now at a fifteen-degree angle. An angle that steepened as they started to slide downwards. Horrible groans, hissing, and twisting came from the ship as cold seawater water flooded up from the flooring. They were rolling over and sinking.

Adam grabbed her arm. "Toward the bow!"

But with the floor becoming a wall as the *Widow* rolled, cold water poured in under pressure, and Grace found she was falling to her knees against what used to be a bulkhead. Water rapidly rose outside the portholes, and to her horror, Grace saw the last gleams of golden sunset disappeared under murky green water as they sank out of reach.

Chapter 32

The electric lights failed with the motor blowing up. Total darkness. Grace couldn't walk against the water pressure pushing her off her legs. She felt hard, flotsam painfully hitting her face and body as she sank under water, swallowing a salty mouthful. Someone yanked at her arm. It was Adam pulling her up into the air. Grace choked then painfully bumped on what felt like a table floating in the water. Adam was pulling them towards what Grace knew to be the masters cabin in the bow. An air pocket.

They could breathe for a while–until they used up their oxygen and the water rose to drown them. Grace had to stop thinking like that, but bobbing in the cold darkness, she felt she was blind and being buried alive. Grace reached to the silver chain around her neck, feeling Freya's lucky coin. A lot of good that had done her! Yet just fingering the warm, rough silver gift of a friend, gave Grace a feeling of Freya's endless, loving protection. Touching the coin leached away some of her terror, giving Grace a chance to think.

She hit something plastic with her foot. In the other compartments, there had been emergency battery flashlights, plugged into outlets on the bulkheads. "I'm getting something under the water." She told Adam, and he let go of her. Using her arms, she pushed herself down, hooking her feet under something sticking out, which was hard with the water wanted to push her back up. With her palms flat Grace frantically spread them along the brocade-covered wall, her lungs were bursting for air, but she felt it, a flashlight still in its bracket! She pulled it free and then bobbing back into their air bubble. Breathing deeply Grace felt for the plastic slide and switched the blessed light on.

She didn't know if the darkness was more terrifying than the sight before them. Their air bubble ended just above her breasts and the men's shoulders. In the yellow light, the water had an oily sheen with an effluent smell that sickened her. Fuel oil? They might not die by drowning or aspiration; with a pounded spark, they might roast alive in an explosive fire.

"I demand to be rescued immediately!" Huang stated loudly.

Both Adam and Grace just looked at him, water dripped from the parquet floor that was now their ceiling.

Adam reached for the flashlight. "Let me see if I can wedge it up there."

Something above painfully reverberated as it bounced against the outer hull. Grace looked for some tool to help them break out. Was there a fire ax? Adam was just watching Huang. Another fish or rock hit the hull, but they didn't seem to be descending anymore or could she tell?

"Can we break through the hull? She asked Adam.

Adam kicked underwater, and then using his hands he ripped a corner of the fancy paneling away. Helping him, Grace pulled with all her might, until they had peeled back it back. In the flashlight, Grace saw that it was gray hull. "Metal?"

"Probably carbon fiber–monocoque hull---might as well be steel," Adam said.

Pounding, resounding against the hull. Grace looked at Adam. "A fish?"

Adam shook his head, as he was looking all around desperately.

Grace prompted, "There were portholes?"

Adam shook his head. "Not helpful..."

"Before the ship blew up, I saw Deborah abandoning ship in the dingy. She might be getting help?" murmured Grace, not really believing it.

"That hatch was deliberately jammed." Adam still looked about, but his expression was growing more hopeless.

"There was an explosion." Her ears were still ringing from it. "It must have been heard throughout the harbor. Someone would have looked up and seen *The Merry Widow* sinking."

Huang just wrapped himself up in a ball, at the highest point of the bow.

Adam spoke slowly. "They'd see a ship to the South sinking, but even if they had been looking right at us, they still could only point in the general direction of the center of the harbor. They won't be able to tell the Coast Guard much."

"With a plane..."

"We might not be too deep to be seen from above, but since the sun has set, they won't send out a plane in the dark."

"Then we have to break out ourselves out." She looked about, why wasn't Adam moving? They can't give up!

Two loud bangs resounded against the hold.

Adam looked up puzzled. "What in the hell is that?"

Another bang. A measured silence. Then another echoing bang.

Grace tried to remember. "Universal distress, SOS. Morse code. Is it three short–three long-three short? Or three long, three short, three long?"

Adam looked up. "Three dots–three dashes–three dots."

"How do you bang out a dash?" Asked Grace.

Looking around desperately, Adam had grabbed a floating chair. He used it to pound against the bulkhead, methodically. Three bumps. A spacing. Three double bumps, a spacing then a steady three bumps. An agonizing wait...then Adam started again.

When he stopped, they listened. Water dripped from the floor that was now their ceiling, splashing around their shoulders. Then from outside came fast, steady bangs, spaced in groups of three, nine altogether.

Huang looked up. "Tell them in bang code I want out of here!"

Still a steady pounding from the top, but another pounding. Below her feet, was there a greening of the water? "I'm diving." Grace took a deep breath, then jackknifed into the water. The salt burned her eyes which were nearly useless in the dark, but ahead she could see a faint light coming in from one of the portholes.

With numb fingers, Grace grabbed at the smooth brass porthole, desperately struggling to open it. Someone with an underwater flashlight was outside. Her lungs felt tight, and she needed air. She took her knuckles and banged frantically on the glass, but the sound she made was small, muffled by the water and her knuckles hurt.

Vainly she clawed at the porthole—it wouldn't open. Grace tried kicking it, but she was floating up again. She pulled on the brass trim both hands, dragging her face against the porthole and sticking it against the flat, unyielding glass. Even if she couldn't see them, they might see her. Should she lose more air and mouth that they were trapped? Hell, whoever was out there knew that! Grace pulled back. The silhouette of a large, male hand waved across the light outside.

Her lungs nearly bursting, Grace reluctantly let go and bobbed back up into the air pocket.

Sucking air, she choked out, "Adam! We're saved!"

Surprisingly he didn't look reassured.

"Down by the porthole, I saw a light. A hand. I'm sure he saw me, but we've got to get the porthole open!" Her excitement was causing her to shake.

Huang shouted, "Me first! I escape first!" He looked at Adam. "This is understood! I am the most valuable to Oyster River Research!"

Grace looked from that idiot to Adam. "I can't force the porthole open alone. Adam, if we both pulled at it?"

"The pressure outside will be holding it down," he said in a flat, emotionless voice.

They had a chance to live, and he was just floating there, explaining physics to her? What the hell was the matter with him? "But if we both tried." She looked to Huang, "If two strong men tired?" Huang had curled himself in the corner, back in almost a fetal position.

She could hear more bangs as if someone was kicking at the hull way below them. Grace took a deep breath and tried to plead her case calmly. "Adam, we both have to try together. We can open that porthole!"

He looked at her pityingly. "Grace, those portholes are only for decoration and sunlight. They probably have never been opened."

"But if we could smash it open, maybe we could escape through it!" Grace hated that she sounded like a desperate, babbling fool.

Adam continued in that flat voice, comfortless voice. "Those portholes are approximately twelve inches in diameter, and even a woman as thin as you couldn't get your shoulders through."

He was right. Why hadn't she realized it? Panic? Okay, there was manic bangings down below against the hull. Should they bang back? Adam followed her gaze. "This boat is stern down. We seemed to be trapped in an air bubble at the bow."

"If they can break the hull?"

"*The Merry Widow* was constructed for rough, ocean seas. If they had an acetylene torch outside, maybe they could cut their way into us if we didn't fry first."

"If we could swim to the stern..."

"Where the hatch is locked? Before the ship sank, the two of us couldn't break that hatch open."

"If we could swim down and press at the hatch, the outside people could help us..."

"We wouldn't have air to swim to the bow, escape, and swim up. We'd drown before we reached the surface."

She was dying, and that idiot was dispassionately giving facts, facts that a part of Grace's mind knew were correct, but she just couldn't give up! "Somebody knows we're here. They will call the Coast Guard. Get a rescue ship, with an acetylene torch."

Adam sounded like he pitied her. "Grace, how long will it take for them to get here?"

How long? "There is a town police boat in the harbor."

"A glorified zodiac, with a few life preservers and fire extinguishers? It's after dark now, how long to get real rescue equipment?"

Huang began to quietly sob in the corner. For his benefit, Grace said, "They are working on freeing us–shortly."

Adam relentlessly continued. "Our air bubble is decreasing. I've tried to mark a line on the bulkhead, but the ship keeps tilting, distorting the water level. With this small air pocket and the three of us breathing, I think we've got less than twenty minutes of air."

There must be something they could do! Grace quietly asked, "How deep are we?"

"I estimate we sank for fifty or so seconds before we reached neutral buoyancy. We will sink farther, as we use up the air bubble. Or drift into the channel current–which will wash us out to sea beyond help."

The banging on the ship's hull had stopped. Had their rescuers just gone away? Maybe they hadn't seen her? Maybe they thought a rescue attempt was too dangerous to their own lives? God, if Huang would just stop crying, she could think! Grace closed her eyes and leaned her head against the wet bulkhead fabric. Should they shut off the flashlight to save the batteries? Why bother? The air would go first.

Adam recited something softly, *"Shema Yisrael, Adonai Eloheinu,*

She should answer him. What was he saying?

" Adonai Echad.

Barukh Shem k'vod malkhuto l'olam va-ed

V-ahavta et Adonai.."

Finally, she recognized what he was saying. A Hebrew prayer.

Did she have any prayers? She had been forced to attend church as a child, but being among groups of people always made her want to run away. Did she believe in God? The people she most admired like Eric Larsen had felt that a belief in an all-powerful being who cared about you personally was illogical, wishful thinking. Still, she never gave it that much thought, and sometimes in the darkest times of her career, Grace had felt that something beyond her ken had helped her, supported her. However, if there were a God counting how many times you attended church or how much you chipped in on the collection plate, he wouldn't be listening to Grace Farrington.

And if this was the end of her life? There was still so much she didn't know and hoped to find out, the total mechanics of how genes created the vast behavior patterns of the animal and plant kingdoms. With her *Popcorn Gene* theory, Grace had famously explained genetically controlled switches, now she desperately wanted to fully understand the mechanics of genetically controlled behavior. And epigenetics, the amazing environmental controlled changes in genes, another world of questions she wanted to study.

Huang was glaring at Adam. "It is your position to do something to save me!"

Adam just ignored him. Then mercifully, both he and Huang were silent.

She never got her Nobel, and they don't award it

posthumously. Never had a husband, but she always thought she might marry someday. David? Kurt? Never had children, but she wouldn't have known how to raise one if she did. Her research studies were her children–her immortality, which seemed pretty empty at this moment. In fact her whole life seemed to have been a failure.

But it hadn't. Her discoveries had contributed immensely to the work of others and would continue to do so! She did have friends: Freya, Bobby, Sara, Gail. Afterward...they would go through her computers and get her recent research. Could Bobby carry it on? Maybe he could publish it for someone else to finish?

Damn, the computer files on the new line of research were passworded. Nobody could access her notes. Why hadn't she gotten a safety deposit box and written all the passwords down? Maybe she could write the passwords on the bulkhead? They might find and raise this hulk and find her body, afterward...after the crabs ate at her. Don't think about that! She had to leave them the passwords. But she didn't have a pen, maybe scratch it out? With a fingernail, she tried scraping the wet brocade, but it just bends her nail. It was getting harder to breathe. Not the lack of air yet, just her panic. Grace closed her eyes, touched her silver necklace, and pictured Freya's early dawn '*ohmmings*' to the sky. Her body relaxed, and Grace opened her eyes.

Bobby could break the password or find someone who could. She should have left all passwords and account numbers in her will. Her only will still had her grandmother as heir because after Grandma had died, she never got around to changing it. No money to leave really, well, there was her personal lab equipment, which was worth quite a bit. That could have been something for her friends, some family jewelry, her car, but not much to leave for a '*successful*' lifetime.

Well, there were the students she'd answered

questions for, they would miss her.

Again heavy banging sounds from below, was the ship drifting? The stern hitting rocks? The water muffled sounds, echoing them strangely like the ringing a wooden bell of doom.

Through the dark water below her, came a rush of small bubbles breaking the surface. Oh, God, was the boat sinking faster?

Chapter 33

Grace saw a murky green light come up from below. The white-lighted tunnel of death ocean style?

A spot-light broke the surface, and its brightness burnt her eyes. A grotesque, inhuman monster face. No-a diver, with a spotlight on his forehead, and a very human face behind a plate and scuba mask– she recognized Kurt MacKay!

Grace pushed forward, off the chair rail, sinking in the water, and kissed his cold glass faceplate.

He pushed it upon his head as breathing heavily Kurt said, "Later, lady."

"There was an accident..." Grace started.

"Wasn't an accident. Had to break free a car locking bar that was holding the main hatchway closed. Somebody set out to kill ya," he said grimly.

The ship shifted again, the water sloshed around them.

Kurt spoke quickly. "She's floating toward the riptide. Gotta get out of here!" He held out his mouthpiece to Grace as he looked at all of them. "All of you, kick your shoes off and anything constricting. Bobby and I have two almost empty air tanks. We'll buddy breathe up. Bobby's outside after I take Grace out, he'll come in and get the next one. Then I'll be back for the last guy. Grace, you'll put the mouthpiece in. Breathe deeply. You'll get some water, jes swallow it. Breathe twice. We swim, and when I tap your shoulder, we stop. You'll take a deep breath, then pass the mouthpiece back to me. After I breathe, I'll pass it back to you. Understand?"

She nodded just wanting to be out of here.

But Huang grabbed the mouthpiece out of Kurt's hand, tightly pulling the airline across Kurt's throat until it looked like it would break.

"Me first!" Huang looked at Adam. "I am most

important! I am a black belt! Save me first!"

Adam looked stunned. Grace realized, that with Huang panicking so badly it might be best to get him out. Grace looked at Kurt, nodding her head. "Him first..."

Kurt ignored all of them, glancing down in the water as he seemed to be moving his feet into a solid position. Braced, he looked back up, hauled back his fist, and punched Huang in the mouth.

Huang screamed, letting the air hose go, and grabbing his face with both hands. There was black nose blood seeping through his fingers, watered down as it dripped over his mouth. Adam swam behind him restraining Huang's arms in a bear hug. "Get the woman out first!"

Kurt rinsed the mouthpiece.

Grace looked at it, "I never learned to scuba!"

"You are now." Kurt forced the mouthpiece between Grace's teeth. "Easy, take a slow breath. Then another. When I tap it, you **must** pass it back to me. Swallow the water. Got that?"

With her mouth painfully plugged, she just nodded.

The ship moved another two degrees. Grace looked up in panic, but Kurt just gave a confident smile. "Lady, I'll be in your bed tonight."

She nodded, kicking her other sneaker free.

"Okay." With her on the tank, he inhaled and exhaled deeply twice in the bubble, and then strong arms were pulling her down. Water closed over her head, and Grace was terrified. With one arm around her, Kurt was swimming downwards, batting floating furniture out of their way, seeing by only the weak illumination from his head spotlight. She pathetically tried to kick to help him as he was now using his other hand to pull part of the boat, pushing them down into the sunken stern. Grace gave a wide kick and painfully hit her shoeless heel against wood. She took smaller kicks next time.

They stopped at the now open hatchway. Another light outside, Bobby? Kurt tapped on her shoulder, she was supposed to take the mouthpiece out and then let it go. Without air–she'd die! Her lungs were closing. She couldn't–Kurt roughly pulled it out of her mouth. Foolishly she opened that mouth to yell and expelled the life-giving air within. Grace locked her jaw shut and tried to swallow the salty water. The boat doors framed blackness as Kurt took his airline back. Then he pushed her out the hatchway.

From outside, someone grabbed her shoulder painfully. It was Bobby, pulling her out. Suddenly she was out of the boat by herself floating free in a terrifying black void with no air. Then Kurt swam beside her and put his warm, hairy arm around her waist. He was pulling the mouthpiece out of his mouth and feeding its bubbles to her. Grabbing the mouthpiece with two hands, she shoved it in, swallowed more water, but she had air.

He gave her a thumbs up, and hand signaled Bobby, who swam into the hatch trailing bubbles. She took desperate breaths, but Kurt was tapping her shoulder again, reluctantly she passed the life-giving mouthpiece back. Then Grace started to swim for her life, but Kurt grabbed her.

He was swimming downwards!

Grace shook her head, twisting away, trying to pull him back.

He locked his arm around her waist and started to kick strongly, ever downwards.

She fought, but he was stronger. The water outside the boat was even colder, and with a lack of oxygen, Grace was weakening. Kurt just kept kicking steadily.

Exhausted by fear and oxygen deprivation, Grace stopped fighting. He was pulling them both down to the dying depths. He'd come to rescue her only to drag her down to die. Maybe it wasn't Kurt–maybe it was a water sprite taking his form, coming to drown her. Maybe this escape was all a nightmare, and she was still dying in the *Widow's* bow, just hallucinating from a lack of oxygen.

Black, black water closing ahead of them—then they were out! Her head was in the air! Kurt was ripping the mouthpiece from her mouth, and she sucked in warm, clean, fresh air. Grace was dazzled by the starry sky, with millions of stars she'd never appreciated before! She just wanted to bob in the waves and look up. Kurt, with his one arm around Grace, hauled her toward the green starboard light of his anchored boat. "C'mon, lady. Ain't gonna lose you here."

"I thought you were pulling us down!"

"Easy to get turned around down below. Now, get hold of that ladder, you gotta climb. My boat is floating free, it's just tied to that diver's buoy that's attached to the *Widow*. If the *Widow* keeps sinking and goes too deep, you'll have to cut the *Big 'Un* free before she sinks too! The knife's in my Jacket's pocket on the deck."

They'd reached the ladder on the side of his lobster yawl. "You're coming too?" She asked, terrified at the answer.

He had already fitted the mouthpiece back in his mouth as Kurt shook his head. He was going down to die! She loved him, she couldn't lose him now! "Kurt–don't go! I'm too weak to climb–help me!"

Giving her a last swat on her behind, he then swam off, getting his hand on the thin, taut rope line off the stern, sinking down with it beneath the cold water.

Weak, but wanting to get out of the water, Grace grabbed the steel rungs of the ladder with both hands. They were even colder than the water as she dragged herself painfully out of the sea. Where she had kicked wood, her bare foot hurt badly, but as she made it on to the bobbing diesel's deck with its weak illumination of red and green running lights.

She limped to the cabin. Besides the throttle and

steering wheel, a ghostly green-lighted scanner screen still held a large yellow blip. The *Widow* below? But it was drifting, almost off the screen. Engine controls, she just wanted to start up and go full speed anywhere but here. No! With numb, uncooperative fingers, Grace fumbled for the radio. It was on the Coast Guard channel. "Coast Guard. We need help!" No response. She looked down, she'd forgotten to release the mike's handset so someone else could talk. Grace released top button.

A crackling voice came over. "Coast Guard. What is your position?"

With wet fingers, Grace pushed in on the handset button. "I'm–a researcher. Researcher of DNA at ORR." *Why the hell were they asking that?* She released.

A professional but exasperated voice crackled back. "Where is the position of your emergency?"

"Oh." Damn. "Uhh–Oyster River Harbor. On the *Big 'Un*." She desperately looked about, where the hell were they? "Off the Research center's point, near the Wilshusen's mansion." She released.

The voice crackled again. "Do you have GPS?"

"Yes. Kurt does. I know he did have." Grace looked at the bewildering clutch of dials and screens. She dropped the mike and then had to fish at the coiled cord to pull it up again. "I don't know how to..."

No answer.

Then she remembered to release the slide on the microphone. Another voice cut in reassuringly familiar. "Grace, this is Ben, town police. We know where you are–Kurt called in the coordinates. Where is Kurt? Grace, remember to release the microphone handset when you finish talking!"

God, it was so good to hear Ben's voice! Grace took a deep, calming breath. "*The Merry Widow* has sunk. Two more trapped aboard. Adam–Adam Greenfield and Huang

Wong. Kurt and Bobby are trying to get them out." She released the microphone.

"It'll be okay, dear. We're a coming. Just hang on," Ben responded.

The screen no longer had the *Widow's* green blip. Her whole body was shaking. It really wasn't that cold, so she must be going into shock. Grace looked around for a blanket or towel. Found nothing. She picked up some cloth on the bottom of the boat. A jacket. Big. Bobby's? She pulled it on, where the hell were they? Why was it taking so long! She needed to help them! The boat was dipping a bit to the side.

Should she cut the buoy line that was pulling at the bow? Not yet, but soon. Grace found Kurt's knife and started searching the boat for another oxygen tank. Bobby must have gone into the *Widow*, if Wong was going crazy, Adam would have said to take him first. But Grace had fought Kurt because she was disoriented and wanted to swim downwards, what if Wong or the stronger Adam did the same with Bobby? In the lights, she could see that small diver's buoy bobbing below the water, pulling the rope tighter...she should cut it, but that would lose the last contact with the *Widow*.

They're drowning, Kurt, Bobby, Adam...

All four of them would die. Grace kept tearing open compartments, looking for another scuba tank or a spotlight, anything that would help. She pulled out a medical kit, and she found three more tanks–all empty.

The sound of water splashing. Grace looked up and ran to the side. She sickened as the boat leaned starboard with her sudden weight, but she could barely make out two heads in the lobster yawl's bow green running light.

Two big heads breaking the water, one with a headlamp. As they swam closer, Bobby's voice called out to her. "Give him a hand up!"

Not taking her help, Adam managed to pull himself aboard. He quickly turned to help Bobby up.

Bobby shook his head. "No, I'm going back to help Kurt!

"You're out of air!" said Adam.

Bobby looked at the gauge. "Must be like a car, when the gas gauge says empty, there'll still be something left." He popped the mouthpiece back in, swam back to the buoy through floating flotsam of plastic cushions, then as he sank, following the line down, his feeble head-lamp was swallowed by dark water.

Grace suddenly knew that she would never see him again, that his three kids were fatherless. What would she tell Sara? Adam was wiping his nose, moving stiffly over to the cabin. He spoke flatly. "Bobby was going to take Huang up first, but our hero has decided he's not leaving the safety of the ship until the Coast Guard comes."

Grace had moved to beside him. Adam was in the cabin checking the fish finder screen, it was just an empty, glowing green. He made some adjustments and seemed to be sweeping a larger area, with some small blips, then he got a hit. Big one.

"The *Widow*?" Grace asked, realizing she had been holding her breath.

"Think so." But just as he had it, the yellow blurb started to slide rapidly off-screen. Adam turned a knob and numbers came on screen. "That boat is shifting and sinking deeper! Faster"

"It's moving away?" asked Grace feeling that terror return.

Adam sounded grim. "The fool's gonna die and take Bobby and Kurt with him. As soon as the wreck drifts into the channel's full current, it will start rolling and really sinking deeper."

"Maybe if I went down..."

"Grace, there's nothing you can do!"

"But if Huang won't leave..."

"Kurt isn't going to spend much time arguing."

"Huang's afraid. Panicking..."

"Remember how Kurt persuaded him to let you go first?"

"Kurt got a sucker punch in, but Huang is a world-class, black belt! He said so. In his curriculum vitae, he said his hands are registered as weapons!"

Adam looked down at her and said drily, "My money is on Kurt Mackay."

Air horn sirens hooting in the darkness, and Grace looked out of the cabin. In the distance, a small figure of the town police boat was cutting through water, white waves at its bow. That would be Sheriff Ben. She could see farther out the rotating blue and red lights up the harbor from the seaward side. The Coast Guard? Would they have diving gear?

But from the darkness, the sound of another boat chugging. Closer. A wood boat with a huge figurehead of a tall, flowing-haired Viking woman at its bow. No figurehead–Freya was at the prow. Freya and Mac were coming!

Adam shouted out to them. "**THREE DIVERS IN THE WATER!**"

Mac cut the engine, still coming in too fast on his momentum. He and Freya grabbed up boat hooks to catch Kurt's craft. Adam was up and hefting one of Kurt's boat hooks.

Freya shouted. "**GRACE**?"

"Here! And Adam!"

They pulled Freya's boat alongside Kurt's boat. Tying the boats together, a joyously Freya shouted. "I've brought hot chowder!"

Like a looney Grace started to laugh uncontrollably. "You had time to fill a thermos?"

"Just pulled the pot off the stove!" Freya said

joyously.

Mac was throwing a line, as Adam asked: "Can you scuba?"

"You got a tank?"

"No."

Mac was pulling off his shoes. "Where are they?"

Adam pointed southeast of the boats, wherein the eerie green light they could see floating debris, an oil slick, and that taut rope attached to its sunken buoy, the *Big 'un's* bow was pulling deeper in the water, to the side. "We got to cut the rope!" Adam said. "Where's Kurt's knife?"

"It will cut the *Widow* free!" babbled Grace but she held out the knife.

"They're either out now–or they aren't getting out." He said climbing forward and, sawing at the rope.

Mac pulled off his shirt, then he jackknifed from his boat. He was gone in a dark wave and splash of gray foam. In the dark water, Grace peered down. Was that feeble light? Or just some luminous jellyfish? Mac couldn't hold his breath long enough to get down to the wreck. The *Big 'Un* bounced up a bit, freed of the *Widow's* dead weight. Grace looked back, to find Freya was gathering up rope attaching it to a life-saving ring. Also useless unless Kurt and Bobby could get Huang out of the ship in time. Huang must be like a horse, desperately seeking security by running back into a flaming barn. Fear does terrible things to the mind. Before she had been afraid that Kurt would leave Huang to die, but if it meant Kurt and Bobby would die with him, Huang Wong could go to hell!

Splashing. A head. A big one. Mac coming up for a breath twenty feet off of the boat. Then he dived again.

The police launch with its red and blue rotating lights was closing. Freya boomed out in her deep, resounding, Wagnerian voice, **"FOUR DIVERS IN THE WATER!"** Ben cut the launch's engine and drifted to the side of Freya's boat. Ben was on the radio, updating the Coast Guard cutter as it closed.

Then quiet. Grace moved back to the sonar scanner. Adam was tying the *Big 'Un* up to Freya's boat, while Freya tied to the police launch on the other side. The sunken *Widow* had drifted off the screen. She tried to center it again like she saw Adam had...finally, Grace got a yellow blip, but it was moving much faster, the current must have caught it. Kurt, Bobby, and Huang were being washed out the channel, beyond anyone's help!

Chapter 34

Splashing. In one porpoise move, Mac surfaced for a breath and dived again.

Then nothing. Just the rocking and groaning rubbing of tied boats. Grace heard chatter on the police radio as Ben's powerful searchlight beam swept over the waves.

Then more foam and splashing. Dark heads, thirty feet off, caught just before the light beam moved on. Grace yelled, "Ben! Move the light back! Back where you were–over there!"

Mac surfaced to the left of them. Freya yelled, "Mac! Port side!"

He swam to the three heads bobbing in the waves. Huang had an air tank on his back, but his head was flopped forward. Bobby with his tank had one shoulder, and Kurt had the other as they swam to boat. With powerful strokes, Mac reached them by the ladder. Huang was like a limp, rag doll, pushed from below by Mac and Kurt as Adam and Grace hauled him aboard.

Grace let Adam drag Huang to a seat, as she reached down eagerly for Kurt. Then they both helped Bobby aboard. Mac swam back to Freya and his boat, as the Coast Guard was arriving.

Starting to cry, Grace grabbed Kurt's wet, hairy chest and hugged him, kissing him on his stubbled cheek. He turned his face and kissed her back with open lips and thrusting tongue. Suddenly realizing they had an audience, Grace pulled back, saying, "I thought Huang would kill you."

"Nope," he said with contempt.

She pressed. "Adam said Huang wouldn't leave the cabin."

Loading the tanks, Bobby smiled grimly. "Kurt persuaded him."

Huang looked up, pointing at Kurt, yelling bitterly,

"That man assaulted me!   He hit me twice! I want him arrested!"

From the other side, Adam pointed out. "Actually, Kurt, you should be covered under the 'Good Samaritan law.'" Freya was untying the *Big 'Un* from her boat.

"I make civil suit!" ranted an irate Huang.

Grace whispered to Kurt. "That's covered under the truism that no good deed goes unpunished."

Sitting on the bench Kurt lounged back, just shook his head, and he started to laugh, as he squeezed a strong, warm arm around Grace's jacketed shoulders. "Bobby, can you get us back to the town dock?"

"Sure." He headed for the cabin saying bitterly. "Huang had to have Kurt's tank for himself. Kurt and I had to buddy breath up."

Kurt nodded. "And I had to teach Huang how to breathe." To Adam, he said, "Your Head of Maritime Research doesn't know how to scuba. Doesn't even know how to swim." Kurt looked at Grace. "But then he didn't panic, get turned around in the water, and try to pull both of us down to Davy Jones' locker!"

"Oh, God." She had. So thankful to be alive Grace snuggled her head against his shoulder.

A tall figure loomed up before Kurt. It was Adam Greenfield. The President of the Board of ORR Directors seemed to be having trouble getting the words out. "You know, Kurt,...we haven't always gotten along...I thought you were a real...." He stopped, then said with his voice choking up, "but what you did for me today..." Unable to continue, Adam just stopped and clumsily, reached out a big hand.

Kurt shook it. "Any time. And hell, Adam, you better not go soft on me! Locking horns with you is usually the highlight of my day!" To break the emotion of the moment, Kurt looked around. "That clam chowder I smell?"

"Best thing to settle ya down," Freya yelled. She

passed the pot over to Bobby just before Mac pushed the boats apart. Passing the pot to Kurt, Bobby headed to start the *Big 'Un's* engines.

There was so much Grace wanted to say to Kurt, did he feel the same way? They'd lost so much time in their lives. She touched his arm. "Kurt, we have to talk."

Weary eyes looked back her, searching her face as if trying to memorize it. "Aaup. Tomorrow. Now, we got to get you ashore, Lady."

There was going to be a tomorrow–that thought was a true marvel for her. She looked around the harbor. Lights, moving towards them. Boats. "Rubberneckers, coming for a view?"

Kurt drank two-handedly from the Freya's pot, and then looked around. "Taint worth the price of gas to cast off. These are harbor folk knowing one of their own is in danger, and they're turning out to help."

With the town police launch escort, Bobby swung the *Big 'Un* toward the town's lights. Grace leaned back on Kurt's wooden bench, preferring not to shout over the engine. But when the town police launch, Kurt's diesel, and Mac moored up to the town dock, Grace headed to the two policemen.

"You've got to arrest Deborah Forbes," she said.

Chapter 35

Mac looked shocked. "Mrs. Forbes? Her family's been here for generations? Why would I arrest her?"

"She locked us in, then set a bomb to sink *The Widow*."

Adam had followed her "Probably not a bomb. From the smell, she just spilled some fuel on deck and set something like a lit cigarette in a book of matches for a fuse, so she would have time to get away in the dingy."

Mac stared at them as if weighing their sanity after their near death. "Are you sure?"

"I think she killed Eve Dupree too," Grace explained. "And she was afraid that I would figure it out."

Mac still looked puzzled. "Because of the Ponzi scheme? Because she lost some money?"

"No, I think Deborah had realized the relationship between Eve and Jack Stuart was closer than business partners, and I think she was insanely jealous."

Kurt had come up behind them. "That's why we broke up. Deborah had a jealous streak wider than a whale's tail."

Grace tried for Mac's attention again. "You should also bring Jack Stuart in for questioning because I think he's going to skip the country."

A puzzled Ben looked at her. "Was he was part of Eve's murder?"

Grace shook her head. "No. That was shock and genuine grief on his part, but he was in on the embezzlement I'm sure."

At that Mac said carefully, "Jack claimed he didn't know anything about the Ponzi, that it was all his partner Eve?"

Again Grace shook her head. "I don't think anything that he said can be trusted. I did DNA tests on a sample from Kurt's boat that I believe is DNA from Eve Dupree. I need your police laboratory investigation specimens to confirm that. I also did a sample that I'm pretty sure comes from Jack Stuart. Your people are going to have to resample him for the chain of evidence, but Eve and Jack's profiles shared multiple loci. They shared 20 identical markers."

Still sounding puzzled, Mac asked, "Can you translate that to English?"

"It is not proof, but it's an accumulation of evidence that supports a very fragile hypothesis. Several of their geographic related markers result in very fair complexioned skin, natural light, blond hair, and blue eyes. Standard Scandinavian profile, Eve had it and so did Jack."

"He was dark-haired," said Mac.

"No, I'm pretty sure he dyes his hair, unusual for a man unless he's grey-haired or in the entertainment business, but Jack is neither. He also had several genes for blue eyes, but he wears brown contact lenses." Grace continued, "Eve and Jack displayed to the world as unrelated business partners, but they shared multiple genes that were passed from parent to child. So they probably had the same mother, and although its harder to tell, I think they shared the same father.

"Eve once told me she tried to have a child with her lover, but they were too close genetically to produce a living baby. Eve had the gene for Trisomy 18, that is a recessive gene, so she was a carrier, but Jack has it too, which means together they probably couldn't produce a viable child."

As a cop, Ben was cautious, "Brother and sister? Some people are given up for adoption. Maybe they were related but didn't know it?"

"Possibly," said Grace, "but unlikely. They could have been unaware of the relationship, but the names and backgrounds they gave us, the hidden hair and eye color, all seemingly carefully crafted to hide their true birth relationship. That was probably done for a reason, and I think they were not only brother and sister, but they were also lovers."

Mac police instincts picked up what was important to the police. "Jack and Eve were both were running the Ponzi scam?"

"I think so," confirmed Grace.

They'd gotten a crowd around themselves, with Kurt adding, "She kinda smelled like she didn't jes have a sisterly relationship with Jack."

Listening to them, Freya happily nodded. "The seance! Isis and Osiris were sister and brother and lovers. The jealous cat goddess was Deborah, see, Grace, the spirits **were** warning you!"

Oh, God, she didn't want to start with this now. Grace turned to Mac, "Look, if you looked into the Ponzi scheme, with Jack not as a befuddled victim but as a willing participant, you might find some of the missing money. He told me he was going to Ontario, Canada to check *Alcom's* mining leases, but I think that was another lie."

Ignoring his wet clothes Mac nodded. "I'll tell the detectives!" He was gone.

Ambulances were arriving. Bobby just wanted a ride home from Ben, but Grace found herself being firmly bundled in for a trip to the hospital by Kurt. She started to protest, but it was easier not to fight, and she suddenly felt so tired. Now in the back of the ambulance with Adam and Kurt, Grace just rested in Kurt's arms and closed her eyes.

But soon she had to talk to Kurt. Change the direction of the life she still had.

The white and yellow Volunteer ambulance took Grace, Kurt, and Adam the few miles to Stamford hospital. Fortunately, Huang, screaming on his Gurney, was loaded into the second, red Fire department's ambulance.

At Stamford hospital, Mac met them again, helping Grace down out of the ambulance. Wrapped in a nubby blanket, she walked into the beige tiled ER under her own steam. Ahead she saw Margey and Fritz Wilshuen, each on one side of a sobbing woman.

The woman's back was to her, but Grace recognized the hysterical voice. "Why did I live? Grace Farrington- the world's lost her genius! Huang-his valuable research! Adam Greenfield, I've known him since high school! Why wasn't I killed instead of them? I wish I were dead and that they were alive!"

Fritz was facing Deborah and could see behind her to the doorway as Grace walked in. After a stunned reaction, Fritz started to smile widely. "Deborah, honey, it looks like you got your wish!"

Mac had moved past Grace and was signaling to the hospital guard as Deborah slowly turned. Her tear streaked face morphed from hideous grief to hard fury as she looked from Grace to Adam. Deborah quickly looked at the exit and started to turn as Mac closed the distance between them. "Ma'am, Mrs. Forbes, could you come with me, please? The police detectives would like to talk with you."

"I'm too ill." Deborah was paling as she spoke. "I have to go back to my hospital room."

Mac looked at the desk nurse, who pointedly said, "Ms. Forbes has just been released on her own sign-out."

"Mam, I'm afraid I must insist," continued Mac, using his body to block her path to the exit, then Mac actually recited her Miranda rights.

He was finishing up as she declared, "I am leaving here. I have an important appointment. You have no right to hold me! No crime has been committed." She forced her voice to calm, as she further explained, "There was an explosion on my ship. I should have tried to reach the others down below, but the ship was sinking so fast! I just panicked and jumped in the dingy." She seemed to think about it, and then loudly proclaimed, "I was rushing to get help for all of them!" She looked to Fritz for confirmation.

He just looked confused. "When we found you, you just said your ship had hit the rocks and sank. You didn't mention an explosion? Or anyone else on board?"

Deborah wet her lips. "I panicked. I ran for my life! That isn't a crime!"

A stern Mac was looming over her. "Mam, you leased *The Merry Widow* from Giordano's shipyard. Just to start with that's a valuable item lost, and there is some question of whether it was deliberately sunk."

Deborah just stood there rigidly.

Moving closer Grace took a chance. "Why did you kill Eve?"

Deborah turned on Grace, her face white with hatred. "Jack was mine! Everybody knew it! He wanted me, not Eve! Then I was walking at night behind that mansion he lived in, and I saw them through the window--together! Kissing!" She stopped, then spoke brokenly, "Later, in front of everybody, Eve was climbing on to Kurt's boat. She was going to sleep with Kurt! He was mine too!" Suddenly, Deborah seemed to come out of her trance, her face collapsing, she looked up at Mac and closed her mouth tightly.

Mac nodded. "Mam, either you come with me willingly, or I'm taking you into custody."

Deborah Forbes raised her chin in defiance, coldly pronouncing, "I'm not saying anything more until my lawyer is present!"

As Mac marched her past Grace, Deborah's eyes were distant.

Then they all could hear Huang screaming as the EMS lifted his gurney out of the Fire Department's ambulance. A nurse guided Grace to a green-curtained, emergency room bed where she waited while she listened to Huang holler. He seemed to have gotten his strength back with furious screams.

"I sue you! MacKay hit me! Sue Board of Directors! Sue hospital!"

Well, things were getting back to normal. Grace settled back on the ER bed to wait for her turn with the doctor. Tomorrow, was soon enough to change her life.

Chapter 36

The Emergency Room was busy that night, so it was hours before they could get to her. She only had some bad bruises, and shallow cuts that didn't need stitches. After sleeping a bit, Grace woke up, refused a sleeping pill, and then she told the doctor she didn't want to stay in the hospital any longer, well by the time he got to her it was just before sunrise. Checking herself out of the E.R. Grace was wondering how she was going to get home when a voice boomed alongside her. "Grace!"

Freya hugged her with massive arms. "Oh, thank Odin! I was so worried!"

Her friend must have been there all night. Her loyal friends, her research, and Kurt, that's what mattered in life. Why had Grace been letting it all slip past her? "Adam and Kurt?"

"Rachel picked up Adam a half-an-hour ago, and they gave Kurt a ride back to his boat at the town dock."

Freya must have seen the disappointment in Grace's face, so she continued, "Kurt was worried about you, and he went in your room a few times, but you were sleeping. The nurses said you were going to stay under observation for a day, so I told him I would wait for you to wake up. He said something about having to get back to his diesel, to dip some early morning water samples?" a puzzled Freya finished.

"Yes, for a marine salinity study he's doing." Grace looked around. "Last night, how did you and Mac know to get out on the water?"

"Oh, I had such a bad, restless feeling last night, and I didn't know why. Mac keeps the Coast Guard channel on one of the radios running in his apartment. I went downstairs, and I heard Kurt's call for assistance. If that bigoted bum hadn't been out there...." Freya's voice started to break.

Grace didn't want to think about it. "Huang stopped screaming?"

"He kept waking up, so they had to keep increasing his sedation. He's going to sue Deborah, the Harbor, the Board of Directors, Stamford Hospital, the Emergency Room personnel, and the President of the United States..."

Grace found herself laughing, with a tinge of hysteria.

Freya continued, "Mac called me just an hour ago. Deborah is not talking, but the police are moving fast. They are going to have State Trooper divers looking over *The Merry Widow*. And you were right about that other rat jumping ship. The police caught Jack Stuart in Miami. "

"Miami?"

"He made the mistake of using his cell phone. They arrested him online for a plane to Belize."

Why Belize? Grace thought and said, "Belize has no extradition treaty with the U.S.?"

"They have one, but if you have enough money, it can be gotten around. Jack was traveling with a passport under a different name, and the Miami police found a bunch of stuff in the lining of his suitcase, cash, unreported emeralds, and more importantly flash drives. He's refusing to give the passwords, but they think they can break 'em. Mac thinks they will show some offshore accounts."

"Does Mac thinks the investors will get their money back?"

Freya shook her head. "The Ponzi's been going on for years. Eve and Jack came here for new blood. And the money they were taking in, with the mansions, the fancy Jaguars, first-class jet trips everywhere, her clothing and jewelry-- they had one hell of a rich lifestyle. Mac thinks the leftover pie will be really sliced thin when its passed around."

"I was hoping David would get his money back," Grace said sadly.

"David Gardiner doesn't have to worry about money,

why don't you just marry him?"

Grace looked over at the entrance. Another ambulance coming in. An elderly woman was being unloaded, a poor old woman totally by herself, Grace didn't want that. "Actually, when I was trapped in that hull, knowing that I was dying, thinking what my life could have been... Freya, I'm going to make a change."

"Marry David?"

"David couldn't handle my research. From a wife of his, he wants a total commitment to himself, and I can't do that."

Freya looked at her strangely, another of those times when she just seemed to '*know,*' "But you are thinking of marriage. To who? Not that blooming barnacle! Not Kurt!"

Grace smiled. "When I was drowning in that dark hold, he was Sir Lancelot in a shining wetsuit!"

"Oh, Grace, even if he saved you, he's still a red-necked moron! Don't do something you'll regret!"

"It's been a long night." Grace gave her a lopsided smile. "Can you drive me home?"

Epilogue

But at her request, Freya left Grace off at her laboratory because as always, Grace had to check how her results were coming. To her surprise, Inger was in early, sorting the hard copy printouts. "I heard the news last night, and I didn't think you be in at your regular time. Should you be out of the hospital?"

"I'm okay." Grace looked around the lab, everything seemed older, more beaten up, but it was hers!

Inger was still talking, "Adam called. He didn't expect you in and didn't want me to disturb you unless you did come in. He's arranged a press conference at the Roost, in..." She looked at her watch. "An hour. He says he's trying to head off bad publicity." Inger looked puzzled. "He was very emphatic about this, he said that if you came in, you should just tell the story of being on the boat, hearing an explosion, and getting trapped below decks. He said to focus your answers on Dr. Mackay's rescue?" Inger was looking questioningly at her.

"I'm not going to the press conference." Grace sat down at an outer table, her legs still felt a bit rubbery at the memory of that water burying her. She opened up her laptop but just couldn't calm down as she kept seeing scenes from her life like she had viewed them in that trapping hull. Finally, unable to stand it, Grace got up and walked outside.

Cars were starting to drive in and park behind the Captain's Roost, and she could see several reporters climbing the back stairs to the mansion. To avoid them, she crossed over the road and kept walking on the grass toward the little closet like guard booth, at the top of the dock ramp.

She could see the Channel Eight's mobile news van pulling in ORR, and several other t-v vans were already parked near the Roost. Adam Greenfield wasn't going to keep the lid on this one. That red-headed reporter was there, looking down at her, trying to catch her eye, but Grace just turned to walk down the gangplank. She would call Sam later, but there were limits, and Grace had reached hers.

Even after last night, breathing sea air helped center her so she could see how Kurt loved living on his boat. Of course, that boat was a lot tighter than even her small apartment. According to Kurt, it was '*cold as a witch's tit*' in January, but he loved that sailboat, so whoever he married would just have to get used to living on it.

Grace could see two of the student boats were out if they were unfamiliar with boating we're they drowning now? She found herself hesitating before stepping on to that floating dock, not wanting to feel that bobbing surface under her feet. Not wanting to ever be trapped inside a boat again—well, she'd have to get over that! Grace determinedly stepped on to the float. What would happen to Deborah Forbes? At this point, Grace didn't much care.

Small pea green waves slapped against the hull of the sailboat Kurt's lived in, but his lobster yawl was out. She walked to the end of the pier and stood watching black-backed seagulls dive and skim the water, finding even the ageless seawater looked different, new, vital. She was grateful to be alive, but for the first time in her life '*alone*' was lonely.

In the marshes below the road, a white egret tucked its neck back, unfurled its long wings, and flew across the emerald green grass. Grace looked down at the water, in the shadows of planks of the docks she could see a gray crab scrabbling up mussel infested pilings. The wind changed, and she could hear the steady chugging of Kurt's lobster yawl across the harbor.   It needed a tune up or something, contentedly she just stood watching him cross, with white foam at his bow. Soon Kurt maneuvered into the slip and Grace tied him up. He jumped on to the dock beside her, then just stood there looking into her eyes, saying sternly, "Lady, before I left, I peeked in and saw you sleeping. The nurses said you were staying in the hospital!"

"Hate hospitals, the smells, being confined inside and the sounds... "

"Huang still screaming?"

"They gave him some pills," said Grace.

Kurt chuckled. "Maybe we can get hold of a bottle of those pills, for when the fool starts mouthing off again."

"You think Huang, and we are all staying at ORR?"

"Aaup, and now I've got Adam Greenfield in my corner, he thinks I'm God's right-hand man."

Grace laughed. "That'll wear off."

"Not with a Jew! He'll remember who saved him the rest of his life." Kurt looked at the cars and satellite topped trucks parking behind the Roost as more news people gathered. "I guess attempted murder and near-drownings brings out more press then announcing new cancer therapies."

She set her shoulders. "We should go up and talk to them."

Kurt looked in that direction and shook his head. "No, we've done enough for Oyster River. Grace, I've been doing some thinking, we have to talk." He took her hand in his big, callused one, and they walked in the other direction, towards his sailboat home. When they were down below in his cabin, he asked, "Can ya stand being in a boat after last night?"

She looked around his sailboat and realized it kind of felt safe, like home, because it was his home. "I'm okay."

He smiled approvingly. "Coffee? Whiskey?"

"Tea."

Kurt busied himself filling a kettle and putting it on the propane stove. Grace wrapped her arms around her. Actually, it wasn't that close in here, and she'd get used to it. Grace looked over to where the police had cut out the dinette bench's upholstery. "You know, Kurt, Sara's handy with fabric. We can probably re-upholster that built-in couch for you and get the rest of Eve Dupree's brains off it."

He nodded. "Appreciate it, but I figure we'll be living in your condo when we marry."

"What?" She was thinking about them living together, but he just said it outright like it was a done deal.

"That's what we're here to talk about," said Kurt, his dark eyes staring into hers. "Leastwise I am. Yesterday, Bobby and I were doing salinity tests out in the harbor. Knew you guys were meeting on Deborah's boat. Saw ya anchor and wondered why Deborah had moored so close to the channel with the tide going out, but Deborah never was much of a sailor. I saw the dingy cast off with just her, and I wondered about that.

"Then I saw that explosion, that sailboat going up in a ball of yellow flame. It kept burning in the water as *The Merry Widow* sank. No way you guys could've gotten out. You were gone, and I'd lost you." His voice choked up.

"Part of the reason she killed Eve was jealousy over you," Grace said just to redirect the intensity of the moment. "Was she a good lover? Deborah Forbes?"

"Go to bed with her once, and she owned you. Expected you to report in daily. That business didn't last long with me."

"And Eve Dupree?"

"Never had the chance to have the lady," he said regretfully. "But she sent me out for white wine and special condoms, so I figured the wind was blowing my way. Then she was killed."

"You're using condoms now?"

"That always depended on the lady I am with, and I'm usually more comfortable with you."

She blushed deeply, and he only chuckled. "You're always so open, so straight forward about everything, and then you go all maidenish."

Grace wanted to change the direction again. "When

we heard the explosion, Adam and I pulled at the door, but it wouldn't budge. The water was fountaining up through up the floorboards."

"When the gas tank blew, took off most of the *Widow's* stern."

"We couldn't get out. I thought my life was all over." Not being able to look at him, she walked to his galley and pulled out a mug and found herself an English breakfast tea bag.

"Aaup, Deborah really planned it well. If I hadn't been keeping an eye on you, the Coast Guard wouldn't have found you until next sunrise. Your ship sank fast with so little flotsam, if I hadn't had the fish finder to locate the wreck underwater, I couldn't have found you meself. ?We just lucky underwater be able to tie a line on the *Widow* in time."

Grace moved to him, starting to cry, she wrapped her arms around his chest. He put his muscular arms around her and kissed the side of her face. "If you and Bobby hadn't taken that stupid risk and dived to save me. Then going back for Adam." She looked at him. "And Huang?"

"Aaup," he gravely agreed. "That was a mistake." He looked at her with a lopsided grin. "Saving Huang that is. Could have left him aboard and in a minute or so that bottom feeder woulda been washed out to the open Sound."

"And in all that time, floating in that cabin, I did a lot of thinking. About what's important in my life," she said slowly.

"So did I," he said, with total seriousness.

Grace stepped back and looked around the cabin. "I can live here in spring and summer–but, maybe during the winter months, we could move into the condo?"

"That'll work for me," he agreed.

"As prominent scientists, we're a role model to the students and some teenagers, so I think we should make it legal, but we'll need rules. If we get married, could you ever cut down to one woman?"

He still kept holding her at a distance. "When I was married, I was totally faithful."

"You're kidding?"

"Honest to God." But that quirky smile again. "I will admit it's going to be quite a change, and a lot of ladies around here are going to be very disappointed."

"Aaup," she responded. Then thought about it more. "With you up before dawn to take your morning studies, and me in my lab until eleven at night, we are going to have to schedule time just to see each other. Lunch?"

"Maybe a quickee instead?" He agreed. "We've done that in the past, this time we'll make a rule: a minimum of sex and three dinners out together a week."

She looked in askance at him. "With our schedules, we'll be lucky if we can make one."

He amended, "Whal, I could bring take-out to your lab?"

Actually, that sounded rather nice. "Okay."

"And travel, Lady. You do a lot of conferences. Well, when I thought you were gone, I kinda was thinking of those fantasies of mine. Of taking Skipper up on his offer to stay with him in Tokyo. The two of us honeymooning in the Imperial Palace. What do ya say?"

"Guests of the Japanese Imperial family?" That seemed a bit daunting.

"Okay," he said. "Let's start off a little less grand. Can you come along on that São Tomé trip for the cable show taping?"

"You missed that."

"Nope. They've been in touch. Since they already got tape on me, they want me for the rest. And my daring underwater rescue of three people from a sunken ship is sure to be included in the show! Jes waiting for Judge Rubin to clear my travel." His tone went from teasing to serious, "Come with me, Grace."

"I can't just leave everything for a week..."

"Two weeks." He held up two fingers.

"Two weeks... no." She started and then felt that cold black water around her body. Of her life being over, with nothing to show but some mention of her name in a dry textbook. "Actually, I can do...one week. A week with you on the beach. Yes, I've got some money in the budget."

He smiled widely. "They'll pay for my assistant, I've already asked them."

She continued, "You can come along to some of my conferences, I've got one in Orlando coming up."

"Orlando? What about my harbor studies?"

"Bobby can do them–he'd love more over time."

Kurt looked to the side. "Orlando? One of those big amusement parks."

"Yes, they're paying for the Tree House Villa at the Saratoga resort, lots of privacy. I'll do some lectures, we'll do an evening reception or two, and then we'll have the rest of the time together."

"Nobody is going to refer to me as 'Mr. Farrington'. It's gonna be Grace MacKay." He insisted firmly.

"Grace Farrington-MacKay?" She tried getting used to the idea.

He shook his head ruefully. "All these rules and concessions, taking all the fun of it! This tying up is gonna need major negotiations. You're the most independent, go her own way woman I know. Babe, marriage means big, hard changes for the both of us."

Kurt held her in his arms, and they stood silently for a moment, then Grace said, "And you know, it was pretty good before. We had each other, and our own lives...we just should have worked harder at getting together more often."

"Getting together," he said, running his rough hand

down her arm. "I'm in favor of that." Where he touched her skin, she tingled, and then Kurt said, "Look, heavy negotiations take time. Until we have the binding marriage compact set up, how about, we agree to leave it just as it was before? I stay on the boat..."

Nodding in agreement, Grace moved away she poured the kettle into her mug of tea. "And my condo's not a far walk for you."

He watched her carefully. "Then I still get Gina and Alpine, no questioned asked?"

Okay. Two could play this game. "And I'll have evenings with David or whoever..."

He narrowed his eyes a bit. "Sauce for the goose–sauce for the gander, aaup. We might have to make some changes further down the line, but right now let's go back to that queen sized bed in the bow and just work on enjoying being alive today."

She thought about it, set her tea mug down and said, "Sounds good to me."

The End

For further books
see www.lynnmarron.com

To comment or talk with the author
I'm at lynn@lynnmarron.com

Other books by Lynn Marron
   All Published in Print and
   E-book editions of Kindle and Nook

ORR: THE NOBEL PRIZE MURDER
(The first in the Grace Farrington Mysteries)
Turned down for this year's Nobel Prize, fortyish genetics pioneer Grace Farrington finds out the new Head of Research at Oyster River is the man who stole her research! When Dr. Marshall is murdered on ORR's houseboat, Grace finds herself chief suspect and is further implicated, when following an1800's witch's *Curse of Three*, two more people die in Oyster River Harbor. While finding herself romantically involved with a wealthy patron and a red-necked colleague, Grace must use her scientific reasoning and her eclectic group of friends (scientists, cops, psychics and some other slightly eccentric New Englanders) to solve the murders before she's arrested or killed herself.

THE PSYCHICS' SEAPORT MURDER
(The first in the Mystic Triplets Mysteries)
After the 'suicide' of their witch mother, the young triplets, Holly, Frost and Noel Corey were separated for seventeen years. The day of their long-awaited reunion in Mystic, Connecticut, a New England seaport, a murdered man is found on their mansion grounds, making brother Frost the police's chief suspect. Knowing nothing of her Old Craft heritage, Holly starts to learn the skills of her ancestors as she struggles to open Witch House as a viable Bed and Breakfast. To save Frosty, she must also find the murderer haunting her family, while she is so thoroughly distracted by the tall, muscular police sergeant, Paul Travinski.

ADAM'S UNORTHODOX, UNNATURAL LAW PRACTICE

(A Paranormal Adventure)

Inheriting his Great Uncle Quentin's unconventional law firm in Missouri Adam Martin finds himself defending the rights of a succubus, a semi-senile seer, mermaids, zombies, and gorgons. Soon he is writing contracts for werewolves, consulting with ghosts, and protecting unfairly accused fire starters. While this is going on, he is trying to stand up to his six foot tall *'Cherokee'* law secretary, and deal with his staid, disapproving family of conservative lawyers led by the formidable, 'hang them high' Judge Jeremiah Martin. Still, while struggling to save his clients, and his law practice, Adam has time to romance some very intriguing and unusual females.

CENTAURESSES OF THE SILVER DRAGON

(The first in the Fantasy Warrior Saga)

The Regiment follows the hoof prints of Jace, a ruggedly handsome centaur of Clydesdale proportions. Warriors winning on their last field, but betrayed by treacherous princes, these sword-wielding mercenaries are outlawed. To keep his band together, the legendary fighter finds a patron in the stunningly beautiful Silver Star, a long-legged centauress with sea-foam white hair, a luxurious silky tail, and ominous cloven hoofs. The Lady promises a vast treasure, if the Regiment but free her rich mines from a rampaging dragon, but Jace knows dragons do not exist. His officers think this silver siren is leading his regiment to death! Yet still, Jace stubbornly marches on.